DEADLY CHOICES

DEADLY CHOICES

Chris Black

Mill City Press, Inc.
212 3rd Avenue North, Suite 570
Minneapolis, MN 55401
612.455.2294
www.millcitypublishing.com

ISBN - 978-1-934937-49-5
ISBN - 1-934937-49-5
LCCN - 2008941775

Cover Design by Fred Kylander
Typeset by Peggy LeTrent

Printed in the United States of America

To my family, Kris, David, William and Sarah Catherine, thanks for your support and belief.

To my friend, Nelle, thanks for your help and encouragement.

- Prologue -

Gerald Warren leaned back in his rich, Corinthian leather desk chair and propped his feet on the corner of his desk. He inhaled deeply from an expensive Cuban cigar and blew rings of gray smoke that drifted silently to the ceiling.

"Gentlemen, come in," he said, motioning with his hand, "I've been expecting you." He turned up the corners of his mouth in a Grinch-like smile. "I believe we've found our nurse."

Bob Carlson closed the door and nervously followed Tim Alford across the lushly carpeted office. Gerald pushed his humidor across the desk and opened the lid.

"Sit down, boys," he said, "and fire up one of Cuba's finest. We've got reason to celebrate."

"Cut the crap, Gerald," Bob snapped. "Who's the nurse?"

Gerald thumped the ashes from his cigar and smiled.

"Kind of testy today, aren't you, Bob?" he asked. "Think I should send Tim down to the pharmacy and get you a Valium?"

"I don't need a Valium," he grumbled. "It's just that you're so damn cavalier about this whole thing. I don't mind telling you I'm not very comfortable with what you're asking us to do."

Gerald put his feet on the floor and sat up straight in his chair. He took another deep drag from his cigar and gently blew a stream of smoke toward Bob.

"You don't have to be comfortable, Bob, just cooperative,"

he said. "Same with you, Tim. The two of you just do what I tell you and I'll take care of the rest. No one will ever know about your past transgressions."

Tim stared coldly at the hospital administrator. His face remained expressionless as he unbuttoned his white lab coat. "You say you've found a nurse?" he asked.

"Actually, Tim, I believe I said 'we've found a nurse', but that gets into semantics and that's not why we're here."

"We've found a nurse," Tim replied sarcastically.

"Yes, we have," Gerald confirmed.

"Who is she?" inquired Bob anxiously.

Gerald folded his arms across his chest and rocked back and forth in his chair.

"Young nurse by the name of Alex Lowe," he replied. "She hasn't been working here long, but I'm confident she's the one."

"How'd you pick her?" Bob asked.

"Actually, Dillard recommended her," Gerald replied.

"Is she involved?" Tim asked.

Gerald raised his eyebrows and confidently nodded. "She is now."

"How'd you convince her to go along with your plan?" Tim asked.

"Same way I did with you two. Just dug up a little dirt on her." Gerald flashed a confident smile and chuckled softly, shaking his head. "It's amazing how cooperative people can be when you discover the skeletons they've hidden in their closets."

"How much does Dillard know?" Bob asked.

"About as much as you two," Gerald replied.

"What makes you think the Lowe girl will cooperate?" Bob asked.

"Oh, she'll cooperate," Gerald boasted, "especially when she sees these tapes."

He opened the center desk drawer and flipped a switch. The mahogany paneled wall behind his desk parted revealing a room with a panel of television monitors.

"Watch the screen on the top left," he instructed.

Bob and Tim leaned forward in their chairs and stared at the screen.

"Who's the patient?" Tim asked.

"A young man dying with AIDS, Jackson I think," Gerald replied, "but that's irrelevant. Watch the nurse."

The three men stared at the monitor as the young nurse entered the patient's room. After glancing nervously about the room, she pulled two glass vials from her pocket and filled a syringe with their contents. She quickly placed the empty vials back in her pocket and injected the contents of her syringe into the patient's I.V.

Gerald smiled as he rolled his cigar between his thumb and forefinger. He had found his nurse.

- 1 -

Her father had tried to warn her, but she wouldn't listen. Now as Alex Lowe stood outside the double doors of the ICU her heart raced wildly. With each forceful beat the blood pulsed within her ears. Her breaths were quick and shallow. A light perspiration covered her brow and palms. She knew when she accepted the job that the demons could still be there, but she had hoped the passage of time had locked them away in impenetrable vaults. Now, five years after her mother's death, the painful memories she had worked so hard to bury slithered forth from the recesses of her brain. As soon as the double doors of the ICU swung open Alex felt a tightness in her throat and a heaviness in her chest. The sounds and smells of the ICU reminded her of things she'd tried so hard to forget. Images of her mother seizing and vomiting, images that had haunted her for so long after her mother's death, reared their ugly heads.

"Are you okay?" asked Patsy Carter, the staff nurse assigned to train her. "You look pale."

Alex swallowed hard and buried her face in her hands.

"Yeah, I'm fine," she lied, shaking her head, "just a little lightheaded. I think I need to sit down for a minute."

Patsy took her by the arm and led her to the small break room in the center of the ICU. Alex's legs felt weak as she collapsed onto the hard plastic chair. Her hands trembled as she sipped a soft drink and wiped her face with a damp washcloth. If only she'd listened to her father. Why didn't she listen to him?

"Are you sure you're okay?" Patsy asked. "You don't look good. If this were Halloween I'd swear you'd seen a ghost."

Alex swallowed hard and stared uncomfortably at the floor. What should she say? In her mind she had seen a ghost, but was she ready to confide something so personal in someone she barely knew? She could continue to feign dizziness and no one would ever know. But before she realized it, she'd blurted out the truth.

"I did see a ghost," she whispered breathlessly.

Patsy pulled a chair away from the table and sat down. She leaned forward and rested her hands on Alex's thighs.

"You saw a ghost?" she asked, shaking her head doubtingly.

Alex wiped the tears from her eyes and slowly raised her head until her eyes met Patsy's.

"Five years ago," she whispered, "I was sitting in room three with my mother when she died. When those ICU doors opened, everything came rushing back. It was so vivid, so real. I saw her laying there hooked to the ventilator, and the chest tube, and her sunken eyes..." Her voice trailed off as she wiped the tears from her eyes.

"I'm so sorry," Patsy replied softly. She lightly squeezed Alex's leg. "I had no idea."

"It's not your fault," Alex replied. "You didn't know. Dad tried to warn me but I wouldn't listen. It never bothered me during nursing school so I thought I had put it behind me. I thought I was strong enough to handle it."

"Nobody's that strong," Patsy said.

"I was with her the afternoon she died," Alex continued. "Dad had sat with her all night and most of that day. He looked so tired. I got here right after school and offered to sit with her while he took a break. He didn't want to leave her, but I insisted, so he and Elizabeth went to the snack bar for a Coke. They couldn't have been gone for more than two or three minutes when Mom started seizing and vomiting. The nurses rushed in to help her, but there was nothing they could do. She gasped for air and then she stopped moving. I've never felt so helpless in all my life." Alex closed her eyes tightly and bit her lower lip as she tried to hold back the tears. "I'm sorry," she said, "I shouldn't unload all of this on you."

"No, I'm the one who's sorry," Patsy replied. "I was only kidding about seeing a ghost. I had no idea."

"Don't apologize," Alex replied, shaking her head. "You didn't know. I didn't know. I guess I knew there was a chance when I took the job it could happen, but I never imagined it would be so vivid."

"She must've been young when she died. Was it cancer?"

Alex nodded her head as she took a tissue from her pocket and wiped the tears from her eyes.

"Yeah," she replied, "colon cancer. She was only forty-three when they found it. She was so vibrant and healthy, or at least that's what we thought. She was never very heavy, but then she started losing weight and having abdominal pain. Mom never complained but we knew there was something wrong with her." Alex paused and wiped her nose with the tissue. Her eyes locked on Patsy's eyes. "Did you ever know a Dr. Jim Curry? He was her doctor."

Patsy rolled her eyes toward the ceiling and rubbed the back of her neck.

"Yeah, I knew him," she replied. "He was your mom's doc?"

Alex nodded her head and chewed nervously on her bottom lip.

"Something tells me you weren't too fond of him," she remarked.

Patsy folded her arms across her chest and pressed her back firmly against the chair.

"I don't like talking about people when they're dead," she replied, "but I was never much of a Jim Curry fan. I saw him put more dying patients through unnecessary tests than I care to remember."

Alex's eyes widened. "If you were working ICU five years ago, then you probably saw him torture my mother before she died."

Patsy lowered her chin and raised her eyebrows. "He tortured your mother?" she asked skeptically.

"Not intentionally," Alex replied, "but that's not how it seemed when I was seventeen. Dr. Curry was a personal friend of Mom and Dad. He was the one who diagnosed the cancer and ordered the CAT scan that showed it had already spread to her liver. Surgery was never an option because of the liver mets, but he told us that with chemotherapy, if she was lucky, she might live a year or two."

Alex chuckled half-heartedly and shook her head.

"Something funny?" Patsy asked.

"Not really," Alex replied. "I was just thinking of Dr. Curry's choice of words. 'Lucky' he said. If Mom was lucky, she might live a year or two."

"How long did she live?" Patsy asked.

"Few months," Alex replied, "but it was anything but lucky. The chemotherapy was horrible. She had terrible nausea and vomiting and developed painful ulcers in her mouth and throat. They had to put in a central line just to feed her." Alex shook her head. "It was a nightmare. Mom cried just swallowing her saliva. She tried to hide the pain, but we knew how much she was suffering."

Patsy shook her head and patted Alex's arm. "I'm sorry I brought it up. You don't have to talk about it if you don't want to."

"No, Patsy, I need to talk about it. If I'm going to work here I can't run from my past."

"Well, one thing's for sure," Patsy replied, "you won't run into Jim Curry."

Alex nodded her agreement.

"Did you say he died?" she asked.

"Yeah, last year in a car wreck," Patsy replied. "Hit and run they say. I heard he was still alive when they got him to the emergency room but his head injuries were so severe that his wife refused to put him on a ventilator."

"Then I guess it's true what they say," Alex replied.

"What's that?" Patsy asked.

"There is no justice. If anyone ever deserved to suffer, Jim Curry did for what he did to my mother. When her condition deteriorated, he laid a guilt trip on Dad and convinced him to do everything possible to keep her alive. It got so bad I'd pray at night for her to die just so she wouldn't have to suffer any more."

Patsy pushed her chair away from the table and stood up. "I'd love to sit and talk," she said, "but we've got work to do."

"Yeah, let's ride the bike," Alex replied.

"Excuse me?" Patsy said.

Alex smiled and shook her head as she rose to her feet. "Inside joke," she replied. "Let's get back to work."

- 2 -

Alex leaned her head back and inhaled deeply of the enticing smell of smoke from a barbecue grill.

"Smells like hamburgers," Elizabeth said.

"Has to be," Alex replied. "Doesn't Dad claim that's his specialty?"

"That and anything else he cooks on the grill," Elizabeth joked. "He's always thought he was a master chef."

Philip Lowe walked around the corner of the house and waved at his daughters. The girls smiled at one another and chuckled, amused by his apron and chef's hat.

"Looking good, Dad," Alex chided.

"Feeling good," he replied. "Makes me feel good just knowing the two of you could fit your old man into your busy schedules. Come on in."

"You know we wouldn't miss one of your barbeques for anything in the world," Alex teased.

"Well, I know your mother would want us to be together today," he said. "You know how much she treasured family time. Before she died, I promised her we'd celebrate her memory, and what better day than this?"

"I couldn't agree more," Alex replied.

"Me either," Elizabeth chimed in. "Haven't seen you much lately, Dad. How's work?"

"Same as usual," he replied. "Buy some stocks, sell some bonds. Make a little money by making a few rich folks a lot of money. How are your grades this semester?"

"Better," Elizabeth replied, smiling, rolling her eyes.

"That's it?" he asked. "Better? I certainly hope they're better. They weren't very good last semester."

"Yes, sir, I know," Elizabeth replied softly. "You've told me several times. But law school is tough."

"I don't doubt that, but you didn't apply yourself last semester. You're not a "C" student. If Alex had been satisfied with "C's" she wouldn't have been accepted to nursing school and..."

"And she wouldn't have graduated with honors," Elizabeth replied sarcastically finishing his sentence.

"Well, she wouldn't," he replied gruffly. "Would you, Alex?"

Alex smiled and winked at Elizabeth.

"No, Dad, probably not," she replied.

"Speaking of nursing school, how's the new job going?" he asked.

"Fine," Alex replied. "Technically, I'm still going through orientation and not officially on the job, but to answer your question, it's going fine."

"No demons roaming the halls of the hospital?" he asked with a smile.

Alex returned his smile and shook her head.

"No, sir, not that I've seen," she replied.

Elizabeth stuck her nose up in the air and sniffed.

"Something smells good," she said. "What's for supper?"

"Your favorite and my specialty," her father replied, "hamburgers. And if you two will excuse me for a minute, I need to flip the burgers."

Elizabeth followed him to the patio and closed the sliding glass door behind him.

She quickly turned around and confronted her sister.

"No demons?" she asked, raising her eyebrows.

"Nope, no demons," Alex replied.

"C'mon, Alex," Elizabeth said. "I saw the look in your eyes. Maybe Dad didn't but I did."

"I don't know what you're talking about, Lizzy," Alex replied, shifting uncomfortably from one foot to the other.

Elizabeth folded her arms across her chest and rolled her eyes skyward.

"You can't lie to me. I know you too well."

Alex returned the look and shook her head.

"I wish I knew what you were talking about," she replied, "but Lord knows I don't. Trust me. There aren't any demons lurking in Richland's hallways."

"I think they're done," Philip announced suddenly as he poked his head inside the door. "If you girls will help me in the kitchen, we'll be ready to eat in a few minutes."

"Don't think our conversation is over, because it's not," Elizabeth whispered as she rose and followed her sister to the kitchen.

"What's all the whispering about?" Philip asked.

"Girl stuff, Dad," Elizabeth replied. "You wouldn't understand."

Philip smiled as he placed the plate of hamburgers on the counter.

"Probably not," he admitted. He crammed several slices of dill pickle in his mouth. Juice ran from the corner of his mouth and trickled down his chin. "Have you decided which area of the hospital you're going to work in?" he asked Alex as he wiped the pickle juice with his apron.

"It's still early in my orientation," Alex replied, "but I might see if I can work in one of the critical care units. I started my orientation in the ICU today. It's high pressure, but it's exciting. The patients are so sick."

"How long was Mom in the ICU before she died?" Elizabeth asked.

"About a week," Philip replied. "Why?"

"Just wondering," Elizabeth said. "It seemed longer."

"Now she was in the hospital for about three weeks," he replied, "but Dr. Curry kept her on the oncology floor the first two weeks."

"I heard today that he died last year," Alex said casually.

"I'd heard that," Philip replied, nodding. "Died in a car wreck."

"He had a car wreck," Alex replied, "but he didn't die in the wreck. The nurse orienting me said he was still alive when they got him to the emergency room, but he had a severe brain injury and would've been a vegetable if he'd lived."

"I hadn't heard that," Philip replied. "I always assumed he'd died in the wreck."

Alex shook her head and pressed her lips together tightly.

"Patsy heard he'd made his wife promise she wouldn't keep him alive if he were ever in that type of situation, otherwise they probably could've saved him."

Philip squeezed a wedge of lemon in his glass and stirred the tea with his spoon. "It's probably best he died if his brain was that severely damaged. No reason to keep a person alive if there's no hope for meaningful survival."

Alex placed her half-eaten hamburger on her plate and pushed the plate away. She took the napkin from her lap and placed it on the table beside her plate. "Do you really believe that?" she asked.

Philip stopped chewing and wrinkled his forehead.

"Believe what?" he asked.

"That there's no reason to keep someone alive if they've got no hope for meaningful survival."

"Of course I do," he replied.

"When did you change your mind?" Alex asked.

Philip wiped his mouth and swallowed hard. He stretched his neck as he took a sip of tea to wash down his food. "I haven't changed my mind," he stated. "I've always felt that way."

Alex pushed back from the table and folded her arms across her chest.

"Then why'd Mom have to suffer so much?" she asked, emotion breaking her voice.

Philip gnawed nervously on his lower lip and scratched his scalp. "I'm not sure I understand what you're asking, sweetheart."

"If you've always felt that people shouldn't be kept alive if there was no hope for meaningful survival, then why'd you let Dr. Curry put Mom through so much before she died?"

"Your mother had cancer," Philip replied. "She didn't have a brain injury."

"That's not my point," Alex said, angrily. "When Mom coded and was transferred to the ICU, we all knew she was going to die. But you and Dr. Curry wouldn't let her."

"I didn't want your mother to die," Philip replied softly.

"You think I did?" Alex asked. Her voice grew louder. "I didn't want her to die any more than you did, but I didn't want her to suffer. I prayed for God to let her die if that was the only way to end her suffering."

Philip lowered his chin to his chest and ran his fingers through his hair.

"Jim wouldn't take no for an answer," he said, his voice just above a whisper. "I asked him to back off, to just keep her comfortable, but he wouldn't listen. When she coded, he and I had a long talk. I told him we didn't want any more heroics; we just wanted to keep her comfortable. But he bargained with me. Just give him a week. That's all he asked. If she weren't better by the end of seven days, then he'd back off. Just seven days. He gave me his word."

"But even if she improved, even if she got to go home, she was going to die," Alex replied. "For crying out loud, Dad, she had metastatic colon cancer."

"I knew that, honey, but I didn't want to face life without her. And because of that, I let Jim influence my decisions, decisions that determined whether or not your mother lived or died and whether or not she would continue suffering. What was I supposed to do? He was the doctor."

"Can we please change the topic?" Elizabeth interrupted. "I thought the reason we came over was to celebrate Mom's memory, not for the two of you to argue over why she didn't die sooner."

Philip nodded his head and wiped a tear from the corner of his eye.

"You're right," he said, composing himself. He picked up his glass of tea and held it in the air above the table. "To your mother and my wife," he said, "may our memories of her be pleasant and remind us of the beautiful woman who loved each of us and who was in turn so deeply loved."

Elizabeth lifted her glass and lightly brushed it against her father's glass, but Alex sat silently, staring blankly ahead as tears trickled slowly down her cheeks.

- 3 -

The pungent smell of burning flesh filled the small cramped room in the corner of the ICU. Beads of sweat dripped from the nose of the physician performing chest compressions and landed silently on the hairy chest of the lifeless old man.

"Everybody clear!" shouted the young intern. "Turn up the voltage to three hundred joules." He pressed the paddles of the defibrillator firmly against the old man's chest. "Everybody clear!" he shouted again.

The torso of the old man jerked violently as the surge of electricity exploded through his body. His tongue hung limply from the corner of his mouth on his unshaven face. Saliva slithered down his chin like a glass snake.

"He's still in V-fib," the doctor yelled. "Everybody stand clear."

Alex pushed her way through the crowd of medical personnel and craned her neck to get a better view.

"If I were you," the doctor said, "I'd quit leaning on the bed rail unless you want to get your pants knocked off."

Alex blushed and backed away from the metal railing.

The old man's body jerked again, rising completely off the bed as the defibrillator discharged its load of electricity. The old man lay completely still. All eyes in the room stared at the cardiac monitor above the bed. Flat line.

"We're losing him," the doctor shouted. "Give him an amp

of epinephrine and one of bicarb. He can't die on my shift."

Alex felt a cold, glass cylinder in her hand and looked back over her shoulder.

"Why don't you give him this amp of epi?" Patsy asked her. "You've done this before haven't you?"

"Yes, ma'am," Alex answered as she inserted the needle into the I.V. line. "But I'm not sure I understand why we're doing this."

The young physician looked at her and shook his head in disgust.

"Is this your first code?" he asked condescendingly. "Surely you know why I'm giving epinephrine. Don't they teach you that in nursing school? Epinephrine is a fancy name for adrenaline. When someone's heart stops, we give it to try and jumpstart the heart. Maybe you should get your book out and read about it."

"I'm very familiar with epinephrine and why you ordered it," Alex shot back. "I just don't understand why we're doing this?"

"You don't understand why we're doing what?" he asked, unable to hide his aggravation.

"Why are you coding this old man?" she asked. "Why don't you let him die?"

The physician squinted his eyes and wrinkled his brow.

"Why am I coding him?" he asked.

"Yes. Why are you coding this old man?" she repeated.

"It's my job," he replied, shrugging his shoulders. "I'm the doctor in charge so it's my duty to take care of him."

"I understand that," Alex said, "but why are you coding him? Why don't you let him die?"

The small room was quiet, the silence interrupted only by the sound of the respiratory therapist rhythmically squeezing the ambu bag. The young doctor smiled and shook his head.

"So you're not asking why I in particular am coding him, but rather why anyone would want to keep him alive. Is that right?"

"Yes, sir," Alex replied, "that's what I'm asking. Look at him. He's so emaciated and frail. He must be ninety years old."

"Actually, he's only seventy years old," replied a chubby nurse standing at the foot of his bed reading his chart. "He probably looks so old because of the metastatic lung cancer and the chemotherapy."

Alex shook her head.

"All the more reason to let him die," she replied.

"Give him another amp of epi," the doctor shouted, cutting his eyes toward Alex. "I take it you're not familiar with the rules governing life and death within the confines of a hospital."

Alex stared blankly at him.

"No, sir, I guess I'm not," she said.

"The rules say that if you're a patient in a hospital, regardless of age, race, sex, condition or prognosis, and you elect to die, you're not allowed to do so without prior approval of your attending physician. That is to say that should you decide to die while in the hospital, we will try to snatch your butt from the jaws of death unless you have previously informed us of your desire to die without heroics. As should be obvious here, this old geezer did not get the prior approval necessary to be allowed to die."

Alex stared coldly at him, her eyes locked on his. "I don't find that very funny."

"It wasn't meant to be funny," he snapped. "I don't enjoy coding these old gomers but I don't have a choice. If a patient isn't a 'No Code' and they die, then we're obligated to try to revive them. If this old man didn't want us pounding on his chest and charring his flesh with electricity then he or his family should have made him a 'No Code'."

"Well, I think those rules stink," Alex said. "If we could use some common sense, we'd let these old people die with a little dignity."

The physician smiled. He was too tired to argue but he liked her spunk.

“I couldn’t agree more,” he said, “but most people don’t have common sense so we have to make rules. Now, if you’ll excuse me, I’ve got a life to save. Keep pumping on his chest and give him another amp of epi.”

Alex bit her bottom lip and walked hurriedly from the room with Patsy following closely behind.

“Are you okay, Alex?” Patsy asked, as she caught up with her in the hallway.

“Yeah, I’m fine, just disillusioned. I can’t understand why we torture these patients when nothing we do is going to change the outcome. If that old man survives the code, so what? He’s dying with metastatic lung cancer. It’d be a blessing for him to die. You know he’s got to be in pain if the cancer has spread.”

“I’m on your side,” Patsy replied, “but it’s not our decision. Dr. Nichols was being sarcastic, but unfortunately, truthful. If a person dies in a hospital and hasn’t been made a ‘No Code’, our society expects us to try to resuscitate them. Until we can change the way society views life and death and change the perception people have of what modern medicine has to offer, we’ll be forced to try and keep all of these people alive.”

“Even if they’d be better off dead?” Alex asked.

Patsy nodded her head. “Even if they’d be better off dead,” she replied. “I’ve seen a lot of patients who I thought should’ve been allowed to die but for whatever reason they were denied that chance. Most of the time it was a family member who refused to give the physician permission to withhold treatment, but there have been times when I’ve seen a physician convince family members to press on, dangling a false hope in front of them like a carrot in front of a mule.”

“Like Jim Curry?” Alex asked.

“Excuse me?” Patsy replied, seeming startled.

“Like Dr. Curry. He convinced Dad to let him try and keep Mom alive even when we knew there was no chance for her to recover.”

Patsy frowned and silently nodded her head.

"He had a way of doing that," she replied. "He believed if one of his patients died he had failed, and failure wasn't an option. I saw him put his cancer patients through so much without ever considering their feelings. Several years ago I took care of one of his patients who was dying with metastatic disease. Severe pain. Suffering. Had just weaned from the ventilator when her lung collapsed. Would've been the perfect opportunity to let her die, but not Curry. He wouldn't allow it. Convinced her husband to let him insert a chest tube and re-expand her lung, knowing damn well that putting a chest tube in wasn't going to change the outcome. I felt so sorry for her husband. He didn't want to put her through it, but he was afraid to let her go and Curry used his fear to convince him there wasn't another option."

"When was that?" Alex interrupted.

"I don't know, four, maybe five years ago," Patsy replied.

Alex pursed her lips and shook her head. A tear formed in the corner of her eye.

"That was about the time my mother died," she replied. "And she had colon cancer. On the day she weaned from the ventilator, she developed a pneumothorax and Dr. Curry convinced Dad to let him put a chest tube in. Do you remember anything else about her?"

"Not really," Patsy replied, uncomfortably. "I mean, I've taken care of so many patients through the years. And sadly, so many of them were terminally ill."

"This particular patient, how old was she?"

"I don't recall. Forty? Fifty? I don't remember."

"What about her hair?" Alex asked. "What color was it?"

Patsy closed her eyes as if in deep thought. "What color was your mother's hair?" she asked.

"Brown," Alex replied, "long and brown."

The corners of Patsy's mouth turned upward in a smile of relief. "She was bald," she replied. "I do remember that. Her head was as slick as an onion. It couldn't have been your mother."

Tears rolled slowly down Alex's cheeks.

"What's wrong?" Patsy asked.

"Mom lost her hair during chemotherapy," Alex replied. "She was completely bald and refused to wear the wig Dad bought her. You took care of my mother before she died."

Patsy forced a smile as she quickly shook her head from side to side.

"A lot of cancer patients are bald. I'm sure it's coincidental."

"Was her name Betty Lowe?" Alex asked.

"I don't remember," Patsy replied, shaking her head and rising suddenly as to end the conversation. "And even if I could, what would it matter? It wouldn't change anything."

"No," Alex replied, noticeably dissatisfied with Patsy's answer. "It wouldn't change anything, but at least I'd know."

As the two of them walked in silence back to the ICU, Patsy's mind drifted back to an earlier encounter with Jim Curry. Even though it had happened years before, in her mind it was as if it were yesterday. She could still picture the frail, diminutive man in bed three. His skin was the pale, sickly white she had come to associate with death and his breath had the strong smell of baker's yeast, a sure sign of Candida overgrowth in his mouth.

"Has his family signed the permit for the bone marrow biopsy?" Dr. Curry asked.

Patsy's heart lodged in her throat. She had felt the wrath of Jim Curry before and she knew she was about to feel it again.

"No, sir," she replied feebly.

"And why the hell not?" he asked, his tone denoting his aggravation.

"I haven't asked them," she replied softly.

Jim Curry pushed up the white sleeve of his lab coat and shook his wrist until his gold Rolex watch spun to the top of his wrist.

"I made rounds at 7:00 a.m. and told you I planned to perform a bone marrow biopsy on him at 2:00 p.m. I ordered the biopsy tray and I told you to get the permit. I did my job. Now why in the hell haven't you done yours?"

"I didn't ..."

"Have you seen his family today?" Dr.Curry asked, cutting her off in mid-sentence.

Patsy chewed nervously on her lip and nodded. "Yes, sir."

"Then why didn't..."

"Because I didn't think it was necessary," Patsy interrupted. "He's ninety years old and he's got leukemia. I've visited with the family every day for the last three weeks. They don't want anything done. They just want to keep him comfortable."

"They don't know what they want or what he needs," Dr. Curry quipped. "They don't have the medical background necessary to make life and death decisions. That's my job. I make the tough decisions that save lives."

"He's dying, regardless of what the bone marrow biopsy shows," Patsy replied.

"Everybody is dying," Dr. Curry snapped, "some just sooner than others. Now, are you going to get the permit signed or do I have to do it myself?"

Patsy shook her head. She knew better than to say what she was thinking but she couldn't help herself.

"Would you do it if he didn't have insurance?" she inquired softly.

"I don't care if he has insurance or not," Dr. Curry ranted. "That's got absolutely nothing to do with it. I make my decisions based on my medical training, not based on the patient's ability to pay."

"Miss Gomez didn't get a bone marrow biopsy before she died last week," Patsy offered.

"And she didn't have leukemia," Curry shot back.

"No, sir, but she was anemic and had thrombocytopenia," she replied.

"She had brain mets from her colon cancer. A bone marrow biopsy wasn't going to save her life."

Patsy walked to the foot of the bed and stared out the window, her back to Dr. Curry. "Do you really believe anything you learn from a bone marrow biopsy will prolong his life? He's ninety years old."

"How dare you question my decisions! If you're not going to get the permit signed, give me the damn thing and I'll do it myself."

Patsy turned around quickly and handed him the clipboard with the permit on it.

"You wouldn't be doing this if he didn't have insurance," she said.

"I've had enough of your attitude!" Dr. Curry yelled, shaking his finger at her. "You'll hear from Lib Dillard and from Gerald Warren. The very idea that you'd accuse me of showing preferential treatment to insured patients just to make money for this hospital."

Patsy sat down beside the old man's bed and watched as Dr. Curry disappeared through the doors of the ICU. She'd never accused him of doing things just to make money for the hospital. But now it was beginning to make sense.

~ ~ ~

"You okay?" Alex asked. "You sure got quiet all of the sudden."

Patsy shook her head to clear the cobwebs. "Yeah, yeah. I'm sorry," she replied. "I'd just gotten lost in some old memories."

- 4 -

Alex's heart pounded when she pushed open the door to the medical records room. Her palms were sweaty as she approached the elderly lady seated behind the metal desk.

"Excuse me," she whispered politely, "but I need to have a chart pulled."

"Name and date of birth," the worker replied without looking up from her magazine.

"Betty Lowe. Two, five, fifty-four," Alex replied.

The lady folded the page she was reading and dropped her magazine on the floor beside her desk. Her fingers moved quickly as she typed in the information. She shook her head while staring at her computer screen.

"You did say two, five, fifty-four, didn't you?" she asked.

"Yes, ma'am," Alex answered. "Is she not in the computer?"

"Betty Lowe?" the lady asked, looking up at Alex.

"Yes, ma'am. Is she not in there?"

"I've got a listing for her. Do you know her room number?"

"She's not in the hospital," Alex replied. "She's deceased."

The woman smiled and sighed.

"That's what the computer said, but I don't trust these things. You know, they're only as good as the operator," she said chuckling. "Garbage in, garbage out. At least that's what they say. I always hate to tell a person someone's dead if they aren't. People don't deal well with death, you know."

"Yes, ma'am, I know," Alex replied. "So, you do have a chart on her?"

"I sure do. If you'll hang on a minute, I'll get it for you."

She disappeared among the aisles of charts and returned with a thick, manila folder. She smiled when she handed the heavy chart to Alex.

"You think you're strong enough to carry this?" she asked.

"I hope so," Alex replied. "It sure is thick."

"It is that," she replied. "She was either hospitalized a lot or real sick. You don't have a chart that thick if you're healthy."

"No, I guess you don't," Alex replied. "Is there some place where I can look at this?"

"There's a table in the back room," the lady replied, pointing at the door behind her. "The doctors never use it when they're doing their dictations. I'm sure they won't mind. I notice by your nametag that you've got the same last name. Was she a relative?"

"Yes, ma'am," Alex replied. "She was my mother."

"I'm sorry. She must've died young."

"Yes, ma'am," Alex replied, nodding. "She was only forty-three."

"Don't mean to be nosy," the lady said, "but what'd she die from?"

"Colon cancer," Alex replied. "By the time they found it, it was too late. She only lived a few months."

"Same thing happened to my Earl," the lady replied, wiping a tear from her eye. "Lived about six months after they found his lung cancer. Course, Earl smoked himself to death. Don't guess your mama smoked, did she?"

"No, ma'am," Alex replied, shaking her head.

"Well, Earl did. Two packs a day for as long as I can remember. Dr. Curry said Earl didn't have no one to blame but himself."

"Dr. Curry took care of your husband?" Alex asked.

"He sure did," the clerk replied, smiling and nodding. "Earl hadn't seen a doctor in thirty years, but when he started coughing up blood, we knew something was wrong. I took him to the emergency room and they suspected it was cancer. Dr. Curry put him in the hospital and ran tests on him. That's when we found out the cancer had spread to his bones and his brain."

"I'm sorry to hear that," Alex replied. "I guess there wasn't anything to do but keep him comfortable at that point."

"Oh, no," the old lady replied, "not with Dr. Curry taking care of him. That man did everything you could imagine for Earl. Gave him chemotherapy and radiation and when he got to where he couldn't breath, he kept him alive on a ventilator while he tried to figure out if there was anything else he could do. If Dr. Curry hadn't been Earl's doctor, Earl would've been dead within two or three months. That's one doctor who sure knew how to cheat death. Earl lived for six months after they found his cancer. Can you imagine? Six months!"

Alex clutched her mother's chart tightly against her chest and rocked back and forth, shifting her weight uncomfortably from one foot to the other.

"I know you were glad to have those six months with him," she said sympathetically.

The lady momentarily lowered her head but quickly looked up, staring in silence at Alex. Tears filled her eyes. She took her knuckle and wiped the tears from her right eye.

"You'd think so," she admitted, "but they were the worst six months of my life. Earl would've been better off if he'd died that night in the 'mergency room. For six months he lay awake at night crying from the constant pain of the cancer eating away at his bones. I asked Dr. Curry to keep him comfortable and let him die, but he wouldn't do it. Even when Earl's mind left him, after the cancer got in his brain, Dr. Curry wouldn't give up. He said life was a battle against death and he was the quarterback on life's team. He wouldn't let Earl die because if Earl died, then he had failed." The old lady wiped her tears again and regained her composure. "I'm sorry," she said. "I didn't mean to get off on Earl like that."

"No need to apologize," Alex said, patting her on the arm. "I know how you feel. When Mom was dying, Dr. Curry did the same thing to her. Did Earl suffer very much?"

The old woman closed her eyes and shook her head.

"Oh, honey, you can't imagine how much he suffered. His pain was unbearable. Dr. Curry filled him with narcotics, but it didn't control his pain. I reached the point of wishing he could die just so he could stop hurting. And then I felt guilty for wishing he were dead."

Alex squeezed the old woman's hand. Her thin, wrinkled skin was covered with age spots and small bruises. She curled her bony fingers around Alex's hand.

"When Earl died, I cried, but it wasn't because I was sad. I knew I'd miss him since we'd been together for forty-five years but it was such a relief knowing his suffering had ended and that he'd moved on to a better place. I don't know what you believe, young lady, but I believe I'll see Earl again one day. And when I do see him, I believe he'll have a new body free from cancer and pain."

Alex smiled and nodded her head.

"I don't know what happens after we die," she said, "but I hope you're right. I'd love to see my mother again and know that she's been restored to health."

"Honey, you'll see your mother again. You mark my word. Now, you go on over there and look through your mama's chart. If I can do anything for you, just let me know."

Alex squeezed the lady's hand again and nodded her thanks. It took both hands to carry her mother's chart to the table. Her hands shook as she opened the manila folder and began reading.

~ ~ ~

This is the second Richland Memorial admission for this unfortunate forty-three year old female with metastatic colon cancer unresponsive to chemotherapy. She has been experiencing severe pain at home uncontrolled by oral medications and accompanied this past week by nausea, vomiting and dehydration. She is being admitted to the oncology service at this time for pain control and correction of electrolyte and nutritional abnormalities with intravenous fluids.

Alex closed her eyes and gently massaged her temples. She wasn't sure she was ready to learn the details of her mother's final days of life. She flipped the pages of the chart until she located the nurses' notes. At the bottom of the page, she saw Patsy Carter's signature.

- 5 -

Elizabeth was sitting in the shade of a large oak tree in the center of Richland Park when Alex arrived. Two large, gray squirrels chased one another carefree in the branches above her head. Dead leaves crunched noisily under Alex's feet as she approached the tree where her sister was sitting. Children playing on monkey bars laughed and squealed joyfully in the distance.

"I picked up a couple of deli sandwiches and some soft drinks for lunch. Hope you haven't eaten," Elizabeth said.

"I haven't," Alex answered, "but I'm not very hungry."

"You're not getting sick are you?" Elizabeth asked.

"No, I feel fine. Do I look sick?"

"No, you don't look sick, but it's not like you to not be hungry."

"I've had a lot on my mind lately," Alex admitted.

"Work?" Elizabeth asked.

"Work's going okay, but...."

"But what?" Elizabeth interrupted.

"Well, the nurse who's training me in the ICU, Patsy Carter, she...."

"Let me guess," Elizabeth interrupted again, "she doesn't know as much about critical care medicine as you do?"

Alex smiled and quickly shook her head from side to side.

"Oh, no, nothing like that," she said. "She very competent and she's an excellent teacher."

"Then what's the problem?" Elizabeth asked.

"She made some comments the other day which led me to believe she'd taken care of Mom before she died."

"What sort of comments?"

"She described a patient who sounded a lot like Mom, a patient with cancer who'd been on a ventilator and had a chest tube and ended up..." Alex stopped in mid sentence and shrugged her shoulders.

"And ended up what?" Elizabeth pressed. "Dying?"

"Yes, she ended up dying."

"Did you ask her if it was Mom?"

"I tried to," Alex said. "I told her Mom's name, but she said the name wasn't familiar."

"I'm not surprised," Elizabeth replied. "That was five years ago. You couldn't very well expect her to remember a patient's name from that long ago."

"But when I told her Mom's name she seemed startled, almost as if she recognized the name but didn't want to admit it."

"That's silly," Elizabeth replied. "Why would she not want to admit it?"

"Maybe she was afraid I'd ask her questions about Mom and what went on with her before she died, questions she didn't want to answer."

"You're grasping for straws," Elizabeth said between bites of her sandwich.

"Then why'd she lie to me?" Alex asked angrily. "Why wouldn't she admit she took care of Mom?"

Elizabeth shook her head and leaned back against the tree.

"How do you know she lied?" she asked. "You don't have any proof she took care of Mom."

"Oh, but I do," Alex answered, eagerly leaning forward from the large oak tree. "After work yesterday, I went to the medical records department and had Mom's chart pulled. Patsy worked the day shift and took care of Mom while she was in intensive care. There's documentation where she cleaned Mom's decubitus ulcers, gave her pain medicine and assisted Dr. Curry with the chest tube. Elizabeth, she was the nurse who got Dad to sign the permission slip for the chest tube. That's why she looked so familiar when I first met her. You and I were with Dad when he signed the permit. I saw Patsy that day."

Elizabeth shrugged her shoulders as she popped the top on her soft drink. She tore a small piece of crust from her sandwich and tossed it on the ground to a squirrel that grabbed it and ran quickly up the tree behind her.

"So she was one of the nurses who took care of Mom," Elizabeth said. "So what?"

"So what?" Alex asked loudly. "Is that all you can say? So what? So everything. Elizabeth, she knows what Mom went through before she died."

"We all know what Mom went through before she died," Elizabeth replied softly. "You know. I know. Dad knows. We all know what she went through. I don't understand why it's so important to you that you're working with a nurse who took care of her before she died."

"Remember the other night when we were eating dinner at Dad's house and you thought I'd lied to Dad about the demons at Richland?"

Elizabeth rolled her eyes and nodded her head. "I can read you like a book, can't I?"

Alex batted her eyes and nodded. "You knew I was lying, didn't you?" she asked.

"I told you as much that night. I don't know why Dad didn't pick up on it. You don't lie very well."

"I've never had the need to," Alex replied.

"Have your memories of Mom returned?" Elizabeth asked.

Alex lowered her head and sighed.

"I did fine on the med-surg floors, but as soon as I walked through the double doors of the ICU..." She paused and took several slow, deep breaths. "Liz, my heart started racing, my palms got sweaty, I had trouble breathing. It was just like when I was having the nightmares."

"Does anyone know?" Elizabeth asked.

"Patsy knows. She was with me that first morning in the ICU. As soon as I walked through the double doors and smelled that ICU smell, she saw the look in my eyes and knew that something was wrong. She wanted to know if I had seen a ghost."

"And you told her everything."

"Well, what was I supposed to do?" Alex asked. "I was practically in tears, and like you said, I don't lie very well."

"So, what'd you tell her?" Elizabeth asked.

"I told her that I'd seen a ghost, that Mom had died in the ICU several years before and that when I walked through those double doors, every thing came rushing back. Elizabeth, I saw Mom as clearly as I see you right now. She was connected to the ventilator and had the chest tube coming out of her side. Her skin was so pale. And she was bald. It was so real."

"Is that the only time you've seen her?" Elizabeth asked.

Alex bit her bottom lip and closed her eyes.

"No," she admitted, shaking her head. "I've seen her several times, but the first time was the most vivid. Now, every morning when I walk down the hall to the ICU, I get this terrible sensation. When those double doors swing open, my eyes automatically look at bed three to be sure Mom's not there."

"Alex, Mom is dead. She's not suddenly going to appear in the ICU."

"I know that, but I can't help it. It was so real that first morning."

"Are you having the nightmares again?" Elizabeth asked.

"I've had some dreams about Mom," Alex replied, "but not the nightmares. I don't think I could deal with them again."

"How long before you finish your ICU rotation?" Elizabeth pressed.

"Just a few more days."

"Do you think they'd let you skip the last few days and

work somewhere else?"

"Probably, but I'm not sure I want to," Alex replied.

Elizabeth frowned, surprised by Alex's answer.

"Why wouldn't you?" she asked. "Especially if it helps keep your sanity?"

"First of all, I'm not going crazy," Alex replied. "And second, I like the ICU."

"You like the ICU?" Elizabeth asked, raising her voice. "Listen to yourself. You just admitted that every time you get near the ICU your heart races and your palms get sweaty. Even the smells bring back memories."

"I know," Alex replied, "but that doesn't mean I don't enjoy working there. There's something about a critically ill patient teetering on the brink of death that excites me. I like working with Swan-Ganz catheters and monitoring heart rhythms. I thrive on pressure."

"You may thrive on pressure, but do you thrive on the memories of Mom?"

"I don't thrive on them, but I'm not going to run from them," Alex replied. "And besides, they don't last very long. Once I get involved in my routine and start taking care of patients, I'm fine."

"Well, I hope they don't assign you to work in the ICU when you start your job."

"I should get to choose where I'll work."

"And have you decided?" Elizabeth asked.

Alex nodded. "If I had to choose today, I'd choose the ICU."

Elizabeth shook her head and stared at her sister in disbelief.

"Unbelievable," she said. "You have a panic attack every time you go near the ICU and yet you'd purposefully choose to work there. I hope you know what you're doing."

Alex lowered her head and drew in the dirt with her finger.

“I know it’s hard for you to understand,” she said, “but the challenge of taking care of critically ill patients is very satisfying and challenging. With time, I’ll put the demons back in their place.”

“For your sake and for your sanity, I hope you’re right,” Elizabeth replied.

Alex smiled and patted her little sister on the arm.

“I’ll be fine,” she said. “Trust me. Now, how about passing me one of those sandwiches.”

“Have you found a roommate, yet?” Elizabeth asked, as she handed her the remaining sandwich.

“No, but I’m not sure I want one,” Alex replied. “It was nice living with you in the dorm, but I’m enjoying having my own apartment with a little peace and quiet.”

“Are you insinuating that I was noisy?” Elizabeth asked grinning.

“Of course not,” Alex replied smiling back, “and I wouldn’t give anything for the two years we lived together. But when you graduate, don’t expect to move in with me.”

“So, I’m on my on?” Elizabeth asked.

“Yep, just like me, you’re on your own,” Alex replied, taking a bit of her sandwich.

- 6 -

Patsy poked her head inside the drawn curtain of the tiny ICU room.

"Alex, are you busy?" she asked.

"Not really," Alex replied as she broke the top off a vial of medicine. "What do you need?"

"If you'll help me get Mr. Holland bathed, we can call transportation and have him taken to the morgue."

"Just a sec," Alex said, "as soon as I administer this Rocephin to bed two."

Patsy pulled back the sheet covering the old man and stared at his emaciated body. The bright sunlight coming through the window accentuated the paleness of his skin.

"Are you okay, Patsy?"

Startled by Alex's voice, she blinked her eyes and reached into the basin for a washcloth.

"Oh, yeah, I'm fine," she replied. "Did you give Miss Roberts the Rocephin?"

"Yeah," Alex replied. "I diluted it in normal saline and piggybacked it into her I.V. line. Are you sure you're okay? You looked like you were in another world when I walked up."

"Thanks for asking," Patsy replied, "but yeah, I'm fine. I was just thinking about something you said yesterday."

"Something I said?" Alex asked, wrinkling her forehead.

Patsy squeezed the soapy water from the washcloth and nodded.

"When Mr. Holland coded yesterday, you asked the doctor why he was being coded. At the time, I thought it was a ridiculous question. You're a registered nurse. You knew why he was being coded. And then I heard Dr. Nichol's answer and I finally understood your question. Now, less than twenty-four hours later, he's dead and I'm asking myself, why did we code this man? Look at him. He's nothing but skin and bones and decubitus ulcers. Nothing we did yesterday, or last week, or last month was going to change the fact that he was going to die from lung cancer. We added several thousand dollars to his hospital bill, which his family will have to pay, broke a few ribs with our chest compressions and burned his chest with jolts of electricity. And for what? So he could live another day. I've been a nurse for ten years, and I've finally realized there's something wrong with our system. Why can't we let these people die?"

"Are you asking my opinion or are you talking just to be talking?" Alex asked.

"Just talking," Patsy replied. "I think I know the answer. We're afraid of death. We can't accept the fact that we're not immortal. I saw a forty-five-year-old, mother of three die last week from injuries sustained in a car wreck. As I stood by her bed and watched her die, I broke down and cried. I wasn't emotionally attached to her, but I realized she and I were the same age and it could just as easily have been me. I think it finally dawned on me that the immortality of my youth never really existed. We're all going to die one day. I only hope when it's my turn, my family and my doctor will let me die with my dignity."

Alex gently pulled the piece of tape from the back of the old man's hand and removed the I.V. catheter. The dark, deoxygenated blood oozed from the site until she covered the puncture wound with a Band-Aid. She connected a syringe to his Foley catheter and deflated the small balloon, allowing her to pull the catheter from his bladder. She took a washcloth from the basin and went through the motion of washing the old man's chest, shaking her head as she bathed him.

"Look at these bruises. I wonder how many ribs they cracked during the code?" she asked.

"It's hard to tell," Patsy replied. "They might have broken all of them as long as they coded him. Bones get brittle when they're full of cancer. Have you removed all of his tubes?"

"Done. He only had the I.V. and the Foley," Alex replied. "If you're finished bathing him, I'll ask Wanda to call transportation."

Patsy sighed deeply as she pulled the sheet up to the old man's chin.

"Is Miss Roberts stable?" she asked.

"Yep," Alex answered, bobbing her head. "I gave her the Rocephin so she's basically on auto pilot for the rest of the shift."

"Then why don't we grab some lunch?" Patsy asked. "I need to get out of here for a few minutes."

"Sounds good to me," Alex replied. "Cafeteria or snack bar?"

"Cafeteria," Patsy replied without hesitating. "It's usually quieter than the snack bar at this time of day."

The two of them walked in silence to the hospital's cafeteria. Patsy was right. There were very few people eating. The two of them found an open table in the corner of the large room and sat down. The metal table rocked back and forth on uneven legs.

"You'd think after all these years I'd get accustomed to patients dying," Patsy said, "but it never gets any easier."

"Why should it get any easier?" Alex asked.

"I don't know. I guess it shouldn't," Patsy replied, "but I know so many nurses and doctors who seem unaffected by death. They have a patient die and it's no big deal. When one of my patients dies, I feel like a small part of me dies with them."

"That's because you haven't allowed the heartaches of medicine to harden you," Alex replied. "You still care about your patients. I saw that from the first day I worked with you.

You're different, and I mean that as a compliment."

Patsy took her napkin and swallowed hard. "That's sweet of you to say. I only hope it's true."

Alex took a bite of salad and washed it down with a sip of her soft drink.

"From what I've seen, it's true," she replied.

"Thank you," Patsy replied. "It's nice to know you feel that way."

Alex took another sip of her soft drink and nervously cleared her throat.

"When I got off work yesterday, I went by the medical records office and pulled my mother's chart," she said.

Her voice trailed off softly, hoping Patsy would ask her why. But her mentor sat with her head down, picking at the food on her plate, seemingly unaware of Alex's remark.

"When I read Mom's chart," Alex continued, "I found your name in the nurse's notes."

The older nurse lifted her head and looked at Alex. "You did?" she asked.

"Yeah, I did. You took care of Mom while she was in the ICU."

"I know," Patsy admitted. "I remember her well."

"Then why'd you say you didn't remember her?" Alex asked. "Why'd you lie to me?"

"I don't know," Patsy replied, shaking her head. "I guess when I saw how disturbed you were that first morning, I thought it'd be best if I didn't admit having cared for her. Why bring up those old memories?"

"Because I can't bury them if I can't face them," Alex replied. "I need to know what she went through before she died."

Patsy took a slow, deep breath and pushed back from the table.

"Are you sure you want to know?" she asked.

"I don't have a choice," Alex replied. "I've got to know so I can put it behind me."

"All right," Patsy replied, "but stop me if you don't want to hear what I have to say."

Alex nodded her head. "Fair enough," she said.

"You looked familiar the first morning you were assigned to work with me. You've changed some. Your hair is longer and you've filled out, but I remembered you. I wasn't sure why I knew you at first, but when you started asking questions about your mother, I remembered. How old were you when she died?"

"Seventeen, almost eighteen," Alex answered.

"I was thinking you were younger," Patsy said, "but that doesn't matter. I've taken care of a lot of patients through the years, most of whom I can't remember, but your mother was different. She was close enough to my age to make me realize it could just as easily have been me dying with cancer. I had two kids and a husband just like she did and at the time, I'd been losing weight. The only thing I could think of was I had colon cancer, just like she did. Fortunately for me, it turned out to be an overactive thyroid."

"Mom was already on the ventilator when she was transferred to the unit wasn't she?" Alex interrupted.

"As I recall, she was," Patsy replied. "She'd coded the night before and had been placed on the ventilator during the code. When I took report that morning, I was assigned to take care of her. I remember thinking how sad her situation was. When I went into her room to do my assessment, I got tearful, which was unlike me."

"Was she suffering?" Alex asked.

Patsy shook her head. "I don't think so. Not when I first saw her. The first day or two after the code she wasn't very alert."

"But after she regained consciousness? Did she suffer much?" Alex asked.

"She had a lot of pain, if that's what you're asking."

Alex inched her chair closer to the table. "What kind of pain?"

"I don't know," Patsy replied. "I just remember that whenever we turned her or bathed her she appeared to be in pain. I do remember she had large decubitus ulcers on her buttocks. One morning I walked into her room and found Dr. Curry scrubbing the ulcers. She was in tears because of the pain, but he wouldn't stop. I offered to help but he told me he was capable of cleaning a wound and wanted to know why I thought I could do it any better."

"What'd you say?" Alex asked.

"Not much. I'd already had a few run ins with him. We didn't see eye-to-eye on a lot of things and he didn't particularly care for me. He told Lib Dillard and Mr. Warren that I had accused him of prolonging lives and performing procedures just to make money for the hospital."

"You did that?" Alex asked, astonished by Patsy's boldness.

Patsy shook her head and chuckled. "No, I wasn't that brash, even when I was younger. But I did have my concerns about why he did what he did."

"What was he doing?" Alex asked.

"I never had any proof but it was almost as if treated insured patients more aggressively than non-insured patients, that he tried harder to keep them alive and did more procedures on them."

"Why would he do that?" Alex asked.

Patsy rubbed her index and middle fingers against her thumb in a circular motion. "For the almighty dollar I presume."

Alex's eyes lit up as if a light had been turned on in her brain. "That's got to be it. Why else would he torture patients the way he did?"

"I don't know," Patsy replied. "It's just my theory."

"What'd you tell him after he questioned you about cleaning Mom's decubitus ulcers?"

"I told him I wasn't any better at cleaning wounds, but I could certainly be gentler. He gave me his go to hell look and kept right on scrubbing. As soon as he left the unit I gave her a shot of Demerol. She slept the rest of the morning. I made a point after that to keep her ulcers clean so he wouldn't have any reason to mess with them."

Alex bit her bottom lip and blinked back the salty tears that burned her eyes.

"In one of your notes you documented the insertion of Mom's chest tube. I don't know if you remember, but that's when I first saw you."

"Oh, I remember," Patsy assured her. "I couldn't understand why Dr. Curry would want to put a chest tube in her. She was dying with cancer. What good would the chest tube do?"

"That's how we felt," Alex said. "We didn't understand his reasoning."

"When I asked him why we were doing it, he got mad. I remember his words as if it were yesterday. 'We are not putting in a chest tube,' he said. 'I'm putting it in.' He was so arrogant about it. 'Just because this lady has cancer and decubitus ulcers is no reason to deny her the right to live. Miss Carter, death is failure and failure is not an option for me.' He told me to order the chest tube tray and have your father sign the permit."

"Do chest tubes hurt?" Alex asked.

"I've never had one," Patsy replied, "but I'm sure they must."

Alex pressed her back against her chair and stared blankly into space, avoiding eye contact with Patsy. "Did Mom ever ask you to let her die?"

Patsy paused and took a deep breath before answering.

"She didn't ask me directly," Patsy recalled, "but I was in the room when she told your father she wanted to die. She'd just come off the ventilator and couldn't even whisper. Your dad, bless his heart, couldn't read lips if his life depended on it. He asked me to see if I could read her lips. There was no doubt about what she was saying, but how could I tell him she was asking him to let her die? I told him she was trying to tell him she loved him, but she kept shaking her head and crying. Finally she whispered to let her die. The look in your dad's eyes was unmistakable. It was like he'd been stabbed in the heart. I felt so sorry for him."

Alex buried her face in her hands and cried softly.

"I'm sorry," Patsy said, "maybe I shouldn't tell you any more."

"No, no," Alex pleaded, "please, go on. I want to hear this. I need to hear it. Every morning when I see the doors to the ICU, I want to turn and run away. It terrifies me knowing Mom died in the unit but not knowing what happened to her during the last few days of her life. If I can hear the truth then maybe I won't have to be a prisoner to my imagination."

"Are you sure you want to hear it all?" Patsy asked.

Alex nodded and swallowed hard.

"I'm sure," she said. "You were in the room when Mom died weren't you?"

"Yes, I was," Patsy replied softly.

"I was there, too," Alex replied.

"I know," Patsy replied. "I tried to get you to go to the waiting room while we worked with her."

"So that was you?" Alex asked.

"Yeah, it was me. You don't remember?"

"I remember being told to leave the room, but I didn't remember it being you," Alex replied.

"You were pretty adamant about not leaving your mother's side."

"I'm sorry."

"Don't apologize. I was simply stating a fact."

"I couldn't understand why Dr. Curry didn't come," Alex said. "Mom was his patient and she was dying."

"That's why he didn't come," Patsy said. "She was dying. When your mom and dad agreed that she'd be a 'No Code', he quit trying. He couldn't accept death and if a patient elected to be a 'No Code', they'd accepted death. And he couldn't handle that."

"Did he know Mom was seizing?"

"Oh, yeah," Patsy said, rocking back and forth in her chair. "He knew exactly what was going on. We called him as soon as the seizure started. He said we could give her some Valium for the seizure, but he was eating lunch."

Tears filled Alex's eyes.

"For some reason," she said, "I knew that. Maybe I overheard one of the nurses that day and had suppressed the memory, but somehow I knew he refused to leave his lunch to help Mom. How could a doctor refuse to help a dying patient?"

"Because he was Jim Curry," Patsy replied. "That's how."

Patsy took Alex's hand in her hand and gently patted it.

"Come on," she said. "We could talk all day, but we need to get back to work."

Alex took a tissue from her pocket and wiped the tears from her eyes.

"Thanks, Patsy," she said. "Thanks for what you did for Mom and for what you've done for me."

- 7 -

Alex had closed the apartment door and was putting her key into the tarnished, dead bolt lock when she heard the telephone ring. She glanced anxiously at her watch. Ten-fifteen p.m., still plenty of time before she'd be late for work. As she pushed open the heavy door, the multicolored mat just inside the door rolled up in a ball. She pushed the mat aside with her foot and walked hurriedly across the small room to the coffee table where her phone was sitting. She plopped down on the edge of the worn, corduroy sofa and pressed the receiver against her ear.

"Hello," she answered.

"Hey, sweetheart. It's Ben. Are you getting ready for work?"

"Yes, Benjamin," she replied, thrilled by the assuring voice of her boyfriend, Ben Folmar, a recent pharmacy school graduate and the newest employee of the Richland Memorial pharmacy. "I was on my way out the door when you called."

"Then I won't keep you," he replied, "but I did want to wish you luck on your first night."

"Thanks, Ben, but after six weeks of orientation it doesn't feel like my first night."

"I hope you know what you're doing," he replied. "Elizabeth told me you'd been having some problems in the ICU."

Alex rolled her eyes and looked out the large window behind the sofa. The thin sliver of moon smiled at her from behind the clouds. Her mother stared lovingly at her from a picture on the coffee table.

"Ben, I'm fine," she said. "I don't know if Elizabeth told you, but one of the nurses I work with took care of Mom while she was in the hospital. She told me all about Mom's illness and what went on before she died. It was hard for me to hear, but I think it helped me put it behind me."

"I hope it did," he replied. "You know we're all concerned about you working in the ICU."

"Really, Ben," Alex replied, "I'm fine. Before I talked with Patsy, my hands would get sweaty and my heart would race if I went near the ICU. But since our conversation, I haven't had any problems."

"I hope you're telling me the truth."

"I've got no reason to lie. Trust me, Sweetie. I'll be fine."

"Well, I wish you didn't have to work nights."

"I didn't have a choice," Alex replied. "I'm low nurse on the totem pole. Hate to run, but I don't want to be late for my first shift."

"And I don't want you to be late," Ben replied. "I hope it goes well."

"Thanks, Ben. I love you for being concerned about me."

"I love you, too, Hon," he replied. "Call me tomorrow. I'm covering the day shift for Jeff but I should be home by six."

"I will, and don't worry, I'll be fine."

She hung up the phone and turned off the black halogen floor lamp beside the couch. A swarm of butterflies danced nervously in her stomach as she flipped off the porch light and closed the door behind her. The cheap, brass doorknocker clanged loudly in the still night.

The evening ICU shift nurses were gathered around a small table in the conference room giving report when Alex arrived. Cardiac monitors and ventilators beeped rhythmically outside the conference room. Inside the small room, the strong smell of perfumes masked the medicinal smell of the ICU.

"Sorry I'm running late," Alex said, "but my boyfriend called to wish me luck as I was leaving. He was worried about my first night on the job. You know how protective some guys can be."

The charge nurse smiled and nodded her head to Alex.

"Only the caring ones," she replied. "You better hang on to him. Anyway, you haven't missed much. We were just getting started. You'll be taking care of Mr. Sheffield tonight. He should be fairly easy. He's a seventy-year-old admitted last night with congestive heart failure. He's put out about four liters of urine today after I.V. Lasix and is breathing comfortably now. Should transfer out of the unit in the morning." She paused briefly and looked at Alex. "Unfortunately, your other patient isn't so simple. I hate to give him to you on your first night, but we're short staffed and Patsy has been singing your praises."

Alex tried to suppress her smile. She was glad to hear Patsy had said good things about her.

"That's fine," she said. "What's he got?"

"He's a seventeen-year-old male with closed head trauma from a motorcycle wreck two days ago," she replied. "Should've gone to neuro-intensive care, but they didn't have an open bed so we got him down here. He had an exploratory laparotomy yesterday where they removed his spleen and sutured a liver laceration. He's also got fractures of his left femur and left tib-fib as well as several broken ribs."

"Sounds like a train wreck," Alex interrupted.

The charge nurse held up her hand and shook her head.

"It gets better," she said. "A CAT scan this morning showed a large subdural hematoma which probably explains his lethargy. His biggest problem on evenings has been his blood pressure. One minute we're using Dopamine, the next minute he's back on Nipride. Wish I didn't have to give him to you, but I know you can handle it. Kendal has the patient in the next bed. I'm sure she'll help if you need her. Hope you have a quiet night."

"Thanks, Pam," Alex said. "And don't worry, I'll be fine."

The butterflies in her stomach flapped their wings excitedly as she made her way to her first patient's room. Walter Sheffield was resting quietly with his eyes closed. His breathing was rhythmic and unlabored. She lightly grasped his shoulder and gently shook him.

"Mr. Sheffield, I'm Alex Lowe," she said. "I'll be taking care of you tonight. How are you feeling?"

"Like I don't need to be in the hospital," he replied. "Couldn't breathe when I got here, but they put something in my I.V. last night and I've peed like a race horse all day. I feel like a new man."

"I'm glad you're feeling better. Is there anything I can get for you?"

"You got any spare blankets in this hotel?" he chuckled. "Skinny old man like me ain't got much fat meat to keep him warm. It's cold enough to slaughter hogs back here."

"It is kind of cool. Let me check on a blanket," she replied.

Alex returned a few minutes later and placed an extra blanket on his bed and tucked it beneath his chin.

"That better?" she asked.

Mr. Sheffield smiled and nodded.

"That's fine," he replied.

"Anything else I can get for you?"

"A million bucks," he replied.

"Only if you'll split it with me," Alex replied, smiling.

"Deal," he said with a wink.

Alex turned off the overhead light and placed his call button within his reach.

"Call me if you need anything," she said, pulling the curtain closed behind her.

"Bed three's alarming," the unit clerk called over the intercom. "Who's got bed three?"

The repetitive beeping of the alarm was coming from the next room. Alex's throat tightened when she realized it was her patient. As she rushed into the room her eyes were drawn to the heart monitor above the bed. The thin, green line on the EKG monitor was flat. Why hadn't the monitor tech called a code? She reflexively looked at the blood pressure monitor. One twenty over seventy-four. How could his pressure be normal if he was flat line? She stepped back and took a deep breath to calm herself. The tight vise on her throat relaxed its grip as she watched his chest rise and fall with each breath. He couldn't be flat line, not if he was breathing and had a blood pressure. She took her stethoscope from around her neck to listen for a heart beat.

"How'd he come off the monitor? I didn't think he was moving anything."

The voice startled her. She turned to find Kendal standing behind her staring at the monitor.

"I have no idea," she replied. "Pam said he hasn't moved all day."

The rapid beating of her heart slowed as the rhythmic beating of his heart reappeared on the monitor when she reattached the leads. She felt foolish for not realizing what had happened but was thankful he wasn't dead. Her first crisis had been averted. She closed her eyes and offered up a silent "Thank you, Lord." Baptism by fire was not how she preferred to get broken in.

By the time of her two o'clock break, she had settled into a routine. Her confidence grew with each medication administered, each dressing changed, and each set of vital signs recorded. The rumors that more patients deteriorated and more codes occurred on the night shift seemed unfounded and she found herself enjoying the solitude of the night shift. With few physicians around and even fewer family members to deal with, it was easy to get her work done. She was enjoying her turkey sandwich in the break room when all of that changed.

"Code Ten, ICU. Code Ten, ICU," cried the raspy voice of

the night operator over the intercom.

Within minutes, the ICU filled with people responding to the code. Alex placed her food back in her lunch bag and made her way toward the commotion.

"Who has bed three?" yelled a doctor in green scrubs. "Where's the nurse taking care of three? Someone get me his chart and find his nurse!"

"I've got bed three," Alex yelled as she ran toward the room. "His name is David Watson. He's seventeen years old and was involved in a motorcycle wreck yesterday. He's had a CT of his head showing a large subdural, an exploratory lap to repair his liver and remove his spleen, a broken tib-fib, a comminuted fracture of his left femur, and several broken ribs. He had blood pressure problems earlier in the day but he's been stable on my shift."

She looked up at the monitor. Flat line.

"See if he's off the monitor," she said anxiously. "He came off earlier tonight."

"We've already checked," Kendal replied. "It's not that simple this time."

"Get me a straight blade and a light," ordered the doctor. "I need a number 7 ET tube."

Alex recognized the on-call physician. Blake Nichols had run the first code she ever participated in and even though he had been abrupt with her that day, she found herself attracted to his California surfer good looks. She watched as he inserted the endotracheal tube and placed his stethoscope on David's chest to listen for breath sounds.

"Tube's in place," he yelled. "Let's bag him with oxygen. Get me a set of gases and some stat lab work. Have we got a rhythm or a blood pressure yet?"

"Dr. Nichols, he's got a weak pulse," replied one of the nurses.

"Stop compressions."

Blake Nichols stared silently at the monitor. An occasional

blip on the screen confirmed the weak pulse.

"Give him an ampoule of epinephrine I.V.," he ordered, "and hang a dopamine drip."

Alex rummaged quickly through the crash cart until she found the medications. Her hands trembled as she inserted the needle into the plastic tubing and administered the epinephrine.

"Epi's in," she yelled as she pulled the needle out.

"Dopamine's hanging and infusing, Dr. Nichols," replied another nurse.

Dr. Nichols folded his arms across his chest and smiled weakly as he looked at the blood pressure reading on the Dynamap. He brushed back his long, blond bangs with a quick flip of his head.

"Looks like we can back off on the dopamine," he said. "Titrate the Dopamine for a systolic pressure greater than ninety."

His eyes drifted to the pulse oximeter. He shook his head from side to side.

"Why is our oxygen saturation only in the eighties?" he asked. "Is he on a hundred percent oxygen?"

"Yes, sir," replied the respiratory technician.

Dr. Nichols placed his stethoscope on the patient's chest and listened for breath sounds. He shook his head as he draped the stethoscope around his neck.

"It's not tube placement," he said. "He's got good breath sounds bilaterally. Are you sure he's getting the oxygen?"

The respiratory therapist nodded her head.

"Yes, sir. Hundred percent," she replied. She handed him a piece of paper. "Here are his blood gases."

Dr. Nichols took a deep breath and looked again at the pulse oximeter.

"Gases are terrible," he said. "Saturation is only eighty-three percent. With that femur fracture, he may have thrown a fat embolus to his lungs. See who's on call for nuclear medicine. He needs a lung scan. If he's got an embolus, and we can't ventilate him, he'll need an embolectomy."

"An embolectomy?" Alex asked, surprised. "Do you really think they'd do an embolectomy with his head injuries and such a poor prognosis?"

Dr. Nichols wrinkled his forehead and stared at her.

"Why wouldn't they?" he asked.

"Well, it's just that," Alex stammered, "well, I was under the impression that his chances for any kind of meaningful recovery were rather slim considering his head injuries. I guess I was wondering how aggressive his family would want to be."

Dr. Nichols angrily shook his finger. "If they don't want aggressive treatment, then he should've never been coded in the first place. Now, somebody get me the radiologist on the phone. We need to get this lung scan going."

Alex stared in silence as once again the unpleasant memories and bitterness buried years before crept silently from the recesses of her brain. She shook her head to clear her mind and told herself that this was different from what her mother had been through. This was a healthy seventeen-year-old with traumatic injuries and not cancer. With the resilience of youth on his side, maybe recovery was possible.

"Excuse me, Dr. Nichols," interrupted the unit clerk, "but Mr. Watson's family is here. I asked them to wait in the conference room."

The small conference room adjacent to the ICU was lit only by the light of a cheap ceramic lamp in the corner of the room. Elevator music drifted softly from the speaker in the ceiling. Alex stood quietly behind Blake Nichols. She strained her eyes in the dim light, unable to clearly make out the facial features of the boy's parents.

"Mr. and Mrs. Watson?" Dr. Nichols asked, as he extended his right hand.

The frightened couple nodded their response.

"I'm Dr. Nichols and this is ..."

He stopped in mid sentence as he looked at Alex. There was

a brief but awkward silence as he struggled for Alex's name.

"... this is the nurse taking care of your son," he continued. "Your son stopped breathing a short time ago. And when he stopped breathing, his heart stopped beating. We worked very aggressively with him and were able to re-establish a heartbeat and a blood pressure. He still isn't breathing on his own so we've had to intubate him and place him on a ventilator."

The boy's parents stared silently at one another with puzzled looks on their faces.

"Doctor, we were told that David was stable when we left the hospital earlier in the evening. What happened?" asked Mr. Watson.

Dr. Nichols took a deep breath and cleared his throat.

"We're not really sure, Mr. Watson," he said, "but we think your son may have thrown a fat embolus to his lungs. Even though he's intubated, we're still having problems with his ventilation."

"I'm sorry, Dr. Nichols, but I'm not sure I understand what you're saying," Mr. Watson apologized. "David's not fat."

Dr. Nichols shook his head and held up his hands.

"No, no," he replied, "It has nothing to do with his size. David broke his leg, his femur. The long bones of the body, of which the femur is one, have fat in the bone marrow. On rare occasions when the bone is broken, fat can escape from the bone and enter the blood stream. We feel this may have happened in David's case with the fat embolus making its way to the lung." Dr. Nichols paused and nervously wiped his forehead. "Any type of embolus, whether it's from fat or from a blood clot, can damage the lung by blocking off the blood flow to that area. When that happens, it makes it difficult for the lungs to supply the rest of the body with sufficient oxygen. We're making arrangements to perform a test and see if that's what has happened."

"You said you were having trouble ventilating him," Mrs. Watson said softly.

"Yes, ma'am. We're giving him oxygen, but we're still having difficulty maintaining adequate levels of oxygen in his blood stream. If the test confirms an embolus, David may need surgery to remove it."

"What if the test shows an embolus and he doesn't have surgery?" Mr. Watson asked.

"There's always a chance his body can reabsorb the fat," Dr. Nichols replied. "If that happens, he'll do fine. But if his body can't absorb the embolus and his oxygen level stays low, then..." Dr. Nichols took a breath. "Well, I'm afraid he would die."

Alex watched helplessly as the couple hugged one another tightly.

"When will we know the results of the test?" asked Mr. Watson.

"Hopefully, within an hour," Dr. Nichols replied. "As soon as we find out something, one of us will let you know."

Dr. Nichols shook hands with the Watsons and left the conference room leaving Alex behind. Alex wrinkled her brow and shook her head, wondering if she'd really seen what she thought she saw. Surely Dr. Nichols hadn't winked at her on his way out. She dismissed the thought and moved closer to the family.

"I'm Alex Lowe," she said. "I've been taking care of David tonight. Let me check in the back to be sure everything is okay and I'll let you come back to visit him."

Alex stood silently at the foot of the bed as she watched the young man's parents hover over him. Tears trickled down their cheeks as they held his hands and ran their fingers through his hair.

"David, can you hear us?" his mother called softly. "We love you, honey. You're going to be all right. The doctors are doing everything they can, but you've got to help them."

It was four in the morning before Dr. Nichols returned to the ICU waiting room to inform the Watson's of the results of the VQ scan. The couple was sitting alone in the dimly lit room.

"The lung scan shows several areas in your son's lung which appear to have emboli," he said, "which explains why we're having so much difficulty ventilating him."

"Will he need the surgery you spoke of earlier?" asked Mr. Watson.

"No, sir," Dr. Nichols replied lowering his voice. "When I reviewed the scan with the radiologist, he thought the emboli were too small and too distal in the pulmonary vasculature to be removed by surgery. The only thing we can do is keep him on oxygen and hope his body can reabsorb the emboli. The surgery would be high risk and probably not very beneficial."

"But can he survive without having the surgery?" Mrs. Watson asked.

"Ma'am," Dr. Nichols replied, shaking his head and running his fingers through his sun-bleached, blond hair, "I don't know if he could survive even with the surgery. I don't mean to be blunt, but I do need to be honest with you. His injuries are critical and regardless of what we do, his chances for survival aren't good. I wish we had more to offer him, more to offer you, but we don't. I'm sorry."

Alex caught his eye and smiled to signal her support and encouragement. The weary physician smiled weakly and nodded his appreciation as he left the room. As she watched him walk away, she reminded herself to call Ben later.

- 8 -

As the days turned into weeks, David continued his struggle to survive. Repeat CAT scans showed his brain was severely damaged with parts of his brain turning into soft mush. He remained dependent on the ventilator for his oxygen and had a tracheotomy tube protruding from the surgical incision in his neck. His nutrition was given through a gastrostomy tube inserted through his abdominal wall directly into his stomach. A Foley catheter drained his bladder. His dark, yellow urine collected in a drainage bag hanging from the side of his hospital bed. Despite the exceptional care he received from the ICU nurses, areas of skin on his back and buttocks broke down and formed large, painful decubitus ulcers.

With each passing day, the physical and emotional strain etched new creases in his parents' faces. Mr. Watson often showed up in wrinkled clothes with unkempt hair and a five o'clock shadow. Mrs. Watson began wearing heavy make up as she tried to hide the deep wrinkles brought about by six weeks of constant worry. Clothes, which only a few weeks earlier had stylishly outlined her shapely body, now hung slipshod from her thin frame. There was no mistaking the look of hopelessness and despair in their faces when they entered the ICU that night.

"I understand David has had a good day today," Alex

said cheerfully. "His blood pressure has been stable and his temperature has been normal for the past twenty-four hours. I heard if his improvement holds, he may transfer to the intermediate care unit later this week. If he does well there," she rambled on, "he might be able to transfer to that nursing home on the south side of town. I can't remember the name of it, but it's the only one in town that accepts ventilator patients."

Mrs. Watson covered her face with her hands, sobbing uncontrollably.

"I'm sorry," Alex apologized. "I didn't mean to upset you. I thought you'd be pleased to hear he might be getting out of the hospital soon. You and Mr. Watson could spend more time with him then."

"Don't apologize, honey," Mrs. Watson replied. "It's nothing you said. I'm just tired. It's been a tough six weeks and we got more bad news today."

Alex placed her arm around Mrs. Watson shoulder and handed her a tissue. Tears filled Mr. Watson's eyes as he watched his wife cry silently as she stroked their son's face.

"I was fired today," he said. "Seems that my boss thinks my performance has slipped lately and I'm expendable. He knows what we're going through with David, but he doesn't seem to care. We don't know what we're going to do. Our health insurance only pays so much and we've about wiped out our savings. Each day here is costing us about two thousand dollars." He paused and blew his nose in his handkerchief, then wiped his eyes and shook his head. "But that's not your concern," he continued. "You've got enough to do taking care of these sick patients."

"Mr. Watson," Alex replied, "sometimes the best care we can give a patient is to provide a listening ear. Since David hasn't spoken since his accident, the least I can do is provide a listening ear to you and Mrs. Watson."

She put her arm around his waist and patted him on the back.

"This is without a doubt the hardest thing we've ever been through," Mrs. Watson said. "But the worst part is dealing with the guilt. We love David very much, but that's not our son laying there." She paused briefly and glanced at David before turning back to Alex. "Can we go outside?" she asked.

Alex nodded and moved toward the door. "Let me find someone to cover for me for a few minutes," she replied.

"We don't feel comfortable talking in front of him," Mrs. Watson whispered, following behind her. "I'm sure you understand."

Alex nodded without speaking. Tales of comatose victims awakening and telling of conversations about them were commonplace.

"Jerry and I aren't wealthy by any means," Mrs. Watson continued once they reached the hallway, "but we've lived within our means and had managed to build a nice nest egg through the years. Since the accident we've totally depleted it. Now with Jerry getting laid off, and with our savings gone, we don't know what we're going to do. But we'll get by. We always have." She paused and took a deep breath, glancing at her husband before she resumed speaking. "I suppose what bothers us most is that we find ourselves thinking selfishly how we'd all be better off if he'd died in the accident. It hurts us to see him laying there, kept alive by a ventilator. He wouldn't want to live like this."

Alex wiped the tears from her own eyes and hugged Mrs. Watson.

"I can sympathize with you," she said. "I lost my Mom to cancer several years ago. She suffered for weeks and it took a toll on all of us. There came a point when we decided she'd been put through enough. She was tired of the pain and suffering and so were we. It was a tough decision, but we backed off and allowed her to die with what was left of her dignity. They kept her comfortable with narcotics until she died. I think we all had some feelings of guilt, but especially Dad. He put up a good front, but he couldn't hide his feelings. He said we were only doing what was best for Mom, that we were doing the right thing, but I think he felt like he'd betrayed her by backing off on her treatment."

"Did you think he let her down?" Mrs. Watson asked.

"At the time, I wasn't sure," Alex replied. "It hurt watching her suffer like she did, but I'd reached the point where I just wanted her to stop hurting. Selfishly, I wasn't prepared to give her up. Even when you know someone's dying, there's no way to prepare yourself for death."

"Do you ever regret the decision your family made?" Mrs. Watson asked.

Alex shook her head and smiled weakly.

"No ma'am," she replied. "My only regret is that Mom suffered as much as she did. When we realized her cancer had spread, we should've tried to keep her comfortable. We should've worried more about her than about how long she'd live."

- 9 -

The sun was climbing into the morning sky as Alex made her way home to her small apartment. She replayed her conversation with David's parents over and over in her mind as she drove. She understood their feelings. They were the same feelings she had experienced years before. The same feelings of helplessness which she had experienced as she stood by her mother's bed, watching her mother seize, aspirate and die, came rushing back. The same unanswered questions and the same sense of anger toward God returned. How could a loving God let one of His children suffer so much when there was no chance of recovery?

She pulled the shades in her bedroom to block out the bright, early morning sun, but even in the darkness, she tossed and turned, unable to shut out the vivid pictures of a young man kept alive by machines. The nightmares she had fought so hard to bury, the ones that had taken months to overcome, reared their ugly head. She saw her mother's baldness and ghostly white skin silhouetted against sunken, hollow eyes. She pictured herself tied to a chair helplessly watching as her mother's body jerked violently from the seizure.

"Help me, Alex! Why won't you help me?" her mother screamed, her face distorted in pain.

Alex sat straight up in bed, her clothes soaked with a cold

sweat. Her chest felt as if it were going to explode, her heart pounding as though she were running. Everything had been so vivid. She sat for a moment on the side of her bed, breathing heavily as she tried to calm herself. Trembling, she made her way to the bathroom and wiped her face with a cool washcloth. As she stared at herself in the mirror, tears filled her eyes and spilled over her lower lids to stream down her cheeks. She closed her eyes and lowered her head. Why, after all these years, had the memories resurfaced? Why not pleasant memories of her mother in the days before the cancer?

She made her way back to her bedroom and opened the shades, hoping to chase away the memories as the sunlight chased away the darkness. Her hands shook as she picked up the phone and dialed Ben's number.

"Ben, are you busy?" she asked, her voice trembling.

"Not if you need me," Ben replied as he propped the phone on his shoulder. "Matter of fact, I was hoping you'd call. You've been so busy with your new job, I was afraid you'd forgotten about me. What's up?"

"I need to talk to you."

"I'm all ears, sweetheart."

"Not over the phone," Alex whispered, breathlessly. "Can I come over?"

"Of course you can come over," Ben replied, "but what's so secretive that you can't tell me over the phone?"

"I just need to see you," Alex replied. "It'll take me about ten minutes to get there."

~ ~ ~

Alex was pounding anxiously on the cold, metal door when Ben opened it. Her eyes were red and puffy from her tears. Black mascara traveled like small highways down her cheeks. Without saying a word, Ben placed his arms around Alex and held her tightly as he led her into the dimly lit apartment. There was a chill in the room from the lack of insulation in the cinder block walls.

"You sounded so upset on the telephone," he said. "Are you okay?"

Alex nodded her head and pushed back from Ben.

"I'm okay," she replied. "There's just been a lot going on at work lately. I guess I'm stressed out."

"Well, you look like hell and your voice sounds like it's more than just stress. Now what's going on?" Ben asked.

Alex wiped the tears from her eyes and ran her wrist beneath her nose as she sniffed the drops of salty water back into her nose.

"Remember me telling you about the young man I've been taking care of, David Watson?" she asked.

Ben pressed his lips together and nodded. "Vaguely," he replied.

"He's been through so much," Alex continued. "The doctors say he's got no chance for recovery because of his brain injury. He just lays there day after day, unresponsive and unaware of anything going on around him. Last night I knew his parents were upset, but I couldn't figure out why because his condition hadn't changed. Then Mr. Watson told me he'd been fired and that he and Mrs. Watson were struggling financially. It's costing them two thousand dollars a day to keep him alive, and for what? He'll never be normal. And he'll probably never leave the hospital. The more they talked, the more I started thinking about Mom and all the suffering she went through. And then I went home and tried to go to sleep and..."

"And," interrupted Ben, "you had a nightmare about your mother, didn't you?"

Alex nodded silently.

"Your dad and Liz were afraid you'd have problems. So you're having the nightmares again?"

Alex stared silently at the floor, shaking her head up and down. Ben wrapped his powerful arms around her and gently pulled her tight against his chest.

"For several weeks now," she replied, "usually when I

try to sleep after working all night. Last night was the worst. Sometimes I see David and Mom standing together pleading for help. When I wake up, I'm physically and emotionally drained. I'm losing weight and I'm always tired."

Ben led Alex across the small den and sat down with her on the ugly, green and red plaid love seat. He draped his arm around her shoulder and ran his fingers through her long, brown hair. Her black mascara rubbed off on his starched, white shirt.

"Have you talked to your supervisor?" he asked.

"I've tried, but she doesn't listen," Alex replied. "We're so short staffed right now that there really aren't many options. I've asked to take care of someone other than David, but I'm stuck with him. He's the most depressing patient we have in the unit and no one wants to take care of him. Since I'm new, I get dumped on."

"Well, you can't go on like this," Ben replied. "If you don't do something soon, you'll end up in the hospital yourself. Can't you change shifts or take a few days off?"

Alex shook her head quickly from side to side.

"I wish it were that simple," she said, "but I haven't been working long enough to take any time off and as far as changing shifts, third shift is less stressful than the others. I just can't understand why working nights or taking care of David would cause me problems. Caring for him isn't any trouble. And with him in a coma, dependent on a ventilator, the only things I have to do are check his vital signs, pour a couple of cans of Ensure down his feeding tube and give him a bath. I don't see how that could trigger memories of Mom."

Ben tilted his head and looked inquisitively at Alex.

"Do you think he knows what goes on around him?" he asked.

"Not really," Alex replied. "His eyes are open, but he doesn't respond except to pain."

"You think he responds to pain?" Ben asked.

"I know he does," Alex replied. "He withdraws from the

needle every time they draw blood. And sometimes when I turn him during his bath, he frowns like he's in pain."

"Maybe that's the problem," Ben said. "Maybe you associate his pain with the suffering your Mom went through."

Alex blinked several times and nodded. "You may be right. It does bother me thinking he might be suffering and knowing I can't do anything to help him. And I guess it bothers me knowing how much his parents are suffering. I didn't know what to say when his mother told me last night that they'd all be better off if he'd died in the wreck."

Ben shook his head. "I can't imagine a parent ever saying that about a child," he said. "How could you ever wish that your own flesh and blood was dead?"

"I did," Alex replied. "I wanted Mom to die so she'd quit hurting, so we'd all quit hurting."

"But your own child?" Ben asked.

"There are things worse than death," Alex replied softly. "And for a lot of people, the pain and suffering of a loved one lingering near death is one of those things. The Watsons love David and they'd grieve if he died, but this has destroyed them emotionally and financially. With time, they can recover from the emotional hurt, but financially, I doubt they'll ever recover."

Ben slid to the edge of the love seat and squeezed Alex's thigh.

"I know you've already talked to your supervisor," he said, "but you've got to do something to change your responsibilities at work. I can't help but believe the stress of taking care of David is causing your problems."

"You're probably right, but with the staffing like it is I'm not sure I have an alternative," Alex replied.

"Well, promise me you'll at least try," he replied. "Your family and I are worried about you."

"I will. And if I have more problems, you and Liz will be the first to know."

Ben took his arm from around Alex's shoulder and looked

deep into her eyes.

"How'd you feel about staying with me for a while?" he asked. "You know, just until things kind of settle down."

"That's not necessary. You don't have the room and your work schedule is crazier than mine. I'd just be in your way. Besides, you're such a neat nick," she kidded.

"It was only a suggestion," Ben replied, turning down the corners of his mouth in a playful pout as he jumped up to clear off a stack of old newspapers at one end of the sofa.

"I know, and thanks, but no thanks. I'll be fine," Alex said.

"I'm not really that messy, am I?" Ben asked, grinning.

"You tell me," Alex replied. "Unless you've got a roommate, the mess in this den belongs to you."

Ben smiled broadly as he glanced about the room at the clothes strewn on the floor and the dirty dishes sitting on the coffee table. He leaned down and picked up two crumpled magazines off the dingy, beige carpet and arranged them neatly on the end table next to the love seat.

"If you're finished critiquing my housekeeping abilities, let's go out and grab a bite to eat."

"I'd love to, Benjamin, but I've got some errands to run before work," Alex replied as she stood up. "Let me take a rain check."

Ben smiled and nodded.

"Call me in the morning, just not too early," he said. "And if I'm slow to answer the phone, it's probably because I'm cleaning my apartment."

Alex smiled as she playfully wrote her name in the dust on the coffee table.

"Thanks, Ben. I love you," she replied, opening the door.

"I love you, too," he replied, planting a kiss on her cheek. "Hope you have a good night at work."

"I will," she called over her shoulder as she rushed out the door, "and don't worry, I'll be fine."

Ben smiled as he watched her hurry across the parking

lot. “And stay away from those young interns,” he hollered playfully.

- 10 -

As the night shift ICU nurses gathered around the conference room table, Alex sat at the far end of the table mentally rehearsing the speech she would use when assigned to take care of David. She would request reassignment not because she couldn't cope with his situation, but because she needed a change of pace, something more challenging. No one could get upset or accuse her of dumping on them, not if she were asking to take care of a more difficult patient. David was low maintenance and unchallenging from a nursing perspective. It would be easy for the other nurses to understand why she was bored caring for him.

"Now, let's see," said the charge nurse, tilting her head back to see through the bottom half of her bifocals. "Alex, you've been taking care of bed three. Do you have any problems taking him again tonight?"

Alex scrolled quickly through the recesses of her brain but the rehearsed speech was gone. Before she realized it, she blurted out, "No, I'll be glad to."

As soon as the words left her mouth, she felt a fullness in her chest. She wanted to retract her answer but the right words wouldn't come. David would be her responsibility for at least one more night. She sighed deeply. At least her patient in bed two shouldn't be difficult. He was an older gentleman hospitalized with congestive heart failure and pneumonia. From the charge nurse's report, he sounded stable.

When change of shift report ended, Alex made her way toward David's room. She licked the dryness from her lips and wiped the moisture from her palms on her pants. The fullness in her chest made it difficult to take a deep breath. For several moments, she stood between rooms two and three, glancing back and forth at the two doorways. She knew she'd have to check on David, but the discomfort in her chest made her stop outside his door. She turned abruptly and walked quickly to room two. The old man looked at her with small dark eyes and smiled. The vise in her chest eased its grip as she returned his smile and patted him on the leg. He seemed to be a pleasant old man. At least one of her patients would be enjoyable.

As she walked the short distance between the rooms, the fullness in her chest returned. The pulsations of her racing heart echoed in her ears. Beads of sweat collected on her upper lip as she checked his blood pressure and counted his pulse. She softly called his name but as on the many nights before, there was no response. She closed her eyes and nodded silently to herself. Barring any problems, she'd keep her contact with him to a minimum.

Three hours into her shift, the repetitive beeping of an alarm drew her attention to room two. She stood at the foot of the old man's bed and stared at his heart monitor.

"Do you feel those extra beats?" she asked. "You're throwing a few PVC's."

The old man smiled and shook his head.

"No, ma'am," he replied. "The only thing I feel is a little bit hungry. I don't suppose you could get me a ham sandwich, could you?"

"I could try," Alex replied, "just as soon as I figure out why you're having these PVC's."

She pulled his chart from the rack and reviewed his labs. His physician had noted the low potassium level earlier that day but his order to administer IV potassium had apparently been overlooked on the evening shift. She smiled to herself and nodded. A little potassium should take care of his PVC's. She made her way to the supply room and filled a syringe with potassium.

On her way back to his room, a soft blue light coming from David's room distracted her. She thought it was the glow of the television but when she looked past the partially drawn curtain the television screen was black and the overhead lights were off. Her hands trembled as she pulled the curtain back. There, sitting motionless in the chair beside David's bed, was her mother. A soft, pale blue light radiated from her face. Her eyes were bright against her deep olive complexion. Long brown hair flowed from her scalp. Alex was overcome with fear and turned toward the door.

"Don't go."

The voice was soft and reassuring, just like she remembered. She wanted to run but felt frozen in her tracts.

"Don't be afraid," her mother said, "I'm here to comfort you. Now, close the curtain."

Alex's breathing quickened as she pulled the curtain.

"I know about your nightmares," her mother said, "and I'm sorry. It hurt me knowing what you've been going through so I had to come see you. I'm at peace now. Look at me. My body is healed. I don't hurt anymore. There's no pain, none at all. Everything is okay. It's time for you to bury those bad memories and get on with your life."

"I had them buried," Alex said. "For years I had them buried, but they came back. Why'd they come back, Mom? Why?"

"Because of David," she replied, shaking her head from side to side. "He's suffering and so is his family."

"Is he hurting, Mom?"

"No, baby. He's not hurting, but his family is. His parents are fighting those same demons that tormented you after I died.

They're questioning the decisions they've made to prolong his life. Alex, they know he has no future."

"Is he going to die?" Alex asked.

Her mother closed her eyes and slowly nodded her head. "He wants to die. And, yes, he's going to die, but not soon. Not without help. If nothing changes, he'll live for several more years in a nursing home."

"Help? What kind of help? What do you mean?"

Her mother rested her head against the chair and looked up at Alex.

"Sometimes we allow people to make mistakes which influence fate," she said, softly. "And at other times we work with troubled souls here on earth to alter the course of another individual's life."

"I don't understand," Alex said, shaking her head.

Betty Johnson interlocked her fingers and extended her index fingers where she rested her chin. "Do you remember the night when I was in the hospital and your father received the phone call telling him I'd taken a turn for the worse?" she asked.

"You mean the night you coded?" Alex asked.

"Yes, dear, the night I coded," she replied, smiling. "I still picture you as a seventeen-year-old school girl and forget you're a nurse."

"Yes, ma'am, I remember," Alex said.

"I coded that night because one of the nurses administered the wrong medication. She'd been allowed to tempt fate. I should've died that night, but unfortunately the physicians were able to resuscitate me. Even so, in the long run, it hastened my death and lessened my suffering."

Alex shook her head.

"Who is 'we'?" she asked. "You said sometimes we are allowed to work with troubled souls."

Her mother's eyes twinkled as she and rocked slowly back and forth.

"We," she replied, "are the spirits of people who had to

suffer unnecessarily, either physically or emotionally, before we died."

Alex shook her head with a pained look on her face. "This is all so confusing. What do you mean when you say you're allowed to work with troubled souls?"

"That's difficult to explain," her mother responded, "but one day you'll understand."

"Alex, are you in three?" someone called from outside the room.

Alex pulled the curtain back a few inches and looked out. "Are you looking for me?" she asked.

"Yeah, I was," her coworker replied. "Did you know bed two is having PVC's?"

Alex nodded silently and offered a weak smile. "Yeah, I know," she said. "I'll be right with him."

The nurse stared at Alex and walked closer. Alex pulled the curtain tight against her face.

"Are you okay?" the nurse asked. "You don't look good."

"No, I'm fine," Alex answered nervously. "I'll be right with him."

She closed the curtain and turned around. The room was dark except for the silvery light of the moon coming through the blinds in the window. The chair beside David's bed was empty. Trembling, she made her way around the bed and sat down in the vinyl chair. The normally cold vinyl felt unusually warm. Chills ran down her spine and covered her body with goose bumps. The hairs on her arms stood straight up. Maybe this was the beginning of the end, the beginning of a nervous breakdown. How else could she explain what she thought she had just seen and heard?

Still sitting in the chair, she tried to steady her hands as she removed the cap protecting the needle on her syringe of potassium. Her hands trembled as she inserted the needle into the plastic I.V. tubing and injected the potassium. David withdrew his arm and contorted his face in pain as the potassium burned his vein like a blazing fire. Alex jerked the needle from the I.V. and quickly slipped the syringe into her pocket. Without intervention, the potassium bolus would kill him. Confused and afraid, she wanted to run. She took several deep breaths and walked briskly from David's room to the supply room to fill another syringe with potassium. She went quickly to room two and injected the potassium into the intended bag of I.V. fluids. Her heart pounded as she looked anxiously around the ICU. Everything appeared quiet. Her mistake had gone unnoticed. She gathered herself and headed for the break room, hoping to find it empty.

"Hey, Alex. How's it going?" asked a nurse seated at the table sipping on a cup of coffee.

Alex interlocked her fingers behind her head to hide her trembling. "Fine. Why do you ask?"

The nurse shrugged her shoulders and took a sip of coffee. "No reason," she replied, "just making conversation. The unit secretary was looking for you. Did she find you?"

"Yeah, she found me," Alex replied. "Wanted to let me know that Mr. Jamison was having a few PVC's. His potassium level was low on his earlier lab work. Dr. Black had ordered IV potassium when he made rounds but it never got hung. It's running now." She paused for a moment. "Could I ask a favor of you?"

"Sure," the nurse replied. "What do you need?"

"Nothing much," Alex replied. "I wanted to go to the snack bar and grab a bite to eat. Just need someone to keep an eye on my patients while I'm gone."

The nurse nodded her head. "I'll be glad to," she said. "Who do you have?"

"Beds two and three," Alex replied. "They're both stable. Neither have had problems tonight except for the low potassium and PVC's on bed two, and he's got potassium hanging now. I won't be gone long."

"Take your time. It seems pretty quiet around here tonight."

As Alex walked toward the double doors, she glanced at the monitor above David's bed. The QRS complex showing the electrical activity of his heart was beginning to widen. His heart was feeling the effects of the potassium bolus. She bit her bottom lip and shook her head. She knew what was coming. The complex would continue to widen until it looked like a wavy rope on the monitor. If nothing was done the heart would stop. The monitor would be flat line. David would be dead. She pressed the automatic door opener and walked hurriedly from the ICU.

Tears ran down her face as she sat in silence sipping a Coke in the deserted snack bar. At any minute she expected to hear "Code Ten, ICU" over the intercom. How could she sit by and do nothing? How could she let him die rather than admit her mistake so measures could be taken to counteract the effects of the deadly potassium bolus? With each passing minute, she became more anxious. Her palms grew sweaty and her heart raced. She tapped her feet nervously beneath the table and drummed her thumbs rhythmically on the tabletop while she stared at the large, round clock on the back wall of the snack bar. Ten minutes passed but no code. Perhaps her mistake wasn't as costly as she had expected. As the minutes crept slowly by, her anxiety gave way to curiosity. She pushed back from the table and looked around the room. No one was present but the young girl behind the counter. She slipped her hand into her coat pocket and clutched the empty syringe. In one smooth motion, she dropped the syringe into her paper cup. She crumpled the cup around the evidence and tossed it into the trash can, breathing a sigh of relief as she headed back to the ICU.

As the automatic doors of the ICU swung open, Alex saw several physicians and nurses hovering outside of David's room. It wasn't what she had expected to find. Why wasn't there the bustle of activity she had expected to see with a code? She quickly scanned the faces, searching for expressions of concern while secretly hoping to see Dr. Nichols. She was disappointed he wasn't among the group.

"What's going on?" she asked nonchalantly.

"I'm afraid David died while you were on your break," one of the nurses replied. "You hadn't been gone more than two minutes when the monitor tech noticed he was in ventricular fibrillation. I was about to call a code when Beth saw the sticker on his chart indicating his family made him a 'No Code' this afternoon. I spoke with the on-call physician and he ordered some lidocaine, but it didn't help. He fibrillated for a few minutes and then went flat line. He was pronounced dead just before you came back."

"Do his parents know?" Alex asked.

"They're on their way. We called and told them he'd taken a turn for the worse and that they should come in. Didn't want to tell 'em over the phone that he had died. It seems so impersonal."

Alex shook her head and sighed loudly. Her heart raced anxiously in her chest. "Any idea as to what happened?"

"Not really. He may have herniated from cerebral edema with his head injury. But that doesn't usually cause V-fib. Makes you wonder if he had an electrolyte imbalance. We probably could have saved him with CPR if he hadn't have been a 'No Code'."

"He's been through so much," Alex replied. "He's probably better off this way. I've gotten close to his family over these past few weeks so it might be best if they hear the news from me."

"Sounds good to me," the on-call doctor replied from the table where he sat writing the death note. "I was dreading facing his parents alone."

The double doors of the ICU flew open and banged loudly against the metal doorstops. Alex recognized the hospital's chaplain from an earlier encounter with a dying patient. He was an older man with silver hair and a salt and pepper goatee. His presence when death called was always welcomed.

"The Watson family is here," he said in a soft, reverent voice. "Should I bring them back or wait with them in the conference room?"

"Why don't you put them in the conference room," answered the tired, sleepy resident. "I'll be in to talk to them shortly." He shook his head and sighed deeply. "God, I hate this part of the job. I haven't had any sleep tonight. I look like crap. And now I've got to tell two people whom I've never met that their son is dead. I wonder why they didn't tell us about this glamorous part of the job in medical school?"

Jerry and Alice Watson rose in unison to meet them as they entered the conference room. In the dimly lit room, their faces looked even more tired than Alex remembered.

"Mr. and Mrs. Watson," the doctor began, "I'm Dr. Jones, the resident on call tonight. As you know, your son began having problems with his heart rhythm a short time ago. From a technical standpoint, he experienced ventricular fibrillation. When a person's heart stays in ventricular fibrillation, it makes it almost impossible to perfuse the body's vital organs. There are medications which can sometimes correct the arrhythmia but when a patient is made a 'No Code' we're not allowed to administer those medications."

Mr. Watson held up his hand to interrupt the doctor.

"He didn't make it, did he?" he asked.

"No sir, he didn't," Dr. Jones replied. "With him being a 'No Code', our hands were tied. There was very little we could do."

Alice Watson buried her face against her husband's shoulder and sobbed softly. Her knuckles turned white as she squeezed his hand.

"Driving to the hospital we had the feeling he might have died," Mr. Watson responded. "It may have been something in the young lady's voice who called us to tell us he'd taken a turn for the worse, but my wife and I both had the feeling he was gone."

"I'm sorry to have to tell you this," Dr. Jones replied, shifting uncomfortably from one foot to the other. "I understand he's been struggling for quite a while. I wish we could've done more."

"We appreciate everything that's been done," Mr. Watson replied. "We've known for some time now that his chances for recovery were very slim."

"Yes sir," Dr. Jones replied, nodding his agreement. "I'm not completely up to date on his case but in reading his chart, it sounds like his head injuries were rather extensive. Again, I'm very sorry. If there's anything we can do for you, please let us know."

He extended his right hand and firmly shook Mr. Watson's hand. His job was over. It hadn't been as painful as he expected.

Alex took Mrs. Watson's hand in her hand. For several minutes the three of them sat quietly in an awkward silence.

"I'm not quite sure what to say," Alex said. "I know this has been difficult for the two of you."

Mrs. Watson put her finger to her lips.

"It's okay, Alex," she said. "Jerry and I have known all along that David wouldn't recover. Our son died weeks ago in the accident. His body has been kept alive artificially and now, it's finally over." She paused and looked at her husband. "Please don't take this wrong," she continued, "but in all honesty, we're relieved that it's over. Maybe now we can get on with our lives. Call it a mother's intuition, but I had a feeling, probably ten minutes before the phone rang, that David had died. I'd been restless all night and was staring at the ceiling when a sense of peace and tranquility came over me. It was almost as if David had stopped suffering and the peace he felt filled my body."

Alex guided the Watson's through the double doors of the ICU and into their son's room. His tubes and lines had been pulled. The white bed sheet had been tucked neatly under his chin. He appeared to be asleep. She stood by silently as his parents ran their fingers through his hair and reached under the sheet to hold his hands. Tears trickled down their faces.

"At last, he's at peace," Mrs. Watson said. "Thank you for everything you've done. You've been so sweet through all of this. You've helped make a desperate situation bearable."

Mrs. Watson wiped the tears from her eyes and hugged Alex's neck. She kissed her son's cheek and then took her husband's hand and walked out of David's room. The double doors of the ICU closed quietly behind them. Their ordeal was finally over. Alex's was just beginning.

- 11 -

The sun dancing through the tinted glass of the windshield cast a pale blue hue on Alex's white uniform as she drove toward her apartment. An uncomfortable feeling came over her as she pictured the strange, blue glow she had seen in David's room before she saw her mother. She felt frightened and confused. Was she going crazy? Was she having a nervous breakdown? What if it wasn't her imagination? What if her mother had been in David's room? The words she had heard, whether real or imagined, played over and over in her mind.

"Sometimes people are allowed to make mistakes which influence fate."

The voice had sounded so real. She couldn't have imagined the words she had heard. Only sick people heard voices.

"It's difficult to explain, but one day you'll understand."

No, it couldn't be. Surely she hadn't been allowed to make a mistake to change fate.

"Sometimes we're allowed to work with troubled souls here on earth..."

Oh, God, she thought! Was she a troubled soul?

The morning air was crisp and cool, but sweat dripped from her hands. The throbbing in her temples matched the pounding in her chest. Her breaths were fast and shallow. She sobbed uncontrollably as she sped down the freeway. Her mind raced widely. She had to tell someone, someone who would understand. She could tell Ben, but would he really understand? She whipped her car into the right lane and zipped down the exit ramp toward Elizabeth's apartment. Elizabeth knew about her nightmares. Surely she'd understand.

As she pulled into the parking lot, Elizabeth was getting into her car. Alex blew her horn and waved her arm wildly outside the car window but her sister didn't see her. As Elizabeth began backing out of the parking space, Alex slammed on breaks, skidding to a stop just before slamming into her car. Elizabeth threw open her door in anger.

"What in the hell are you doing?" she screamed.

"I'm sorry, Elizabeth," Alex said, "but I had to stop you. I've got to talk to you, now."

"This had better be good, Alex, the way you were driving. You're acting like some kind of fool and I'm late for class. What is it this time? More dreams about Mom?"

"Worse," Alex admitted, shaking her head. "I saw her at work last night. She spoke to me."

"Get a life, Alex," Elizabeth replied shortly. "Mom's dead. It's one thing to see her in your dreams, but to have a conversation with her at work. For heaven's sake, Alex, listen to yourself."

"I know it sounds crazy," Alex replied, "but it was so real. She was in David's room. I thought it was the glow of the television at first but the T.V. wasn't on. When I looked in the room, she was sitting in the chair at the head of the bed. I didn't want to believe it, but she was there and she looked different. She had a new body and her cancer was gone. Liz, she looked so healthy."

Elizabeth shook her head in disgust and frustration.

"Did anyone else see her?" she asked sarcastically.

"I'm not sure," Alex replied, "but I don't think so. The curtain in the room was drawn and no one came in while she was there."

"Tell me you didn't discuss this with anyone else," Elizabeth said.

"Are you kidding?" Alex asked. "They'd think I'm crazy."

"What about Ben?"

"Your apartment is closer," she replied, quickly shaking her head from side to side.

Elizabeth pressed her lips together tightly and slowly shook her head. "Ohhhh, Alex."

"Tell me I'm not crazy," Alex pleaded. "Tell me it could happen."

"I don't know what to tell you. You obviously had some sort of experience. But think about it. You not only saw a ghost, you talked to it."

"Not a ghost, Elizabeth. I saw Mom. I know it sounds crazy, but I swear she was there."

"Maybe it's the stress," Elizabeth reasoned. "Maybe you're so stressed out that your mind played a trick on you. I told you to talk to your supervisor about transferring to another unit."

"Believe what you will, Liz," Alex replied, angrily, "but I know the truth and I'm not going to argue with you about it. Mom came to visit me last night."

"You're losing it, Alex."

"Losing it or not, Mom was there." She paused momentarily and looked at her sister. "There's something else I've got to tell you."

Elizabeth shook her head slowly from side to side.

"And what would that be?" she asked.

"During our conversation Mom said sometimes people are allowed to make mistakes to influence fate. Shortly after she vanished, I made a terrible mistake. I was so upset after I saw her that I gave one of my patients a dose of medicine that was intended for another patient."

"Everybody makes mistakes," Elizabeth replied. "It's no big deal. I don't see your point."

"David Watson died last night," Alex replied.

“So?” Elizabeth said, shrugging her shoulders.

“So,” Alex replied, “he died because I gave him the dose of medicine which was intended for another patient. I was allowed to make a mistake that influenced fate. Don’t you understand?”

“I understand you need help if that’s what you believe. Are you’re telling me you killed a man last night?”

“I didn’t kill anyone,” Alex whispered. “I was just a participant in the master plan, an unwilling and unknowing participant.”

Elizabeth rolled down the window and closed the car door.

“Have you told Dad?” she asked as she cranked her car.

“No. And don’t you,” Alex ordered. “He doesn’t understand things like this.”

“Neither do I, Alex, neither do I.” Elizabeth bit her bottom lip as she shook her head at Alex. “Look, I hate to run, but you’re delusional and I’ve got a test to take. I’ll call you when I get home.”

Alex climbed back into her Volkswagen convertible and made her way across town to her apartment. She was physically and emotionally exhausted from the night’s ordeal and longed for sleep. Her legs quivered beneath her as she wearily climbed the steps to her apartment. It had been a long night. Sleep would be welcome.

She pulled the shade to block out the bright morning sun and crawled into her bed. Her eyelids were heavy and sleep came quickly. For eight hours, she enjoyed a deep, restful sleep. There were no nightmares or apparitions, only sleep. She awakened refreshed and could only wonder if her imagination had played a trick on her.

- 12 -

David's death was never mentioned. His family declined the right to an autopsy and assumed his fatal arrhythmia was the result of cerebral edema with herniation of his brain stem. The passing of time healed Alex's feelings of guilt. In her mind she rationalized that if her mistake had contributed to his death, then it was for the better. His death had put an end to the unnecessary suffering. Perhaps fate allowed her to make such a serious mistake. Fate. Allowed to make a mistake. Such a thought scared her.

Conrad "Prince" Christopher was old and withered. His family said he'd smoked for a hundred years, rolling his own cigarettes before they were available in the store. His nickname was given because of the Prince Albert tobacco he used so often as a young man. His fingernails were stained a dirty yellow from years of heavy tobacco use. His skin had the look of old shoe leather that had been soaked in turpentine and allowed to dry in the summer sun. Its dusky color conveyed to the trained eyes of the medical world his diagnosis of emphysema. His doctors had warned him for years to stop smoking or risk developing chronic lung disease and dying the miserable death of emphysema. He'd spent his last few years dependent upon supplemental oxygen, attached to an oxygen tank by a ten-foot piece of plastic tubing. Now his lungs were failing. When he was admitted through the emergency room, a chest X-ray revealed bilateral lobar pneumonia. Because of his advanced age and end-stage lung disease, his physician had encouraged the family to not place him on a ventilator should his condition worsen. Mr. Christopher himself had requested that he be given 'Do Not Resuscitate' status and had convinced his family to go along with his wishes.

"I've lived a good life," he said, "and I've got no one to blame but myself. These last few years have been hell. I feel like I'm on a leash attached to that damn oxygen tank. If I can't get better, then I'd just as soon die."

Each night Alex stood at the foot of Mr. Christopher's bed and watched his barreled, emphysematous chest rise and fall with each labored respiration. When he'd awaken with the sensation of choking, she'd gently thread a suction catheter through his nostril and down the back of his throat so she could suction out the thick, tenacious mucus which threatened to obstruct his airways. He was a crusty old man, but she developed a sense of respect for him. She understood that he'd scorned medical advice for years and had smoked himself to death. But now rather than beg for help from the very ones he'd defied, he chose instead to face death, if that's what fate held for him. He wasn't going to live on a ventilator or have his life prolonged through unnatural measures. For days it appeared as if he would get his wish. The oxygen concentration in his blood remained precariously low as his body waged war with the pneumonia. When even his family began to think he wouldn't survive, he began showing signs of improvement. His color improved and his respirations became less labored. It became clear he'd turned the corner when his physician decreased the flow of oxygen but yet the oxygen concentration in his blood stream remained adequate.

Alex was in good spirits that night as her shift began. The evening was quiet with several vacant beds in the ICU. Her assignment that night, as it had been for many nights, was

Mr. Christopher. With only one patient, she had time to read through his chart and visit with him.

"I've lived a long, good life," he told her. "I grew up in a simpler time, a time when life wasn't so hectic. Back when I was a boy, a family was two parents, one male and one female, raising children and teaching them to respect their parents and authority. Ain't like that today. Damn kids these days don't respect nothing. Hell, they don't even respect life. Most of 'em just as soon kill you as they would to look at you. When I was a boy, you rebelled against your parents by skipping school and sneaking down to the creek to smoke a cigarette, not by killing folks. I guess that's how I got started smoking. Basically I was a good kid. I didn't really smoke to rebel against my folks but more just to go along with the gang. I suppose I was more afraid of having my friends laugh at me for not smoking than I was of getting a good old-fashioned whipping. Besides, Daddy was a smoker, and I figured if it was good for him, then it should be good for me. It's funny looking back now. I still remember that first cigarette. My buddy, Hudson, showed me how to roll it and how to smoke it. He looked like a pro the way he could dangle a cigarette from his top lip and let it bounce up and down while he talked. I imagined I'd look like James Dean with a cigarette hanging from my mouth, but when I took that first drag, I coughed so hard and long I thought I'd cough up my toenails. But like any fool, I kept trying until eventually I could smoke with the best of them. You know, back then we didn't have any warnings that smoking could be, how does the surgeon general put it, hazardous to your health? Hell, we didn't even know what a damn surgeon general was. By the time my doctors advised me to quit smoking, it was too late and I was addicted to nicotine. If I had it all to do over, I'd never have started in the first place. But I'm not bitter. Ain't got no one to blame but myself for this miserable life I'm living. You ain't no smoker are you?"

"No, sir. I smoked a cigarette or two when I was a young

girl just to see what it was like, but I'm not a smoker," Alex answered.

"Good for you. Hope you never start."

"I've been looking at your chart tonight," Alex said, changing the subject, "and it sounds like you might be transferring to the floor tomorrow. Who knows, if you continue to improve, you might be home in time for Thanksgiving."

"I might go home," he replied in his husky smoker's voice, "but I'll always be hooked to an oxygen tank like a mutt on a leash. I'm just a burden on my family, keeping them tied down while they take care of me. If I had a Thanksgiving wish it'd be to die in my sleep, just slide on out of this life. I don't know what's on the other side, but odds are it's better than what I've got here. Either way, I'm willing to take my chances."

Alex patted the old man on the leg and lightly squeezed his bony thigh.

"Oh, Mr. Christopher, don't talk like that," she said. "I'm sure your family doesn't consider you a burden."

"Well, I am one whether they consider it or not," he replied. "I look forward to the day I die and I bet they do too."

His comments made Alex feel uneasy but she understood how he felt. In his mind, emphysema with its chronic sensation of shortness of breath was a sentence worse than death.

- 13 -

Mr. Christopher's bed was neatly made and unoccupied when Alex reported for work the following evening. She smiled to herself and nodded. She was right.

"Did Mr. Christopher transfer to the floor today?"

"Yep, moved out on day shift," the charge nurse replied.

"Was he still on oxygen?" Alex inquired.

"Yeah, but only two liters," the nurse replied, "but with his chronic lung disease I'll be surprised if he ever gets lower than that."

"Probably not," Alex replied, "and that's a shame. He's really a nice old man. I hope he does well and gets out of here for Thanksgiving."

When her shift ended, Alex clocked out and made her way to the parking deck. She was thankful it had been a quiet evening. As she opened her car door, she heard someone calling her name. Turning around, she recognized the weathered face of Eloise Christopher.

"Hello, Miss Alex," called the old lady.

It was pleasant but strange how polite some of the country people were. It didn't feel right being called 'Miss' by someone three times her age.

"Prince may get to go home today," Mrs. Christopher said. "I know he ain't never gonna be well, but at least he's a goin' home."

"I'm glad to hear that Mrs. Christopher," Alex replied. "I hope he does well at home."

"Will you be taking care of him today?"

"No, ma'am. I'm just finishing my shift so I'm on my way home. I only work in the intensive care unit so I didn't see him during the night. Please tell him I said hello and to take care."

"I'll do that Miss Alex. And I want you to know how much me and him appreciate all the kindness you showed him back there in that ICU. He reckoned you was about the best nurse he'd ever had take care of him and believe me, he's had his share of nurses in his life."

"Thank you, Mrs. Christopher," Alex replied. "It's easy to be kind to nice people. Wish him well for me."

She patted Mrs. Christopher on the shoulder and got into her car. It felt good to be appreciated. How many times had she taken care of patients and never received so much as a thank you?

~ ~ ~

The face in bed one looked familiar when Alex entered the ICU that night. The room was lit only by the glow from the television and the patient's face was partially obscured by the ventilator tubing connecting the endotracheal tube to the ventilator, but still, the face looked familiar. The traffic had been unusually heavy on the freeway so she had arrived a few minutes late for her shift and didn't take the time to see who was behind the tubing.

"Sorry I'm running late tonight," she said, "but there was a wreck on the interstate and traffic was backed up forever. Who have I got tonight?"

"You've got bed two, an eighty-five year old lady with pyelonephritis," the charge nurse replied. "She was admitted earlier today and was put back here because she was hypotensive, probably from dehydration, although she might be septic. She was stable last shift. You've also got Mr. Christopher again in bed one."

"Mr. Christopher?" Alex asked, surprised. "I spoke to his wife this morning and she thought he was going home today."

"He was supposed to," the nurse replied. "Apparently he'd been discharged but while he was waiting on someone to come with a wheelchair to take him to his car, he stopped breathing. They called a code and had him intubated before they realized he was a 'DNR'. His family isn't real happy about the situation. It seems he'd made it quite clear that he never wanted to be on a ventilator."

"Yeah," Alex replied, nodding her head, "he made that clear while I was taking care of him. He had such a miserable existence that he was ready to die. Looks like he missed a good opportunity today."

"Well, his family has requested that he be taken off the ventilator, but you know regulations. It'll take an act of Congress now to pull the plug. I think the plans are to taper the ventilator as fast as possible tomorrow without checking gases and then pull the tube. He'll either fly or die without the tube."

"I'm glad they're waiting until tomorrow," Alex said. "I don't think I could bear to watch him struggle when the tube is pulled. Why'd he code?"

"They're not sure. He was poorly responsive, slumped on the floor when they found him. A CAT scan was done after he was resuscitated and showed a large bleed in the right side of his brain. Could have coded because of the bleed or he might have had a respiratory arrest and hit his head when he passed out. Either way, he's paralyzed on the left side of his body. It's really a sad situation."

Alex made her way into Mr. Christopher's room and stood at the foot of his bed, staring silently at him. She fought hard to hold back her tears as he looked at her with his big blue eyes. He tried to speak but only gagged on the ET tube. His right arm was tied to the bed rail to keep him from pulling on his I.V. lines and ET tube. His left arm lay flaccid at his side. She watched as the ventilator filled his lungs with oxygen every five seconds.

"Are you getting enough air?" she asked.

The old man turned his head to the side to avoid eye contact. What a stupid question. He hadn't had enough air in years.

"Are you hurting anywhere?" Alex asked.

Again, the same response. Alex felt helpless. She wanted to comfort him but didn't know what to say. She knew the last thing he wanted was to be kept alive on a ventilator. And now to be paralyzed as well.

"You know, they plan to get you off this ventilator tomorrow," she said, "and then it won't be long before you go home."

Tears filled his eyes as he shook his head. He had no desire to go on living even before the stroke. Why would he want to go home now and be an even bigger burden on his family?

The gnawing, empty feeling in the pit of her stomach grew to the point where she thought she was going to vomit. Haunting memories of life's unfairness crept back into her mind. Just when she was about to burst into tears, she began arguing with her subconscious. This wasn't one of life's unfair sentences. He had brought this on himself. He was the one who had smoked all of his life. Even the stroke that landed him back in ICU could be related to his smoking. She wanted to blame it all on him but his pleading blue eyes drew on the compassion which separated her from so many of the nurses who had cared for him before.

The tears Alex had fought so hard to control came rolling down her face. Right or wrong, fair or unfair, self-induced or bad luck, it really didn't matter. She couldn't stand by idly and watch another human being suffer.

"Mr. Christopher, can you hear me?" she called softly.

The old man nodded his head.

"I know you've got to be uncomfortable with your right arm tied down so tightly. Now if I untie you, I don't want you to pull out your I.V. or your endotracheal tube. Do you understand?"

Again, he nodded his head, this time, closing his eyes in a long blink.

"You understand," she said, "that if you pull out your tube, you could die. So whatever you do, you must not pull out your tube. Did you hear me? You could die."

Again he shook his head in acknowledgment. He understood. She was giving him the option of living or dying. It would be his choice.

Alex walked from his room to the lounge and fixed herself a soda. The intensive care unit was quiet. When she was certain no one was watching, she went back to his room and loosened the restraint on his right wrist.

"Now, doesn't that feel better?" she asked. "I'm going to leave the restraint on your wrist but I'm going to leave you untied. Remember, don't pull your tube out. I've got to check on my other patient, but I'll be back in just a few minutes."

She walked next door and occupied her time by checking the old woman's vital signs. No fever. Blood pressure and pulse were both normal. She glanced at the clock above the bed. Only three minutes had passed, much too soon to return to Mr. Christopher's room. She made small talk with the unit clerk as she stalled for time. Five minutes passed. Still not ready to return to his room, she walked to the lounge, never looking toward Mr. Christopher. Nervously, she pulled the wrapper from a saltine cracker and poured herself a Coke. What would she do if he were still on the ventilator? What would she do if he had extubated himself?

An uncomfortable pressure swelled like a balloon within her chest as she made her way to his room and slowly pulled back the curtain behind the open sliding glass door.

"Come in."

The voice was low and hoarse, more like a guttural whisper.

Prince Christopher was holding his endotracheal tube in his right hand. His wrist restraint dangled loosely from his thin wrist. His thin lips curled upward in an evil smile.

"Look what you've done!" Alex cried. "I can't believe you!

I leave you alone for just a minute and you manage to get untied and pull out your ET tube."

"What's wrong, Alex?" called a coworker as she raced into the room. "I could hear you next door. Is there a problem."

"It's Mr. Christopher," she replied, shaking her head. "I'm out of his room for maybe five minutes and he transforms himself into Houdini and manages to get out of his restraint and pull out his ET tube."

"Should we call anesthesia to get him reinsulated?"

"No," Alex replied, "and that's what upsets me so. He's a 'DNR' and can't be reintubated. I guess we'll have to put oxygen on him and see if he flies."

"Well, call me if you need any help."

"I will," Alex replied.

She closed the sliding glass door and pulled the curtain behind her.

"I know you could get in trouble for what you did," Mr. Christopher growled in his gruff voice, "and I want to thank you. You did the right thing. I won't be a burden any longer."

Nothing more was said, but Alex understood. She patted the old man on the leg before leaving his room to notify the physician. She rehearsed her lines as she slowly dialed the number of the on-call room. The young intern sounded sleepy and aggravated.

"What do you mean he extubated himself?" he asked. "I thought he was restrained."

"He was," Alex replied, "but he managed to get his hand untied and pulled out his ET tube."

"How in the hell can a man paralyzed on one side free up his good hand and pull out his tube?" the doctor asked. "These old gomers never cease to amaze me. Is he a 'No Code'?"

"Yes, sir, he is," Alex replied.

"Well, put a Venturi mask on him with about fifty percent oxygen and see how he does," the doctor replied.

"Should I check some blood gases on him?" Alex asked.

"Why?" he asked. "He's a 'No Code'. We can't reintubate him if his oxygen saturation drops so why do gases. You might as well discontinue his pulse oximeter, too."

"Yes, sir. Anything else?"

"Yeah, how about calling his family and letting them know what happened. They might want to come on in. I'm not sure how long he can hang on without a ventilator."

Mrs. Christopher was sleeping when she got the call. Her false teeth sat in a glass of water by her bed. She spoke with a lisp without her teeth. "Hello," she answered, sleepily.

"Hello, Mrs. Christopher, this is Alex Lowe, in the ICU at the hospital. I'm sorry to call you at this time of morning, but the doctor wanted me to let you know that Mr. Christopher pulled out his breathing tube tonight."

"Did he get over his stroke?" the old woman asked.

"No, ma'am," Alex replied, "he didn't get over his stroke. He's still paralyzed on his left side."

"But his hand was tied down when I visited him earlier tonight. How'd he pull it out?"

"I'm not sure," Alex said, shaking her head in an attempt to sound more convincing. "I was out of his room for only a few minutes working with another patient and when I returned he had extubated himself."

"You know he don't want to go back on the breathing machine, don't you?" Mrs. Christopher asked.

"Yes, ma'am. I've discussed it with the doctor and he understands that Mr. Christopher is not to be reintubated."

"Is he breathing on his own?"

"Yes, ma'am. We've put some oxygen on him and he is breathing on his own, but he isn't breathing well."

"You reckon I oughta come see him or just wait til the morning?"

"Well, if you're asking for my opinion, I'd say you should come on now. I can't play God, but I'm not sure he'll survive until visiting hours in the morning."

Alex hung up the phone and returned to check on the old woman's husband. His breaths were already becoming more rapid and shallow. He would tire soon. His body and stroke riddled brain were too weak to maintain the rapid respiratory rate. She knew the scenario well. As he tired, his respiratory rate would slow as the rising levels of carbon dioxide took their toll on his brain. As the carbon dioxide level rose, the brain's respiratory center would be depressed and he would eventually stop breathing. The acids would accumulate in his blood stream as his respirations slowed and his heart would stop. Death would have its victory, and Prince Christopher would be at peace.

The clock over his bed showed that it was four o'clock in the morning. An hour had passed since he had pulled out his ET tube, at least forty-five minutes since she had talked to his wife. She was surprised he had lasted this long. Perhaps his will to live was stronger than she had expected, but it wouldn't be long now. His heart rate had slowed to twenty beats per minute. The QRS complex on the monitor was beginning to widen. Soon it would deteriorate into a continuous wavy line. After that, flat line and death.

Eloise Christopher looked frightened and tired as she tried to push open the automated doors of the ICU. The smile from the day before was gone. Her gray hair was flattened on one side of her head where she'd been sleeping. She hadn't taken the time to apply make-up to cover her pale face. When Alex pressed the metal plate on the wall, the double doors flung open, startling the old lady and almost making her fall. Alex caught her by the arm and guided her to her husband's room.

"Prince? Prince, can you hear me?" she called in a trembling voice.

"I'm afraid he's not able to hear you," Alex replied. "He hasn't responded to my voice for about the past fifteen or twenty minutes."

"Is he still alive? He ain't moving at all. Is he breathing?"

"Yes, ma'am," Alex said, "he's still alive, but he's not breathing much. I don't think he can hang on much longer."

"You reckon he's a gonna die?" Mrs. Christopher asked.

"Yes ma'am," Alex answered, nodding her head and draping her arm around Mrs. Christopher's waist, "and I don't think it'll be very long."

No sooner had she finished her sentence, than the wavy line on the monitor deteriorated into a flat line. He lay perfectly still. Prince Christopher had his wish. Death had its victory.

Mrs. Christopher stood there, her expression unchanged. Alex ushered her towards the conference room adjacent to the ICU and asked the unit clerk to call the chaplain.

"Why can't I wait in the room with Prince?" she asked. "You said that he couldn't last much longer and I want to be at his side when he dies."

"Mrs. Christopher," Alex said apologetically, "I'm afraid your husband died just before we left the room. We've paged the on-call physician to come and check him. The chaplain will wait here with you."

The physician was entering Mr. Christopher's room when Alex returned to the ICU. She watched as he felt for a pulse and then placed his stethoscope on Mr. Christopher's chest to listen for a heart beat and breath sounds.

"No breath sounds, no pulse and no apical heart beat. The man's dead and I'm going to bed. Write the official time as 4:08 A.M. Now, if you'll excuse me, I'm going to get a little sleep."

"Are you going to speak to his wife?" Alex asked.

"Nope," he replied, shaking his head. "You're a big girl. I think you can handle that. He was a 'No Code' so she must have been expecting the old gomer to die. I haven't had much sleep tonight and I'm not about to lose any more by wasting time telling some old granny I've never met that Gramps is dead. When the sun comes up, your shift will be over and you'll go home. But for me, I've been on duty for twenty-one hours and have another fifteen hours to work before I go home. So if you can handle that, I'm going back to the call room and get a few more winks. I'd appreciate it if you'd try not to call me again tonight."

Alex wanted to say something to the young doctor about his cavalier attitude as he strolled cockily out of the ICU, but she knew it wasn't worth the effort. She hadn't placed him on his pedestal and she wouldn't be the one to knock him from it, at least not tonight. She shook her head as the heavy metal doors closed and wondered if arrogance was an inherited or an acquired trait.

The chaplain sat with Mrs. Christopher in the conference room, holding her left hand as she wiped tears from her eyes with her right hand. Alex sat down beside her and patted her knee.

"He's gone, ain't he?" Mrs. Christopher asked.

"Yes ma'am," Alex replied. "I'm sorry but he is. But Mrs. Christopher, you can be thankful that he didn't suffer."

"Honey, he'd suffered for so long with his bad lungs that he deserved to not have to suffer any when he died. I wasn't ready to give him up, but I know he was ready to die. He's been just plain miserable for the past four years. I was always so scared that he'd get tired of his misery and kill himself. I'm just thankful he died naturally. I don't know if I could've kept going if he had killed himself."

"Do you have any children or family members we can call for you?" the chaplain asked.

"No, we wasn't ever able to have no babies and I'm an only child. Prince had an older brother but he drank himself to death while he was still a young man."

"Could we get one of the hospital's social workers to help you in any way?" he asked.

"I'll be okay," she replied. "I've been expecting this for a long time. I ain't got no family by blood left living, but I've got lots of friends who'll help me through this."

"I'm sorry it had to end this way," Alex said, "but he's better off, Mrs. Christopher. He wouldn't have wanted to go on living if he was going to be paralyzed on one side."

"I know he wouldn't, and I'm gonna miss him, but I know he's better off tonight than he's been in a long, long time. Now, you dry those tears in your eyes and get back to your work. You did everything you could for him. And him and me both appreciate it. Now, go on. You got sick folks to take care of."

Alex hugged the elderly woman tightly.

"We'll get him cleaned up and then you can come back and see him. You call me if I can do anything for you."

- 14 -

When Alex entered the ICU she saw a strange blue light glowing softly behind the closed curtain of Prince Christopher's room. It reminded her of the light she'd seen when David Watson died, the same eerie light which had surrounded the vision of her mother. Afraid of what she might find in his room, she went to the break room to gather her courage. She poured herself a cup of coffee and joined several other nurses gathered around the table.

"Sid, could you help me get Mr. Christopher cleaned up before they take him to the morgue?" she asked. "I need to pull his lines and get a clean gown on him if you don't mind."

Sid nodded and took a sip of coffee.

"Let me finish my coffee and I'll be right with you," he replied.

Unwilling to enter Mr. Christopher's room alone, Alex went to the room of her other patient. Methodically, she rechecked the patient's vital signs, trying to delay as long as possible her trip to Mr. Christopher's room. She sat down outside the room to record her findings, but as she tried to focus on her notes, her eyes were drawn toward Mr. Christopher's room. She glanced anxiously toward his room. The eerie blue glow which had frightened her so was gone. She breathed a sigh of relief and stretched her neck to see if Sid was still in the break room. The firm grasp of his hand on her shoulder startled her.

"My word, Sid," she said between deep breaths. "You scared me."

"Sorry," he replied with a grin. "I thought you were expecting me. Are you ready to get him cleaned up?"

"Yeah, I'll be right with you."

Sid had already disconnected the I.V. and was bathing the corpse when Alex entered the room. The television was on with the volume turned down. The light from its picture cast a soft bluish hue on the dead man, a strange bluish glow that only minutes before had filled her with fear. Alex shook her head. She felt foolish for having been so frightened.

"Thanks for your help, Sid. I probably could've done it by myself but I've still got to bathe Miss McCurdy and change her dressing before I finish my shift." She paused as she squeezed the water from her washcloth. "Did you notice anything out of the ordinary when you came in the room to bathe him?"

"Depends on what you mean by out of the ordinary," Sid replied.

"I know this sounds crazy," Alex said, "but when I came back from speaking with his wife, his room looked like it was glowing." She shrugged her shoulders and frowned. "Just gave me an eerie feeling."

"You can be a strange girl sometimes," he replied, "but to answer your question, no, he wasn't glowing nor was his room. The only thing that seems a bit unusual to me is his body temperature. He sure seems warm for a dead man."

Alex placed the back of her hand against his bare shoulder. He did feel warmer than she expected, but then again, she hadn't felt a lot of dead bodies. She slid her hand up his neck and placed her fingers over his carotid artery.

"I've already checked," Sid said with a chuckle. "No carotid pulses and no heart beat. He's dead."

Alex laughed softly.

"You know, it wouldn't be the first time one of our junior

doctors has pronounced someone dead before their time," she replied.

"Yeah, I know," he replied. He dropped his washcloth in the basin and dried his hands. "Can I help you with anything else before I go finish my work?"

"No," Alex replied, "that's all. Thanks for your help."

Sid stood on his tiptoes and stretched his long right arm to turn off the television before leaving the room. As the T.V. screen faded to black, Alex felt the hairs on the back of her neck stand on end. A chill ran down her spine. She followed quickly behind him to the workstation in the center of the ICU. As she waited for someone from transportation to take the body to the hospital morgue, the uneasy feeling she'd felt earlier returned. She lowered her head and glanced out of the corner of her eye toward the dead man's room. The eerie soft, blue light again glowed behind the partially drawn curtain. She balled up her fists and pressed them against her eyes. She'd watched Sid turn off the television. For what seemed like an eternity, she sat at the desk with her face buried in her hands. Afraid, but feeling drawn to the light, she pushed her chair away from the desk. Her legs quivered as she stood up. She wondered if they were strong enough to carry her the short distance to the room. Hesitantly, she made her way across the ICU. She paused outside the room and took a deep breath before grasping the curtain. She looked anxiously around the ICU. No one was watching her. After taking several deep, calming breaths, she slipped behind the curtain and closed the glass door.

Betty Lowe was sitting in the chair beside the dead man. She was the picture of health. The soft blue light radiating from her skin illuminated the room. David Watson stood behind her. He, too, the picture of health.

"Hello, Alex. You look lovely," her mother said. "You remember David, don't you?"

Alex shook her head and closed her eyes. How could she not remember someone she had tried so hard to forget? She opened her eyes and stared at him. He looked so different. There were no tubes running from his body, and his cheeks were full and rosy. There was a sparkle in his eyes that Alex had never seen before. The same soft blue light radiated from him.

"I brought him back to let you know it was all right," her mother stated. "See how good he looks? Look at that twinkle in his eyes. He's been restored to the wonderful health a young man deserves. Oh, and Alex, he fits in so well with the rest of us. This is the first time he's been allowed to return. He got special permission to come with me."

Alex sat in silence, stunned by what she was seeing and hearing. She closed her eyes and took another deep breath. Common sense told her that her mind was playing tricks on her. Maybe it was the stress of seeing a dear patient and friend die that was allowing her imagination to run wild. Maybe when she opened her eyes they'd be gone. Maybe this wasn't happening. But when she opened her eyes, there they were, smiling and waiting patiently.

"What do you want?" she pleaded. "Why are you here? Why won't you leave me alone?"

"Alex, please don't be angry with your mother and me," David said softly. "It was my idea to come back with her. I had to thank you. Your kindness let me escape my pain and suffering and move on to a better place. I would've reached the other side eventually, but without your intervention I was scheduled for many more weeks of torment. I'll always be grateful to you."

He paused and whispered in Betty's ear. She smiled and nodded.

"He's not sure of the rules yet, so be patient with him. Go ahead and tell her. I think she needs to know."

"My parents are doing well," David said. "They grieved like any parents would who've lost a child, but they made it through the struggle. But if you hadn't intervened, they wouldn't have done so well. Mom was on course to have a nervous breakdown if I'd survived another six or eight weeks in the ICU. Now she and Dad are really doing quite well. They're making a financial come back, too. You were a life saver." He chuckled softly and glanced at Betty. "Guess that's sort of an oxymoron isn't it? Taking someone's life and being a life saver."

"Yes, David, it is somewhat ironic," Betty replied. "By giving you the potassium, Alex took one life and saved two."

"Stop this! Stop all of this nonsense," Alex yelled angrily. "I don't know why you're here or for that matter, if you're even here. For all I know, you're just a figment of my imagination. Now leave! Real or imagined, I want you to leave. I want you both to leave now!" She stopped and looked directly at them. "Besides, I didn't kill David," she added in a much softer voice.

"Please calm down, dear," her mother said gently. "We're not here to upset you, and we're not accusing you of killing anyone. As I explained before, Alex, some people are chosen and given the chance to alter destiny. It's their choice as to whether or not they participate. You were allowed to make a mistake that altered the course of David's life, or in this case, David's death. He came back tonight to assure you that you didn't do anything wrong. Both he and his parents benefited from your mistake. Now, whether we're real or whether we're an elaborate confabulation of your imagination is something you must decide for yourself. If you want to ask me any questions regarding your life before my death I'll be more than happy to answer them, but I'm not allowed to discuss events on earth that occurred after my death. That's why David was uncertain as to whether or not he could tell you about his parents."

"But why me?" Alex asked her mother, wiping the tears from her eyes. "Why not Sid or Jane? Why did you choose me?"

"Actually, the Council chose you. You were chosen because of your compassionate nature. You're very caring and loving. You always have been, even as a child. It's obvious that you feel the pain of the people you care for and because of that you were the clear choice."

"But how'd the Council know I'd respond favorably if given the chance?" Alex asked, suspiciously.

"Oh, we didn't," her mother replied, shaking her head. "We chose you and then arranged to have you put in a couple of situations to see how you'd respond. And I must say, you have exceeded our expectations in both situations."

"What do you mean by that? What two situations?" Alex pressed, desperate for more information.

"When you were taking care of David you understood his pain. When you gave him the potassium, you stopped his pain. Tonight you untied Mr. Christopher's hand and let him pull out his tube. You gave him the choice of life or death. There were other options short of death that you could've chosen but you made decisions which allowed your patients to have the ultimate relief."

Alex paced nervously in the small room, trying to make some sense of the situation.

"I don't know what you're talking about," she confessed. "I made an honest mistake with David. I had no intention of giving him I.V. potassium to end his life. Anyone could've made the same mistake. And as far as Mr. Christopher is concerned, I untied his hand so he could be comfortable. I didn't know he'd pull his tube out. How could I have known he'd pull his tube out?"

"You're right dear," her mother replied. "You couldn't have known for sure that he'd extubate himself but it must've crossed your mind. But that's beside the point. When arrangements were made for you to take care of David and Mr. Christopher, we hoped you'd give them a little extra pain medication or maybe turn the oxygen down a tad lower than was ordered. But you were more creative. We're very pleased with your performance."

"Are you telling me I had no control over my actions? That some outside force caused me to administer the potassium to David?"

"Oh, no, dear," her mother responded. "We aren't allowed to cause people to make mistakes. We can only help prevent mistakes. It's difficult to explain, but I'll try. There are times when people are about to make mistakes and something deep in their brain, something in their subconscious stops them. You might say we are that something. We plant that little seed of doubt that makes the person rethink their decision. Now, at other times, as in your incident with David, we see someone about to make a mistake, but we aren't allowed to intervene. The individual then goes ahead with their initial impulse."

"Who decides when intervention is allowed?" Alex asked, clearly puzzled.

"I'm afraid I'm not at liberty to divulge that information," her mother replied, shaking her head.

"Is it the Council?" Alex asked.

"Our councils and committees are no more efficient than your committees here on earth. You've got to realize that these are split second decisions. There's no way for the committee to make decisions that quickly. I can't tell you anything more, so please don't ask."

"Will I always be asked to alter fate?" Alex asked.

"Periodically you'll have the opportunity to make decisions which can alter another person's life. And as with David, you may be allowed to make mistakes which will alter destiny. The choice, however, will always be yours. We'll never try to influence your basic values or beliefs."

Alex shook her head and buried her face in her hands. When she opened her eyes seconds later the room was dark. The eerie, blue light was gone. The chair beside the bed was empty. She squinted in the darkness, struggling to see the outline of the figure in the bed. Prince Christopher's corpse was still there. She placed the back of her hand against the old man's neck. He was cold and stiff. The hairs on the back of her neck stood up as she shivered to the realization that no living person shared her secret. She hurried from the room to escape her fear.

- 15 -

Elizabeth wiped the sleep from her eyes and tried to focus on the red, block numbers of the digital clock as she reached for the telephone. Who would be calling at such an early hour?

"Elizabeth, hope I didn't wake you but I've got to talk to you."

"No, no, Alex," Elizabeth replied, sleepily. "I was awake, just laying here for a few minutes before I got up. What's up? Have another rough night?"

"Yeah, pretty rough," Alex replied. "Are you going to be home when I get off work?"

"Yeah. Why?" Elizabeth asked.

"I need to talk to someone."

"I'm listening."

"I'd rather not discuss it over the phone," Alex stressed. "Are you sure you don't have plans?"

"Gheez, Alex, it's not even seven o'clock. No, I don't have plans. Besides, I've got some news to share with you, too."

Elizabeth got out of the bed and quickly showered. It would take Alex at least twenty minutes to drive from the hospital to her apartment, plenty of time to shower and eat breakfast. She was spreading grape jelly on a slice of toast when she heard the slamming of a car door. It had only been sixteen minutes since she'd hung up the phone. The look on Alex's face when Elizabeth opened the door was one that she'd seen only once before.

"You saw her again didn't you?" she asked.

Alex threw her arms around her sister and buried her face in her shoulder. Her body shook uncontrollably. Her voice cracked as she tried to speak.

"I was taking care of an elderly gentleman last night. While I was on break, he pulled out his endotracheal tube and because he was a 'DNR', we couldn't reintubate him. He couldn't survive off the ventilator and died after just a short while."

"What's so upsetting about that?" Elizabeth asked. "There's nothing you could've done to prevent it."

"I untied his hand," Alex replied. "If I hadn't untied his hand, he couldn't have pulled out his tube."

"But you couldn't know he was going to pull out his tube," Elizabeth said. "That was his fault."

"I knew he wanted to die," Alex replied, softly.

"But even so, you couldn't have known he was going to pull out his tube, could you?"

"It did cross my mind."

"Then why would you untie his hand if you thought there was a chance he'd extubate himself?" Elizabeth asked.

"Because he wanted to die," Alex answered. "He'd made his family promise that they'd never put him on a ventilator and now, here he was with a tube rammed down his throat and a machine keeping him alive. He was dying and they were taking away his dignity."

"So you killed him?" Elizabeth asked with a troubled look on her face.

"No!" Alex shot back. "I didn't kill him! I gave him the opportunity to determine his own destiny. And he chose death."

"Then are you upset because he chose to die?" Elizabeth asked.

"Heavens, no," Alex said, shaking her head. "He's better off dead than he was alive."

"Then why are you so upset?"

"Because after he died, Mom came back to see me."

Elizabeth shook her head. "Oh, no, here we go again! So our Mom, who's been dead for how many years now, came to see you in the hospital last night?"

"I know it's hard for you to believe," Alex said, "but please hear me out."

Elizabeth nodded her head and stared deeply into Alex's eyes, searching for what she hoped wasn't true. "You haven't told anyone else, have you? Like Ben?"

"No," Alex replied quickly. "I wasn't sure he'd believe me."

"But you thought I would?" Elizabeth asked, smiling and raising her eyebrows as she shook her head. "I don't know if that's a compliment or an insult."

"It's not meant to be either," Alex answered. "You're my sister. Who am I supposed to turn to?"

Elizabeth took her sister's hand and led her from the small den to the tiny eat-in kitchen. "I'll hear you out but I've got to make us some coffee. It's hard for me to concentrate without my morning caffeine."

Alex pulled a ladder back chair away from the glass top table and sat down while Elizabeth brewed a pot of coffee.

"Go ahead, I'm listening," Elizabeth said.

"After Mr. Christopher died, there was this strange, blue light coming from his room. The only other time I'd ever seen the light was just before the first time I saw Mom. I was scared to death. I looked away for a moment and when I looked back, the light was gone. It still bothered me, so I asked an orderly to help me clean Mr. Christopher so he could be transferred to the morgue. When we went in the room, the television was on and it gave off a soft blue glow. I felt sort of foolish but still a little uneasy. I asked Sid if he'd noticed anything peculiar before I came in the room. The only thing he noticed was that the corpse felt a little warmer than he would've expected. Once we got the body ready for transport to the morgue, Sid turned off the television and we left the room. I was sitting at the nurses' station talking to someone in the transportation department when I got a strange feeling. It was almost as if someone or something was calling me and turning my head back toward Mr. Christopher's room. When I looked up, there was no mistaking the blue light coming from inside his room. I had just watched Sid turn off the television, so I knew what it was."

"Let me guess," Elizabeth said with a hint of sarcasm. "This time it was Mom."

"Of course it was Mom," Alex replied. "Please don't interrupt me."

Elizabeth shook her head and poured herself a cup of coffee. "I'm sorry," she said, "but this is a little difficult to believe, especially since I've never had an encounter with a dead person. Okay, I'm sorry. Please, finish your story."

Alex took a deep breath and continued. "I made certain no one was watching, and I went back to his room. When I went in, Mom and David Watson were both in the room, surrounded by the blue light."

Elizabeth poured another cup of coffee and handed it to Alex.

"Drink this. Maybe it'll sober you." She hesitated. "Am I supposed to know David Watson?"

Alex frowned. "I'm not drunk, and yes, you're supposed to know him. He's the young man who died when I accidentally gave him a bolus of potassium."

"Oh, yes," Elizabeth said, rocking back and forth, "now I remember. You were in his room the first time you saw Mom, weren't you?"

"Yeah, and it was her visit that caused me to make the mistake with the potassium."

Elizabeth dropped two square lumps of sugar into her cup of steaming coffee and added enough milk to give it a light chestnut color. In deep thought, she stirred it several times and tapped the spoon on the side of the cup. "Have you seen Mom any other time besides tonight?" Elizabeth asked.

"No," Alex replied, quickly shaking her head, "but I saw Mom and David tonight and they were both the picture of health. David said he came back to assure me that my mistake had worked out for the good of everyone involved. He assured me he was in a better place and his parents were putting their lives back together. He told me that if he hadn't died that night, he'd have lived in a coma for several months, and his mother would've had a nervous breakdown."

Elizabeth raised her eyebrows. "So," she said, "your mistake saved his parents lives and allowed him to pass to the other side where his body was made whole."

"Please don't be sarcastic," Alex pleaded. "This is very difficult for me to discuss and you're the only person I feel I can turn to."

Elizabeth placed her cup of coffee on the saucer in front of her and looked at Alex.

"I'm sorry," she said, "but put yourself in my shoes. This is hard to believe. Very hard."

"I realize that," Alex admitted, "and if I hadn't seen it with my own two eyes and heard it with my own two ears, I probably wouldn't believe it myself."

"So, let me get this straight," Elizabeth continued. "Mom and David came to see you last night to tell you that everything was all right. Correct?"

"Yeah, but that's not all," Alex replied. "That's why David came, but Mom came to tell me that I'd been chosen to alleviate pain and suffering."

"And who chose you?" Elizabeth asked suspiciously.

"I'm not sure, but according to Mom, I was chosen by some higher council of beings who, like Mom, were forced to endure pain and suffering before they died."

"Did she say why they chose you?"

"That's what I wanted to know. Why not one of the other nurses in the ICU? Or why not you or Dad?"

"Yeah," Elizabeth said raising her voice. "Why not one

of us?"

Alex leaned back in her chair, pushing the front legs of the chair off the floor. She gripped the edge of the table to steady herself. "Mom says I've been found to have a very caring and compassionate spirit; not that you don't, of course."

"Of course," Elizabeth echoed.

"Rather than stopping me, the council let me make the mistake of giving David the potassium. Then they purposefully put me in the situation with Mr. Christopher to see how I'd respond. I did even better than they had hoped for."

"And exactly what was it they had expected?" Elizabeth asked.

"They hoped I'd do something to allow him to die."

"Well, you certainly did that," Elizabeth replied as she poured herself another cup of coffee. "They, whoever they are, must be pleased. You're two for two in the dying category."

Alex leaned forward, gradually lowering her chair until the front legs again rested on the tile floor. She rubbed her hands nervously in front of her face.

"Oh, I think they're pleased," she said, "maybe too pleased. Mom says there'll be other situations where I'll have the chance to influence destiny, situations where people are having pain and suffering. It's all so frightening, but Mom says I'll always have a choice. I'll never have to do anything I don't want to do."

Alex stopped talking and took a sip of her coffee. She tapped her fingers softly on the table and waited for Elizabeth to speak.

"I'm not sure what you want me to say," Elizabeth replied.

"Just tell me I'm not crazy, Elizabeth. Tell me it could happen."

Elizabeth shook her head and frowned.

"Alex, I don't think you're crazy," she said, "but listen to yourself. You say you had a conversation with two dead people who told you that you've been selected by a council of dead people to make decisions which will influence how much pain and suffering certain living people will have to endure. Does any of that sound crazy to you?"

Alex pushed away from the table and walked to the sink. She stared out the window as she poured her coffee down the drain.

"Elizabeth, I know it sounds crazy," she said, "but you've got to believe me. Mom and David were in that room last night and I had a conversation with them."

"I want to believe you, Alex, I really do, but it's hard. Maybe it's stress or maybe it was a dream. With you working nights you may have dozed off for a few minutes."

Alex turned on the water and rinsed the stainless steel sink, all the while shaking her head. "Why can't you just believe me?"

"Because it's too strange for me to even imagine," Elizabeth replied. "But if what you describe happened, then I still have trouble understanding why you were chosen and not someone else? What makes you so special?"

"It's not that I'm special," Alex replied, "but I'm compassionate and hate to see people suffer. Nothing more than that."

"And you're sure you haven't told anyone else about this?" Elizabeth asked.

"Absolutely. If word of this ever got out, I'd be run out of the hospital," Alex replied. "Can you imagine administration hiring a nurse who talks to ghosts?"

With the tension finally broken, they both laughed.

"Well, now that we've got my problems solved," Alex said, "what'd you want to tell me?"

"With your apparitions, I almost forgot," Elizabeth replied. "Guess who's got a date with the best looking intern at Richland Memorial?"

"You've got to be kidding! Blake Nichols asked you out?"

"Friday night. Movie and dinner."

"How'd you meet him?" Alex asked.

"His sister, Leigh, and I have some classes together in law

school. He was meeting her for lunch last week and she asked me to join her."

"Well, you must have made quite an impression for him to ask you out," Alex replied.

"Actually, I think you're the one who made the impression," Elizabeth answered, smiling.

"And what's that supposed to mean?" Alex questioned.

"When Leigh introduced us, Blake said he thought he recognized me from the hospital but that I had cut my hair."

"No, he didn't," Alex oozed.

"I swear," Elizabeth replied. "He said we had worked a code together."

"Well, I did work a code with him," Alex said, "but I don't think we look that much alike." She paused and ran her fingers through her long hair. " And I was afraid I made him mad during the code."

"What did you do?"

"I questioned something he did to revive an elderly patient."

"I don't know if you made him mad, but you must have made an impression because he remembers you."

Alex smiled as she pictured the handsome, young doctor in her mind. "One thing is for sure," she said, quickly shaking her head, "he's a cutie. I wouldn't mind going out with him myself."

"And what about Ben? I'm not sure he would like that. You two aren't on the outs with one another, are you?" Elizabeth asked.

"No, nothing like that. But we haven't seen much of each other lately, even with us both working nights at Richland. Maybe we can both take a long weekend and spend some time together."

"That would probably do your relationship good," Elizabeth said with a wink, "provided the council will give you the time off."

- 16 -

Six Months Later

"Alex, you'll be taking care of Billy Jackson tonight. He's a twenty-three year old male who transferred to us from five main after his pneumonia worsened. He'd been in excellent health until about eight months ago when he tested positive for HIV."

"How'd he get it?" Alex inquired. "Homosexual activity?"

"Drugs," the charge nurse replied. "Went to college on a football scholarship, but he began experimenting with drugs and this is what he's got to show for it. It's a sad situation. His family is well known in the Richland societal circles and this has devastated them. Billy says they've practically disowned him. And while they're destroying him emotionally, the AIDS is destroying him physically. He's six foot four and says he weighed two hundred fifty pounds when he played football. Now he probably weighs a hundred and fifty pounds soaking wet. He's lost four pounds since we got him three days ago. I hope you don't mind taking care of him."

"No, I don't mind," Alex replied. "He's no different than anyone else with an incurable disease."

Billy's skin was unusually pale against his dark hair and widely set, piercing black eyes. A five o'clock shadow couldn't hide the thinness in his face. A large purple discoloration, a Kaposi's sarcoma, covered much of his left lower leg.

"What are you staring at?" he growled.

His gruff voice startled her.

"I'm sorry," Alex replied, extending her hand to greet him. "I didn't mean to stare. My name is Alex Lowe. I'll be taking care of you for the next few nights."

"Well, somebody's got to do it," he said. He turned away from her and stared out the window. "What happened? Did you draw the short straw?"

"What's that supposed to mean?" she asked.

He slowly turned his head until his eyes met hers.

"Didn't they tell you?" he asked. "I've got AIDS. In the past eight months I've yet to find anyone in the health care field who wants to take care of me. Most people I've come in contact with are afraid to even be in the room with me. I'm surprised you aren't wearing gloves."

Alex folded her arms across her chest. Her head rocked from side to side as she spoke.

"Well, I'm not scared to be near you," she stated sternly, "and no, I didn't draw the short straw. I could've refused to take care of you, but I didn't. Now if you want a different nurse, I'll be delighted to have someone take my place. I don't need any extra grief from you tonight. I've got enough worries of my own without having to baby sit an ingrate."

Billy dropped his chin to his chest and batted his eyes.

"I'm sorry, Miss," he said, glancing up at her name tag, "Miss Lowe. It's just that..."

"Please," Alex interrupted, "call me Alex. "I'm not old enough to be Miss Lowe."

Billy smiled and nodded. His dark black eyes twinkled.

"Okay, Alex," he said. "It's just that since I was diagnosed with AIDS, I've been rejected by everyone. I've been in and out of this hospital for the past eight months, and you're the first nurse who's not been afraid to touch me without those damn latex gloves."

"I apologize, too," Alex replied. "It was very unprofessional of me to lose my temper with you. If I'm going to take care of you, we need to try to get along."

Billy grabbed the bed rails and pushed himself up in the bed. Alex stared at his thin chest, unconsciously counting the number of visible ribs.

"When I was diagnosed with AIDS," he said, "my life changed drastically. Childhood friends disappeared. Associates at work began avoiding me. But worst of all, my parents disowned me. I can't tell you how many times I've been in and out of the hospital since I was diagnosed and my parents have yet to visit me. I call them on the telephone and always get the answering machine. Even though I leave messages, they never return my calls. Sometimes I think they use the answering machine to screen calls to make sure they don't have to talk to me."

"I can't believe they'd disown you just because you're sick," she said.

"It's not just any sickness," he replied. "I've got AIDS. It's a socially unacceptable disease and Mom and Dad have always prided themselves on being in the upper echelon of society. Now I'm an embarrassment to them. People who once invited them to parties now whisper about them behind their backs. They feel like society has turned its back on them, so they've turned their back on me. It's ironic, but Mom was the one who really pushed Dr. Smith to find out what was wrong with me. After the diagnosis was made, I heard her tell him that it would've been better for me to have cancer. At least then I wouldn't have ruined their lives. In her words, they'd be better off if I were dead. And truthfully, I think I agree with her. Every morning I wake up and wish I were dead."

Alex shook her head.

"Don't talk like that," she said. "Every person is of value to someone. I bet if your parents knew how isolated you feel they wouldn't feel the way they do."

"Oh, they know," he said, shaking his head, "they know. I've written them letters and left plenty of messages on their answering machine. Believe me, they know how I feel."

"Would you mind if I called your mother when my shift ends? I want her to know how you feel and try to educate her about AIDS. Maybe if she and your father understood more about AIDS, they'd feel differently about you."

"Go right ahead," Billy replied. "But don't hold your breath. I've ruined my life and theirs, too. The only way they can deal with it is to deny my existence."

Alex had clocked out and was almost to the parking deck when she remembered her promise to call Billy's mother. She was eager to get home, but a promise was a promise, and the thought of parents completely ignoring a child for any reason disturbed her. She felt certain Billy was exaggerating but there was only one way to find out. She turned around and slowly walked back to the ICU.

She found the phone number on Billy's chart. Her heart raced as she waited for someone to answer. After the fourth ring she heard the recorded message of the answering machine. She waited for the tone and began speaking. As soon as she stated her name, she was interrupted by a voice on the other end.

"Hello."

"Is this Miss Jackson?" she asked.

"Yes it is."

"Miss Jackson, my name is Alex Lowe. I'm a nurse in the intensive care unit at Richland Memorial Hospital. I'm calling to let you know that your son, Billy, is in the ICU with pneumonia."

"Did he put you up to this?"

"Ma'am?" Alex asked.

"Did Billy put you up to this? Did he make you call us?"

"No ma'am. I asked his permission to call you. He's rather sick with pneumonia and I thought you and Mr. Jackson would want to know."

"Young lady, I appreciate your concern, but I'm really not interested in his affairs. I don't suppose he told you he has AIDS."

"Yes, ma'am," Alex replied. "I'm aware of his condition. We had a long discussion last night about his AIDS and his family situation."

"What about his family situation?"

"Mrs. Jackson, Billy feels very isolated and alone," Alex explained. "He needs your support. He's suffering physically from AIDS, but his physical pain is nothing compared to the emotional pain of being separated from you and his father."

"Is that what he said?"

"Yes, ma'am, it is," Alex replied.

"Young lady, did he tell you that his illness has destroyed our lives? Caswell and I worked for years to secure our position in this community and he managed to take it all away. We're the laughing stock of high society in Richland, all because of him. Did he tell you that?"

"Yes ma'am," Alex responded, "and he's very sorry for hurting you. Mrs. Jackson, Billy would do anything in the world to restore his relationship with the two of you."

"Honey, the best thing he could do for us would be to die. At least then we could bury our problem and get on with our lives. Now, I hope you have a good day, and please, sweetie, don't call here again."

Alex hung up the phone and sat in silence, stunned by what she'd just heard. How could a parent have so much hatred toward their own child? She wanted to run from the ICU, to avoid Billy, but he'd seen her talking on the telephone.

"Guessing from your expression," he called to her, "I'd say you talked to Mom."

"Yeah, I did."

"Pretty much confirmed what I'd told you, didn't she?"

"Unfortunately, she did," Alex confessed.

"Did she answer or did you get the machine?" Billy asked.

"I got the machine. But as soon as I spoke, she picked up the phone."

"That's what I figured," he said. "I've had other people call for me and the same thing happens. I'm sure that's how they screen their calls." He lowered his head and tried to conceal the tears filling his eyes. "I've tried every way I know to reconcile our differences, but nothing's worked. I guess it's hopeless. I'm to the point of wishing it all could end. I'd be better off dead. At least then I wouldn't have to hurt so badly in here."

He took his hand and pounded on his chest.

"Are you not afraid of dying?" Alex asked.

"I've never given it much thought," he replied. "But the way I see it, whatever waits for me after death has got to be better than this. I've thought about suicide, but that's the coward's way out. And of the many things I am, a coward is not one of them."

"What would you say if I told you I've seen the other side?" Alex suddenly blurted.

Billy raised his eyebrows. His eyes brightened. "You've had a near death experience?"

"Not me personally," Alex said, "but I've been visited by people who have died."

"People who've had near death experiences?"

"No, no," Alex said, "I've actually had encounters with people who've died. They've returned from beyond and spoken to me. Their bodies have been made whole again. They feel no pain."

Billy chuckled and shook his head. "What were you smoking at the time?"

"I wasn't smoking anything," Alex replied, condescendingly. "I don't do drugs."

"Well, even when I was doing drugs," he replied, "I never had conversations with dead people."

"Well, I have," Alex insisted, nodding her head. "I've been visited by my mother and by a young man I cared for until he died. I tried to convince myself it was only my imagination, but I know it happened."

"Better you than me," Billy replied, smiling. "I'd probably pee in my pants if I saw a ghost."

"Oh, I was scared the first time I saw her," Alex confided, "but it was comforting, too. Mom died with cancer and looked so wasted when she died. When I've seen her since then she's looked vibrant and healthy. The same way with the young man who died."

"Why are you telling me this?" Billy asked, puzzled.

"I don't know. I guess to let you know that from what I've seen, what awaits you after death may be better than what you're going through right now. There is a light at the end of the tunnel."

"I hope so," Billy said, forcing a weak smile. "It couldn't get much worse. Thanks, Alex. Now go home. I know you're tired."

"Hope you get to feeling better," she replied. "I'll see you tonight."

- 17 -

Billy's room was dark when Alex arrived that evening, but even in the darkness, she was able to make out the silhouette of his body in the hospital bed. She stood quietly outside his room and watched him breathe. His breathing was deep and slow, interrupted only by an occasional barking cough.

"Hello, Alex," he called weakly from the darkness. "You plan on standing out there all night?"

Alex slid the curtain back and walked into his room, closing the glass door behind her.

"I couldn't tell if you were sleeping, and I didn't want to disturb you," she replied. "How are you feeling?"

"Like I always do," he answered.

"And how's that?" she asked.

"Like I'd be better off dead, and so would everyone else."

"Don't talk like that," Alex snapped.

"Well, you know it's true," he replied. "You told me so yourself just this morning."

"I said you'd be better off dead?" she asked.

"Not in so many words," Billy replied, "but I can read between the lines."

Alex shook her head. "I don't think so," she replied curtly.

He sat up and turned on the overhead light.

"There's a light at the end of the tunnel," he replied. "What awaits you after this life may be better than what you're going through right now. Isn't that what you said?"

"Well, yeah, that's what I said," she replied, "but I didn't mean you'd be better off dead."

"Could've fooled me," he replied.

"Well, I'm sorry if you took it that way, because that's not what I meant."

"No problem," Billy said. "How was your day?"

"Good," Alex replied. "Uneventful but good."

"Glad to hear that," he replied, nodding his head. He lowered his head and raised his eyebrows. "Have you had a chance to look at my chart tonight?"

"Not yet," Alex replied. "Why?"

He tapped on his chest with his finger.

"I made myself a 'No Code' today," he replied proudly.

"Oh, really?"

"Yeah. I was afraid my breathing might worsen with this pneumonia and I couldn't stand the thought of being placed on a ventilator."

"Do you feel like you're getting worse?"

"No, not really," he replied, "but I'm certainly not getting any better. But it's a moot point. You know as well as I do that whether I get over this pneumonia or not, I'm dying. From the day I stuck that needle in my arm and contracted AIDS I've been dying."

Alex struggled for the right words. She wanted to tell him no, that he wasn't dying, but she knew he was right.

"Well, your blood pressure and heart rate don't look like someone who's dying," she said as she placed a temperature probe in his ear. "No fever either. Looks to me like you're making some improvement. I'm going to close your curtain and let you get some rest. Call if you need anything."

"You know what I need, don't you?" he asked as she slid open the glass door.

Alex stopped in her tracks and stared at him. The puzzled look on her face surprised him.

"You do know, don't you?" he asked, wrinkling his brow and tilting his head playfully.

She shook her head and poked out her lips. "Apparently not."

"I need to die. I want to die." He tapped his fingers nervously on the bed rail. "Have you given any more thought to my request?"

Alex closed the sliding glass door and pulled the curtain behind her.

"If you're referring to your request for me to kill you, no, I haven't."

"I didn't ask you to kill me," Billy replied, "just to help me die sooner rather than later."

"What's the difference?" Alex asked indignantly.

Billy laughed softly, his stomach bouncing as he suppressed the chuckle.

"I'm dying," he said. "Whether you or anyone else does anything at all, I'm going to die."

"Like I said, what's the difference?" Alex asked.

Billy slowly pulled his legs up under him and shifted the weight of his frail body in the bed.

"Killing is an act of hatred," he explained. "I'm simply asking you to commit a random act of kindness. How much more compassion can you show a fellow human being than to alleviate their pain and suffering?"

"Billy, I can't do it," Alex said uncomfortably. "It's not ethical."

"You don't really believe that do you? It goes on all the time in hospitals everywhere."

"I'm afraid I don't know what you're talking about," she replied.

He smiled weakly and stroked his chin with his finger.

"Mistakes are made in hospitals every day," he said, after recovering from a racking cough. "Patients are given the wrong medications. Surgical procedures are botched. Patients who are listed as stable unexpectedly take a turn for the worse. The mistakes are hidden by telling families that patients have deteriorated in spite of everything that's being done. No mention is ever made of the blunders that caused the deterioration. That's all I'm asking for, just a little medication error. Slip me a big slug of morphine and just let me slide on out of here."

"Like I said," Alex replied, avoiding eye contact with Billy, "I don't know what you're talking about."

"Oh, give me a break," he replied. "You're going to stand there and tell me that you or someone you know has never given the wrong medication or made any mistakes that have harmed a patient?"

"That's exactly what I'm going to tell you," Alex quipped.

"Watch your nose, Alex, looks like it's starting to grow."

Alex closed her eyes tightly as she slid the door open. There was no way Billy could've known of her past encounters. She grasped the handle of the dagger and tried to pull it from her heart, but it was in too deep.

"I'll check on you in a little while," she said, fighting to hold back her tears. "Let me know if you need anything."

He smiled and nodded, slipping back into a restless sleep.

- 18 -

Elizabeth was sitting in the snack bar when Alex arrived for her 2:00 A.M. break. Alex pulled up a chair and engaged in small talk while she gathered the courage to discuss her recent conversation with Billy. "How was your date with Dr. Nichols, I mean Blake?" she asked.

"It was great! He's such a nice guy."

"He must have kept you out pretty late for you to be stopping by at this time of night," Alex replied.

"We were supposed to go to dinner around six and then to a movie, but he called saying he had gotten hung up making afternoon rounds and was running late. Rather than having him drive across town to pick me up, I offered to meet him here. We finally got to the restaurant around nine and went to the late movie. He dropped me back by here to get my car and I thought I'd stop in and surprise you."

"Well, I'm glad you did," Alex replied, her voice taking on a more serious tone. "There's been something I've been needing to ask you."

Elizabeth slid her chair closer to the table and propped her chin on her on her palm. "What's up?" she whispered.

Alex glanced quickly around the snack bar to insure that no one was within hearing distance. "Have you ever been asked to do something that you knew was wrong but felt tempted to do it anyway?"

"Am I going to have to play twenty questions or are you going to tell me what's going on?" Elizabeth asked.

Alex tapped her fingers nervously on the table and took a deep breath.

"There's this young man," she said, "a really nice guy, in the ICU, who's dying from AIDS. I really feel sorry for him. When his family found out he had AIDS they disowned him. His friends have deserted him. He's depressed. He's completely lost his will to live."

"So what's that got to do with being tempted to do something that you know is wrong?," Elizabeth asked.

"That's what I'm getting to if you'll give me a minute," Alex replied harshly. She scanned the small snack bar again to be sure no one was listening and leaned forward toward Elizabeth. "Promise me that you won't speak a word of this to anyone," she said.

"Okay, I promise," said Elizabeth with a nod.

"Promise, promise?" Alex asked.

Elizabeth grinned.

"Yes, Alex. I promise, promise."

A promise, promise. It was the absolute guarantee of a promise the two of them had used since childhood. Only torture or the threat of death could allow someone to break a promise, promise.

"The patient asked me to help him die tonight."

Elizabeth's mouth fell open. "I can't believe you would even consider something so wrong," she whispered.

"If you could only talk to him and understand how lonely and miserable he is," Alex replied, "you'd feel differently."

"But Alex, that's murder," Elizabeth replied.

"It's not murder," Alex said, shaking her head in disagreement. "Murder is something that's done in anger. If I helped him die, it'd strictly be an act of compassion and mercy."

"Yeah, well try telling that to the judge," Elizabeth replied sarcastically. "Maybe you'll get life instead of the electric chair."

Alex glared coldly at her sister. Her voice dropped to a low whisper.

"I knew better than to ask your opinion," she said. "You don't take care of patients. You're just learning how to manipulate the facts to fit your needs."

"Now what in the hell is that supposed to mean?" Elizabeth asked angrily. "I haven't even finished my law degree and you're taking jabs at my chosen profession."

"You know good and well what it means," Alex shot back. "Lawyers take on clients regardless of whether they're guilty or innocent and twist the facts to suit their needs. They hide behind the law and profit at the expense of society with runaway jury verdicts. Lawyers can choose to not get involved in their clients lives and sufferings."

"And nurses can't?" Elizabeth asked angrily.

"Well, well..." Alex stammered. "If you could spend just fifteen minutes with this patient you'd see why I'd consider helping him. It's like it was with Mom. Death would be less painful for him than life."

Elizabeth pushed back from the table and folded her arms across her chest. "I didn't mean to make you mad," she said, shaking her head, "but this is serious. If you help him end his life, you could be charged with murder."

"Not if it was a mistake," Alex replied. "Not if no one ever found out about it."

Elizabeth shook her head and rose from her chair.

"I'm obviously wasting my time trying to reason with you," she said. "I've got to go home and get some rest so I can stay awake in my truth twisting class tomorrow. But think about it, Alex. Think long and hard."

Alex sat alone and watched as Elizabeth disappeared down the hallway. After seeing her reaction, she knew there was no use in asking Ben for his opinion, much less asking for his help in obtaining the morphine. But maybe Elizabeth was right. Maybe it was crazy to even consider Billy's request. Why should she risk her or Ben's future for someone she'd only known for two days?

Alex's heart thundered nervously as the double doors of the ICU swung open. She walked quickly into the medication room, hoping no one would see her. Her palms were sweating as she reached in her pocket and fingered the ring of keys, one of which would unlock the narcotic cabinet. As she placed the keys in the lock, she rehearsed the lines she would use if someone walked in on her.

"I'm drawing up some morphine for Mr. Davis. Poor man is dying with prostate cancer and has constant pain from his bone mets."

The lines sounded good. It was only his second night in the unit and she'd taken care of him both nights. No one could possibly know whether or not he was having pain. If she got caught, she'd simply give him a small dose of morphine. No one would ever know.

Alex's hands trembled as she fiddled with the lock on the narcotics cabinet. The click of the lock opening echoed loudly in the small room. She swallowed hard, but the lump in her throat would not move. With sweaty fingers, she grabbed two vials of morphine and placed them in her pocket. The hinges on the cabinet squeaked as she closed the door. The closing click of the lock seemed even louder than the opening click.

She took a deep breath and waited anxiously, hoping no one had heard her. When no one came, she breathed a sigh of relief. Mistakes are made. Surgical procedures are botched. Patients who are stable suddenly take a turn for the worse. Families never know what happened. People make mistakes that influence destiny.

Billy was sleeping soundly, snoring loudly when Alex entered his room. She stood silently at the foot of his bed, watching the sheet rise and fall as he breathed. She called his name softly but there was no response. Maybe it was better if he didn't know. Her hands trembled as she placed a white washcloth over the two clear vials and snapped off the tops, taking care not to drop any slivers of glass on the floor. There was no room for mistakes. There could be no evidence. She quickly drew up the contents of the two vials into a syringe and placed the empty vials in her pocket. She crimped the I.V. line above the point where she inserted the needle. How much morphine would it take to suppress his respiratory drive? It didn't matter. She'd give him the contents of both vials. Beads of sweat formed on her forehead as she pressed the plunger. As she pulled the needle from the I.V., doubt crept into her mind. If she acted quickly she could reverse the morphine with Narcan and save his life. She looked down at him and shook her head. This was what he wanted. It wasn't her idea. She would've never done it if he hadn't asked her. It was unfair to make him suffer any longer. If he could've gotten the morphine he would've administered it himself. And he wouldn't have reversed it with Narcan.

With the task accomplished and her heart pounding from the rush of adrenaline, Alex peered from behind the drawn curtain and scanned the empty hallway. Satisfied that there were no watching eyes, she quickly left the room, confident that no one would ever know what had transpired.

- 19 -

Billy's bed was empty when Alex returned to work the following evening. Its fresh, crisp, white sheets were turned down in preparation for its next occupant. Billy had been pronounced dead at 10:43 A.M. His mother had sounded more surprised than upset when she received the call telling her that he'd died. It only confirmed Alex's belief that what she'd done was for his own good.

The night shift ICU nursing staff had finished taking report and was receiving assignments when the director of nursing appeared on the unit. Lib Dillard was a pleasant, middle-aged lady who'd worked her way through the ranks at Richland Memorial. She began her career as a nurse's aide while attending night school to get her degree. Now she had dominion over all of the hospital's night shift nurses. While it wasn't unusual to see her patrolling the units, it was unnerving. There was always the fear that her appearance meant a reprimand for some poor soul who'd made a mistake, been written up by one of the physicians or had a formal complaint registered by a patient or family member. Alex saw Miss Dillard approaching out of the corner of her eye and hoped the nursing director wasn't going to speak to her.

"Hello, Alex," she said. Her voice was warm and friendly. "How are things going?"

"Going well, Miss Dillard," Alex replied, with some relief. "Thank you for asking."

"Are you enjoying the night shift?" she asked.

"Yes ma'am, I am. There's a quieter, more relaxed atmosphere at night and fewer staff and family members to deal with."

Miss Dillard nodded her agreement. She could remember working night shifts as a staff nurse.

"Have you been able to adjust your circadian rhythms so you can sleep during the day?"

"For the most part," Alex replied. "I still have trouble sleeping at times but it's rare. Overall, I enjoy working nights."

Miss Dillard glanced over her shoulder and moved closer to Alex.

"Alex, how about walking down to my office with me for a few minutes," she said. Her warm, friendly voice took on a more threatening tone. "I've made arrangements with the charge nurse to have someone cover for you for a short while."

Alex's stomach churned. The ball of cotton in her throat made it difficult to swallow.

"Do I need to let them know I'm leaving?" she asked.

"No, dear," Miss Dillard replied, shaking her head. "I've taken care of that. Now come with me."

"Have I done something wrong Miss Dillard?" Alex asked, following a step behind her supervisor. "I mean, we always assume that when you come around, one of us is in trouble."

Miss Dillard continued walking, never looking back at her.

"I'm not sure, Alex," she replied. "We've got some concerns regarding a couple of patients you've taken care of recently but we wanted to hear your side of the story before making any judgments."

Alex flipped through the Rolodex of patients stored in her mind, trying to imagine which patients were to blame for this. Had she done something to a patient or had a physician registered a complaint against her?

There were three men sitting in Miss Dillard's dimly lit

office. Alex recognized the older, gray-haired gentleman sitting behind the desk from a picture she'd seen in the hospital's lobby. He was Gerald Warren, the hospital administrator. The other two men she'd seen, but didn't know their names.

"Miss Lowe, I'm Gerald Warren, the hospital's administrator. This is Bob Carlson our chief financial officer and this is Tim Alford, our director of pharmacy. And you know Miss Dillard. Thank you for agreeing to meet with us. Please, have a seat."

She didn't know what to say. She hadn't agreed to meet with them. It hadn't been an option. She had no idea why she'd been called to meet with the hierarchy of the hospital, but there was obviously more at stake than a reprimand for poor patient care or a physician's complaint.

"Miss Lowe," Mr. Warren continued, "I'm not going to beat around the bush with you. We have some very serious concerns regarding several patients who've recently been under your care. Here at Richland, we try to run a very efficient yet technically superior facility. Our overall mortality rates when adjusted for age, socioeconomics, and severity of illness are quite low in comparison to the national average. The reason we've called you here is because you've been directly involved in the care of several patients who have recently died."

Alex sat perfectly still. Her expressionless face hid the tide of fear growing within her.

"I'm not sure what you're driving at," she said calmly. "As a nurse, I've had the opportunity to take care of quite a few patients whose conditions have not responded to treatment. When treatments fail, Mr. Warren, people die."

"Miss Lowe, let's not play games," he replied. "Do you remember a young man by the name of David Watson?"

"Yes, sir, vaguely," she lied.

"Mr. Watson, as you might recall, was an unfortunate young man who'd been critically injured in a motorcycle wreck. The odds for his recovery were exceptionally slim, and I guess no one was surprised when he died. In fact, his death would have gone completely unnoticed had not a worker in the snack bar turned in an empty syringe on the night that he died."

Alex shifted nervously in her seat, crossing and uncrossing her outstretched legs.

"The worker," he continued, "reported seeing a nurse, whom she later identified as you, dispose of something inside a paper cup. That something, Miss Lowe, was a syringe. Normally, the young lady in the snack bar would have paid no attention to the incident, but on that night she thought the nurse looked rather upset and, I believe in her words, suspicious. She retrieved the cup and took the syringe to nursing services the following morning."

"That's when I became involved," Miss Dillard interrupted. "I must admit that our initial concerns were way off base. We were afraid we had a nurse on our hands who was abusing controlled substances. Why else would a nurse dispose of a syringe in such an unusual way? Needless to say we were quite surprised when the laboratory tests on the drops of liquid in the syringe revealed potassium chloride and not a narcotic. We probably would have dropped the investigation there and instructed you in the proper disposal of needles and syringes were it not for the death of Mr. Watson."

Mr. Warren leaned forward in his chair.

"Miss Lowe," he said, "we pride ourselves in our low mortality rate. And because of that, we have a committee of physicians and nursing personnel who review the chart of each patient who dies, looking specifically for errors or system failures that we can improve upon. Again, this case would have been lost in the shuffle had not Miss Dillard been a member of the committee. The review of the records from Mr. Watson's chart showed that he died from ventricular fibrillation. You'll have to excuse my ignorance regarding medical terminology and in what age groups you expect to find certain medical conditions, but apparently it's unusual for someone as young as Mr. Watson with no history of heart disease to die from ventricular fibrillation. Is that correct, Miss Dillard?"

"Yes, sir," the supervisor replied. "It's not unheard of, but it is unusual. Wouldn't you agree, Alex?"

"Yes, ma'am," Alex answered softly.

"From what I've been told, Miss Lowe," the administrator continued, "the most common cause of ventricular fibrillation in a young patient with no prior history of heart disease is elevated potassium levels. Would you agree?"

"Yes, sir," she replied.

"Excuse me, Gerald, but if I could go on from here?" Miss Dillard interrupted.

The administrator nodded his approval and leaned back in his chair.

"Alex," Miss Dillard began, "when I reviewed work schedules and the timing of events, I became concerned that perhaps you had administered a bolus of potassium to Mr. Watson which caused his ventricular fibrillation and ultimately led to his death. We only have circumstantial evidence, but we feel we have a fairly strong case against you. My question to you is whether this was an accident or whether it was intentional. "

Before she could stop herself, Alex blurted out, "It was an accident."

"So you do admit you administered the potassium bolus which caused his death?" Miss Dillard asked.

What could she say now? She had already admitted that she'd accidentally administered the potassium. Changing her story at this point would only get her into more trouble.

"Yes ma'am," she answered nervously. "I'm afraid I did." Tears pooled in the corners of her eyes and slowly trickled down her cheeks. "It was an honest mistake," she sobbed. "It could've happened to anybody."

"We understand that, Alex, and to be blunt, that's not why you're here," Miss Dillard said, her tone much less threatening.

Alex looked puzzled. "Then why am I here?"

"After that incident, we began watching you," replied Mr. Warren. "It wasn't that we didn't trust you; but rather, we wanted to try to keep you from making other serious mistakes. Now, what we tell you behind closed doors is not to leave this room. Is that understood?"

Alex nodded.

"Miss Lowe, we have surveillance cameras strategically placed throughout the hospital, including the ICU. The cameras are rather inconspicuous so that most employees are unaware of their presence. We have a central monitoring station where we can directly observe the work habits of our employees. This helps us maintain a very streamlined and efficient operation. Employees who are found to be dishonest, unethical or downright lazy are dismissed."

"What's all of this got to do with me?" Alex asked.

"I'm getting to that," he replied. "We have taped footage of you working with several patients over the past few months, and I must commend you for your work ethics and your show of compassion. However, there are two encounters that concern us. You took care of an elderly gentleman by the name of Alfred Christopher. I believe you knew him as Prince. He was suffering from emphysema and later in the course of his illness, I understand he had a stroke. Our footage shows you untying his right hand, his good hand. Shortly after that, Mr. Christopher pulled out his endotracheal tube. Since he had a do not resuscitate order, he could not be re-intubated and died shortly thereafter."

Alex nodded her head, wondering where this was headed.

"I remember Mr. Christopher very well. When I untied his hand, I had no idea he'd pull his tube out. It never crossed my mind. The only reason I untied him was to make him more comfortable. I was very upset when he died, but I had nothing to do with his death."

"Alex, may I call you Alex?" he asked, coyly.

Alex stared coldly at him. She was feeling more uncomfortable and suspicious about the whole meeting.

"Apparently not," he said, answering his own question. "Miss Lowe," he continued, "we're not accusing you of doing anything wrong. We're merely pointing out the facts as documented by our videotape. Now, the other encounter is a little more disturbing, from both an ethical and a legal standpoint. Mr. Carlson, if you would show the tape, please."

Alex looked on in disbelief as she watched herself on the television screen. The tape showed her pulling the two vials of morphine from her pocket, filling the syringe with morphine and inserting the needle into Billy Jackson's I.V.

"Mr. Carlson, if you would fast forward the tape a little bit, please," he said. "Miss Lowe, observe closely the respiratory pattern of Mr. Jackson. Do you notice anything out of the ordinary?"

"No, sir. He appears to be quite comfortable," Alex replied. "His breathing is certainly not labored."

"Can you count his number of respirations per minute?"

"No, sir. I can't really see his chest movement."

"We enlarged the pictures and followed his progress, or rather his deterioration, over several hours. After you administered your medication, his respiratory rate gradually declined, finally to the point of respiratory failure and death. Because of our concern over the possibility of foul play surrounding Mr. Jackson's death, we performed an autopsy. As you can imagine, the cause of death was respiratory failure. Does that surprise you?"

"No, sir," Alex replied, trying to appear calm. "As I recall, Mr. Jackson had AIDS complicated by a severe case of pneumonia. He'd stopped responding to medical treatment with a worsening of his pneumonia. It's not uncommon for a patient with pneumonia to die of respiratory failure. Your videotape shows me administering a medication, Mr. Warren. I'm a nurse and administering medications is part of my duty, so I'm not sure what you're concern is."

"Miss Lowe, there were very high levels of morphine found in Mr. Jackson's body, levels high enough to cause a respiratory arrest."

"Are you insinuating that I gave Mr. Jackson morphine?" she asked, indignantly.

Miss Dillard reached into a briefcase and pulled out a hospital chart. She thumbed through the chart as she spoke.

"Alex, Mr. Jackson wasn't on morphine," she said. "There were no antibiotics or other intravenous medications ordered for administration at the approximate time you injected the medication that was captured on the tape. The chart also shows that you didn't document in your notes or elsewhere that you administered any I.V. medications during your shift. Alex, you're one of our most conscientious nurses when it comes to documentation, so for you to not document something as important as an I.V. medication is most unusual. The bottom line is that we believe you had morphine in that syringe and by administering a large enough dose, you killed Billy Jackson."

Alex sat silently. What could she say? She knew the evidence against her could send her away for life. If only she had listened to Elizabeth. What if she had told Ben? Maybe he could have stopped her.

"I can't believe you're accusing me of these things," she replied, "but I don't think I should answer any of your questions without my lawyer being present."

"Miss Lowe," Mr. Warren said, "we haven't gone to the authorities and at present, we don't have plans to do so. But to keep us from doing that, we will need your cooperation."

"I'm afraid I don't understand," Alex replied.

"Miss Lowe, Richland Memorial is struggling financially. We're finding ourselves in a "Catch 22" situation. We pride ourselves on our low mortality rate, but by prolonging survival in many of our elderly and chronically ill patients, we run up enormous expenses." The administrator rose from his chair and walked over to the window. He turned his back to Alex and stared out at the darkness. "Often these patients survive long enough to leave the hospital," he continued, turning around to face her, "only to be readmitted a few days later in a much worse condition. They then enter into a downward spiral, a spiral that is often irreversible and consumes our valuable financial resources. If our hospital is to survive these changing and difficult economic times we must eliminate this drain on our resources. And that Miss Lowe, is where we need your cooperation."

He placed his hands on the desktop, and leaned toward Alex, looking straight into her eyes.

"Miss Lowe," he said, "we're in the process of putting into place a resource utilization team. Our goal is to limit financial loses by eliminating those patients who in reality have no chance for long term or meaningful survival outside of our institution. Ideally, we could do this simply by denying admission to certain patients. But we could never get away with that. We would be paraded in front of our community as being racist and discriminatory, which would mean almost certain financial ruin and subsequent closure of our facility. As you are undoubtedly aware, having grown up in our community, Richland Memorial serves not only our town but also the surrounding county. If our hospital closes, then the nearest health care facility will be in Covington, almost one hundred miles from here. We can't afford to let that happen."

He paused for a moment, stood fully erect, and folded his arms across his chest.

"Miss Lowe, are you beginning to get the picture?" he asked, gesturing with a nod of his head.

Alex shook her head. "No, sir, not really. I understand that as a business, the hospital has to run efficiently and try to save money, but I'm not sure I understand what you're asking me to do. I'll be more than happy to work with your resource utilization team and give my opinion as to what we can do in the ICU to save money. It might be beneficial to have training meetings for the nursing staff to discuss ways in which we could become more cost efficient. And I certainly don't know much about the finances of the hospital, and it may be something that the administration is already doing, but the committee could check into government funding for small hospitals as well as see what types of research grants might be available."

Mr. Warren smiled and shook his head.

"Miss Lowe, I appreciate your willingness to serve on our resource utilization team and yes, the administration has explored other options for funding our institution. But I'm afraid you're not getting the picture here. We're not trying to save a few dollars here and there by improving utilization, although I readily admit that cutting cost is important. Our goal is much larger. Our goal is to try and prevent or, perhaps eliminate is a better term, patients who realistically have no chance for long term survival yet require vast sums of our health care dollars to keep them alive."

Alex squirmed in her chair, shifting her weight from side to side. Her palms were moist.

"How do you propose to eliminate these patients?" she asked. "You've already told me you can't prevent their admission to the hospital. Surely you're not suggesting that they be killed."

Mr. Warren shook his head rapidly from side to side.

"We prefer not to use that term," he said. "It carries such harsh connotations. What we propose is to, well, let me use your patient, Mr. Christopher, for example. Mr. Christopher, by all accounts, was a pleasant old gentleman. Unfortunately, he had basically smoked himself to death and nothing anyone could do was going to change the fact that he was going to die from his emphysema. The only question was how long would he survive? Do you know how much it costs us to take care of an ICU patient for a single day? A minimum of a thousand dollars. Well, with Mr. Christopher, then, your act of kindness enabling him to extubate himself and hasten his death saved our facility thousands of dollars."

Alex raised her hand to interrupt him. She shook her head as she spoke.

"I can't believe what I'm hearing," she said angrily. "You call me in here and accuse me of being involved in the deaths of these patients but then tell me if I'll cooperate with your patient elimination plan you won't go to the authorities. You compliment my work ethic and compassion and then you have the audacity to sit there and ask me to kill patients to save the hospital money!"

Mr. Warren wrinkled his forehead and squinted.

"I wish you wouldn't use that term," he said. "We're not asking you to kill anyone."

"Well, I'm sorry," Alex replied, raising her voice, "but that's sure as hell what it sounds like to me, and I won't be a part of it."

Gerald Warren lowered himself onto the seat of the firm, leather chair behind the desk and leaned back, scratching his head. He chewed on his lower lip, trying to control his rising emotion.

"Miss Lowe, let's be reasonable," he said. "You know as well as we do that there are a lot of people in the hospital who live for months without any hope of recovery. I imagine you've had the privilege, or perhaps misfortune, of taking care of some of them. Many of them want to die. They're suffering, and their families are suffering. They realize that life has nothing left to offer them but pain and misery. Others don't even realize they're alive. They're kept alive in vegetative states by families who refuse to give up hope, even when there is none. We can't continue throwing money away keeping these patients alive, not if we're to continue providing state-of-the-art care to the people who really need it, not if our institution is going to remain open to serve our community."

"I'm sorry, Mr. Warren," Alex stated firmly, "but I can't be a part of your team. No matter how you explain it, it still sounds like you're assembling a team to kill patients."

Mr. Warren smiled and looked at Bob Carlson who was shaking his head.

"Miss Lowe, I was hoping you'd understand our reasoning and be willing to participate, but I respect your opinion. Unfortunately, if you don't participate we'll have to turn over our tapes, as well as the syringe, to the authorities. We can't afford to have staff nurses running around our hospital killing people. It just doesn't look good."

"That's blackmail!" Alex shouted, rising from her chair.

"Call it what you will, Miss Lowe," he replied threateningly, "but that's my offer. I suggest you think about it for a day or two before making your final decision. And should you decide to discuss it with anyone, everything you've heard tonight would be adamantly denied and you'd look quite foolish and vindictive. Now, do you have any further questions?"

Alex stared at the floor and stubbornly shook her head.

"No, sir," she replied. "I don't think so."

Mr. Warren smiled and rose to his feet.

"Thank you for coming to meet with us," he said, dismissing her. "You may return to the ICU now."

Alex walked slowly to the door, shuffling her feet as she walked. The weight of the world pressed down on her shoulders. She pulled the door to close it but felt someone pulling from inside the room. Lib Dillard followed her into the hallway.

"I want you to know this isn't my idea," she said, "but there are some things in my past, things I'm not proud of, that he knows about. I had no choice. Either I went along with his operation and helped find a nurse to implement his plans, or he'd go public with my past. My life would be ruined. I'm sorry you were the one selected but Gerald felt that he'd built the strongest case against you. With the syringe and the videotape in his hands, he's prepared to press charges against you for murder if you don't go along with him."

"Miss Dillard, do you think I killed those people?" Alex asked.

"I don't know. I think you're basically a good, kind-hearted person, but if I were in your shoes, I'm not sure I'd want to stand before a jury. They're willing to play hardball in there. Now, I've made arrangements for you to be off work the remainder of the night. I know if I were in your shoes, I couldn't concentrate on my work, and the last thing you need right now is another incident they could use against you."

- 20 -

The cool night air was refreshing as Alex drove through the city. She had no desire to go home and sit alone in her apartment. She wanted to call Elizabeth or Ben but was afraid of what might happen if she crossed her accusers. Their threat of prison was real, and she knew it. At that moment she hated herself for having not listened to her sister. As she drove, she tried to rationalize the actions that had put her in this predicament. She wasn't a bad person and she wasn't a murderer. She was a compassionate human being who had made decisions based on other's needs. She'd taken action to prevent further suffering for people who were unable to help themselves. She hadn't killed Prince Christopher. He made the decision to pull out his endotracheal tube. She'd merely untied his hand to make him more comfortable. David Watson had died because of her mistake, but there was no intent to take his life on her part. There was nothing premeditated. It could've happened to anyone. Billy Jackson's death was more difficult to rationalize. No matter how she pictured it in her mind, the truth was that she'd purposefully given him the morphine to end his life. And that was murder, even if he did want to die.

Tears rolled down her face as she pressed the gas pedal to the floor, sending the tiny Volkswagen racing down the highway. The speedometer only registered eighty-five miles per hour but with the needle completely out of view, she knew she was exceeding that. If she jerked the steering wheel sharply to one side, the small car would flip over and possibly end her life. Or maybe she could slam into the concrete support columns of the overpass. A violent crash like that should end her life. She couldn't face life in prison and there would be no disgrace in death by a car accident. Just as she was about to veer off the road in an attempt to roll her car, the intruding, troublesome voice of doubt spoke to her.

"What if you flip the car or crash into one of the concrete supports but don't die? What if you end up with severe injuries or in a persistent vegetative state? What if you wind up on a ventilator aware of your surroundings and can never be weaned? Who will be your angel of mercy? Who will challenge fate in your defense?"

She took her foot off the gas pedal and allowed the car to gradually slow down. She turned on to a dirt road and followed the winding, washboard road down to the river. Outside she could hear the crickets chirping and the frogs croaking. The reflection of the moon on the water was so peaceful. Death was not the answer. The only way out was to go along with Mr. Warren. If she cooperated then maybe she could have some input into which patients were denied resources. And if he were true to his word, then he wouldn't be asking her to deny resources to patients who had a chance for recovery. She would simply do what she had done before and put an end to people's pain and suffering. It was for the good of the hospital and community that she participate.

Early the next morning she placed a call to Mr. Warren and arranged to meet with him. His office was impressive with expensive walnut furnishings. Plaques honoring him for various civic activities adorned the walls. In her eyes, he looked more like a corporate lawyer than a hospital administrator with his slicked back, gray hair and his stylish, charcoal gray suit with a starched white shirt. Alex was casually dressed and found it amusing that he was wearing a bright red, paisley power tie for their meeting. As she entered the room he made his way toward her and extended his right hand. She stuck her hands into the pockets of her tight blue jeans.

"I was hoping I'd hear from you," he said, tracing her slim but shapely frame with his eyes, "but I wasn't expecting it to be so soon. I trust you've given some thought to our conversation last night."

"Yes, sir, I have," Alex replied.

Her face remained expressionless as she stared at him.

"And?" he prompted her.

"And I've decided to join your team."

He smiled and took a deep breath.

"I must say, I am delighted and believe you've made a wise decision. Now, if you'll permit me, I'll call the other members of our team so we can begin preparations to implement our cost saving operation."

"Mr. Warren," Alex said, "I want you to understand that my willingness to participate does not in any way insinuate that I believe I've done anything wrong. Are we clear on that?"

"Crystal," he responded.

Within minutes, the other team members, each of whom carried a black satchel and a note pad, joined them. Mr. Warren locked the door to his office and notified his secretary that he was not to be disturbed. Alex sat with her arms folded across her chest and her legs crossed with her right leg swinging up and down.

"As you're aware," he began, "for the past two years our institution has operated in the red. Our losses last year alone were over one point six million dollars. We've taken measures to cut our losses, but unfortunately, three months into our current fiscal year, we're still operating at a deficit. Our own internal audit has shown conclusively that the vast majority of our losses can be directly attributed to the ongoing care given during the last three months of life to many of our patients. In particular, we focused our attention on our elderly population as well as our trauma victims and cancer patients." He paused and looked each of them in the eye. "If we can limit the resources we spend on these dying patients then I believe we can not only trim our losses, but potentially turn a profit for this hospital. And each of you knows, as well as I do, that we must have those profits to renovate our facility and update our equipment. If we continue to operate at a loss, the hospital will be forced to close and that will leave our community without a medical facility. The task at hand is, for us as a group, to set up a series of guidelines to determine which patients and in what manner our resources will be withheld."

"I may be speaking out of turn," Alex said, raising her hand, "but do you feel we're qualified to make those decisions? I mean, shouldn't we have a physician's input into this."

"I understand your concern, Miss Lowe," he replied, "but to answer your question, no, at least not at this point. Let me assure you that we have personnel throughout the hospital who are eavesdropping on our physicians trying to gather information about beliefs and attitudes. If or perhaps, when we find the proper physician, we'll sit down with him and discuss our purpose. I'm sure you must realize that we have to be very cautious in our approach to this problem."

"Yes, sir," Alex replied. "I'm well aware that your operation could blow up in your face, especially if word gets out of what you're doing. I can only imagine the field day the news media would have if they found out patients were being killed at Richland Memorial to cut costs."

"Miss Lowe, need I remind you that you're a part of this team? If it comes unraveled, you'll be implicated along with everyone else. As I recall, it was your decision to participate. No one held a gun to your head."

"You didn't have to hold a gun, Mr. Warren," Alex said. "Your threat of blackmail was motivation enough."

"Blackmail, Miss Lowe?" he asked, sounding alarmed.

"No one tried to blackmail you. We were strictly looking out for the interests of our hospital and the care that our patients receive. Our biggest concern was that some of your actions had produced very questionable outcomes."

"Can we get on with this?" Miss Dillard asked angrily. "The two of you bickering over who's at fault or why everyone agreed to participate isn't going to solve anything. The fact is we're all involved and if any of us chooses to go public with our operation, we'll all suffer the consequences."

"I couldn't agree more, Miss Dillard," Mr. Warren replied. "If it's okay with Miss Lowe, I'd be more than happy to continue."

He focused his cold, piercing eyes on Alex and waited for her response. She stared back at him and nodded her head.

"Now, Miss Lowe, to get back to your concerns. If possible, we will have physician involvement in the future, but for now we must rely on Miss Dillard's expertise, as well as your own. While it's impossible for such a small group as ours to review each hospital admission, we have set some guidelines, which we believe will be helpful in spotting potential over-utilizers. We'll attempt to review the charts of anyone admitted to our hospital who is over the age of seventy, carries an admitting diagnosis of cancer, undergoes open-heart surgery or is admitted to our surgical trauma team. From past experiences, these groups tend to have the highest numbers of patients who have prolonged hospitalizations as well as the highest probability of dying without ever leaving the hospital."

"That's still going to be a large group of patients. What I want to know is how are you going to decide who dies?" Alex asked.

"When we have a consensus among us that someone's chances for meaningful survival outside of a hospital are nil, then we'll limit their resources. Or on the other hand, if we become aware of a situation in which the physician believes his patient should not receive certain treatment options, such as dialysis or open heart surgery, but is forced into pursuing these treatments because of family pressures, then we may take it upon ourselves to ensure that such options are not pursued."

"Why don't you stop all of this double talk?" Alex asked angrily. "The bottom line here is that we'll be taking people's lives, either actively or passively, to save the hospital money."

Mr. Warren shook his head, looked at Alex, and smiled.

"In order to be successful," he said, "we must make some changes and special arrangements. Our first priority will be to move you from your permanent position as a night nurse in the ICU to flexi-pool. Only then can we fully utilize your expertise and abilities. I apologize for any inconvenience this may cause you in your lifestyle and daily routine, but it's necessary if we're to succeed. When we feel we've found a suitable candidate, we'll assign you to that floor and make arrangements, when possible, for you to take care of that patient. There will undoubtedly be occasions when we need to limit resources but are unable to assign you to the case without drawing attention to you. On those occasions we'll need total team cooperation. When you're not working for the team, you'll be assigned to one of the nursing units as usual."

"I'm still not sure I understand what you expect me to do once a victim has been identified," Alex said.

"Don't worry about that. When the time arises, you'll be given explicit instructions and provided with the necessary equipment and medications. Mr. Alford will be on call twenty-four hours a day to assist with any pharmaceutical supplies you may need. We've made arrangements for you to have a few days off, starting today, before you begin your new job. Any other questions?"

"No sir," Alex replied. "I think you've answered them all."

"Very good. You're free to go. We have several charts to review today but we'll be in touch with you soon. Miss Dillard will take care of finding someone to work in your place in the meantime."

Alex walked quickly from the room and pulled the door closed behind her. She reached her hand into the pocket of her coat and turned off the small tape recorder.

- 21 -

Lib Dillard opened the heavy wooden door and looked out. The outer room was empty except for his secretary, who sat at her desk busily typing, oblivious to the gathering behind the closed door. The nursing supervisor closed the door and took her seat with the others.

"She's gone," she reported.

"Are you sure?" Mr. Warren asked.

"Positive. There's no one out there but your secretary, and she's too busy typing to concern herself with us."

"I think we've got to watch the girl closely," he said. "She makes me nervous. I'm not sure we can trust her. If I didn't know better, I'd swear she kept baiting me, trying to make me say we wanted her to kill someone for us."

"Don't be ridiculous, Gerald," Lib replied. "Put yourself in her shoes. She just wants to know what will be required of her. After all, you did use blackmail to get her to agree to participate in the first place."

"I used blackmail?" he asked harshly. "You're as much a part of this as I am. This is a we situation. You're the one who recommended her. Surely you remember that."

"Yeah, I remember," she replied, "and I remember how you blackmailed me to get me to participate."

Bob slammed his fist on the desk and rose to his feet.

"Enough, already," he roared. "We're all in this together. How and why we participate is irrelevant. But I agree with Gerald. The girl worries me. We better watch her closely and the sooner we get her actively involved, the better off she'll be, the better off we'll be. Who's got the list of prospective patients?"

Tim opened his black satchel and pulled out a yellow legal pad.

"These are the names with diagnoses and number of days in the hospital as of yesterday," he said. "I took the liberty of pulling up their medication profiles and jotting them down. I think we've got at least three strong candidates. In bed two of the open heart unit there's a Mr. Elrod. He's seventy-nine years old and has been in the unit for six weeks. He appears to have severe underlying lung disease and hasn't been able to wean from the ventilator. He has no family and shouldn't be missed if he dies. The second option is a young man in the ICU who was involved in a car wreck. He's been in the hospital for almost two months. He's stable hemodynamically but has a severe head injury. He's been unresponsive since he was admitted and is being kept alive with tube feedings. His parents won't take him home and we can't find a nursing home that's willing to take him. According to the nursing notes his parents haven't visited him in about three weeks. Right now he's costing us about twelve hundred dollars a day. The last patient is a ninety-four year old lady who was sent in from a nursing home. She's got multiple medical problems including an infection with methicillin resistant staphylococcus. She's too sick to go back to the nursing home but not sick enough to die. She's only costing us about six hundred dollars a day but she might be our best bet. She's got no family and she's a 'No Code'."

Gerald nodded his approval.

"What do you think, Lib?" he asked.

"I'd have to agree with Tim," she replied. "I looked over the charts earlier and felt she'd have the fewest tracks to cover."

"How about you, Bob?" he asked.

Bob folded his arms across his chest and shook his head quickly from side to side.

"I've already told you how I feel," he replied. "I don't like what we're doing and I'm not going to make any decisions regarding who dies. I've got no medical or pharmaceutical knowledge. I'm a number cruncher, remember?"

"How could we forget?" Gerald asked. "You remind us every time we have a meeting. Then, if everyone agrees, the old lady will be our first participant. Now, what we've got to decide is how we'll limit her resources."

"Gerald, I'm sorry if I sound like the girl," Lib interrupted, "but can we stop playing word games. It's ridiculous to sit here and talk about limiting resources when in effect we're discussing how to take someone's life. I understand your caution when she was with us but not now."

"Okay, Lib. How do you propose we end her life?"

"I think we should give her a large bolus of intravenous morphine," she replied. "She's already so poorly responsive that no one would notice a change in her mental status. It would appear as if she just died in her sleep."

"How should we arrange it?" he asked.

"I've thought about that," she replied. "I suggest we assign Alex to the fifth floor, supply her with a syringe of morphine and let her do the rest."

"How can we be sure she'll be assigned to take care of the old lady?" Tim asked.

"It won't matter whether she takes care of her or not," Lib replied. "Our nurses generally assist one another with patient care so she should have ample opportunity to be in and out of her room. It might make her less uncomfortable and less conspicuous if she isn't actually assigned to care for her. My biggest concern is getting her the morphine. Narcotics are closely monitored on the nursing units."

"That shouldn't be a problem, should it Tim?" Gerald asked.

"No, sir," the pharmacist replied. "I'll make arrangements in the pharmacy to supply any medications we might need. It'll be a lot easier to alter my invoices than to try to obtain medications on the units."

"When should we do it?" Gerald asked.

"The sooner the better," Lib replied. "The less time she has to contemplate, the less time she has to back out. I say we bring her back tomorrow night with the fifth floor assignment."

"Why the night shift?" Gerald asked.

"Lighter staffing with more sharing of responsibilities," Lib explained. "It'd be much easier at night for her to find a reason to go into the old lady's room without raising anyone's suspicions. Long term, however, I think we should vary her shifts. That should make it more difficult for anyone to detect a pattern surrounding patients' deaths."

Bob stretched his legs and crossed his ankles. His face turned bright red.

"The three of you make this whole damn thing sound so impersonal," he said in a loud voice. "Does the old lady, as you insist on calling her, have a name?"

"I'm sure she does," Gerald replied, "but I'm not sure it matters."

"Damn it, Gerald, it'd matter if she were a friend or one of our relatives," Bob replied.

"Maggie Cooper," Tim said. "Her name is Maggie Cooper."

"You know her, Bob? She's not your mother is she?" Gerald taunted.

Bob cut his eyes at his friend and shook his head.

"No, Gerald, I don't know her," he replied coldly. "And no, she's not my mother."

"Wonderful," he replied, nodding his head. "Do we have your permission, then, Mr. Carlson, to terminate Miss Cooper?"

Bob folded his arms across his chest and stared at Gerald.

"One of these days, Gerald, one of these days," he replied angrily.

Gerald smiled and chuckled under his breath.

"Bobby, Bobby, Bobby. What am I going to do with you? Now, where were we? Oh, yes, the morphine. Tim, if you can get the syringe of morphine then we'll be all set for Miss Cooper," he said with emphasis on the old lady's name. "I'm sure you can determine how much medication will be needed."

"Yes, sir. That won't be a problem," Tim replied, "but how am I going to get the syringe to the girl?"

"Good question. Any ideas, Lib?"

"That all depends," she replied. "How hard would it be for you to dispense an extra vial of morphine to the fifth floor tomorrow night?"

"Dispensing the morphine shouldn't be a problem," Tim replied. "I'd be more worried about the girl getting caught while drawing up the morphine into the syringe. I think it'd be less risky to have a syringe already filled with morphine. She could come by the pharmacy and pick it up or better yet, why not put it in her locker prior to shift change."

"Good idea," Gerald replied. "Do we have access to her locker?"

"I can make arrangements for the two of us to have dual access to a locker in the nurse's lounge," Lib replied. "We've got several empty lockers. I'll put a keyed lock on one and make sure Alex has a key. We could leave medications and correspondence in the locker."

Gerald lightly slapped his hand on his desk and nodded his agreement.

"If that's agreeable with everyone, then that's what we'll do. As far as any written correspondence, we have to make every effort to keep it to a minimum. We can't afford to have a paper trail for anyone to follow if this thing falls apart. And we've got to limit our phone conversations since you never know who may be listening. If you have to leave anyone a voice mail, be careful what you say. Is that clear?"

With the nod of a head, they all agreed. The less said, the better.

"Lib, you're in charge of contacting the girl and discussing the assignment with her. If there are no more questions, then you're all dismissed."

Bob leaned back in his chair, raising the front two legs off the floor as he watched Lib and Tim leave the office.

"I've got my doubts about Dillard," he said as the door slammed shut. "She worries me as much as the girl does."

"You worry me, Bob," Gerald replied. "You're too paranoid. Neither Dillard nor the girl will give us any trouble. We've got too much on them."

"I hope you're right."

"Trust me. Once you do some creative accounting and we share some of the revenues we're saving, we won't have to worry about anyone getting out of line."

"How much you gonna' give 'em?" he asked.

"I'm not sure," Gerald replied. "I guess whatever it takes to pacify them. Hell, I think I've got enough dirt on the two of them that they should pay me just to keep me from having them arrested."

He paused and looked at Bob.

"How much is your cooperation going to cost me?" he asked.

"I haven't given it much thought," Bob replied. "With what you had me do five years ago, I'm not sure I'm in a position to demand any money. If the truth were known that Jim Curry's wreck wasn't an accident, I could be ruined and you would deny everything."

Gerald shook his head and chuckled softly. "I hate you feel that way, but I'm glad you understand who's in charge here. And as far as what we did back then, it was for the good of the hospital and it didn't hurt anyone."

"Jim Curry is dead because of it," Bob replied, shaking his

head solemnly. "And what about the patients and their families. Don't you ever wonder how much they suffered under Curry's care?"

"Those patients were dying. So what if they suffered a little bit more before they died?" Gerald replied coldly. He tapped his fingers rhythmically on his desk as he thought. "Curry was the best damn doctor we had at keeping patients alive, and all he had to do was amend his ways after reimbursements changed. If only he would have been willing to terminate those patients who were costing us money…" His voice trailed off as he gazed out the window. "Life is precious. Those patients and their families should have been thankful for the few extra days of life we gave them. If we hadn't arranged for Curry to be involved in their care those patients and their families wouldn't have had that extra time together."

"But did Curry have to die?"

"We didn't have a choice. He knew too much and was willing to blow the whistle." Gerald gently massaged his eyes with his thumb and index finger. "Before these damn DRG's, we benefited by prolonging life and ordering tests. If we hadn't kept those patients alive, Richland might have folded. We were just fortunate Curry agreed to cooperate."

"With the dirt you had on him, he didn't have a choice."

"And neither do we. We didn't have a choice back then. And we don't have a choice now.

- 22 -

Alex stared at the flashing red light on her answering machine. She hoped the message was from Ben but subconsciously she knew it probably wasn't. She took a deep breath, hesitating briefly before listening to the message. Her body went limp when she heard Lib Dillard's voice.

"Alex, this is Lib Dillard," the message began. "You've been assigned to work the night shift on fifth floor Thursday night. Part of your responsibility will be to evaluate the resource utilization of Maggie Cooper, room 535. Call me in my office at 426-6790 before your shift tomorrow to finalize your work schedule. It's imperative that I speak with you before your shift."

Alex took the small tape recorder from her pocket. She replayed the message, this time recording it on her recorder even though there was nothing inflammatory or suggestive in the message.

The next thirty-six hours passed slowly, as if she were a child waiting for Christmas. But unlike the anticipation and excitement of gifts on Christmas morning, there was the dread and fear of the unknown. When she called Miss Dillard, she was told that the parking deck security guard would have an envelope for her containing a key to locker thirteen in the nurses' lounge. Her final instructions would be in a manila envelope inside the locker.

The security guard watched her as she pulled her red Volkswagen into the parking deck of the hospital and made her way toward the crosswalk. As she approached him, he reached into his pocket and pulled out a key.

"Are you Alex Lowe?" he asked.

"Yes, I am," she replied. "Why do you ask?"

"Some lady, I think she's a nurse, left this key for you. Said she found it in the nurse's lounge and it had your name on it. She told me to be on the lookout for you tonight, but I was about to give up. You're the fifth person I've asked tonight if they were Alex Lowe."

"Well, I'm glad you found me. I couldn't have done my job tonight if I couldn't get into my locker. I certainly appreciate your help."

"It's my pleasure, ma'am," he replied. "I'm just glad I could help out. I hope you have a good night."

"Thank you," Alex replied. "I hope I do too, and you as well."

She breathed a sigh of relief after opening the door of the nurse's lounge and finding the room empty. She took the key from her pocket and opened the lock on locker thirteen. She glanced nervously about the room before opening the locker door. As she'd been told, there was a manila envelope inside the locker. Its metal clasps were folded down, but the flap wasn't sealed. Her hands trembled as she opened the envelope and withdrew its contents. She hurriedly placed the syringe in her coat pocket before reading her instructions. The short, handwritten note instructed her to administer the medicine to Maggie Cooper in room 535. She folded the note several times and placed it in her purse. An uneasy feeling came over her as she made her way to the fifth floor to take report.

"Darlene, you'll be taking care of Maggie Cooper in room 535," the charge nurse said. "She was transferred to the hospital from a nursing home. She appears to be septic with a urinary tract infection and has been unresponsive except to painful stimuli. She's a 'No Code' and as far as we know, she has no family. The state-appointed legal guardian didn't accompany her to the hospital but apparently told her physician to call him only if she died."

Alex closed her eyes and uttered a silent "Thank you". At least they'd chosen an easy first victim. Half of the shift had passed before she found the courage to enter Miss Cooper's room. The sight of the old lady unnerved her. She was expecting a frail, shriveled up, elderly woman. Instead she found a plump, rosy-cheeked, grandmotherly figure with shimmering white hair who appeared much younger than her ninety-four years of age. Alex called her name and patted her shoulder. There was no response. She took her knuckle and pressed firmly against the old woman's sternum. The old lady grimaced but made no effort to grab Alex's hand.

Alex placed her hand in her pocket and held the syringe lightly in her fingers. Her pulse quickened. A cool, anxiety provoked perspiration beaded up on her forehead. She walked quickly to the doorway and looked out. There was no one in the hallway. She pulled the door closed and walked back to the bedside. After a deep, calming breath she withdrew the syringe from her pocket and inserted the needle into the I.V. port. Her heart pounded as she hurriedly injected the medication. She recapped the needle and placed the syringe back in her pocket. Resource utilization by Maggie Cooper would be ending soon.

She was sitting at the nurse's station charting on another patient near the end of her shift when a nurse's aide approached her.

"Are you the nurse taking care of 535?" the aide asked.

"No," Alex replied. "I think Darlene's taking care of her."

"But I thought I saw you coming out of her room earlier in the shift," the aide replied.

"You might have," Alex replied, nervously, "I heard her I.V. beeping and I went in to check on it. What do you need? Is there something I can help you with?"

"Yeah, I think she's dead," the aide replied. "When I went to give her a bath she was cold and stiff. Looks like she's been dead for a while."

Alex tried to hide her anxiety as she pushed back from the desk and followed the aide to the room. Miss Cooper was just as she'd been described. Alex felt for a pulse but there was none. She placed her stethoscope in her ears and listened for a heart beat. No sounds except for the forceful pounding of her own heart within her ears. Maggie Cooper was dead, her resource utilization over.

"I'll find her nurse and let her know," the aide said, "if you'll notify the doctor."

Alex nodded and walked back to the nurse's station, the rubber soles of her shoes squeaking as she walked. She sat down and took a deep breath. Death had come sooner than she expected, but no one appeared to expect wrongdoing.

The intern arrived on the floor within a few minutes to examine the patient. He went through the same ritual that Alex had performed. He checked for a pulse, an apical heartbeat and a blood pressure. Satisfied that she was dead, he wrote a brief death note in her chart and asked the nurse to notify the next of kin. He saluted Alex, stated, "I'm outta here", and disappeared on the elevator.

Alex shook her head as the elevator doors closed. Maggie Cooper's death was nothing more than an inconvenience for the young doctor. She was just another old lady who'd outlived her usefulness and died in her sleep. His only concern was how quickly could he pronounce her dead and return to his call room for a few more minutes of sleep before morning rounds.

She propped her elbows on the table and rested her chin in the palms of her hands. Her eyelids felt heavy. When she'd administered the medication to Miss Cooper, she'd felt an incredible adrenaline rush. But now the natural high was gone and she felt drained. There had been fear in knowing she might get caught, but the sensation she'd experienced afterwards had excited her. Now that Miss Cooper was dead and no questions were being asked, she found herself feeling alone and dejected. The doubt that comes from uncertainty crept back into her mind. All she wanted now was for her shift to end so she could go home and sleep.

- 23 -

A light rain was falling by the time Alex clocked out and made her way to the parking deck. The darkness of the clouds only added to her sense of despair. With the radio blaring, she raced from the parking deck. There was nothing she wanted more than to see the silhouette of the hospital shrinking in her rear view mirror. She needed to run, to get away from what she had just committed.

The rain was falling steadily by the time she reached her apartment. As she pulled into the parking lot, she saw a male, soaked to the bone, his hands cupped around his face, looking in her bedroom window. For several minutes, she sat in her car watching the man as he moved from window to window trying to see inside the apartment. His wet clothes stuck to his body. Water dripped from his hair. Not until the intruder turned away from the building and started walking to the parking lot did Alex recognize Ben.

"What are you doing?" Alex yelled, relieved. "You look like a wet rat."

"Where in God's name have you been?" Ben yelled back. "I've been worried sick about you."

"I've been working!" Alex replied. "Remember? I'm a nurse. I work nights at the hospital."

"Well, where were you last night?" Ben asked. "I went

by the ICU to get you to eat with me and you weren't there. I called here early this morning before I got off work to see if you wanted to go biking and you didn't answer. I phoned Liz and your Dad and they hadn't heard from you so I came over here to check on you. Hell, for all I knew, you could've been dead."

Alex unlocked her apartment and motioned for Ben to follow her inside. Water dripped from his wet clothes. Alex looked at him and grinned.

"Don't you look lovely? Here, dry yourself off," she said, tossing him a towel.

"You still haven't answered my question," Ben said angrily.

Alex hung her raincoat on the hook behind the door and stretched out her arms.

"Look at my clothes, Benjamin. I worked last night," she said.

"But I checked in the unit and no one had seen you."

"I wasn't in the unit," Alex replied. "I worked five main."

"Five main?" Ben asked, surprised. "Did you get pulled?"

Alex sat down on the couch and pulled off her white clogs.

"Oh, that feels good," she said, wiggling her toes and stretching her legs.

Ben plopped down on the brown, vinyl chair just inside the doorway. He leaned forward and shook the water from his hair before peeling off his soaked shirt. He quickly dried his muscular torso with the towel.

"I asked you if you got pulled," he said.

"In a manner of speaking, yes, I got pulled," Alex said, sounding aggravated. "Miss Dillard asked me a few days ago if I'd work flexi-pool. I didn't want to, but she kind of pressured me. It's no big deal. I'll still do some work in the ICU, and I'll probably continue to work nights."

"So you're not in the ICU anymore?" Ben asked.

"No. I'm officially a float nurse now. I won't know until I get to work where I'll be assigned."

"Are you happy with that?" he asked.

"Doesn't matter if I'm happy or not," Alex replied. "If I'm going to work at Richland, I'll be working flexi-pool."

"How can she make you work flexi-pool?"

"She managed to find out about a mistake I made on a patient and threatened to go to the nursing board if I didn't cooperate with her. Look, it's no big deal. I'll still get to work some in the ICU."

"How'd she find out?"

"I don't know," Alex replied, "but it doesn't matter. She knows and there's nothing you or I or anyone else can do about it."

"Well, I'm glad you're okay," Ben said. "I was worried thinking something had happened to you. You know it's not like you to not be home when I call at six-thirty in the morning." Ben paused and pointed at phone. "Your phone's ringing," he said. "Aren't you going to answer it?"

"No, let it ring," Alex replied. "The answering machine will get it. It was a long night and I don't really feel like talking to anyone."

Ben shook his head and smiled. "Do you want me to answer it for you and screen your calls? It might be your new boyfriend," he teased.

"No, just let the recorder pick up," Alex replied. "If it's someone I want to talk to then I'll answer it."

"Hello, Alex, this is Lib Dillard. I'm sorry I missed you, but..."

Alex quickly grabbed the phone before Miss Dillard could finish her sentence.

"Hey, Miss Dillard," she said. "I'd just walked in when I heard your voice on my recorder. No, ma'am, no problems. Everything seemed to go just fine. No, I don't think so. Not as far as I could tell. No, ma'am, no plans. Yes, ma'am, if that's what you want me to do. I can certainly use the extra money. Do you think it's wise, so soon? Okay. I'll be in touch."

She placed the phone back in the cradle and sighed softly.

"What was that all about?" Ben asked, curiously.

"Nothing much," Alex replied. "She wanted to be sure my night went okay. I'm sure she feels a little guilty after pressuring me to work flexi-pool." She leaned back on the sofa and opened the blinds behind her. "It's still raining," she said, trying to change the subject.

"Looks like it might rain all day," Ben replied, nodding. "What was that about being able to use the extra money, and doing something so soon?"

Alex shrugged her shoulders. "Nothing really. She promised to try and get me a raise if I went along with her request and apparently the hospital agreed to it."

"What about it not being wise to do something so soon?" Ben asked.

"It's not important," Alex replied. "Don't worry about it."

"Well, now that I know you're all right," Ben said, putting his arms around her, "I'm going home and get some sleep. If it stops raining and you want to go biking this afternoon give me a call."

"Thanks, Ben. I'm sorry I had you worried, but it's good to know you care."

"Was there ever any question?" Ben asked, planting a warm kiss on her cheek.

"No, not really," Alex replied, pulling back from his embrace.

Ben opened the door and leaned against the door frame.

"You seem tense," he said. "Work isn't getting to you, is it?"

"No. I'm fine, just tired," Alex replied, meekly.

"Well, try to get some rest. I agreed to fill in on the nightshift in the pharmacy for the next week or so, so maybe I'll get a chance to see you."

"I hope so," Alex answered. "Call me tonight. Maybe we can eat together."

Alex watched as Ben ran through the rain to his car. As the taillights disappeared in the distance, she dialed Miss

Dillard's number.

"Miss Dillard, this is Alex Lowe. Have you got a minute?"

"Sure, Alex. What's on your mind?" she replied.

"When you called, a friend was here and I wasn't free to talk. Were there any problems with what happened last night?"

"No, Alex," she replied. "None at all. I think it went much smoother than we anticipated. There's nothing but praise for you around here this morning."

Alex cradled the phone between her shoulder and her ear as she straightened the magazines on the coffee table.

"I'm glad to hear that. I'm not afraid to admit I had quite a few reservations about what we were doing. I couldn't imagine what would've happened if I'd been caught."

"That's the beauty of it. If we're careful with our selections, you shouldn't get caught. If anyone had walked in on you last night, you could've said you were giving a scheduled medication. After all, you are a nurse taking care of patients."

"Well, I can assure you it was nerve racking. I've never done anything like that before," Alex replied.

"I'm sure you were nervous, but we both know you've done it before, just not for pay. Now, about tonight, I've got you scheduled to work in the surgical intensive care unit. There's a young man in bed four who was involved in an MVA some time back. He's unresponsive and being kept alive with a ventilator and a feeding tube. He's draining the system dry."

"Isn't that kind of risky?" Alex asked. "I mean, if he's in the intensive care unit there'll be other nurses around. Miss Dillard, it's not easy to sneak into one of those rooms without being seen if you're not the one taking care of the patient."

"You underestimate our resources, Alex. I've already made arrangements for you to take care of him tonight. You won't have to sneak into his room. Your instructions will be in the locker when you get to work. Now, you get some rest. We want you fresh tonight. You've got to be quick and able to think on your feet so as not to make a mistake."

Alex hung up the phone and replayed the taped recording. There was no mention of killing in the conversation but at least there was talk of being careful and not getting caught. With time, one of them would slip up. She had to be patient.

- 24 -

An older nurse with salt and pepper hair sat alone in the locker room smoking a cigarette. Alex looked straight ahead as she walked past her to locker thirteen.

"It's a shame isn't it?" she asked Alex.

"Excuse me?" Alex replied, irritated by the stranger's intrusion into her private thoughts.

"I said, it's a shame. You know, having to sneak off to the locker room to smoke a damn cigarette. It's bad enough having to work nights. Seems like the least they could do would be to let me smoke in the break room."

"Yeah, sure. Whatever you say," Alex mumbled.

"You been working here long?"

"Not too long. You?" Alex responded.

"Twenty years. Twenty long, miserable years working the graveyard shift with nothing to show for it but a gold plated service pin."

"Well, I hope they don't plan on seeing me around here working nights twenty years from now because it's not going to happen."

The older nurse flicked the ashes from her cigarette and coughed deeply.

"You sound like me when I was your age," she said. "In twenty years you'll probably be sitting here one night having this same conversation with someone half your age."

Alex shook her head. "Don't count on it," she replied.

She pulled a manila envelope from her locker, slammed the door and fastened the lock. The older nurse looked on curiously as Alex pulled a folded sheet of paper from the envelope. Alex ran her hand deep in the envelope. As she expected, a syringe lay in the bottom of the envelope. She rolled the syringe between her fingers but knew it was too risky to place it in her pocket with someone watching. She folded the flap on the envelope and secured it with the metal clasps. She had no choice but to take the envelope and syringe with her. She turned away from the nosy intruder and used her body as a shield while she unfolded the paper and read her instructions.

"Whatcha' reading?" the nurse asked.

"Nothing," Alex answered as she scanned the note.

"It's got to be something or you couldn't read it," the nurse replied curtly.

"Look," Alex said glaring at her, "I don't know you and you don't know me. I'm not in the mood to socialize with a stranger tonight and what I'm reading is really none of your business."

The older nurse took one final drag off of her cigarette, flicked the butt into an open toilet and blew an endless stream of smoke toward Alex.

"When I first spotted you," she said, "I thought you were different from the rest. You had an air about you. You held your head a little bit higher than the others. I thought that maybe, just maybe, you were special. But you're not. You're no different from me or any of the others who've been stuck here in this hellhole their entire life. And you'll never get out of here either. Excuse me for intruding on your life."

She slammed her locker and stormed from the lounge without looking at Alex. Alex shook her head and smiled. "What a jerk," she mumbled under her breath. Who'd she think she was and what gave her the right to judge and criticize someone she didn't even know?

The instructions were short and to the point. She was to administer the syringe of medication to the patient in bed four of the ICU. She squirted a small amount in her palm and smelled it. She'd smelled that odor before but wasn't sure where. She placed a few drops on her tongue. The intense, salty bitterness was familiar. Nothing was as bitter as potassium. The patient in bed four would die from hyperkalemia. The potassium bolus would cause the heart to fibrillate, circulatory collapse would follow, death would have another victim, and Gerald Warren's hospital would lose less money than it did the day before.

It came as no surprise when she was assigned to take care of the patient in bed four. His condition was exactly as had been described. Severe head injury, ventilator support, tube feedings and unresponsiveness even to noxious stimuli. An appropriate choice for termination, she thought. Without taking time to clean the medication port, she inserted the needle into the I.V. and injected the deadly bolus of potassium. Her heart raced on another adrenaline high.

Within minutes, the patient's heart felt the effects of the potassium, the heart rhythm deteriorating into ventricular fibrillation. She wondered why the monitor technician wasn't calling attention to it and looked out from behind the curtain. The monitor technician sat in front of the cardiac monitors with her chin on her chest, her eyes closed. She wouldn't be calling a code.

Alex watched and waited as his heart fibrillated. If she waited long enough there'd be nothing that anyone could do to save the dying boy. She walked to the break room and poured herself a cup of coffee. Surely, this was destiny's way of showing her that she'd done the right thing. She sipped slowly on the coffee as she watched the second hand travel around the face of her watch. Five minutes passed, then ten. Confident that intervention couldn't save him, she returned to his room. The coarse, irregular rhythm of ventricular fibrillation had deteriorated further into the slow, wavy snakelike rhythm of a potassium-poisoned heart before it completely stops beating. The Dynamap no longer registered a blood pressure on the monitor beside the bed. Alex threw open the curtain and raced from the room.

"Call a code!" she screamed loudly, "bed four's coding!"

Within minutes, the young man's room was filled with medical personnel working furiously to resuscitate the lifeless body. His body jerked violently with each attempt at electrical cardioversion. The smell of burning flesh saturated the thick air within the small, crowded room.

"Give him another amp of epinephrine and an amp of bicarb," shouted the resident.

Alex rummaged through the drawers of the crash cart searching for the medications.

"May I help you find something?" Miss Dillard asked, leaning against the crash cart beside Alex.

"No ma'am, Miss Dillard," Alex replied. "I found what I needed."

She uncapped the needles and injected the two medications into the I.V. line.

"Everybody clear," shouted the resident.

The boy's body jerked uncontrollably as another charge of electricity surged through his tissues.

"Who's the senior resident here tonight?" asked Miss Dillard loudly.

"I am. Why?" asked a young doctor in a starched white lab coat.

"Have you read this patient's chart?"

"No, Miss Dillard, I haven't. I've been too busy trying to save his life to take the time to read his chart," he replied sarcastically.

"Obviously," she shot back. "I believe if you'd read his chart, you'd stop this nonsense and let him die. He's suffered a massive head injury and is being kept alive artificially because his parents won't allow us to withdraw support. It's interesting that none of his family has visited him in the past six or eight weeks, but yet they want us to keep him alive. I think it's time for you to end this code."

"You may be right," the resident replied. "Stop compressions and see if we've got a rhythm."

All eyes in the room stared at the monitor above his bed. A straight, flat line stretched across the screen. His heart had no electrical activity. The resident turned off the ventilator and listened for breath sounds. There were none. He was dead.

"The time of death is two-fifty A.M.," he announced.

He slung his stethoscope around his neck and sat down beside the bed to write a death note.

"Here are his labs and blood gases," the unit secretary said, handing him a slip of paper. "I guess they're too late to do him any good. I don't know what the hold-up was with the lab."

"I don't believe this," he said, shaking his head.

"What's that?" Alex asked.

"These labs. I don't believe these labs," he replied. "He's got a potassium of nine and a half. If it's accurate, there's no wonder he fibrillated. It's got to be a mistake. Look at these gases. His pH was 7.31 during the code so that wouldn't have run his potassium up. Is he on a potassium supplement?"

Miss Dillard thumbed through his chart.

"Not as far as I can tell," she said.

"Then this doesn't make sense. It has to be a lab error. I bet the blood was hemolyzed."

"You're probably right," replied the nursing supervisor. "There's no way his potassium could be that high. The blood had to be hemolyzed." Miss Dillard lifted her chin and looked around the room. "Who was the nurse assigned to this patient?"

"I am. Why?" Alex asked, glaring at her supervisor.

"Did you see anything out of the ordinary before he coded? Any arrhythmias or blood pressure changes? Anything at all?"

"No, Miss Dillard, I didn't. I'd given him a bath a few minutes before he coded and everything was fine. I went to the break room for a cup of coffee and when I returned, he was fibrillating. That's when I called the code."

"Did he receive any I.V. medications near the time he coded? Was there anything ordered for you to give him?"

"No, ma'am. He didn't receive any medications before he coded. I don't believe he's had anything since six o'clock when he received a Tylenol suppository for a fever."

"You didn't mistakenly give him a bolus of I.V. potassium, did you?" she asked.

"No, ma'am, I didn't," Alex replied angrily.

"Well, it's obvious then that this was an act of God and no amount of resuscitation could've saved him. He's better off now, anyway."

Having made her point, Miss Dillard left the unit. Alex stood in silence, shaking her head, confused by their conversation. She finished preparing the body for transport to the hospital's morgue and sat down at a table to complete her paperwork. The intern who had performed the chest compressions during the code sat across from her shaking his head and mumbling to himself. Alex squinted as she read the name embroidered on his coat.

"What's wrong, Dr. Woodard?" she asked. "You look down."

"I suppose I'm just tired," he said, "but it sure gets frustrating. I mean, here we are, spending all of this time and money trying to keep people alive and for what? I called his parents during the code to tell them that he'd taken a turn for the worse and that they might want to come to the hospital. His father told me that not only would they not be coming in, but he'd appreciate not being bothered by any more phone calls while he was sleeping. I tried to explain that there was a good chance his son could die tonight. Do you know what he said to that? I'll tell you what he said. He said that if his son died we should call Drake's Funeral Home to pick up the body and have someone notify them after eight o'clock in the morning. The nerve of some of these people! It absolutely infuriates me! With a family like that he's better off dead."

- 25 -

Ben was sitting alone at a small table in the back of the cafeteria eating a sandwich when Alex arrived. Alex pulled out an uncomfortable, metal chair and sat down across from him. The table wobbled unsteadily when she put her plate of food down. Ben placed his sandwich on his plate and tapped on his watch.

“Where’ve you been?” he asked, as Alex reached for his hand. “I thought we agreed to meet at three o’clock. My break’s almost over.”

“We did agree to meet at three,” Alex replied, “but we had a code about two-thirty and I just finished up with my paper work.”

“A code?” he asked. “I didn’t hear it. Did the patient survive?”

Alex shook her head. “No,” she said, “but it’s probably a blessing.”

“Why’s that?” Ben asked.

“He had no chance of recovery, plus a bad family situation. His family hadn’t visited him in a couple of months and didn’t even come to the hospital when we told them he was coding. His dad told Dr. Woodard to call the funeral home if he died and to have the funeral home call him after eight in the morning. Can you imagine that? His father was more concerned over his sleep than over his son’s condition.”

Ben took a bite of his sandwich and washed it down with his drink. "What was wrong with him?"

"Car wreck," Alex replied. "Happened several months ago. I think he'd been comatose since he was admitted. Tonight was my first time with him. They were keeping him alive with a ventilator and tube feedings because his parents wouldn't let them back off on his treatment."

Ben wiped his mouth and placed the crumpled napkin on his plate.

"That doesn't make sense," he said. "Why would the parents insist on keeping him alive but not visit him in the hospital?"

Alex pulled her chair closer to the table and leaned forward, catching a faint whiff of Ben's cologne.

"It's all hearsay," she whispered, "but the rumor was if he survived to his next birthday, he'd get an inheritance from his grandparents. Makes you wonder if that wasn't why they were keeping him alive."

"I guess we'll never know, will we?" Ben asked.

"No, probably not," Alex replied. "But it's just as well. I'm sure it'd make me mad if I knew the truth."

"Well, Hon, I'd love to sit here and visit, but I've got to get back to the pharmacy. There's nobody down there tonight but me. I'm glad I got to spend a little time with you."

Alex pushed her plate away and looked up at Ben.

"Have you got just a minute before you go?" she asked. "I need to run something by you."

"Not really," Ben replied, shaking his head as he stood up, "but if you want to walk me to the pharmacy, I'll be glad to listen."

Alex drank the last bit of Coke in her glass and followed Ben from the cafeteria. The hallway was empty except for a muscular, young man stripping the wax from the tile floor. As they walked by Lib Dillard's office, Alex saw a light shining through the partially opened door.

"Hold on just a minute," she said. "I'll be right back."

She tapped lightly on the door, but without waiting for an answer, she pushed the door open. The night nursing supervisor lowered her head and looked over her half glasses at Alex.

"Can I help you?" she asked.

"I've got a few questions I need to ask you," Alex replied.

"Concerning?"

"Concerning me and you and the rest of this damn hospital," Alex replied, angrily.

Miss Dillard placed her glasses on her desk and stood up.

"You sound upset," she said. "Please, have a seat."

"I don't have time right now," Alex replied coldly. "I'm in the middle of a conversation with a friend. Will you be here in about fifteen minutes?"

"I can be," she replied.

"I'd certainly appreciate it," Alex replied. "We need to get a few things straightened out."

"I can expect you in fifteen minutes?" Miss Dillard asked.

"Fifteen minutes," Alex replied as she turned to leave.

Her sudden appearance in the hallway startled Ben.

"Caught you eaves dropping, didn't I?" she asked.

Ben grinned sheepishly and nodded.

"Sorry, but I couldn't help it," he replied. "You sounded upset."

"I am upset with that witch hiding in there behind the supervisor's desk," Alex replied. "I can't believe some of the things she does around here."

"Is that what you wanted to talk to me about?" Ben asked.

"No," Alex answered, shaking her head. "What she does doesn't concern you. I'm just glad she's got no control over you. She can be so hard to deal with at times."

"What'd you want to talk to me about?" Ben asked, taking Alex's hand.

Alex took a deep breath and glanced quickly up and down

the hallway.

"Now, this is all hypothetical," she said, "but I wanted your opinion. Okay? If you found out that one of your coworkers in the pharmacy was doing something unethical or illegal which negatively impacted the well-being of a patient, how would you handle it?"

Ben tilted his head back and wrinkled his forehead.

"How detrimental is it to the patient and is it unethical, illegal, or both?" he asked.

"It's really a judgment call as to whether it's unethical but it is illegal seeing that it ultimately results in the patient's death," Alex replied.

"So you're asking me what I would do if one of my coworkers was doing something illegal that caused patients to die and I found out about it?"

"Yeah, what would you do?" Alex asked.

"That's a no brainer," Ben replied. "I'd turn them in."

Alex pressed her lips together tightly and nodded.

"What if it was someone close to you?" she asked.

Ben folded his arms across his chest and stared at Alex.

"This is starting to sound like more than a hypothetical situation," he said. "Who's doing it?"

"No, really," Alex replied lightly. "It's all hypothetical."

Ben shook his head slowly from side to side.

"I know you too well," he said, "and you don't invent hypothetical situations. Tell me you're not involved in anything illegal."

"For crying out loud, Ben!" Alex said, raising her voice. "What do you think I am, a criminal?"

"I don't think you're a criminal," Ben replied, "but I know you well enough to know that if you're not involved, then someone you know is. And if you're asking my advice, you're obligated to turn them in."

"What if it was a close friend?"

Ben stuck his fingers in his ears and shook his head.

"I can't listen to any more of this," he insisted. "If someone is doing something in this hospital that's causing patients to die, you're obligated as a nurse to turn them in. If I found out that you were involved in something illegal, I'd turn you in."

Alex forced a weak smile and nodded.

"That's what I figured," she replied, "but I wanted to hear it from you."

"I hope you're not involved in whatever you're talking about," Ben replied, the wrinkles in his forehead showing his concern.

"Don't be ridiculous. You know me better than that. We've got the same values and beliefs."

"I just hope you remember those beliefs and values," Ben chided.

The door to Lib Dillard's office was closed, but a ray of light was visible beneath the door. Alex knocked softly on the door and waited to be invited in. When there was no answer, she pushed the door open. The tight hinges groaned as the door swung open. Miss Dillard was sitting with her chin resting on her chest, her glasses hanging precariously on the tip of her nose. Alex cleared her throat and coughed loudly, hoping the noise would startle her. The older woman lifted her head, and looking over her half glasses, motioned for Alex to come forward.

"You need to talk to me about something?" she asked, blinking her heavy eyelids.

"Why'd you quiz me so much about the code in the ICU?" Alex asked. "You practically accused me of causing his death."

"Well, dear, from what I know, you were responsible for his death, now weren't you?"

Alex glared angrily at her.

"Of course I was," she replied, "but only because you and the others put me up to it."

"It really doesn't matter why you did it," Miss Dillard

replied. "The bottom line is you killed him. Now, the reason I questioned you so pointedly was to draw attention away from you. By questioning you in front of everyone in the unit, I was able to make it clear that you had no role in his death. I never doubted that you could answer any question I threw at you."

Alex's chest swelled with anger as she listened to the explanation.

"Well, that's not how it sounded," she replied. "It made me feel as if you were accusing me of causing the code. If you hadn't been the supervisor, I would have slapped the hell out of you."

Miss Dillard smiled and chuckled softly.

"Honey," she said, "you're in way too deep to be thinking about anything like that. You've got to trust us if we're going to be successful and realize that I'd never do anything to jeopardize our goals. As I said, there was never any doubt in my mind that you could adequately answer the questions and effectively prevent any attention which might have come your way later."

"Well, you sure as hell better not let it happen again," Alex snapped. "I may have to go along with whatever you and Mr. Warren suggest, but I don't have to put up with your crap in front of my peers. Rest assured that if I go down, I'm taking you and everyone else down with me."

Miss Dillard pushed her chair away from her desk and stood up, looking down sternly at Alex.

"If that's all you've got to say to me, I've got work to do," she said. "And in case you haven't heard, Mr. Warren wants to meet with everyone in his office at eight o'clock. I suggest you attend."

As the door closed, Miss Dillard reached under her desk and turned off the small tape recorder. Gerald would be pleased with parts of their conversation.

- 26 -

The smell of freshly brewed coffee filled the air of Gerald Warren's inner sanctum. A plate of doughnuts and pastries sat on his desk. Gerald sat in the leather chair behind his desk, his feet propped on the corner of the desk. Tim, Bob, and Lib were sitting in smaller chairs in front of his desk.

"Come in, Miss Lowe," Gerald said, putting his feet on the floor. "We've been waiting on you to get started. Please, have a seat. Could I get you a doughnut or a cup of coffee?"

Alex poured herself a cup of coffee and took a bite of a cream cheese danish.

"Why are we here?" she asked.

Mr. Warren stood up and handed each of them an envelope. He smiled as he handed Alex her envelope.

"As you know," he said, tugging at the collar of his starched white shirt, "our first two attempts at restriction of resource utilization have been overwhelming successes. In both cases, the flow of excess expenditures has come to an abrupt halt. Our estimated savings from these two cases alone, based on probability of survival, estimated length of stay, and previous resource utilization by these two patients, we believe to be in excess of eighty thousand dollars. In the envelope you'll each find a small token of my appreciation for the fine job you've done. I realize that there is some risk involved in our operation so I think it's only fair that each of you benefits from the enormous savings we're affording our institution. I do ask that you don't discuss this with anyone outside of this office and that you don't discuss your rewards with each other. It's extremely difficult for me to place a monetary value on each of your services so I've tried to base your remuneration on your degree of involvement with each case and your overall risk with each incident. Now, I need your input and recommendations regarding further operations."

Alex raised her hand and cleared her throat. Mr. Warren looked at her and nodded his head.

"Yes, Miss Lowe," he said.

"I've got several things bothering me," she replied. "First of all, I'm still not comfortable with what I'm being asked to do. I understand the reasoning behind it and realize that in theory it's for the good of our hospital and our community, but it just doesn't seem right."

"I understand your concern," he said, "and I can sympathize with your feelings. If you look at our operation strictly from a medical viewpoint it may appear that what we're doing is wrong. Given the Hippocratic Oath that physicians take, I seriously doubt we could find a single physician at Richland who would willingly cooperate with our team. With your training as a nurse, you too are trained to alleviate pain and suffering, and much as the physician to 'first do no harm'. I understand that. What I want you to do is to look not only at the pain and suffering you're alleviating, but also at the big picture. No matter how you look at it, two people have died. But is there any doubt in your mind that those two patients and their families are not better off? Their deaths are not the focus of this operation. The survival of our institution is. If our hospital closes, try to imagine the number of lives that will be in jeopardy. Let me give you an example." He stood up and for a moment, stared silently out the window behind his desk. "Last Saturday," he continued, "we had an eight-year-old boy brought to our emergency room after he was hit by a car while riding his bicycle. He suffered massive internal injuries and underwent emergency surgery within minutes after arriving at the hospital. His heart stopped even before the surgery began, but the physicians were able to resuscitate him. During the surgery, his spleen was removed, a tear in his liver was repaired and a collection of blood around his heart was drained. That little boy moved out of the ICU today and will probably go home this weekend. If our institution were closed, he would have died before he could have been transported to the nearest hospital. Miss Lowe, that little boy is my grandson, but he could just as easily have been your little brother or even your son. We're in the midst of difficult times for the medical profession, a time when choices and changes must be made. Here at Richland, we've made the choice to shorten the lives of a few hopeless individuals to hopefully save the lives of countless others."

"But that still doesn't make it right," Alex replied.

Mr. Warren smiled and raised his eyebrows.

"Miss Lowe, was it more right when you took the lives of David Watson or Prince Christopher?" he asked.

His question caught her off guard. In her mind, she believed what she'd done before becoming involved with his project was right. Hadn't David appeared to her to tell her that everyone had benefited from her action, even if she wanted to believe his death was an accident. And Mr. Christopher. Clearly he was better off in death than he had been in life. But they could never understand her reasoning. And they certainly couldn't understand how she'd been chosen to tempt fate. Mr. Warren looked sternly at her and shrugged his shoulders.

"Well, Miss Lowe, was it right or not?"

"Mr. Warren, what I did was out of love for those people," she replied. "You've never had to deal with the kind of suffering which I deal with every day as a nurse. David and Mr. Christopher were suffering more than you could imagine. I acted totally out of love and with compassion when I took their lives. This group is doing neither."

Mr. Warren smiled. At last he had the admission of guilt he needed. It would be much easier to ensure her full cooperation from this point on. He allowed the tape recorder to continue running. It could be edited later.

"I'm afraid that's where we disagree," he said. "I look at our mission as one of humanity. We're alleviating unnecessary suffering and assuring the future of our community. What can be wrong about that?"

Alex folded her arms across her chest and pushed back in her chair.

"I'm wasting my time arguing with you," she said, "so let's just drop it."

Mr. Warren nodded and smiled. He'd made his point and won this confrontation.

"Any other gripes?" he asked.

"After I completed my assignment last night, Miss Dillard questioned me about the code and basically accused me of causing the code," she replied.

"Which you did, of course," he replied.

"Of course I did," she replied angrily, "because I was told to do so, but that's not the point. She knew damn well what had happened since she put the syringe with the potassium in my locker."

"Then what's the problem?" he asked.

"What's the problem?" she screamed. "I'll tell you what the problem is! The problem is that if she doesn't lay off with that kind of crap in front of my peers, I'll blow the lid on this operation and take my chances with the authorities. I've got enough evidence on the three of you to take you down with me. If you don't believe it, just try me."

"All right, all right," he replied, waving his hands above his desk, "settle down. Lib told me about the incident before you arrived and she was severely reprimanded for her actions. Trust me. It will not, I dare say, it cannot happen again. The last thing we need is disharmony among the five of us. It would be tragic for something so petty as ego to destroy our operation. Now, is there anything else we need to discuss?"

"Yeah, there's one more thing," Alex replied. "I didn't feel very comfortable participating in a code which I caused. Using I.V. potassium is too risky. There's too much room for error. Sooner or later someone's going to survive the code and then there'll be a lot of explaining to do."

"What would you suggest?" he asked with interest.

Alex shook her head. "I'm not sure. The morphine sulfate works well if the dose is large enough to suppress respirations, but it could have problems, too, if a patient was on telemetry and managed to survive. Maybe someone else has an idea."

Tim nodded his head excitedly back and forth.

"I didn't want to bring it up until I was certain I could obtain the drug," he said, "but, yes, I do have a suggestion. There's a company in Mexico that sells a mixture of very potent poisons. Best I can tell, it's a mixture of neurotoxins from the poison dart frog, as well as toxins from cobras and coral snakes. It's guaranteed to produce death within thirty seconds after administration. Apparently, cattlemen use it to poison coyotes."

"How long will it take for you to get some?" Gerald asked.

"I've already got it," he replied, obviously pleased with his new acquisition.

"Is it expensive?" Bob asked.

"Not really. A vial costs about thirty-five dollars and contains enough medicine to treat several patients. I only ordered two vials until I could discuss it with the group. I guess the real test comes with the first patient."

"What are its drawbacks?" Alex asked.

"I don't feel there are any, other than the fact that the individual who administers the medication better be careful with their technique. Each vial only contains two milliliters of poison, so it only takes a small amount to be lethal. It's possible that a stick with a contaminated needle could be fatal."

"Any other risks? What about autopsy findings?" Lib asked.

"That's the beauty of these poisons," he replied. "There are no tests available today to detect them, at least not to my knowledge. They tend to attack the central nervous system, particularly those areas of the brain controlling heart rate and respiratory rate. When the toxins attach to the receptors in the brain, the electrical impulses governing the circulatory and respiratory systems are blocked. The heart stops beating, the patient stops breathing and excess utilization of resources comes to an abrupt halt. It's quicker, cleaner and more deadly than anything available in our pharmacy prior to today."

"When's our next mission?" Bob asked.

Alex shook her head. She understood her role and the long-range objective but had difficulty accepting murder as a mission.

"We've already selected our next patient," Gerald replied. "Miss Lowe will be assigned to three west tonight where she'll have the opportunity to take care of Ella Hibbetts. Miss Hibbetts is a widow with no immediate family, save a ninety-three year old sister, who unfortunately, has requested that everything possible be done to save her sister's life. It seems they have no family left except for each other. She was transferred to us from a nursing home three weeks ago with a urinary tract infection. She's done quite well medically and has been awaiting transfer back to the nursing home for the past two weeks. And therein lies our problem. She's consumed her Medicare days and has no funding for placement otherwise. Her care isn't extremely costly to our hospital, about four hundred dollars a day, but there's no end in sight. Our social workers have worked diligently to find an outpatient facility to take her, but there's nothing available for a patient without family or funding. So basically, she's a drain on the system in two ways. We're providing free care everyday and she's occupying a bed in which we could have a paying patient who'd provide us with a chance to generate revenue. The real impact will come over the long run when we're able to eliminate the losses that accumulate from the countless numbers of nursing home patients who are dumped on our institution weekly. She's just the first of many."

"I thought we were alleviating pain and suffering first," Alex said, "and then concerning ourselves with the financial ramifications."

"What's your question, Miss Lowe?" Gerald asked, obviously perturbed.

"Is she suffering, or is she being eliminated simply because of the economic benefits you'll obtain through her death?"

"She's ninety years old," he replied. "She's suffered enough for two lifetimes. She's got one sister who's not going to be alive much longer. She's got a lonely and miserable existence. Miss Lowe, it's not your job to worry about who's eliminated. The four of us will make that decision. You simply need to follow your instructions."

Satisfied with his answer, Gerald rose and ushered the team members to the door. Bob purposefully followed behind the others and waited to speak until they had left the office.

"I can't believe you'd kill Miss Ella," he whispered. "She practically raised you as a child."

The color drained from Gerald's face as beads of sweat moistened his brow. "What makes you say that?" he asked.

"You told me so five years ago when she was diagnosed with colon cancer. Surely you remember. I couldn't understand why you had Lib arrange for Curry to take care of her when the hospital wouldn't benefit from prolonging her life. You told me then that it wasn't about the money. It was about the love you had for Miss Ella and her sister and how your mother was like a daughter to the two of them. You said they had been like grandmothers to you."

Gerald swallowed hard and tugged on the collar of his starched, white shirt. "Times have changed," he said angrily. "She's ninety years old and costing Richland money."

"So, it's not about love anymore?" Bob questioned.

"I haven't heard from her since she was treated for the colon cancer," Gerald growled. "If she still cared for me, I would have heard from her."

"How long has she been in the nursing home?" Bob asked.

"I don't know and I don't really give a rip," Gerald replied. "The only thing I know is that other than when she was hospitalized with the colon caner, I haven't heard from her since Mom died ten years ago."

"Did you ever try to get in touch with her?"

"The rules have changed," Gerald said sternly, ignoring the question. "I didn't change them but I've got to play by them. Miss Hibbetts is costing my hospital money and the only way to solve that problem is to take her life. Now, if you don't have any more questions, I've got work to do."

Bob shook his head and slowly closed the door behind him. "I don't know about the rules, but you've certainly changed," he mumbled.

Gerald sighed deeply and wiped the sweat from his brow. He was doing the right thing. It didn't matter that he would receive a tidy inheritance once the two old maids were dead. It was for the good of the hospital.

- 27 -

Alex struggled to keep her eyes open as she drove home. The night shift with its code and the added stress of her interrogation by Lib Dillard had left her exhausted. Squinting against the glare of the sun, she pulled on her Ray Bans and reached to lower the sun visor. As she pulled the visor down, the envelope from Mr. Warren fell in her lap. Her hands trembled as she opened the envelope and pulled out the stack of crisp hundred dollar bills. She licked her fingertips as she counted them. Ten bills. One-thousand dollars. The adrenaline of newfound wealth chased the exhaustion away.

Still clutching the stack of bills as she pulled into her apartment complex, she leaned her head against the seat and wept. She no longer had the power to choose if and when she would tempt fate to alter another's destiny. It was out of her hands. How could she control someone else's future when she'd lost control of her own life?

She pushed open the door to her tiny apartment. The metal doorknocker clanged loudly as the door closed behind her. Subconsciously she hoped to see the eerie, blue light which had been so frightening only a short time before. But the room was dark and still. No signs of life nor of a supernatural presence. She flipped on the lights and walked across the room to a small chest of drawers. A family picture, taken before her mother's illness, rested on top of the chest. She pressed the picture tightly against her breasts. Tears rolled down her cheeks and fell silently on the tarnished silver frame. She placed the stack of crisp hundred dollar bills in the top drawer. Blood money. How could she allow herself to stoop so low?

She tossed and turned fitfully as she tried to rest that day. When her alarm sounded, she crawled wearily from her bed. She rubbed her tired eyes and stretched. The tight muscles made it feel as if she had not slept at all. The hot shower felt good beating on the achy muscles of her neck.

"Alex."

The soft voice startled her. Through the steam, she made out the silhouette of a woman standing near the bathroom door. Instinctively, she grabbed the towel from the bar and wrapped it around her.

"Don't be afraid. It's only me."

"I'm not afraid, Mama," she replied. "I was hoping you'd come."

"Alex, I don't have long but we knew you were struggling with a lot of unanswered questions."

"I'm so confused," Alex cried. "Are they tempting fate?"

"Yes, dear, in their own way they are."

"Were they chosen, too?"

Her mother shook her head.

"No, dear, they weren't," she replied.

"Then how can they do what they're doing?" Alex asked.

"Sweetheart," her mother explained, "our realm of influence is very small. Most of what happens in this world happens because people are allowed to make decisions without regard for the consequences. We get to work with only a small number of individuals. Within that select group, we can arrange situations to assist them with their mission, but anyone, anywhere, can alter another's destiny through their decisions and their actions."

"But what I'm doing now seems wrong," Alex said. "They paid me a thousand dollars to take someone's life. I feel like a murderer." She paused and looked at her mother. Tears filled her eyes. "Please tell me it's all part of the master plan," she begged.

Her mother shook her head slowly from side to side.

"I wish I could," she said, "but it would be a lie."

The tears filling Alex's eyes spilled over and trickled down her cheeks.

"Was it fate for me to be blackmailed into participating in their scheme?" she asked.

"I'm afraid not, dear," her mother replied. "It was just bad luck. Your life's master plan didn't include this."

"I don't understand," Alex sobbed.

"One day you will, Alex. One day you will."

Alex wiped the tears from her eyes.

"What should I do now?" she asked. "I'm afraid if I refuse to cooperate, they'll go to the authorities and I'll be prosecuted for murder."

"That's a decision you'll have to make. But think it over carefully. We're not pleased that you've been coerced into taking lives, but it can work to our advantage. You've been given more opportunities to prevent suffering and pain than you would have had otherwise. If you've got a problem with the money, then give it to a charity."

"Am I still considered chosen?" Alex asked.

"By all means. Once we choose someone, they're chosen for life. What you must remember is that you'll always have a choice. Whether we arrange the contact or whether they arrange it, the ultimate decision for life or death and peace or pain will always rest with you."

- 28 -

Alex listened closely as patient assignments were made that night. It came as no surprise when she was assigned to take care of Ella Hibbetts in room 543. Everything the team had orchestrated up to this point had occurred as planned. Why should tonight be any different?

As she entered room 543, she was unprepared for what she found. What she had assumed would be a private room with a decrepit, elderly female, turned out to be a semiprivate room with two beds, each of which was occupied. She pulled the curtain between the two beds and looked at the sign above the first bed. "PATIENT IS BLIND AND HARD OF HEARING. SPEAK LOUDLY." The stench coming from the bed left no doubt that the old lady had bed sores weeping with infection. The pungent odor of dried urine and feces was unmistakable. Her dry, scaly skin hung loosely on her cachetic frame. Alex stood silently by the bed and watched as the old lady gasped for air. When she leaned down to speak into the old woman's ear, she saw the thick, dried mucus coating the woman's tongue and smelled the yeast on her breath. At least they'd chosen another patient who'd clearly be better off dead.

"Miss Hibbetts?" she called in a loud voice. When there was no response, she tapped the old lady lightly on the shoulder. "Miss Hibbetts, I've got some medicine for you," she said, pulling the syringe of poison from her pocket.

"I'm Miss Hibbetts. That's Minnie Davis you're talking to and she's deaf."

The warm, sweet voice startled her. She pulled back the curtain between the two beds.

"Excuse me?" Alex replied, completely unnerved.

"I said I'm Ella Hibbetts, honey. That's Miss Davis you're yelling at and she hasn't spoken to anyone since I've been here. Did you say you've got some medicine for me?"

"You're Miss Hibbetts?" Alex asked, clearly puzzled.

"That's right," the elderly lady replied. "Have been for ninety years now, and guess I will be until I die. What kind of medicine do you have for me?"

Alex shook her head.

"I'm afraid there's been a mistake," she said. "I was under the impression that this was intended for the "A" bed. I had better check the chart."

"Whatever you say, honey. It seems strange that I haven't received any medication in over a week and now that I'm doing fine, they start ordering medicine. I guess that's why they're the doctors and I'm just an old lady."

Alex's heart pounded as she made her way to the nursing station. Surely, it was a mistake. The medicine had to be intended for Minnie Davis. She was the one who'd benefit from death. She slipped the note from her pocket.

"Ella Hibbetts. Room 543. Bed 2. Age 90. Born August 3, 1912. Date of admission: 09/11/02."

Alex pulled both charts. The vice in her throat clamped tighter as she compared the information on the note with the admission data on the two charts. There was no mistake. The information on her note matched exactly the information on Ella Hibbetts' chart. The poison was intended for the "B" bed. Alex shook her head in disbelief. There was no logical explanation. Ella Hibbetts was old but mentally alert and in no obvious pain. Her death would be senseless.

"You'll always have a choice." The words from her earlier conversation echoed hauntingly in her mind as she walked slowly down the hallway.

"Well, Miss Hibbetts," Alex said cheerfully, "I'm glad I checked. I was at the right bed, just had the wrong name. This medicine was for Miss Davis and not for you. I didn't see any medicine listed on your chart except for some Tylenol and a sleeping pill."

Miss Hibbetts smiled and nodded.

"I didn't think I'd be getting any medicine," she said, "but you can never tell what these doctors are thinking."

Alex returned her smile and pulled the curtain between the beds. She hesitated only briefly before injecting the life-ending poison into the patient's vein. She left the curtain drawn and walked to the door.

"I'll check on you later tonight, Miss Hibbetts," she called. "Hope you get some rest."

Alex turned out the light and closed the door behind her. Death would come quickly to claim the old lady, but if she discovered her lifeless body too soon, it might draw attention to her and to the I.V. medication. The minutes passed slowly. Shortly after midnight, she returned to the room. Minnie Davis was cold and stiff. Alex peeked around the curtain. Miss Hibbetts was sound asleep and breathing heavily.

Except for the night charge nurse, there was no activity at the nursing station when Alex returned.

"Cindy," she called out as she neared the nursing station, "I was making rounds and found Miss Davis in room 543 dead. I had checked on her about an hour ago when I was getting vital signs on "B" bed and she was asleep. When I went in this time, she was cold and stiff."

"It's probably for the best," the charge nurse replied. "She had such a miserable existence."

"Oh, really?" Alex asked. "This was my first night to take care of her. She did look rather pitiful."

"Yeah, she was. You might check her chart, but I think she was a no code."

"She is," Alex replied. "I remember that from the report I received on her. I'll call the night physician and have him pronounce her."

Dr. Blake Nichols arrived within a few minutes and hurriedly went through the death certifying ritual of listening for heart tones and breath sounds while checking for a pulse. Satisfied that there were no indications of life, he sarcastically announced, "543-A is officially dead. Time of death is 12:26 A.M. Could you get me the chart so I can scribble a death note?"

"I'll be glad to," Alex replied, respectfully. "I know we haven't officially met, but I'm Alex Lowe. My sister, Elizabeth, told me you two were acquainted."

Dr. Nichols took the chart from Alex and began writing. "Nice to officially meet you," he said, without looking up. "You and your sister look a lot alike. My sister stays on my case about working too much so I agreed to meet Elizabeth to put an end to Leah's nagging." He finished his note and looked up at Mary. "I'm glad she stayed on me. I enjoyed the date with Elizabeth and intend to call her again."

"Well?" Miss Dillard interrupted. She squeezed Alex's shoulder as an evil smile curled the corners of her thin lips. "Who died?"

"Minnie Davis, room 543," Alex replied. "I can't say that it wasn't expected. She was in bad shape."

"I'm not familiar with her," Miss Dillard replied, rubbing her chin. "How's Miss Hibbetts doing?"

"Fine as far as I can tell," Alex answered. "She was sound asleep when the doctor pronounced Miss Davis."

The night supervisor appeared surprised, but held her tongue until Dr. Nichols left the nursing station.

"She's still alive?" she growled.

"Yes ma'am. And doing well," Alex replied without looking up at her.

"When do you go on break, Alex?" Miss Dillard asked.

"Any time now," Alex replied.

"Good. How about meeting me in the snack bar in about fifteen minutes."

~ ~ ~

Miss Dillard was sitting alone near the back of the room sipping on a cup of coffee when Alex arrived.

"Pull up a chair," she ordered.

"What's wrong?" Alex asked as she sat down.

"When are you going to take care of Hibbetts?" she asked. "It needs to be done tonight, and sooner rather than later."

Alex sat up straight in her chair. "I injected Miss Davis," she replied.

"You did what?" Miss Dillard asked angrily.

"You heard me. I injected Miss Davis."

"Why, for God's sake, did you do that? Didn't you get your instructions?"

Alex pushed back from the small table and stared at Miss Dillard.

"Yes, ma'am, I got them," she answered.

"Did you read them?"

Alex pressed her lips together and nodded but didn't speak.

"You graduated from nursing school so I know you're not illiterate," Miss Dillard said sarcastically. "Give me the damn note and let me read it myself!"

Alex unfolded the small piece of paper and handed it to her. The night nursing supervisor shook her head as she read the note.

"What part of this did you not understand?" she asked.

"I understood it all," Alex replied. "I just thought..."

Miss Dillard cut her off in mid sentence.

"You thought? You thought?" she said raising her voice. "You're not getting paid to think! Your job is to do as you're instructed, not to think."

Alex bit her bottom lip tightly. "If you'll shut up and listen I'll explain why I did it."

Miss Dillard stared coldly at her.

"Miss Hibbetts was old and feeble," Alex explained, "but she wasn't suffering. I felt there had to be a mistake."

Miss Dillard gritted her teeth and shook her head.

"There was no mistake," she said, "at least not on our part. You terminated a patient with Medicare, a revenue generating patient, and let a no pay, revenue consuming patient live."

"Well, I'm sorry," Alex replied angrily, "but I felt it was wrong to take the life of a spry, elderly lady when I had the option of relieving Miss Davis' pain and suffering. How was I to know that Miss Hibbetts wasn't a paying customer?"

"First of all, it was not an option. And second, it's not your concern or place to know who generates income and who consumes resources. The team selects the clients for you. We don't ask you to think or become emotionally involved, only to carry out your instructions."

Alex sat silently, staring off in the distance. There hadn't been a mistake. They expected her to terminate Ella Hibbetts simply because she was costing the hospital money. It didn't matter that she was doing well for age ninety and was confined to the hospital only because she had no place to which she could be discharged. It didn't matter that Miss Davis was suffering. A wave of nausea swelled in the pit of her stomach.

"Meet me in Hibbetts' room in five minutes," Miss Dillard ordered as she stormed out of the snack bar.

- 29 -

Ella Hibbetts snored softly, unaware of her visitors, her face illuminated by the flickering light of the television. Miss Dillard stepped from the shadows and extended her hand toward Alex.

"Here, take this," she whispered.

Alex hesitated before reaching for the object.

"What is it?" she asked.

"Her medication, the one you were supposed to give earlier this evening."

Alex shook her head.

"She doesn't have any I.V. medications ordered. I've already reviewed her chart."

"You know what I'm talking about!" Miss Dillard responded.

"And you know what I'm talking about," Alex replied. "As her nurse, I'm not giving her anything her doctor hasn't ordered."

"You don't have a choice," Miss Dillard growled.

"That's where you're wrong," Alex insisted. "I'll always have a choice."

Miss Dillard snatched the cap from the needle and crimped the I.V. tubing.

"Gerald will hear about this," she hissed. "And trust me, he won't be pleased."

Miss Dillard inserted the needle into the I.V. but before she could press the plunger, Alex grabbed her wrist. The needle pulled out of the tubing.

"Get your hand off of me!" Miss Dillard whispered angrily. "You've got no right interfering with our plans."

"And you've got no right to take her life!" Alex replied. "You can't play God!"

"I'm not playing God. I'm just doing what's necessary to save my job and this hospital."

She grabbed the I.V. tubing and tried again to insert the needle. Alex reflexively reached for her arm.

"This is wrong! You can't kill her," Alex whispered.

As Miss Dillard jerked her arm away the needle embedded in her left thigh. The plunger depressed partially, injecting the poison into her thigh. Terror filled her eyes. She could still hear Tim's words. "It only takes a small amount. Death is quick."

Miss Dillard pulled the needle from her thigh and gazed at the syringe. Only half of a milliliter had been injected.

"Damn you, Alex Lowe. Damn you!" she shouted.

Before Alex could move, Miss Dillard bolted from the room, still clutching the syringe tightly in her hand.

"Thank you, honey," a kind voice whispered.

"Ma'am?" Alex asked, startled.

"I said, thank you," replied Miss Hibbetts. "I saw what you did for me."

"What did you see?" Alex asked, clearly shaken.

"Everything, dear. I saw and heard everything."

Alex stopped at the door.

"I've got to go help her," she said, hurriedly. "Please don't talk to anyone before I get back."

Miss Dillard was slumped over a chair when Alex reached the nursing station. The syringe had fallen to the floor and rolled beneath the counter. Alex took her foot and pushed the syringe behind a trashcan.

"Call a code," she yelled as she pulled Miss Dillard's body

from the chair and placed it on the hard, tile floor.

"Already did," replied the unit clerk. "You didn't hear it?"

Miss Dillard's skin was mottled with cyanosis around her mouth and in her fingers. She did not respond when Alex called her name and rubbed a knuckle against her sternum. The charge nurse knelt beside Alex and checked for a pulse while Alex listened for breath sounds.

"No pulse," she said.

"Nor respirations," Alex added.

The small workspace at the nurse's station became a blur of activity as the on call physicians arrived and began barking orders.

"Get her on a monitor and start an I.V. We need some blood work and stat ABG's. Do we know anything about her?" shouted the resident in charge.

"She's Lib Dillard, the night nursing supervisor," answered the unit clerk. "I was sitting at the desk when she came running up the hall screaming that she needed a doctor. She was pounding her chest and gasping for air. She collapsed and fell over the chair before I could get to her. I thought she was having a heart attack. That's when I called the code."

"Do we have a rhythm?" the young physician asked, looking up at the heart monitor.

"Looks like V-fib," a second physician shouted.

"Shock her with two hundred joules."

Alex watched helplessly as Miss Dillard's body jerked from the surge of electricity.

"She's still in V-fib!" yelled the physician. "Push an amp of epi and shock her with three hundred joules."

With the higher voltage of electricity, her body shook violently, her head banging against the hard tile floor when her muscles finally relaxed.

"Damn it, she's still in V-fib," the physician shouted. "Turn it up to three sixty and hit her again. She's too young to die."

Everyone in the room watched anxiously as the doctor

placed the paddles on her chest and discharged the electricity. The spontaneous, uncontrollable contraction of her muscles reminded Alex of a grand mal seizure. The smell of her burning flesh was nauseating. The cardiac monitor was flat line.

"How long have we been coding her?" the senior resident asked.

"About twenty minutes," replied the intern.

"Stop compressions and see if she's got a rhythm," he ordered.

"Nothing. She's flat line," replied the intern.

The senior resident draped his stethoscope over his shoulder and shook his head.

"It's no use," he said. "Let's call it off. She must've had something catastrophic happen for us to be unable to establish any kind of rhythm. Has anyone called her family?"

"They're on their way," replied a nurse.

"Let me know when they get here, and I'll speak to them. I hope they'll consent to an autopsy. It'd be nice to know what happened to her."

An autopsy? Alex shuddered at the thought. How long would it take for the poison to break down so that it wasn't detectable? Would they even check for poisons? Could they check for poisons? Why should they? There was no reason to suspect anything out of the ordinary. People die every day, even people who aren't supposed to die.

A bright, orange sun was climbing quickly into a cloudless sky when the shift ended. As Alex took her time card from her purse, she remembered Miss Hibbetts. She had to know how much the old lady knew. She punched her time card and then paced impatiently as she waited for the elevator doors to open.

"Miss Lowe," Mr. Warren called out, "I was hoping I'd catch you before you left the hospital. I left a message on your answering machine earlier this morning. Have you got a minute?"

"I've got to run upstairs for a few minutes but then I'll be free," she replied.

"Stop by my office before you go home," he ordered. "There's something we need to discuss."

"Yes, sir," Alex replied, nodding her head.

She knew it was inevitable, but she never imagined it would happen so quickly. How had he found out about Miss Dillard's death and how much did he know?

~ ~ ~

Miss Hibbetts was eating breakfast when Alex arrived. The smell of bacon and hot biscuits made her stomach growl.

"Miss Hibbetts, is it okay if I come in?" she asked, pushing open the door. "I don't want to interrupt your breakfast."

"No, no, honey," Miss Hibbetts replied. "You come right on in. I thought you'd forgotten about this old lady."

"No ma'am," Alex replied, smiling. "Things got kind of hectic last night and it just slipped my mind."

"Did that other nurse die?" Miss Hibbetts asked, her green eyes twinkling.

Alex lowered her head and stared at the floor.

"Yes, ma'am, she did," she replied.

"I'm sorry to hear that. I've always thought it sad whenever anyone dies. That must have been some powerful medicine she was going to give me."

"Yes ma'am," Alex replied. "It's was."

"Why'd she want to end my life?" she asked. "I've never done anything to hurt her. I just don't understand it."

"It's a long and complicated story, Miss Hibbetts. And if it's all the same to you, I'd rather not get into the details."

"That's up to you, Miss Lowe. That is your name, isn't it?"

"Yes, ma'am, it is. I'm Alex Lowe. How'd you know?"

"You introduced yourself last night, but then there was a man who came by earlier this morning asking a lot of questions. He called you Alex Lowe and described you perfectly." Miss Hibbetts paused and stared at Alex. "You're in some kind of trouble aren't you?"

"What did this man look like?" Alex asked.

"Middle aged. Gray hair. Nice looking man. Seemed real sweet," she replied.

"What did he ask?" Alex asked.

"Mostly he asked questions about the nurse that died. And some questions about you. He seemed real interested in what I might have seen."

"What'd you tell him?" Alex asked nervously.

"I told him I knew you by his description, but I'd never seen the other lady he described. He kept asking me if I was sure I hadn't seen her and I just kept telling him no." The old lady smiled and chuckled softly. "I told the old buzzard he insulted my integrity, doubting my word like that. I told him that when someone my age tells you something, you can believe it. My generation was different from his. We weren't raised to tell lies."

Alex looked puzzled and tilted her head to the side.

"But you told me you saw everything," she said.

"And I did," Miss Hibbetts replied, nodding her head.

"Then you lied to him?" Alex asked.

"That's right, honey. I lied to him. I wasn't raised that way. It's just a little something I developed on my own through the years. Mama taught me that you don't lie, but Papa taught me that you take care of those who take care of you. For some reason you felt obligated to spare my life last night and until I could talk to you and hear your side of the story, I felt obligated to protect you."

Alex breathed a sigh of relief.

"What'd you see last night?" she asked.

"Which time?" the old lady replied.

"What do you mean which time?" Alex asked.

"I mean the time when you gave Miss Davis the medicine or the time when the other nurse tried to give me the medicine?"

"Both times," Alex replied.

"Well, I really couldn't see what happened when you gave Miss Davis the medication, but I knew you were giving her something from what you'd said to me. Whatever you gave her killed her, didn't it?"

"Why do you say that?" Alex asked. "She did die last night, but she was old."

Miss Hibbetts smiled.

"Honey," she said, "it wasn't five minutes after you left the room that she started making these crying noises, sort of like a cat with its tail caught in the screen door. I could hear her gasping for air and thrashing about in the bed. Then everything was quiet. I knew she was dead, but there was nothing I could do about it. And then I saw you come in and check on her. There wasn't much commotion after she died so I assumed you had expected to find her dead."

"But you were asleep when I came in the room," Alex said.

"I was faking it," she replied. "I was too frightened to sleep, afraid that I might be next. I saw you when you checked on me."

"What about when the other nurse and I were in your room?" Alex asked.

"She came in about five minutes before you did. She shined a flashlight in my face and then just sat in the dark, waiting for you. I heard everything. I think that's when I realized that whatever you gave Miss Davis had been intended for me. Who ordered the medication?"

"It wasn't a physician," Alex replied.

"Was it Gerald?"

"Gerald?" Alex asked.

"Yes, I distinctly remember her telling you that Gerald would hear about what you'd done, or what you'd refused to do."

"Do you know Gerald Warren?" Alex asked.

"Gerry Warren?" the elderly lady asked, smiling. "You might say I know him, seeing how I changed his dirty diapers when he was a little boy. His mama and I were friends, God rest her soul. My sister, Ruth, and I lived next door to the Warrens when Gerry was little. Gerry's mother worked so he spent about as much time at our house as he did at his own house. As I got older and it became apparent that I couldn't care for myself, he helped make the arrangements to get me in a nursing home. He used to bring his mama by to visit me, but after she died, he quite visiting. I bet I haven't heard from him in at least five years."

Alex took several deep breaths and glanced at her watch.

"Miss Hibbetts, I need to talk some more with you about what happened last night, but I've got to meet Mr. Warren in his office in just a few minutes. I'll be back later, if that's okay with you."

"That's fine with me." Miss Hibbetts paused momentarily. "Miss, I don't know what you're involved in, and it's really none of my business, but I think you should be careful. The man that was here earlier scared me. He didn't seem too pleased about what happened last night."

"I appreciate your concern," Alex replied, "but I'll be fine. I'll be back later."

As Alex rushed from the room, Miss Hibbetts' mind drifted back to the many times she had taken care of Gerald Warren as a child. She couldn't help but smile when she remembered how he had fondly called her Aunt Ella. But the nostalgia quickly faded as she considered the dangerous situation facing her. Surely Gerald remembered her! He had to. They had been so close. But if he remembered her, then why did he want her dead?

- 30 -

Mr. Warren was sitting behind his desk when Alex arrived. Bob and Tim sat across from him. With his blue suit and gray hair, Bob Carlson matched the description of the man who'd visited Ella Hibbetts earlier that morning. The three of them stared at Alex as she sat down.

"Miss Lowe, are you aware that Lib Dillard died last night?" Mr. Warren asked.

"Yes sir," Alex replied. "I was working five main last night and was there when she died."

"Did you see what happened?" he continued.

"No sir, but I overheard the unit clerk say Miss Dillard came running up the hallway clutching her chest and gasping for air before she collapsed. We worked for about twenty minutes trying to resuscitate her, but nothing we tried worked. Dr. Woodard thought she probably had a massive heart attack. She was a smoker, you know."

"No, I didn't realize that," he replied. "Did you have any contact with her last night?"

"No, sir. The only time I saw her was when I responded to the code and she was already unresponsive by then."

Mr. Warren leaned forward and appeared puzzled.

"Miss Lowe," he said, "is it not unusual for someone of her age, with no major medical problems, to drop dead with a heart attack?"

Alex swallowed hard. "Yes, sir," she answered, "it's a bit unusual, but it happens. It's so sad. Do you know if she had any family?"

"Yes, she has family," he replied, somewhat impatiently. "She was married and has two grown children."

Alex shook her head. "How tragic."

Mr. Warren chewed on his bottom lip and scratched his head.

"Miss Lowe, we gave you an assignment last night to terminate Ella Hibbetts, but according to the admitting office, she's still alive. Why is that? You did get the assignment, didn't you?"

"Yes, sir," Alex replied. "I received the instructions, but after Miss Dillard coded, everything was so chaotic it slipped my mind."

"You will be expected to complete your assignment tonight. Is that clear?"

"Yes sir. Crystal," she replied, nodding her head.

Mr. Warren rubbed his smooth chin, curling his bottom lip over his upper lip.

"Were you aware that a Miss Davis died on your floor last night?" he asked, continuing the interrogation.

"Yes, sir," Alex responded. "I was taking care of her. She was ninety-three years old and in very poor health. It was a blessing for her to pass away."

"So, she just died of old age?" he asked, skeptically.

"That's what I assumed," she replied. "She was barely responsive when I first checked on her. When I went back in about an hour later, she was dead."

Bob stood up and paced back and forth. His face was red with anger.

"Can we stop this nonsense?" he demanded in a loud voice.

"Sit down, Bob. We'll handle this my way," Gerald replied, sternly.

Bob slapped the desk as he sat down. He folded his arms across his chest and stared coldly at Alex.

"Miss Lowe," Mr. Warren said, "we're concerned that you may know more about the deaths of Lib Dillard and Minnie Davis than you're telling us."

"No, sir. I've told you everything I know," Alex replied nervously.

Gerald shook his head from side to side very slowly and rolled his eyes.

"We've built this group on trust, Miss Lowe, and right now we've got reason to believe you're lying to us. We cannot tolerate lying, and we will not tolerate deceit. Now, is there anything you wish to tell us?"

"No, sir," Alex answered, "I've told you everything I know."

Mr. Warren unlocked his desk drawer and flipped a switch. The paneled wall behind his desk parted, revealing a room filled with television monitors.

"You startled me, Mr. Warren," said a young man sitting in front of the screens. "I wasn't expecting to see you again this morning."

"Buster, pull up the tape you showed me earlier."

"Yes, sir, Mr. Warren."

"Move over here, Miss Lowe, where you can see this," he instructed.

Alex slid her chair closer to the panel of monitors and watched stone-faced as the tape showed her injecting the syringe of poison into Minnie Davis.

"Fast forward through this next section, Buster, and stop when Miss Dillard enters the picture. I hope these pictures will refresh your memory, Miss Lowe."

Alex closed her eyes and shook her head when she saw Miss Dillard pull the syringe from her pocket.

"Please watch, Miss Lowe," Mr. Warren urged, "if you can. The pictures aren't of the best quality because of the darkness in the room, but I believe you can see clearly enough."

Alex stared at the monitor as she and Miss Dillard struggled with one another beside Ella Hibbetts' bed. She jerked reflexively as the needle plunged into her supervisor's thigh. Miss Dillard looked directly into the camera. Her face showed the terror of knowing she was about to die.

"Stop it!" Alex shouted. "I've seen enough. You've got the whole damn place monitored, don't you?"

"Almost," Mr. Warren replied, smiling. "Now, would you like to give us your side of the story? Perhaps this time you could tell us the truth. That's all for now, Buster. You may be excused."

"What's there to say?" Alex asked. "You saw what happened."

"We've seen it, but unfortunately, we don't have audio capabilities, yet. We'd like to hear why you killed Lib."

"I didn't kill her," Alex snapped. "She stuck the needle in her thigh, not me."

"Just tell us what happened. Did you get your assignment?"

"Yeah, I got my assignment," she replied. "I expected Miss Hibbetts to be old and debilitated, but she wasn't. When I saw Miss Davis and the terrible condition she was in, I thought there had to be a mistake and that's when I decided to give her the poison. After Miss Davis died, Miss Dillard confronted me and told me the only mistake was mine and instructed me to meet her in Miss Hibbetts' room. I had no idea she was still planning to kill Miss Hibbetts. I argued with her that it wasn't right and told her that Miss Hibbetts didn't deserve to die. That's when I tried to take the syringe from her. You saw what happened after that."

"You lied to us then, didn't you?"

"What was I supposed to do?"

"You were supposed to do your job. That's why you were recruited. That's why you were paid so well. We never asked you to make a decision. If you'd carried out your instructions Lib would still be alive."

"If I'd carried out my instructions," Alex replied, "Ella Hibbetts would be dead, and she doesn't deserve to die any more than Miss Dillard did. It's wrong to take someone's life just to save the hospital money."

"Correct me if I'm wrong," he replied, "but I seem to recall two other occasions where you took someone's life to save this hospital money."

"Those people were suffering," Alex replied. "Taking their lives was the humane thing to do. Whether or not it saved the hospital money was of no concern to me. I could've taken their lives had the opportunity arose whether I was involved in your sick scheme or not."

"You had no problem taking our money for your efforts."

"I didn't ask for your damn money!"

"No one said you did, Miss Lowe; only that you accepted it. In my mind, your acceptance indicated your approval of our objectives."

"I've never approved of what you're doing," she proclaimed. "Have you forgotten that you blackmailed me into participating."

"Blackmail?" he asked. "Those are strong words for someone in your position." He opened the manila folder on his desk and thumbed through its pages. "Was it blackmail that made you kill David Watson or Billy Jackson?"

Alex shifted her weight nervously in her chair but didn't answer.

"Miss Lowe," he continued, "we're convinced you're a cold-blooded killer hiding behind a mask of humanity and compassion. If we hadn't recruited you, you'd still be taking the lives of innocent people. The only difference being that our hospital wouldn't be benefiting from your efforts."

Alex sat quietly and stared blankly at the wall in front of her. She wasn't a cold-blooded killer, at least she didn't think she was. She'd been chosen by a higher authority to direct fate and alter destiny, to alleviate pain and suffering. Her mother and David Watson had told her so. Her visions were real. They had to be. They just had to be.

"We're all deeply saddened by the misfortune of last night," Mr. Warren said. "Lib was a valuable part of our organization. Not only will she be missed, her death will make it much harder for us to ensure that you're assigned where you're needed. But we're working on new arrangements even as we speak. We've made certain that Lib's official cause of death will be recorded as an acute myocardial infarction. It could destroy us if it were determined she died from poisoning."

"Surely, you don't plan to keep going after what happened last night?" Alex asked in disbelief.

"Miss Lowe," he said, "do you remember when you were a small child learning to ride a bicycle? If you fell off, your daddy made you get back on and try again, and the sooner the better. Well, consider me your daddy and last night a tragic bicycle wreck. It's time for you to ride again."

Alex folded her arms across her chest.

"It's not that simple, Mr. Warren," she said. "Miss Dillard died last night trying to take the life of an innocent person. It could just as easily have been me with the needle stuck in my leg. I won't take any more lives for you. I want out."

Mr. Warren shook his head repeatedly from side to side.

"If you'd followed your instructions, the only person who would have died would have been Ella Hibbetts and our hospital would have benefited financially from her death. Your disregard for your orders killed Lib. We've tried to make things as simple as possible for you. We've never asked you to think, only to act. As for you wanting out, that's not an option. You're too vital to our success and know too much about our operation to simply quit. If you need more money, we can discuss that."

"It's not the money," she said angrily. "I never asked for your filthy money. I don't want it! I want out! I want to sleep at night with a clear conscience. I don't want to live my life worrying that the next person you make me kill will be another Ella Hibbetts."

"None of us enjoy what we're being forced to do, Miss Lowe, but it's a matter of survival. We can't continue to spend more money than we receive and as we've explained previously, the only way to stop our losses is to limit utilization of resources by non-revenue generating patients. Unfortunately, some of those patients don't fit your preconceived criteria of who should live and who should die."

"And if I refuse to cooperate?"

Mr. Warren looked at the other two men and smiled. He carefully selected a cigar, lit the tip and slowly inhaled.

"Then we'll be forced to destroy you and your family," he stated matter-of-factly. "We've got enough evidence to put you away for life. There's not a jury in America that wouldn't convict you with the amount of evidence we've gathered. We've got videotapes showing you administering intravenous medications to several patients who mysteriously died shortly thereafter. If that's not enough, we have recorded conversations with you in which you've confessed to your involvement in the deaths of these patients."

"For some reason, Mr. Warren, I'm not surprised, not surprised at all," Alex replied, shaking her head. "But for your information, I'm not afraid of prison or death. I'd rather take my chances with a judge and jury than be used by you to kill innocent people."

"We expected as much. Tim, do you have those papers with you?"

Tim Alford pulled a stack of papers and two clear plastic bags from his briefcase.

"See if you recognize this signature, Miss Lowe," he asked, handing her the papers.

Alex stared at the documents. Lopez Medical Supply Company. Her eyes followed the page down to the bottom line. B.W. Folmar. The signature was very legible. Ben had always taken pride in his penmanship.

"You do recognize your boyfriend's handwriting, don't

you?" he asked.

"Of course I do," she replied, "but what's this got to do with me?"

"Look carefully at the items on the invoice," he directed.

"It's a purchase order for the pharmacy, Mr. Alford," she sneered. "Ben's a pharmacist in your facility and I believe he has the authority to order medications and supplies."

"We're not questioning his authority to purchase items on behalf of the hospital, Miss Lowe. Take a look at the fifth item. It's something I don't normally order when I fill out the purchase requests for the pharmacy."

Alex's eyes ran hurriedly down the list of items. Normal saline I.V. fluids. I.V. tubing. Syringes. Alcohol swabs. Crotalotoxin. Crotalotoxin?

"I'm not familiar with the fifth item," she replied.

"The fifth item, if memory serves me, is crotalotoxin," Mr. Warren informed her. "Since I've got no formal training in pharmacology, perhaps Mr. Alford could elaborate on its contents."

Tim pulled a sheet of paper from his brief case and read aloud.

"We are pleased to inform you that we now carry crotalotoxin. This deadly poison is composed primarily of rattlesnake and cobra venoms as well as toxin from the deadly African poison dart frog as well as trace amounts of several other equally lethal poisons. When given intravenously or intramuscularly crotalotoxin can produce death in a matter of minutes. If swallowed, death can be expected within fifteen minutes."

He paused and looked at Alex. "It's the trade name of what you administered to kill Minnie Davis and Lib Dillard."

"Miss Lowe," Mr. Warren said, "we've got evidence, if you push us, to show the authorities that your boyfriend has been involved with you in your scheme to kill innocent but unfortunate patients. We surmise that it's the crotalotoxin that you've been administering to your victims. What else could act so quickly? And why else would Mr. Folmar be ordering it?"

"I don't believe you!" she shouted angrily. "Ben would never stoop to your level."

"Do you doubt the signature on the paper, Miss Lowe?" he asked.

"I recognize the signature, but I don't believe Ben signed it. I know him too well and he'd never go along with something like this."

Mr. Warren smiled cockily.

"Oh, but that's where you're wrong," he said. "You'd be amazed at how low a drug addict would go to get a fix."

Alex stared in disbelief. Ben, a drug addict?

"You're crazy if you expect me to believe Ben is a drug addict," she said.

"Show her the other stuff, Tim."

Tim took the two clear bags from Gerald's desk and handed them to Alex.

"Look but don't open," he instructed her. "The bag in your left hand contains syringes filled with crotalotoxin and though you can't detect it with your naked eyes, the syringes are covered with Mr. Folmar's fingerprints. In your right hand is a bag containing syringes of morphine. Those, too, are covered with your boyfriend's fingerprints. As you may be aware, federal regulations require all pharmacies to keep accurate records regarding dispensing and utilization of narcotics. Part of Mr. Folmar's responsibility in the pharmacy is to keep the narcotics log on his shift. Over the last three months, we've had numerous vials of morphine mysteriously disappear. Not coincidentally, it's occurred most often when Mr. Folmar has been the lone pharmacist on duty. When we confronted him, he denied it. But when we found where he hid the vials and syringes, he confessed to everything. The drug screen there in front of you confirmed our suspicions. Initially, we were tempted to fire him but then we realized how valuable he could be to our operation. We needed someone to place the order for the crotalotoxin and to prepare the syringes for your use. The threat of prison for morphine theft was enough to ensure his cooperation."

Alex placed her face in her hands and wept bitterly. She'd always considered Ben to be not just her boyfriend but her best friend, someone in whom she could confide. Now she was being told that Ben was not only a junky but was also involved in the same shameful operation that had destroyed her.

"Does he know about my involvement?" she asked.

"Indirectly," Tim replied. "He knows that crotalotoxin is a poison and that it's administered by a nurse to terminate lives, but that's all. With his drug problem, we weren't sure he could deal rationally with the realization that his girlfriend was a murderer."

"So you see, Miss Lowe," Mr. Warren interrupted, "if you choose to expose our operation, you'll destroy both you and Mr. Folmar. The three of us will deny having any knowledge of your operation and our testimonies, combined with our evidence, will make it very difficult, if not impossible, for a jury to return anything but a guilty verdict. I feel certain that your boyfriend would be tried as an accomplice. Perhaps, if you're lucky, the two of you would be sent to the same prison." Mr. Warren chuckled softly and grinned from ear to ear as he leaned back in his chair. "It's your choice, Miss Lowe," he said, "but I suggest continued cooperation on your part."

"If I agree to continue," she said, "when would my next assignment be?"

"The sooner, the better. Ella Hibbetts is still alive and I do believe we have a syringe with her name on it ready to be administered tonight."

Alex winced.

"Does it have to be Miss Hibbetts? I'm just not sure I can take her life. She doesn't deserve to die."

Mr. Warren raised his eyebrows and shook his head.

"No," he replied, "it doesn't have to be her. It could be you.

You could take the syringe, plunge it into your thigh and put an end to your own misery. Or better yet, why not confront your boyfriend, confess your sins to one another, and share a syringe. At least that way, you wouldn't disgrace your family name. You can choose tonight."

Alex rose from her chair and took a step toward the door.

"I hate you," she sobbed. "I hate all of you for what you've done to me."

The three men smiled at one another.

"That's your right, Miss Lowe," Mr. Warren said. "You may hate anyone you choose to hate. But let me assure you, we have no animosity towards you. In fact, we are deeply grateful for what you've done and will do in the future in an effort to preserve this fine institution. And, Miss Lowe, I suggest you don't discuss this meeting with your boyfriend. I'm confident he'd deny our allegations. Drug addicts are notorious liars, especially when confronted with their addiction. If you doubt what we've told you this morning, simply look at his arms. If he's got no puncture wounds confirming his I.V. drug abuse, then everything you've heard is a lie. And if it's all a lie, then I'd encourage you to go to the authorities with what you know. You'll find your assignment and your equipment tonight in the usual place."

With tears streaming down her cheek, Alex walked quickly across the room and out the door without acknowledging his final remark. Bob watched her walk down the hallway. When he was confident she was gone, he closed the door.

"Do you think she bought it?" he asked.

"It's hard to tell," Gerald replied, wrinkling his brow. "She's a pretty sharp girl. I'm sure she'll go straight home and confront her boyfriend this morning. How'd his arms look when you last saw him, Tim?"

"Like a junky," the pharmacist replied. "I convinced him to let me draw blood every other day for the past two weeks or so.

I told him we were doing an in house study on electrolytes in acutely ill patients and needed volunteers to serve as controls. He's so kind hearted and interested in helping others that saying no never crossed his mind. I'm not very good at drawing blood so his veins are pretty messed up. I wish we could've had a longer time so we could have seen some scaring. I think it would've looked more like tract marks then, but even now, he's got puncture wounds on top of puncture wounds. When I drew blood yesterday, I felt confident I had inflicted enough damage to give the appearance of drug abuse. I think when Miss Lowe looks at his arms and remembers the drug screen we showed her, there's nothing the guy can say or do to convince her he's not an addict. We're fortunate with our timing. If this had happened a week ago, we could've been in big trouble. I'm afraid she would have gone to the authorities if it were only her life at stake."

"The fake drug screen was a good idea," Gerald replied, rocking back and forth in his chair. "I'm glad you suggested it. Now, if she does go to the authorities, do we actually have any syringes with Folmar's finger prints on them that we could fill with morphine or crotalotoxin?"

"No, sir, but I think we can get them. I'll leave some empty syringes out tonight. I'm sure he'll pick them up and put them away. Filling them with the medications won't be a problem."

"What if the Lowe girl balks tonight?" Bob asked. "What if she won't kill the old lady?"

Gerald unbuttoned his collar and loosened his tie.

"Then there'll be no doubt about her long range intentions," he said, "and we'll be forced to kill her."

- 31 -

Ben was working in his yard when Alex arrived. Beads of sweat covered his forehead.

"I thought you'd be sleeping," Alex called to him as she got out of her car. "Didn't you work last night?"

"Yeah, but the weather is nice and I've been needing to trim these shrubs," Ben replied. "What brings you by so early this morning. Didn't you work last night?"

"Yeah, I'm just now leaving the hospital," Alex replied. Her eyes drifted toward Ben's muscular arms but the long sleeves on the blue denim shirt were rolled up only to his mid forearms. Maybe they were lying. Maybe there weren't any needle marks on the arms. But why would he have on long sleeves on such a warm morning?

"You look troubled," Ben said, noticing the wrinkles in her brow. "What's on your mind?" He dropped his tools and put his arm around Alex's shoulder.

"Nothing much. I was just stopping by to be sure you were doing okay."

"Come on, Alex," Ben said, "I know you too well. You don't wrinkle your brow and squint your eyes when nothing is wrong. You might as well level with me. What's bothering you? You haven't been yourself for weeks."

"Nothing!" Alex replied. "Really, I was just stopping by

to say hello."

"Well, I'm doing fine and as soon as I finish trimming these bushes, I'm going to grab some breakfast before I go to bed. I'm working again tonight."

Ben gathered his lawn tools and motioned her toward the house. Dirt and sweat covered his forearms. Beads of sweat dripped from his brow. He wiped across his cheekbone with the back of his glove and pushed back the moist curls from his glistening forehead.

"Let's go inside," he invited. "I need to get cleaned up."

Ben pulled off his leather gloves and tapped the bottom of his tennis shoes with the pruning shears. Clumps of dark dirt broke loose from the soles of his shoes and fell silently to the ground. He untied his shoes and set them on the welcome mat outside the door. Alex followed closely behind him as he opened the door and went inside.

"Are you going to keep playing this game," he asked, as he scrubbed his hands in the kitchen sink "or are you going to tell me what's bothering you?"

Alex squeezed his hands and looked into his eyes.

"Have you got a few minutes?" she asked.

Tears filled her eyes and rolled slowly down her cheeks. Ben hugged her and led her to the sofa.

"What's going on, Alex?"

Alex sighed and tried to clear the lump from her throat. She wiped the tears from her eyes and slowly shook her head.

"I'm afraid I'm in trouble, deep trouble," she said.

"What kind of trouble?" Ben demanded.

Alex pushed back and folded her hands in her lap.

"Do you remember when I told you that I knew about someone being involved in something illegal and asked your opinion as to what I should do?"

Ben nodded knowingly as he chewed on his bottom lip.

"Well, I'm that someone," Alex said, her voice trembling.

"Somehow I was afraid you were. What is it? Gambling? Drugs?"

Alex closed her eyes and lowered her head.

"I wish it was that simple," she said.

"What is it then?" Ben asked, wondering to himself what could be worse than gambling or drugs.

"Murder," Alex answered softly.

"Murder?" Ben echoed, his mouth dropping open in disbelief. "You killed someone?"

"They blackmailed me. I didn't have a choice. And now I'm afraid I'm in too deep to get out alive."

"Who blackmailed you?" Ben asked anxiously.

"There are some unethical people running Richland," Alex continued. "They've got surveillance cameras throughout the hospital, cameras that almost no one knows about. They accused me of killing two patients and told me if I didn't go along with their plans, they'd turn me in to the authorities."

"So you went along with them?" Ben asked in disbelief.

"I didn't have a choice. If they went to the police, I could go to prison for life."

Ben massaged his temples and shook his head.

"Who's behind it?" he asked.

"Gerald Warren is calling the shots," Alex replied, "but Bob Carlson and Tim Alford are involved as well. Miss Dillard was involved, but she died last night."

Ben appeared surprised. "The night supervisor?" he asked. "How?"

"I'll get to that," Alex answered. "It's such a long story, and I am in so deep."

"I'm listening," Ben replied, sliding back onto the sofa.

Alex took a deep breath.

"Richland is apparently having financial problems and is on the verge of collapse if some changes aren't made. Mr. Warren decided that the best way to cut cost was to cut expenses. Limiting utilization of resources, that's what he calls it. Patients who don't have insurance or patients whose insurance doesn't adequately cover the costs of their treatment are identified and killed. Dead patients don't consume costly resources."

Ben raised his eyebrows and shook his head.

"Are you telling me that Gerald Warren is killing patients?" he asked.

"Actually, no," Alex replied. "He just selects the patients who should be terminated and then delegates the responsibility."

"So Alford and Carlson are killing the patients?"

"No," Alex replied, shaking her head emphatically. "They help Mr. Warren select the patients."

"Then who in the hell is killing them?"

"That's what I'm trying to tell you, Ben. I've killed the patients. They blackmailed me. I didn't have a choice."

Ben folded his arms across his chest and stared at Alex.

"I don't want to hear this," he said very slowly and deliberately. "How many people have you killed?"

"Not many. The operation, as they call it, hasn't been going for very long. At first, they asked me to kill patients who were suffering, patients who were better off dead than alive. But last night, they wanted me to kill an old lady who wasn't suffering and was aware of everything that was happening to her. They wanted her killed simply because she didn't have insurance and was costing the hospital money."

"Did you kill her?" Ben asked in disbelief.

"No," Alex replied emphatically, "and that's what caused the problem. The patient in the "A" bed was in such poor condition and in so much pain that I gave her the injection that was intended for their victim. After she died, Miss Dillard confronted me and we got into a big argument. I refused to kill Miss Hibbetts and she demanded that I follow my instructions. When I refused, she tried to give the medication. We got into a scuffle and she accidentally stuck the needle in her own leg. I don't think she got a very large dose of the poison, but it was still enough to kill her. Mr. Warren's got everything on tape and he's accusing me of killing her. He's demanding that I terminate Ella Hibbetts tonight or he'll go to the authorities."

"I'm dumbfounded," Ben said, "speechless."

He reached over and placed his arm around Alex. Alex leaned her head against his shoulder and sobbed quietly.

"So Miss Dillard's death was an accident?" Ben asked.

"Yeah," Alex said tearfully. "I swear it was, but it doesn't matter. Mr. Warren said if I'd done what I was told to do, it would've never happened. And I guess he's right. But if I had done what they told me to do, Miss Hibbetts would be dead, and she didn't deserve to die any more than did Miss Dillard. Ben, I've done some things I shouldn't have done, things I regret, but I've never taken anyone's life without honestly believing that they wouldn't be better off dead. When I watched Mom suffer before she died, I realized there were things worse than death and I promised myself that if I were ever given the chance to prevent pain and suffering, I'd do something about it. That's all I ever intended to do."

Ben lifted Alex's head from his shoulder and lightly held her face between his hands.

"Listen to your self," he said sternly. "You're playing God. Who are you to decide who should live and who should die? You don't have that right any more than I do. You've got to turn yourself in and expose Mr. Warren and the others."

Alex pulled away from Ben and shook her head.

"I can't do that. Not with the evidence Mr. Warren has against us."

"Against us?" Ben asked, shaking his head. "I'm not involved in this and the last time I checked, it wasn't against the law to date you."

"Quit lying, Ben," Alex said angrily. "They told me everything. I saw the syringes, the drug test, the order forms, everything."

Ben wrinkled his brow as he stared in disbelief at Alex.

"I don't have a clue as to what you're talking about!" he

insisted. "What syringes? And what drug tests?"

Alex grabbed his hands and extended his arms. She pushed the rolled sleeves up to the middle of his biceps, and placed her fingers near the crease of the elbow and rubbed the puncture wounds.

"I know about the morphine addiction," she said softly, "and how they blackmailed you, too. I'm the nurse you prepared the syringes for."

Ben looked down at his arms and rolled his eyes.

"I don't know what you're talking about!" he said indignantly. "I'm not addicted to morphine and I have no idea what syringes you're talking about."

"Explain these tract marks then," Alex demanded, tapping on his arms.

"Those aren't tract marks," he replied, "they're venipuncture sites. Tim's been drawing blood for some sort of project he's conducting on electrolytes."

Alex smiled and nodded.

"Mr. Warren said you'd deny everything, that addicts have that tendency."

Ben sighed deeply.

"Listen to me," he said raising his voice. "I'm not a drug addict. I'm your best friend. You know me better than that!"

"And I wasn't raised to be a murderer," Alex said tearfully, "but that's what I've become."

"But I'm a pharmacist," Ben yelled. "If I were hooked on morphine, do you think I could continue to do my job? Do you think Tim would let a junky work in his pharmacy with free access to narcotics? If they had proof I was addicted to morphine, don't you think they'd fire me?"

"Oh, they thought about it," Alex replied coolly, "but they knew you could be valuable to their operation. That's why they kept you on, so you could order the poison and fill the syringes."

Ben shook his head and bit his lip to control his mounting anger.

"God knows I wish I knew what you were talking about, but I've never ordered any poison and I certainly haven't filled any syringes with it," he replied.

"But I saw the syringes," Alex sobbed, "the ones with the morphine and the ones with the poison. They said your fingerprints were on them. And what about the order form? I recognized your signature. And the drug screen where you tested positive for morphine? How do you explain that?"

"I don't know what they showed you this morning or what they told you, but I'm not a drug addict and I'm not a part of their operation. I haven't taken a drug screen since my pre-employment physical and I passed that without any problems. I don't know what more I can do to make you believe me."

Alex wiped the tears from her eyes.

"I want to believe you," she said, "I really do, but they've got so much evidence against you."

"Didn't you say they've got evidence against you?" Ben asked. "Evidence that makes it look a lot worse than it really is, that could send you to prison? Don't you see what they've done? They've framed us. If they can convince you that I'm involved in their scheme, then you're that much less likely to go to the authorities. And if you do go to the authorities, they've fabricated enough evidence to convict us both. Can't you see what's going on? They've created the perfect crime. You're doing their dirty work and they're collecting evidence against you, and from what you say, against me."

Alex rose from the sofa and anxiously paced the floor.

"Swear to me," she said, breathing heavily. "Swear to me that you're telling the truth."

"I've got no reason to lie to you," Ben replied, his eyes pleading for her trust.

"Swear it," she repeated, raising her voice.

"Okay! I swear I'm telling the truth."

She stopped pacing and looked at Ben. She wiped the tears from her eyes and stretched out her arms. For several minutes, the two of them stood in silence, tightly holding one another.

"Oh, Ben," Alex said, "I am in so much trouble. You've got to help me."

"You've got to go to the police. The longer you go along with them, the deeper the hole you're digging. Don't you see? Every time you kill someone, they gather more evidence to use against you if their plot is ever uncovered."

"If they find out I've gone to the police, I'm afraid they'll kill me," Alex said, her voice shaking. "You don't know them like I do. You haven't seen the hatred in their faces."

"Then they can't find out," Ben replied. "You've got to tell your side of the story to someone who can stop them, and the sooner the better."

"But Mr. Warren told me I've got to terminate Miss Hibbetts tonight. If I don't follow his orders, he'll know something is wrong."

"Then we've got to go to the police today," Ben replied, collecting their coats.

- 32 -

The short trip from Ben's house to the police station seemed like a cross-country journey as the two of them rode along in silence. Alex stared blankly at the dashboard, her bottom lip clinched tightly between her teeth. Ben patted her lightly on the arm.

"It'll be okay," he said. "Things have a way of working out. Trust me. You're doing the right thing. There isn't another option."

Their hearts pounded as hand-in-hand they climbed the worn, cement steps to the police station. It was stuffy inside the station. An old ceiling fan turned slowly above them but produced no breeze. Alex wiped the perspiration from her forehead.

"Can I help you?"

A middle-aged man with black hair and a five o'clock shadow peered at them over the glasses sitting on the tip of his nose. His desk was littered with paper. A small stream of smoke rose from a cigarette in an ashtray.

"Yes, sir. We need to report a crime," Ben said.

"What kind of crime? Assault? Robbery?" he asked.

"No, sir. Something more serious. Is there someplace where we can discuss this in private? We could get in trouble if the wrong people see us talking to you."

"Hey, Pete," he shouted. "How about manning the front desk for a few minutes while I talk to this couple."

The two of them followed the officer down a dimly light hallway to a small room. The officer took a seat behind a gray, metal desk and motioned for the two of them to sit in a pair of brown, folding chairs opposite the desk. He turned on an old gooseneck lamp and pulled a yellow legal pad from the top drawer of the desk.

"More serious than assault or robbery?" he asked as he scribbled on the legal pad.

"Yes, sir," they said in unison.

He raised his bushy eyebrows and folded his arms across his chest.

"What do you young folks need to report?" he asked, almost condescendingly.

"Sir, I'm Ben Folmar and this is my girlfriend, Alex Lowe. I'm a pharmacist at Richland Memorial and Alex works there as an R.N. What we're about to tell you may be difficult for you to believe."

"I'm listening," he said, unfolding his arms and tapping his pencil on the metal desk.

"It's my problem, Ben. Let me tell him," Alex interrupted.

Ben nodded his approval and squeezed her hand.

"I'm not quite sure where to begin," Alex said.

"Why don't we make this simple," the officer replied. "What type of crime are you reporting?"

"Mur..." Alex swallowed hard against the lump in her throat. "Murder," she whispered.

The word was hard for her to say. Until the previous night, she hadn't considered what she was doing as murder. She was compassionately helping the unfortunate who were unable to help themselves. Not until she was instructed to terminate Ella Hibbetts did she understand that she was committing murder.

"Murder?" the officer asked.

He stopped tapping his pencil and laid it on the desk beside the legal pad. Staring silently at Alex, he took off his glasses and twirled them in his hand.

"Yes, sir. Multiple murders," Alex answered.

The officer held up his hand and pushed back from the desk. "Hold on just a minute, ma'am," he said, rising from his chair. "It'd probably be best for you if I got someone from homicide to hear your story. I'm more accustomed to dealing with less serious crimes. I'll be right back."

The large oak door slammed loudly, echoing in the small, sparsely furnished room.

"I hope I'm doing the right thing," Alex said.

"You don't have a choice," Ben replied.

Alex glanced anxiously around the dimly lit room. An old metal light fixture with a single socket hung above the desk from a thin electrical cord. The bottom third of the cord was wrapped with black electrical tape. Alex pushed her chair against the brown paneled wall behind her and flipped the light switch. There was a bright flash of light and a loud pop as the bulb above her head surrendered under the surge of unexpected electricity.

"Guess that's why he turned on the desk lamp," she said nervously.

Several minutes passed before the large oak door swung open, its pair of rusty hinges squeaking in harmony. A second taller man dressed in a tan, polyester suit with a cheap, clip-on tie accompanied the policeman with the bushy eyebrows and five o'clock shadow.

"Miss Lowe, this is detective Horton, of homicide," the officer said.

"Hello, Miss Lowe," the detective greeted her, extending his large right hand.

His firm handshake comforted Alex.

"Please, call me Alex," she said, "and this is my friend, Ben Folmar."

"Okay, Alex," he replied, nodding his head. "Officer Lloyd tells me you've got information about some murders."

"Yes, sir," Alex replied, "the murder of patients at Richland Memorial Hospital."

The two men looked at each other, bewildered. Sharing a match, they spontaneously lit unfiltered cigarettes, and leaned their wooden chairs against the paneled wall.

"First news I've heard of any murders at Richland," replied the detective, looking at Officer Lloyd who nodded in agreement.

"It all started several months ago," Alex began. "I made a serious mistake one night which cost a patient his life."

"What kind of mistake?" detective Horton asked.

"I accidentally gave him a bolus of intravenous potassium."

"And that killed him?"

"Yes, sir," Alex replied softly.

"Did you know it could kill him?" he asked.

"Yes, sir," Alex answered. "Any nurse knows that."

"Did you try to correct your mistake?"

"No, sir, I didn't."

"Even though you knew it could kill him?" the detective asked, scribbling on his notepad.

"Yes, sir," Alex answered.

"Why not?" he asked without looking up.

"Because he was suffering so much. Anyone who knew anything about his situation would tell you that he and his family were better off with him dead than with him alive."

Detective Horton put his finger to his lips and nodded his head.

"So his death was unintentional but possibly preventable?" he asked.

"Yes, sir, it was preventable," Alex admitted.

"You said murders. Were there more deaths?"

"Not long after that, I was taking care of an elderly man who had made it clear that he never wanted to be kept alive by machines. He'd smoked for years and had horrible lungs. For years he had lived his life attached to an oxygen tank. He felt he was a burden to his family. To make a long story short, on the day he was being discharged from the hospital, he suffered a stroke and quit breathing. The left side of his body was paralyzed. Unfortunately, the first physician to reach the scene didn't know about his wishes and placed him on a ventilator. I knew he was miserable and would rather die than be kept alive by a machine." Alex paused. "So I untied his hand and left his room. While I was gone, he pulled the tube out of his throat. He made the decision to die."

"So by untying his hand you made it possible for him to pull out the tube."

"Yes, sir."

"Did you have any suspicions he'd pull his tube out if you untied his hand?"

"I tried to make myself believe he wouldn't pull it out, but deep down, I knew if given the chance, he'd do it. And if he pulled it out, I knew he'd die."

"So you intentionally untied his hand knowing that if given the opportunity he'd pull his tube out?"

"Yes, sir."

"And knowing that if he pulled his tube out, he'd ultimately die?"

"Yes, sir. But even if he hadn't pulled out his tube, his doctor was planning to taper the ventilator the next day and extubate him. I only gave him the chance to have a voice in his treatment."

Detective Horton rubbed the stubble on his chin and clinched his jaws.

"Miss Lowe," he said, "from what you've told me so far, I'm inclined to believe that you're plagued by very poor judgment, but without your confession there'd be no way to prove to anyone that you've done anything wrong. Why would you want to tell me about these two incidents?"

"So you could understand what I'm about to tell you," Alex replied. She looked nervously at Ben who nodded for her to continue. "Some time after the death of Mr. Christopher, the old man on the ventilator, I was assigned to take care of a young man who was dying with AIDS. He was hospitalized with pneumonia and he wasn't responding to treatment. His parents had disowned him and said he had disgraced them. They wouldn't answer his phone calls and wouldn't even come to the hospital to visit him. One night while I was assigned to take care of him, he asked me to help him die."

"He asked you to kill him?"

Alex shook her head quickly and appeared distressed.

"No, sir," she said, "not really. The way he explained it, killing someone was an act of hatred and violence. He was asking me to show compassion and love for him by helping him end his life. He was dying. From the moment he injected those I.V. drugs and contracted the AIDS virus, he was sentenced to death. The medical community had nothing to offer him but palliative treatment. He'd lost his friends and his family and had no reason to want to go on living."

"Did he make any suggestions as to how you might take his life?"

"Yes, sir. He said I could just give him a big slug of morphine and let him slide on out of this life. Those were his words."

"And did you?" the detective asked.

"At first I had reservations about what he was asking me to do," Alex confessed. "Up to this point I'd done some things which had cost people their lives but I'd never actively done anything to take someone's life. But the more I thought about it, the more I realized that if he could get his hands on the morphine, he'd take his own life. I tried to put myself in his shoes. If I were dying with AIDS or cancer or anything terminal, I'd rather die peacefully with an overdose of morphine than struggle and suffer through the final stages of life. That night I injected two vials of morphine into his I.V. line. He died not long after shift change."

Detective Horton lowered the front legs of the chair to the floor and leaned forward.

"Miss Lowe," he said, "it might be in your best interest if we get you an attorney in here before you go any further. Sweetheart, you've just confessed to a murder."

"Mr. Horton, I don't want to have an attorney present," she replied. "I know what I've done and I came here on my on free will to try to prevent any more deaths. But I didn't murder Billy. It's like he said, murder is an act of violence. What I did was out of love and compassion for a fellow human being who was terminally ill. Regardless of what I did that night, he was going to die. It was simply a matter of timing."

The detective rubbed his eyes and looked at the other officer. They sighed and shook their heads in unison.

"Is there more?"

"Oh, yes, sir," she replied. "What I've told you so far has been leading up to my real reason for coming down here today. The night after I gave my patient the morphine, I was summoned by the night shift nursing supervisor to meet in her office. When I arrived, there were three men waiting with her. One of them was Gerald Warren, the hospital administrator."

"Who were the other two?" he asked.

"Bob Carlson and Tim Alford," she replied.

"I know Warren, but I'm not familiar the others," he replied, scratching his head. "Who are they?"

"Mr. Carlson is the chief accountant and financial officer at the hospital. Mr. Alford is head of pharmacy."

"So, there are five of you at a meeting in the nursing supervisor's office in the middle of the night?"

"Yes, sir."

"Strange time for a meeting."

"That's what I thought. I understood Miss Dillard being there, but not the other three."

"Why'd they want to see you?"

"They knew about the three deaths I've told you about."

"How'd they know?" he asked. "Had you told someone else?"

"No, sir," she replied, "but after I pushed the I.V. potassium, I made a second mistake. I threw the syringe away in a paper cup in the snack bar. I thought if I disposed of it there, no one would ever suspect anything. But the worker in the snack bar thought I looked nervous and retrieved the cup with the syringe from the garbage. She turned it in to nursing services thinking that I shouldn't be disposing of syringes and needles where the general public could possibly get their hands on them. Apparently, there's a policy at Richland that when a patient dies, their chart is automatically reviewed. When this patient's chart was reviewed, the committee was suspicious that he'd died from unexplained hyperkalemia, or a high potassium level. One and one added up to two and pretty soon administration had linked me to his death. After that they monitored my activity without my knowledge. Mr. Horton, people at the hospital don't know it, but Mr. Warren has the entire hospital monitored by video cameras."

"He's got cameras in the hospital?" he asked, sounding surprised.

"Yes, sir," Alex replied. "He claims they were installed in an effort to ensure safety and to improve service, but I have my own opinion."

"And your opinion is?"

"To spy on his employees, to catch people making mistakes, like I did, and blackmail them to make them go along with his plan."

"And what plan would that be?" he asked.

"His plan to selectively kill patients who are costing the hospital money."

The two men looked at one another and raised their eyebrows as if doubting what they were hearing.

"Gerald Warren has a plan to kill patients?" the detective

asked.

“Yes, sir,” she replied. “Two patients have already died and more will die if he isn’t stopped.”

“Miss Lowe, hospitals need patients to survive,” detective Horton noted. “Why would he want to have patients killed? That goes against everything we’re lead to believe about hospitals. The sole reason hospitals exist is to save lives.”

Alex shook her head.

“There was a time when I believed the same thing,” she said, “but it’s not true, at least not completely. Hospitals do exist to save lives, but only if they can make money. Richland has been losing money for the past few years. A hospital can’t operate in the red indefinitely and Mr. Warren knew that.”

“But it’d seem to me that the hospital would need more patients rather than less to cut its losses.”

“It was never a question of numbers of patients,” Alex said, shaking her head. “Richland operates at over eighty-five percent bed occupancy most days. No, sir; the problem wasn’t the number of patients, but the payer mix. Unfortunately, we live in a relatively poor county. The hospital loses money because it has to provide care for a number of patients without insurance or without the ability to privately fund their health care. Mr. Warren felt that if those patients who were costing the hospital money could be eliminated, he could put Richland back in the black.”

Detective Horton held a pencil between his fingers and tapped repetitively on the table with the eraser.

“So, you’re telling me that Gerald Warren, the hospital administrator, the chairman of the board of deacons in my church, and an officer in the chamber of commerce planned to kill patients who couldn’t pay for their health care? Those are very serious allegations, Miss Lowe, very serious.”

“I realize that,” she replied, “but that’s exactly what I’m telling you. Mr. Warren not only planned it, he had his plan carried out. He blackmailed me and the others into participating.

I took the lives of two patients at Richland on his orders, two patients I haven't told you about."

"Let's hear it then," he said, scratching his forehead.

"When we finished our meeting that night, he made sure I understood he'd turn me in to the authorities if I didn't go along with his plan."

"But from what you've said, you didn't believe you'd done anything wrong at that point, did you?"

"I tried to make myself believe it, but when he showed me the tape of me administering the morphine to Billy, I got scared, real scared. Billy wanted to die, and he needed to die. I knew I'd acted out of compassion and love but could I convince a jury of that? I wasn't sure I wanted to take that chance."

"So you cooperated to prevent them from turning you in to the police?" he asked.

"Yes, sir."

"But now you're turning yourself in. Miss Lowe, this doesn't make good sense to me. Why didn't you come clean to begin with?"

"I was scared," she replied.

"What happened after the meeting?"

"I couldn't sleep and thought about his proposal all night. The next morning I met with him and agreed to cooperate with him. But I still didn't understand what I was getting involved in. I knew I'd be taking lives to help save the hospital money, but I thought I'd be dealing with patients who'd benefit from death, patients who were tormented by pain and suffering."

"I take it that wasn't how it turned out?" he asked.

"No, sir," she replied. "The first two patients were perfect and fit my description of people whom I believed would be better off dead than alive. I managed to convinced myself that even if Mr. Warren hadn't forced me to participate, I would've been tempted to take their lives if the opportunity had presented itself. But the third patient was different. She didn't deserve to die. They chose her simply because she was costing the hospital money."

Detective Horton nodded as he scribbled on his note pad.

"We'll get to her," he said. "What about the first two? Who was first?"

"The first victim was an elderly lady who'd been transferred from a nursing home with a kidney infection. She had no family and was in pitiful shape. In my heart, I knew she wanted to die. She was tired of suffering."

"So you killed her?"

"Yes, sir. When I got to work that night, there was a note with her name and room number on it in my locker, and a syringe of morphine."

She reached into her purse and withdrew the note and the empty syringe.

"I saved these," she said. "I never had a good feeling about what they were doing."

Detective Horton took the paper and syringe with a handkerchief and placed them in a clear plastic bag.

"Maggie Cooper," he said, reading the note aloud. "Can't say that I knew her. We'll dust these for fingerprints. You never know who might've had their hand on this."

"I'm sure Lib Dillard was responsible for placing the instructions and the medications in my locker, at least she was until she died."

"Lib Dillard died?" he asked.

"Yes, sir, last night," Alex answered.

"Last night?" he asked. "What happened?"

"I'll get to that," Alex replied. "After Miss Cooper died they wanted to move quickly with their plan. The next night I was assigned to take care of a young man in the ICU who had no chance for survival outside of the hospital."

"Did he fit your profile of someone who deserved to die?"

"Sir," Alex replied, "I don't think anyone necessarily deserves to die, but I think it's unfortunate that some people have to endure so much pain and suffering before they die. I mean, what's the point. If a person is dying, and the medical community has nothing to offer them, why should they have to suffer while they wait to die? But to answer your question, yes, sir, he fit my profile of someone whom I thought would be better off dead than alive."

"Did you kill him?"

"Kill is such a strong term," she answered, looking troubled. "I took his life and put an end to his suffering."

"Did you feel any remorse after he died?" the detective continued.

"Not really. He was better off dead. There was no doubt in my mind about that."

"Did you inject him with morphine like you did the old lady?" he asked.

"No, sir. Mr. Alford decided we should use potassium on him."

"Why the change?"

"I'm not sure. This entire operation was new to everyone. I think Mr. Alford was trying to decide what medication worked best and was least likely to be traced in the event we ever had complications."

Detective Horton blew rings of smoke into the air and shook his head.

"Are you sure you wouldn't like to have a lawyer present?" he asked. "You're building quite a case against yourself."

"No, sir," Alex said, shaking her head as she glanced over at Ben for reassurance. "I'm not concerned for myself. I'm here so I can put a stop to what Mr. Warren intends to do. He's not concerned over pain and suffering. His sole purpose is to prevent Richland from losing money and closing its doors. If he'd chosen his victims more carefully, I seriously doubt I'd be sitting here before you today."

"Really?" he asked, amazed by her honesty.

"Yes, sir."

"So you took the lives of two patients, but you balked on

the third. What made you decide to disobey his orders?"

"After the second patient died, we had a team meeting. Mr. Warren and the others seemed pleased at how well everything was going. He told us how much money he estimated we had saved the hospital by eliminating those two patients. And then he did something that disturbed me."

"What was that?" he asked.

"He gave each of us an envelope with money for the jobs we were doing, as if he were rewarding us. I took the money home and put it away. I didn't want to touch it, let alone spend it. I suppose that's when the realization of what we were doing finally hit me. I was being paid to kill people. No matter how I tried to rationalize what I was doing, the bottom line was that I'd become a paid killer."

"So that's when you decided to come clean?"

Alex blushed and shook her head shamefully. Ben squeezed her hand in support.

"Unfortunately, no," she replied, her lips pressed tightly against one another. "I thought long and hard about it, but Mr. Warren's threat to destroy me and my family terrified me. I was in deep and I knew it, but up until then, I'd taken the lives of two people who needed to die. In my mind I could still justify my actions. It wasn't until last night when they told me to kill Ella Hibbetts that I realized he had to be stopped."

"What made her different from the others?" the detective asked.

"She wasn't suffering or dying. Just old and uninsured. And that's why they wanted her dead. She was costing the hospital money."

"Did you kill her?"

"No, sir. When I went into her room, I saw a decrepit, old lady in poor health. She was nothing but skin and bones, with decubitus ulcers on her legs and buttocks. Her skin had torn open where I.V. lines had been taped to her arms. I called her name several times and rubbed my knuckle on her chest, but she never answered. I was ready to inject the poison when the patient in the second bed answered to her name. The patient I thought was Ella Hibbetts was in reality Minnie Davis. Miss Hibbetts was in the second bed. She was also old, but in good shape for her age. I just knew there had to be a mistake. Surely they didn't intend for me to terminate Miss Hibbetts. The poison had to be for Miss Davis. But when I went back to the nursing station and looked at their charts, there was no mistake. They wanted me to kill Ella Hibbetts."

"But you didn't?"

"No, sir. She didn't deserve to die."

"No one deserves to die. Isn't that what you said earlier?"

"Well, yes, sir. No one deserves to die, but some people need to die more than others. Miss Davis needed to die. She had a miserable existence."

"You could tell that so quickly, even though you had just seen her?"

"Yes, sir, I could," Alex replied.

"Did you kill Miss Davis?"

"I wish you wouldn't use the word kill."

"But you're the one who said you realized you were nothing more than a paid killer. I'm only using your words."

"Yes, damn it, I killed her," she admitted, raising her voice.

"What was it this time? Potassium? Morphine?" he asked.

"Neither. It was a poison mixture Mr. Alford had ordered especially for that purpose. It was much quicker than potassium or morphine and more difficult to trace if an autopsy were ever done."

"So Alford ordered a special poison for the sole purpose of taking patient's lives?"

"Yes, sir."

"What happened to Ella Hibbetts. Is she still alive?"

"Yes, sir, she is. After I administered the poison to Miss Davis, Miss Dillard confronted me. She wanted to know if Miss

Hibbetts was dead. When I told her she wasn't, she wanted to know why. I tried to explain how I thought they'd made a mistake, that I couldn't understand why they'd want her dead since she wasn't suffering. We got into a heated argument and she made it clear that Miss Hibbetts was to be killed because she was costing the hospital money. Miss Davis was being allowed to live because she was a revenue-generating patient. Those were her words. A revenue-generating patient. Miss Dillard told me to meet her in Miss Hibbetts' room and finish the job."

"And did you?"

"I met Miss Dillard in the room, if that's what you're asking."

"Did you finish the job, as you put it?" he asked.

"No, sir," she said, shaking her head. "When I got to Miss Hibbetts' room, Miss Dillard was already there. She pulled out another syringe of poison and told me to give it to Miss Hibbetts, but I refused. She tried to insert the needle into Miss Hibbetts' I.V. tubing, but I wouldn't let her. There was no way I was going to let her take that sweet, old lady's life. As we struggled with one another the needle pulled out of the tubing and stuck in Miss Dillard's thigh. She made it to the nursing station before she collapsed. We tried to save her, but it was no use. The poison acted too quickly. After the code, I went back to Miss Hibbetts' room. I thought she'd been asleep through it all, but she'd seen and heard everything that happened. She knew I'd taken Miss Davis' life, but she also knew I'd spared her life."

"Then you've got a witness as to how Miss Dillard died?" he asked.

"Yes, sir," Alex replied, nodding. "Miss Hibbetts saw it, but so did Mr. Warren. He caught it on tape. He called me into his office this morning and confronted me. I didn't know he had seen everything and tried to pretend I didn't know much about Miss Dillard's death. When he showed me the tape, I wanted to die. He blamed me for her death and said if I'd done my job, she wouldn't have died. But if I'd carried out his orders, Miss Hibbetts would be dead and she didn't deserve to die any more than Miss Dillard did. I told Mr. Warren I wanted out, that I wouldn't take the lives of patients who didn't need to die. But he wouldn't take no for an answer. He threatened to ruin me and my family and even concocted a story about Ben and how he was addicted to morphine. He tried to make me believe he was involved in their plot and was ordering the poison for them. He had everything planned, even fabricated drug screens and pharmacy order forms. He even had Mr. Alford draw blood on Ben each day to make me believe he had needle sticks from injecting morphine. Show them your arms, Ben."

Ben rolled up his sleeves and showed the puncture wounds and bruising in the crease of his elbow.

"Mr. Alford told me he was doing a study on critically ill patients in the hospital and needed to draw blood from me to use as a control," Ben said. "I thought it was an unusual request but didn't really see any harm in it."

Detective Horton stretched his neck to get a better view of Ben's arms.

"And the purpose in doing that was to make your girlfriend believe you were injecting morphine into your veins?" he asked.

"Yes, sir," Ben replied. "The three of them had thought their plan out thoroughly, apparently to protect themselves if anything ever went wrong."

"And now something's gone wrong and you believe they'll try to place the blame on you and your girlfriend?"

"Yes, sir," he replied. "If what Alex has told you is true, I believe they will. I don't agree with what Alex's done, but at least she's had the courage to come forward and try to stop Mr. Warren from killing any more patients."

Detective Horton stopped drumming his pencil on the table and slid his chair back.

"You know it's not every day we have someone come in here and confess to a murder, much less to a string of murders that no one even knows anything about. You do realize that you've implicated the involvement of some very respected and influential men in our community. I hope you can prove your allegations."

Alex reached into her purse and produced several cassette tapes.

"These are recordings of some of my earlier conversations with Mr. Warren and the others. They didn't know I was recording our meetings but they were still cautious during our conversations."

Detective Horton listened to the tapes as Alex and Ben looked on.

"Can you identify the voices?" he asked.

"Yes, sir," Alex replied. "The male speaking on the first tape was Mr. Warren. The female was Miss Dillard."

"The one who died last night?" he asked.

"Yes, sir. The voice on the last tape was Tim Alford, the head of the pharmacy. The other voice was Bob Carlson. He's quiet and hasn't had much to say in most of our meetings. Out of all of them, he seems most troubled by what's going on."

Detective Horton and Officer Lloyd shook their heads.

"These tapes are interesting and certainly suggest some sort of covert operation but it'll be difficult to make a strong case against any of the men based on these tapes alone. We need more evidence if we're to make an indictment."

Alex reached into her pocket and pulled out three slips of paper, each containing a room number and a patient's name.

"These are the instructions they've given me," she said.

"I'm afraid this won't be of much help unless we can prove that these are orders for you to kill someone," Detective Horton replied. "And even then, we'd have to show that one of the three men was responsible for writing and delivering the orders."

"I don't think it was their responsibility. I think Miss Dillard gave me the instructions, and now she's dead."

Detective Horton rose from his chair and walked over to the window. His body silhouetted against the sun gave him the appearance of being even larger than he was. He ran his fingers through his hair and rubbed his eyes.

"You do realize you've just confessed to the murders of six people, don't you? And that you've accused four other people, one of whom is now dead, of being involved in the murders of at least two of these people?"

"Yes, sir."

"Do you also understand that until we have more evidence, we can't arrest any of those you've implicated?"

"But I gave you the evidence and told you what happened," she pleaded.

"But that's not good enough," he replied. "Until we have more evidence, the best we can do is bring them in for questioning."

Alex shook her head and glanced at Ben for support.

"If you bring them in for questioning," she said, "they'll know I've talked. And they'll kill me."

"Have they threatened you?" he asked.

"They told me this morning that if I went to the authorities, they'd destroy me, and my family."

Ben held tightly to Alex's arm.

"If I could speak..." Ben began.

Detective Horton nodded.

"Sir, from what Alex told me this morning, I don't think they plan to kill us but rather to portray us as cold-blooded murderers, and as such, destroy us and our careers. What Alex did was wrong, but in her mind she honestly believed she was doing the right thing. She believed she had in some way been anointed to alleviate pain and suffering, even if it meant taking an individual's life. But they forced her to kill for them. She's not a murderer, but they didn't give her a choice."

"I sympathize with you," Detective Horton replied, "but

regardless of her motive, your girlfriend has confessed to taking the lives of six people. We've got no choice but to place her under arrest. I'd strongly advise her to obtain the services of a good lawyer. I'm afraid she's going to need it. We'll listen to these tapes again and bring the other three in for questioning."

Alex listened in disbelief, shaking her head, realizing for the first time that she was going to jail.

"I should've waited," she mumbled. "At least then, Miss Hibbetts might have survived."

"But I thought she was alive?" mused the detective.

"She is," Alex replied, "but Mr. Warren told me this morning that she had to die tonight. I'd get my instructions and her poison when I reported for work. If I'm in jail and they panic when you question them, I'm afraid they'll kill her."

"What makes you think they'll kill her?" the detective asked.

"Mr. Carlson asked her a lot of questions this morning. She denied knowing anything, but they're worried about her, worried to the point that they'd kill her to prevent her from talking."

"Then we've got a problem, don't we?" he asked. "If we lock you up, then Warren knows you've talked, and if he knows you've talked, then you feel Miss Hibbetts is in danger."

"Mr. Horton, could I make a suggestion?" Alex asked.

"I'm listening," he said, folding his arms across his chest.

"If I can go to work tonight, we can fake Miss Hibbetts' death. You can have one of your female officers working with me."

Detective Horton smiled and shook his head as Alex described her plan.

"I don't know what to say. It's rather unconventional to release a confessed killer, and I could probably get in a lot of trouble, but I'm not sure we have another option. If we release you and follow your plan, we'll have to have an officer nearby at all times. For your safety, we'll make a concerted effort to remain as inconspicuous as possible."

The two officers escorted Ben and Alex from the police station through a back door to an alley.

"Your car is parked at the corner of Maple and First," the officer said. "We towed it there after hearing your confession and your concern that you could be in danger if you were spotted. We'll have an officer follow you at all times so don't do anything foolish. We'll make arrangements to have a couple of undercover agents on duty at the hospital tonight. Now, I'd advise the two of you to get some rest. It may be a difficult twenty-four hours."

- 33 -

A full moon cast a soft, silvery glow across the blackened sky as Alex walked to her car that night. She nervously scanned the parking lot hoping to spot the policeman who'd be following her. She didn't recognize the man in the late model, black Chevrolet and was certain she'd never seen the car before. As she pulled out of the parking lot, the black Chevrolet followed closely behind.

The nurse in the lounge looked vaguely familiar but didn't speak when Alex entered the room. Alex fumbled with her lock and glanced over her shoulder, hoping the intruder would keep her distance. As she removed the lock and opened the door, the nurse said, "Don't touch anything. There may be something we can use as evidence."

"I thought you looked familiar," Alex said. "You were at the police station this morning, weren't you?"

The nurse smiled and nodded her head.

"I'm Maria Sanchez," she replied. "I'll be working five main with you tonight."

"Are you a nurse?" Alex asked.

"No," she replied, shaking her head, "but I'll be wearing a Jackson State nursing student uniform. We've already made arrangements for me to shadow you tonight. Now let's see what's in your locker."

She pulled on a pair of latex gloves before grabbing the manila envelope in Alex's locker.

"If it's like it usually is," Alex said, "there should be a note with Ella Hibbetts name and room number on it and a syringe filled with medication. Be careful with the syringe. If it's what I think it is, you prick your finger and you're dead."

"Bingo," Maria said, looking inside the envelope. "The finger prints on this paper and syringe may be very helpful." She placed the envelope in a briefcase and then placed the briefcase in a locker. "We need to get you wired," she said. "We feel like they'll contact you, but we're not sure when. We'd hate to have you make contact with Warren and not be able to hear the conversation."

Alex sat patiently as the officer taped a small microphone and battery pack under her scrub top.

"It picks up pretty well," Maria said, "but still try to get as close as possible to anyone you want us to hear. The technician in the van will be recording every conversation you have tonight. Don't say anything you don't want on record. Now, let's get to work."

Ella Hibbetts was sleeping when the two of them entered her room. Alex cleared her throat, hoping to arouse the old woman. When she didn't awaken, Alex gently patted her on the arm. Miss Hibbetts batted her eyelids and tried to focus on the two figures standing beside her bed.

"Miss Hibbetts, are you awake?" Alex asked.

"Yes, honey," the old lady replied, still batting her eyes. "I'd just dozed off. I wasn't expecting to see you tonight, you know, after what happened to your associate last night."

"Well, to be honest, I wasn't sure I'd be here tonight," Alex replied. "Miss Hibbetts, I've got someone I want you to meet. This is Maria Sanchez. She's a nursing student who's been assigned to work with me tonight."

"A student?" she asked, raising her eyebrows. "Well, they must think a lot of you if you're given the responsibility of teaching others. It's nice to meet you, Maria."

"It's my pleasure, Miss Hibbetts. Alex told me about you and what happened last night."

"Do you think that's wise?" she asked, wrinkling her forehead at Alex. "With all of those questions they were asking me this morning, I didn't think you'd tell anyone."

"It's all right, Miss Hibbetts," Alex said. "She's on my side."

Miss Hibbetts smiled.

"I'm glad to hear that. You're such a sweet girl."

Alex nodded her approval and returned the smile.

"Miss Hibbetts, we've got a problem," she said. "The same people who wanted me to give you the medication last night are demanding that I give it to you tonight. Right now, even as we speak, they're watching us. Don't look up, but beside the television is a video camera. They can't hear what we're saying but they can see what we're doing."

"Well, honey, why would they want to do that?" Miss Hibbetts asked.

"I really can't explain that right now," Alex replied. "Just trust me."

"Well, I don't understand why they'd want me dead," she said, shaking her head. "I'm so old. I don't have long to live and I'm not hurting anyone."

Alex patted the old lady on the arm.

"I know that," she said, "but they're evil men, Miss Hibbetts. In their eyes, you don't have insurance so you're costing the hospital money. That's the bottom line."

The old lady's mouth dropped open. She opened her eyes wide.

"I just find that hard to believe," she said. "Killing an old lady because she's costing the hospital money? They ought to be turned in."

"They have been," Alex assured her. "That's why we're here tonight. The police needed a little more time to gather information for their case and that's where you come in. The men behind this want you dead. Even though you told them you hadn't seen or heard anything last night, they're afraid of you, afraid of what you might've seen or heard. Initially, it was because you had no insurance, but now it's because of fear."

Miss Hibbetts tried to fight back the tears that filled her eyes.

"Are you going to kill me?" she asked through her tears.

"Oh, no. Lord, no, Miss Hibbetts," Alex said. "If I were going to do that, I'd have done it last night."

She placed the blood pressure cuff on the old lady's arm and showed Maria how to check the blood pressure.

"We've got to perform our jobs so they don't get suspicious. You check her pulse and her temperature, while I straighten her covers. Now, Miss Hibbetts, what we've got to do is make it appear that we've killed you. Maria and I will come back later tonight and inject some water into your I.V. You're to wait about five minutes and then move about in the bed as if you're struggling to breathe. Let a minute or two pass and then lay perfectly still. I'll come back in to check on you. And then, when we're satisfied that you're dead, we'll move you out of the room and down to the morgue. All you need to do is stay still and keep your eyes closed."

"But you're not going to kill me are you?" she asked nervously.

"No ma'am. It'll only be water. I know it's hard to understand, but you'll have to trust me."

"Miss Hibbetts, I'm really a police officer," Maria said, grasping Miss Hibbetts' hand. "What Alex's told you is true. Just do as she says and everything will be okay. She'll knock three times on your door when she returns."

Alex patted the old lady on the head, turned out the lights and left the room. Maria followed her into the hallway.

"She seems like a sweet person," Maria said. "It's hard to believe they'd kill her simply because she doesn't have insurance."

"It's more than just not having insurance," Alex replied. "By their logic, she's a financial drain on the system, a system that's already running in the red. If the hospital keeps losing money, it'll close and a lot of people will be out of work. The only way to keep it open is to make it profitable. One way to make it profitable is to terminate those patients who consume resources in excess of the revenues they generate. She's one of those patients."

"You don't believe that, do you?" Maria asked. "The only way to keep it open is to kill patients who can't pay their bills? That's absurd."

"It might seem absurd," Alex replied, "but it's true. We spend way too much money on individuals in the terminal stages of an illness. We're bankrupting our medical system and torturing the terminally ill."

"Then why'd you refuse to follow their instructions?" Maria asked. "Why didn't you terminate Miss Hibbetts?"

"Miss Sanchez," Alex replied, "I was selected by higher powers to alleviate pain and suffering, not needlessly and willfully terminate lives of happy, productive citizens. I'm not a bad person."

"Higher powers?" Maria asked.

"You wouldn't understand," Alex said, shaking her head. "Just believe me when I say I'm not a cold blooded killer. I've only taken the lives of people who, for whatever reason, would be better off dead."

Maria shook her head. Alex was right. She didn't understand. The only higher authority she knew was God, and the last time she checked, He didn't authorize murder for any reason. She walked behind Alex in silence, following her into the medication room. Alex filled a syringe with sterile water and placed it in her pocket.

"Let's wait about thirty minutes before we go back," she said. "Are you sure someone from your office is available to pronounce her dead?"

"Positive," Maria replied. "He's listening to everything we say. As soon as we determine she's dead we can call him and he'll come right over. We've even arranged to have our personnel pose as transportation workers to move her off the floor. Once we get her down to the entrance by the morgue, we'll have an unmarked car waiting to take her to a domiciliary. If they're taping the activity in her room, it should convince them that you've carried out your job. It'll be up to you to arrange a meeting in the morning and have them admit their involvement."

Miss Hibbetts heard the three soft knocks on her door and waited anxiously for what was about to follow. Alex made her way to the bedside while Maria stood just inside the door, out of the view of the camera. Miss Hibbetts' heart pounded as she felt Alex tug on her I.V. Sensing her fear, Alex turned her back to the camera and spoke to her in a quiet voice.

"Don't open your eyes, Miss Hibbetts," she said, "it's just me. I'm going to inject this water in your vein. You won't feel a thing except for the coolness of the water. Remember what we told you to do. I'll come back in about twenty minutes to check on you. We'll have a physician examine you and then we'll put you on a stretcher to take you away. Everything's going to be okay."

The old woman breathed deeply but didn't move. She could feel the cool water entering her vein. Only after she heard the door close did she realize she was alone. Slowly in her mind she counted backwards from one hundred. Still there was silence. She twitched her left shoulder and then her right. Her mouth dropped open as she gasped for air and clutched her chest. Another violent jerk of her body and then nothing. She was dead. At least she wanted whoever was watching her to believe she was dead. It was difficult to remain still. Her respirations were shallow but rapid, the slight rise and fall of her chest wall beneath the covers undetectable.

After what seemed like an eternity, she heard footsteps outside her room. The three quick knocks on her door were reassuring. Alex walked over to the bed and called her name.

"Miss Hibbetts," she said, "I'm going to gently shake you and try to awaken you. Then I'll listen to your chest and check your pulse. I've got to make everything appear realistic. After I do those things, I'll leave the room for a few minutes and return with a police officer posing as a doctor. He'll confirm that you're dead. After he completes his exam, Maria and I will remove your I.V. and clean you up before we transport you downstairs. Try to lay still and keep your eyes closed."

It was hard for her to keep from flinching when Alex grabbed her shoulder and shook her body, but through it all, she remained perfectly still. She felt Alex checking her pulse and let her arm drop limply to the bed when Alex released her wrist. Alex listened for a heartbeat and appearing satisfied that there was none, she removed the stethoscope from her ears and patted the old lady gently on the brow. For appearance purposes, death had come.

Back at the nursing station, Alex told the charge nurse that Miss Hibbetts had died.

"That was rather unexpected, wasn't it?" the charge nurse asked. "I know she was old, but I was told during report she was stable."

"Yeah, I was surprised," Alex replied. "She seemed fine when my shift started. I certainly didn't expect to find her dead."

She picked up the phone and dialed the number Maria had given her. She didn't recognize the voice on the other end.

"This is Alex Lowe on five main," she said. "Are you the physician covering for Dr. McLeod tonight? One of his patients, Ella Hibbetts, has died. I need you to come pronounce her."

She hung up the phone and waited at the nurse's station. Within minutes, the elevator doors opened and a young man in scrubs got off. His face looked strangely familiar.

"May I help you?" the charge nurse asked as he approached.

"Yes, ma'am," he replied, "I'm Dr. Ellis. One of your nurses called about a patient of Dr. McLeod's who died."

"Dr. Ellis, did you say?"

"Yes, ma'am," he replied.

"I'm Linda Whitmore, the charge nurse on five main," she said. "I don't believe I've ever seen you up here before."

"No, ma'am, you haven't," he replied. "This is my first day here. I'm doing a residency at Bethel Hospital in Union City and came to Richland to do a rotation in family practice. As part of the rotation, I've got to take general medicine call every third night. Can't believe I got stuck with call my first night here."

"Well, Dr. Ellis, welcome to Richland," she replied. "If I can be of any assistance during your rotation, please don't hesitate to ask."

"Thank you. Now, do you know which nurse I spoke to?"

"That was me, Dr. Ellis," Alex said, rising from her chair. "I'm Alex Lowe."

As they shook hands, she realized where she'd seen him. He had driven the black car that had followed her to the hospital. For a policeman, he was very convincing as a physician.

"Where's this dead person?" he asked.

He even acted like a resident. A little bit cocky. A little bit brash and arrogant.

"She's in 543," Alex said. "It's at the end of the short hall."

Except for her coloration, Ella Hibbetts looked dead. From a distance, they were unable to detect her breathing. He placed his stethoscope on her chest and listened. He looked at Alex and nodded his agreement that she was dead.

Dr. Ellis scribbled a death note and assured the charge nurse that once he returned to the resident's lounge he'd give Dr. McLeod a call and tell him that Miss Hibbetts had died. Alex removed the I.V. lines while Maria feebly attempted to give the deceased a sponge bath in preparation for transfer to the morgue. When the two young males from the transportation department arrived with the gurney, Maria called them both by name.

"Members of your office?" Alex asked.

Maria smiled.

"We try to think of everything," she said. "If your story is true, we've got to do everything correctly tonight if we're to get the information we need to arrest the others."

The four of them lifted Miss Hibbetts and placed her on the stretcher. Her arms hung limply off the sides of the narrow gurney. Alex folded Miss Hibbetts' arms across her chest and pulled the sheet over her head. Through it all, the old lady remained perfectly still.

"Miss Hibbetts, there are two young men who will take you downstairs where a car is waiting. The police department has taken care of your living arrangements until they can get you a bed back at the nursing home. I don't know that I'll ever see you again, but I hope you know how much I appreciate what you did for me yesterday."

- 34 -

Gerald Warren's secretary was sipping on a cup of coffee when Alex arrived. She looked at Alex but appeared not to recognize her even though Alex had been in the office on several occasions.

"May I help you?" she asked.

"I need to see Mr. Warren," Alex replied.

"Your name?"

"Alex Lowe."

"Do you have an appointment?" she asked curtly.

"No, but I think he's expecting me."

"And the nature of your visit?"

"It's none of your business. He'll know."

The secretary raised her eyebrows and mumbled beneath her breath.

"Have a seat," she said. "I'll see if he's available this morning. He's a very busy man and usually sees people by appointment only."

Gerald was at his desk reading the morning paper when Alex entered. She was surprised to find the other two not present. She'd assumed all three would be awaiting her arrival.

"Miss Lowe, please come in," he said. "I planned to call you later today. Won't you have a seat?"

She preferred to stand but knew it would be easier to engage him in conversation if she sat down. She chose the chair nearest his desk and pulled it even closer.

"If you'd been here about fifteen minutes earlier," he said, "you could've seen the video tape from last night. I was making sure you carried out your instructions."

"Did you have doubts?" she asked.

Gerald shook his head and smiled.

"I'd be lying if I said no," he replied. "You said some things yesterday that concerned me, concerned us. We were worried that perhaps you'd decided to stop participating in our project. We hoped you'd realize it was in your best interest to continue in your present capacity, but we weren't sure."

"It crossed my mind," she said. "It was hard to believe the things Mr. Alford told me about Ben. It was uncharacteristic of him. He's always been so straight laced."

"Did you confront him?" he asked.

"Yes, sir," she replied. "And everything was just like you said. He denied it all. If I hadn't seen the needle marks in his arms and the drug screen, I probably would've believed him. No matter what I said, he denied knowing anything about the poison or the morphine. He even said the needle marks on his arms were where Mr. Alford had been drawing blood for some type of research he was doing. I was amazed at how far he'd go to hide his addiction."

"How much did you tell him about your activity?" he asked.

"Everything," Alex replied.

He turned his head to the side and narrowed his eyes as he looked at her.

"Everything?" he asked.

"Yes, sir. I assumed he knew everything except who was administering the poison. And with him being a junky, I felt even if he told anyone, they wouldn't believe his story. How many drug addicts do you know whom you can trust?"

"Not many," he replied, "not many. But it still concerns me. We could find ourselves in a lot of trouble if someone found out what we're doing here. Of course, I don't think we have any choice if we're to save this hospital, but people outside of our circle might not agree with our methods."

"Do you think it's wrong for us to kill these patients, Mr. Warren?" she asked.

"I don't like to think of it as killing patients, Miss Lowe."

"But that's what we're doing, isn't it, killing patients who can't pay their bills?"

"You may be killing patients, Miss Lowe," he replied, nodding his head, "but I'm saving a hospital."

"The only patients I've killed are the ones you've ordered me to kill."

Mr. Warren shook his head.

"I clearly recall several patients who died under your care before you joined our team," he said.

Alex sat up in her chair and crossed her ankles. She placed her hand against her cheek as she spoke, resting her chin in her palm.

"You still didn't answer my question, Mr. Warren. Do you think it's wrong for us to kill these patients?"

"I don't condone murder, Miss Lowe, but with today's medical climate, it's survival of the fittest. Richland Memorial can't survive if it continues to run in a deficit position. We must be strong financially."

"So, you don't think it's wrong?" she asked.

"It's not wrong to be a survivor, Miss Lowe," he replied.

Alex smiled at him. There was no way he was going to admit his guilt.

"Will I be paid for Miss Hibbetts' death?" she asked, leaning forward in her chair.

He returned her smile and scribbled on his desk pad.

"Do you want to be paid?" he asked.

"I deserve something," she replied. "After all, you paid me when I terminated the other two patients for you, didn't you?"

"I believe you were well compensated for your work."

"Are you going to pay me for killing Miss Hibbetts?" she asked again.

Gerald pulled an envelope from his desk drawer and slid it across the desk to her.

"This should answer your question," he said.

Alex pulled the stack of crisp one hundred dollar bills from the envelope. She licked her fingers to separate the slick bills. Ten bills. One thousand dollars.

"A thousand dollars," she said. "Why the increase? That's double what you gave me for each of the first two."

"You're right," he said, nodding, "but with Dillard gone, you're even more valuable to us. You're our only link to patient care. If we lose you, we lose all access to the patient. We can't afford that, not if we want to survive."

"And there's nothing wrong with being a survivor, right Mr. Warren?" she asked.

"Right, Miss Lowe. We do what we must to survive."

"How many more patients do you plan to kill?"

"That depends upon the economy and the overall medical climate," he replied. "We envision a long range plan in which we terminate those patients who can't financially afford the quality of medical care which they require in order to survive. When we eliminate our losses, we increase our gains. If we can increase our gains, we can become one of the premier institutions in this area. We can buy state of the art equipment and hire the highest caliber of physicians, physicians who can give us national or even international notoriety. If our hospital does well, the four of us will do well."

"Have you selected the next victim?" she asked.

"Victim," he repeated, shaking his head and smiling. "Interesting choice of words. But to answer your question, yes, we have selected the next participant. You'll receive your assignment tonight."

Alex leaned down to tie her shoe and attached a small

transmitter to the leg of his desk.

"So, you're expecting me to kill someone else tonight?" she asked, sitting up.

"Limit resources, Miss Lowe," he replied, smiling. "We expect you to help our hospital limit the utilization of its resources tonight. Do you have a problem with that?"

"No, sir," she replied, "but if it's all the same to you and the others, could I take some time off after tonight?"

"That shouldn't be a problem," he replied.

"When will I find out the patient's room number?"

"Nothing's changed. You'll find your assignment in your locker when you report for work tonight. Now, if there's nothing else you wish to discuss, I've got work to do."

Alex nodded and quietly left the office. Gerald followed her to the door and watched as she made her way across the receptionist's office and out into the hallway. He locked the door leading to his office and walked back to his desk. Bob and Tim would be pleased to learn that everything had gone smoothly.

Maria and Ben were waiting in the hallway for Alex.

"Did I do okay?" she asked. "Did they hear what they needed to hear?"

"I'm sure you did fine," Maria replied, "but I'm not sure how much they heard. Were you able to place the transmitter?"

"I put it on the leg of his desk," she answered. "Will it work from there?"

"It should," Maria said. "It's state of the art."

Ben put his arm around Alex and pulled her close.

"I think I scored big for you last night," he said.

"I pray that you did," Alex replied, hugging her boyfriend.

"I found four vials of poison hidden in a cabinet in the back of the pharmacy," Ben said, "and a zip lock bag with two syringes filled with a clear liquid. It'll be interesting to see what's in them and whose fingerprints are on them."

Alex smiled.

"It'll be very interesting," she said, "especially with Miss Dillard dead."

"But it gets better," Ben said. "I found purchase receipts for the poison signed by Mr. Alford and a hand written list of hospitalized patients selected for termination."

"How can you be sure it's a list of patients for termination?" Alex asked.

"It can't be anything else," Ben replied. "It's got the patients ranked in order of total revenue lost during the hospitalization and even breaks it down into how much is being lost daily. The third name on the list is Ella Hibbetts. The two names above hers have been scratched off."

Alex's took Ben's hands and looked into his eyes.

"I can't believe I was gullible enough to believe the lies they told about you," she said. "I'm sorry I doubted you."

Outside, the sun was shining brightly as the three of them walked in silence to a waiting, unmarked, black patrol car. Maria took out a pair of handcuffs and placed them on Alex as she opened the back door of the car.

"Are those necessary?" Alex asked.

"I wish they weren't," she replied, "but I'm afraid it's departmental policy."

Alex shook her head as she bent down to get into the car.

"I still believe what I was doing was right. I wouldn't have done it if I hadn't been chosen by a higher authority to alleviate unnecessary pain and suffering. I was only doing my job until they interfered. You've got to believe me when I tell you I'm not a bad person."

"We know you've got a good heart," Maria replied, "or you wouldn't have done what you did last night. You've just been misguided."

Ben leaned down and kissed Alex on the cheek. "I've got to tell your Dad and Elizabeth what's going on," he said. "They'd rather hear it from me than read about it in the morning paper.

We'll get you the best lawyer money can buy."

Maria patted Alex on the shoulder and closed the car door.

"I should've confronted her when she first came to me," Ben said, "but she honestly believes she was chosen and given the authority to do this."

"How could she believe she was chosen to take people's lives, regardless of how much they were suffering?" Maria asked.

"I thought you knew," Ben replied.

"Knew what?" Maria asked, shaking her head.

"About her mom."

"No, she never said anything about her. What's wrong with her?"

"She died several years ago after a bout with colon cancer. Her whole family took it hard, but Alex took it the hardest. She had nightmares for months, and then, after the nightmares stopped, she had visions where she'd see her mother and talk to her. She claims her mother told her that she's been chosen to intervene in the lives of people who are suffering and dying."

"Do you believe her?" Maria asked.

"Would you?" Ben asked. "I mean, I don't think she's crazy because she's so rational about everything else, but she claims she's had conversations with dead people. She's my girl friend, and I love her dearly, but that's not normal. Maybe she never fully accepted her mother's death. I don't know. They'd been so close before her mother got sick."

"So she claims she was chosen to take the lives of those people to put an end to their suffering?"

"Yeah, that's what she believes."

"Do you think she honestly believes it or is she using it as her alibi?"

"No," Ben replied, "she truly believes she's been chosen to alter destiny. I saw her after one of her visions. If you could've seen the terror in her eyes you'd understand."

- 35 -

Gerald had the videotape ready to play when Tim and Bob arrived.

"Gentlemen, come in," he called. "I think you'll be pleased with what you're about to see."

The three men looked on in silence as they watched the replay of Alex injecting the deadly poison into Ella Hibbetts' vein. The tape ended after her body stopped jerking.

"I don't know about the two of you, but I'll certainly rest easier tonight knowing she's a team player. I'll have to admit, I had my doubts about her when she left my office yesterday."

"I think we all did. Did she talk to her boyfriend?" Bob asked.

Gerald nodded and smiled.

"Yeah, she did. Folmar denied everything, just like we told her he would. I think the needle punctures were what really convinced her. We're fortunate. If this had happened a few days earlier, we would've had a difficult time convincing her that her boyfriend was hooked on morphine."

"What about tonight?" asked Bob. "Is she going to take out another revenue loser?"

"She's agreed to carry out one more assignment and then take a few nights off," Gerald replied. "I think the stress is getting to her. I had been thinking we'd terminate the young man in bed four of the ICU, the uninsured fellow who was in the car wreck, but she's still hung up on her belief that it's wrong to kill these patients if they're not suffering. With that in mind, I think our next best option is to terminate the uninsured lady up on four west. She's costing us about seven hundred dollars a day and since she's a stroke victim, our little angel of mercy shouldn't object too strongly. Is that agreeable with the two of you?"

"Fine by me," replied Bob.

"Same here," agreed Tim.

Gerald handed each man an envelope.

"You know," he said, "I almost feel guilty making money by killing these poor people. But hell, I'm doing it for the good of the hospital. And what's good for the hospital is good for our community. In fact, we should get recognized at the Kiwanis Club for our community service."

Their laughter was interrupted by a soft knock on the door. Gerald closed the wall behind him, hiding the surveillance room. He opened the door a few inches and looked out.

"I thought I told you not to bother me when my door's closed," he said angrily.

"I'm sorry, sir," his secretary stammered nervously, "but there are some men here who won't take no for an answer."

"They don't have a choice," he replied. "I will not be disturbed when I'm in a meeting. Do you understand?"

"I tried to tell them, sir, but they're from the police department," she whispered.

"Tell them I'm not here," he said, lowering his voice.

"I can't do that, sir. They can hear us talking. Perhaps it would be best if you let them in."

He turned slowly and looked at his two accomplices. There was no mistaking the fear in their eyes as he opened the door.

"We haven't done anything wrong," he whispered behind the door. "Gentlemen, come in. What can I do for you today?"

"Are you Gerald Warren?" the officer asked.

"I am," he replied confidently.

"Mr. Warren, I have a warrant for your arrest."

Tim and Bob quickly looked away.

"As well as warrants for the arrests of Tim Alford and Bob Carlson."

"There must be some mistake," Gerald protested. "I'm the CEO of this hospital. I haven't done anything wrong. None of us have done anything wrong!"

"Sir, each of you is under arrest for conspiracy to commit murder. Anything you say, can and will be used against you in a court of law. You have the right to an attorney. If you can't afford an attorney, one will be appointed for you."

"I can afford any damn attorney I want," he replied loudly. "But you let me tell you one thing, mister, you're making a mistake, a big mistake. I've got friends in high places, friends who won't take kindly to this. You've got the wrong person and someone will pay for your mistake. I haven't killed anybody or conspired to kill anybody."

The policeman ignored the tirade and placed a pair of handcuffs on Gerald's wrists.

"I'll have your job for this," he shouted. "Do you hear me? I've got some very influential contacts in this town."

The second officer placed handcuffs on the other two men and pulled a piece of paper from his pocket.

"Sir, this is a search warrant, granting us permission to search your entire hospital."

"You look any damn place you want," he replied. "We've got nothing to hide here."

The officer squatted by the administrator's desk and removed the small transmitter. He extended his hand in front of Gerald's face, revealing the tiny listening device.

"I believe this belongs to our office," he said with a smile. "It's amazing how well these little things pick up."

Gerald looked at the other two men and shook his head.

"How long has that been there, Gerald?" Tim asked angrily.

"Hell if I know," he answered.

"Long enough," replied the officer. "Long enough."

"Damn it, Gerald! I knew something like this was going to happen! I just knew it!" Bob yelled.

"We haven't done anything wrong, Bob. Just remember that," Gerald replied. "We haven't done anything wrong."

Bob hung his head, shaking it from side to side as the officer led him out of the office.

- 36 -

The Madison County jail was an aging structure built several decades before. The white paint, which had been used to cover the aging red bricks in the mid-eighties, had not been recoated in a number of years and now was losing its grip on the brick and flaking off in small pieces. The narrow windows, each lined with one inch, solid steel bars, allowed the inhabitants of the six small jail cells a glimpse of the outside world. Each cell was designed to hold four prisoners, with rickety, metal bed frames suspended in pairs on the two side walls of each cell. Rusty, metal springs supported the thin, soiled, cotton mattress on each bed frame. A metal drain in the center of the brown, ceramic tile floor in each cell afforded easy clean up of the facility when each week the removable contents of each cell were placed in the exercise yard to air out while the non-movable items were sprayed with a pressure washer.

There were no designated male and female cells in the jail, and at the time of Alex's arrest, the six cells were filled to capacity with drug offenders, purse snatchers, and deadbeat dads who were either behind or refusing to pay their child support. It wasn't often that Madison County had to incarcerate a female felon, so special arrangements were made to accommodate Alex. The cell closest to the front of the jail was vacated for Alex, its four inmates moved into the remaining five cells. While Alex sat alone, isolated in her private cell, the male inmates were crowded into the remaining jail cells, the overcrowded conditions resulting in verbal hostility directed toward Alex.

"If it weren't for the bitch in the front room getting special treatment," one inmate shouted loudly, "we wouldn't be packed in here like damn sardines, and I wouldn't be sleeping on no damn floor. I wish they'd put me in the cell with her. I'd give her some special treatment."

"Better watch you say," another man responded in a quieter voice, " you might get your wish. You'd be better off in here with the four of us. Odds are, ain't none of us gonna' kill you. You get on her bad list and you might wake up dead. I seen the story about her in the newspaper. That girl killed six or seven people before they caught her."

Alex leaned her head against the wall and closed her eyes. Warm, salty tears ran down her cheeks. They hadn't caught her. She'd turned herself in to prevent Gerald Warren from killing other innocent patients.

"You're shitting me," came the loud reply.

"No hell I ain't."

"That skinny bitch ain't big enough to kill nobody," the first man yelled loudly with a laugh. "I'd like to see her try to pull a gun on me."

Alex forced a weak smile, amused that her heckler had called her skinny. Maybe size was like beauty and was in the eye of the beholder. As a size ten, she'd never thought of herself as skinny.

"She don't use no gun," his cellmate replied softly.

"Well, she damn sho' ain't man enough to cut me with no knife," he yelled.

"Don't use no knife, either," came the reply.

"Well, if she don't use no knife and she ain't packing' a gun, then how in the hell did she kill them people? Does the bitch know kung fu?" he yelled.

A chorus of laughter and the sound of tin cups being pulled across the metal bars of the cell doors followed his question. Alex bit her bottom lip, wanting to reply but not wanting to lower herself to his level or enter into a war of words with someone she could not see.

"The girl's a nurse, at least she was before they caught her," the second inmate replied. "She was killing patients at the hospital, injecting them with poisons according to the paper."

For a brief moment there was complete silence in the Madison County jail.

"Damn, she must be a mean bitch," the first man said in a much softer voice. "A nurse is supposed to help people, not kill them. She must be crazy or mean as hell to do something like that."

"I'm not crazy, and I'm not mean, and I didn't kill those people," Alex screamed angrily. "Those people were dying, and I helped put an end to their suffering."

"Well, I sure as hell hope I don't get sick while you're on duty. I'm too young to die," he called back to her.

Alex buried her face in her hands and sobbed softly. Maybe it was a mistake to turn her self in. Maybe she should've gone along with his plan. Maybe she could've convinced him it was wrong to kill patients who weren't suffering. Maybe they could've seen eye to eye and worked together to alleviate pain and suffering while at the same time saving the hospital money. Maybe when the sun rose tomorrow she'd be named president of the United States and could give herself a pardon. Maybe.

"Having a rough day, huh?"

Alex slowly lifted her head. A young sheriff's deputy, with keys in hand, was unlocking her cell.

"You need to ignore those idiots back there. There's nothing they'd enjoy more than engaging you in a shouting match," he said.

"And I fell right into what they wanted me to do," she replied, shaking her head.

"I suppose you did," he said smiling. "If you feel up to having a visitor, I've got someone here who might brighten your day."

"Daddy," Alex squealed excitedly. "I'm so glad to see you."

"Daddy, oh, Daddy," came the echoes from the other cells. "We're so glad to see you."

Philip Lowe wrapped his arms around his daughter. Her body trembled as the metal door slammed behind them.

"How ya' doing, sweetheart?" he asked.

"Not good," she replied, gently pushing him away. She placed her hands in his hands and looked deep into his pale, blue eyes.

"Daddy, do you think I'm a killer?" she asked.

"No, honey, I don't think you're a killer," he replied.

"Do you think what I did was wrong?"

"Sweetheart, I don't know. You're my child, and as your father, I can never allow myself to believe you would intentionally do anything wrong, especially anything to purposefully harm another human being. I think your intentions were good, but maybe a bit misguided."

"But I was chosen to stop people's suffering," she replied. "Mom told me so."

Philip shook his head.

"I know that's what you believe, and I'd like to believe it, too, but I can't. I'm sorry."

Alex dropped her chin to her chest and closed her eyes.

"So, you think I'm crazy?" she asked.

"Oh, no, no, baby. I don't think you're crazy, just misguided," he replied.

"What if they find me guilty? What then?" she asked.

"I'm not sure I understand your question," he answered. "If they find you guilty, it won't change my opinion of you. It won't make me think you're crazy."

"But will it change how you feel about me? Will you stop loving me?" she asked, tears running down her cheeks.

Philip cupped his hands around his daughter's face and leaned toward her.

"I love you because of who you are. You're my daughter. My love for you is unconditional and unending. A jury's decision won't change my love for you."

~ ~ ~

The two months leading up to her trial passed slowly. She was able to endure the daily verbal abuse hurled at her from the other inmates only because of the frequent visits and encouragement she received from her family and Ben. Now as the setting sun casts hues of orange and pink in her tiny cell she found herself looking forward to the next day and the beginning of her trial.

She had drifted off into a restless sleep when a cool breeze blowing across her face and a soft voice calling her name awakened her.

"Alex, are you awake?"

Through the darkness in her cell, she saw the silhouette of a female moving gracefully toward her.

"Who's there? What do you want?" she asked nervously.

"It's okay. Don't be afraid. It's only me."

"Mother?" she asked, squinting in the darkness.

"I was worried about you," her mother replied. "We knew you were having a hard time dealing with this and with your trial starting tomorrow, well, I was just concerned. We all feel a little guilty about how this has turned out. When we chose you, we had no idea you'd end up in such a predicament. If we'd had our way, you would've never gotten involved with them, but we can't control what happens down here."

"You can't control what happens down here?" Alex asked raising her voice. "If you can't control what happens down here then why was I picked to interfere with fate?"

"Honey, we can't really control things that happen here," her mother replied. "We can arrange for certain people to be placed in situations where choices have to be made, choices which will influence people's futures."

"I can understand those cases where people were suffering

and needed help," Alex replied, "but why I was allowed to get involved with Mr. Warren. He took lives for the wrong reason."

"I'm not sure," her mother said, "but I think you were allowed to get involved so you could stop him. If you hadn't stopped him, how many lives would've been lost? And you did prevent the death of Ella Hibbetts. The council says she's got some unfinished business to attend to before she dies."

"But why me?" Alex asked. "Why not someone else who's caring and compassionate? Why was my life destroyed?"

"If he hadn't chosen you, he would've chosen someone else. And who's to say whether that person would've had the courage to stop him. There could've been a lot of unnecessary deaths if the wrong person were involved. Ella Hibbetts might've died without having had the chance to finish her work, and there's nothing as tragic as someone who dies without accomplishing their life's mission. Sweetheart, we're not the only ones allowed to influence what happens on earth. We like to think we are, but just as there are good influences, there are evil influences. The unrighteous walk among the righteous and the unjust as well as the just are allowed to tempt fate. Sometimes what we have to do is place one of our people, someone like you, in a potentially bad situation to limit the effects that evil influences have over the future."

"So, I'm sitting in jail with the likelihood of going to prison or worse and I had no choice in the matter?"

"You've always had a choice," her mother replied. "You didn't have to do what he proposed. You could've refused to go along with his plan."

"And still ended up right where I am," Alex replied angrily. "If I'd refused to go along with his plans, he would've had me arrested for murder. He blackmailed me. I don't care what you say, I didn't have a choice."

"Sweetheart, I didn't come to argue with you. The decision you had to make wasn't easy nor the consequences pleasant, but the fact remains that you did have a choice. And now you've got to make a choice regarding your future. What are your lawyer's plans?"

"I confessed everything to the authorities when I came forward, so there's no way to deny killing those people," Alex replied. "Mr. Hutchinson thinks we should play on the emotions of the court. He feels if we can make the jurors understand my actions were born out of love for those patients, then maybe they'll be lenient on me. He's as much as told me that the best I can hope for is life in prison. And if I'm sentenced to life, I'll serve twenty years at the most. It's so unfair. I was only trying to put an end to needless pain and suffering, and now I'm the one who's suffering and causing my family pain."

"The council thought your lawyer might pursue a verdict of not guilty by reason of insanity," her mother replied.

"That was my decision," Alex replied. "He recommended it but I refused. I'd rather take my chances in prison than live a life of freedom branded as insane. Besides, if I were declared insane, I'd spend more time in a mental hospital than I'd spend in a prison if I were convicted of murder."

"I'm not here to tell you what to do, but I don't think that's wise."

"Why not?" Alex asked.

"I've spoken to people who've crossed over after experiencing life in prison and from what I've been told, it's not a place where you'd want to spend twenty years of your life. A jury's decision doesn't change the person you are."

"I understand that," Alex replied, "but are you suggesting I should plead not guilty by reason of insanity?"

"I'm not allowed to give my opinion," her mother replied, "but if I were, that's what I'd recommend."

Alex closed her eyes and shook her head. She knew her mother was right. She could never survive in prison, not if she were labeled a serial killer. When she opened her eyes the apparition was gone. The air in the cell felt cooler than she remembered.

- 37 -

The county jail was only five blocks from the courthouse but the ride over the pothole filled road seemed to last for ever. Curious onlookers lined the streets, each one hoping to get a glimpse of Richland's own serial killer. Her arrest and impending trial were the talk of the town. The rumor at Pete's Texaco was that she'd tried to commit suicide in her jail cell by hanging herself with her bed linens. The gossip at the beauty shop was that she'd confessed to six murders at Richland but was a suspect in at least ten more deaths across a five state region. The kids at the swimming pool knew for a fact that she'd eaten body parts of some of her victims.

The courtroom was packed by the time she arrived. The mass of people crowded into the small room buzzed excitedly. The air hung thickly as the air conditioner struggled to meet the demands of the overcrowded room. A hush fell over the crowd as Alex and her lawyer entered and took their places at the front of the room.

The strategies of the two attorneys were clear from the onset. One would attempt to paint a portrait of a kind and gentle female acting out of love and compassion for her fellow man, the other to portray her as a cold blooded killer. Each witness was examined and cross-examined as the two sides built their cases.

"Could you please tell the court your name and your relationship to the accused," the lawyer asked.

"My name is Dorothy Muir," the elderly lady replied softly. "I taught Alex in the twelfth grade."

"So you didn't know her well. Is that a fair statement?" the lawyer asked.

"No, sir, not entirely fair. I taught her English when she was in the twelfth grade, but I also served as faculty advisor for the Centurette study club. Alex was the president."

"Did you spend much time with Miss Lowe outside of school," he asked.

"Yes, sir. The Centurettes were called a study club but truthfully, it was about anything but studying. It was more of a social club."

"A social club?" he asked. "What's the purpose of a social club?"

"This club sponsored various events to raise money so the girls could host two dances a year, dances they could invite the boys to."

"So it was strictly social?" he asked.

"No, sir. Not strictly social," she replied. "They served as a civic organization as well. They often volunteered their services to assist charities with various functions."

"Did you attend these functions with the girls?"

"Most of the time. I was their sponsor."

"How did Miss Lowe behave at these functions?" the lawyer asked.

"The way any self-respecting, well mannered young lady would behave." Miss Muir tilted her head and shook it quickly from side to side. "The two of you have repeatedly asked everyone who's taken this stand to testify about this young lady's character and both of you keep getting the same answers. I never heard her say or saw her do anything to anyone which would make me believe she was anything less than a model citizen. I can tell you that her favorite functions involved the elderly. Two or three times each year the Centurettes would visit

Shady Grove Nursing Home. Took them cookies on Valentine's Day. Sang carols at Christmas. The old folks loved it, but not as much as Alex. She'd pat on those old people and comb their hair and feed them their meals. I don't know that I've ever seen a teenager so full of love for the elderly."

"No further questions, your honor."

"You may step down, Miss Muir."

The attorney took the old lady by the hand and assisted her as she stepped down from the witness stand. Her blue hair caught the sun's rays coming through the window at the front of the room. She limped noticeably as she moved slowly back to her seat, the ravages of polio evident in her left leg. She winked at Alex as she walked by.

"Your honor, I call Eloise Christopher to the stand," the prosecuting attorney announced loudly.

The wife of her former patient walked slowly with a walker, taking several minutes to reach the witness stand. Alex shook her head. Miss Christopher appeared so old and feeble, much like her husband had before he died.

"Miss Christopher, do you know Miss Lowe?" the attorney asked.

"Yes, sir," she replied in a soft, warm voice.

"And how do you know her?"

"She took care of my husband, Prince, when he was in the hospital."

"Did she take good care of him?"

"Yes, sir, real good. Before he died, Prince said she was the best nurse he ever had, and he'd spent many a day in the hospital."

"Before he died?" the lawyer asked. "When did your husband die?"

"Several months ago," Miss Christopher replied.

"Was he in the hospital when he died?"

"Yes, sir, he was."

The attorney placed his hands on the railing and leaned toward the witness.

"I apologize, Miss Christopher," he said. "I didn't need to ask that question because I already knew the answer. In fact, your husband died while Miss Lowe was taking care of him, didn't he?"

"Yes, sir, he did," she replied.

"Miss Christopher, were you aware that Miss Lowe untied your husband's hand the night he pulled out his breathing tube?"

"Yes, sir."

"Did she tell you she had untied his hand before he died?"

"No, sir. I didn't know nothing 'bout it, 'til I read it in the paper."

Alex closed her eyes and shook her head slowly from side to side. She'd wanted to tell Miss Christopher herself, and now she wished she had. At least then she could've explained why she did what she did.

"Did Miss Lowe know your husband had a do not resuscitate order on his chart?"

"Yes, sir," she said, nodding her head up and down repeatedly. "We made sure all the nurses knew that he didn't want no resuscitation."

"Do you believe she understood that if his tube came out he was not be re-intubated and could die?"

"Objection!" yelled the defense attorney. "Witness can't possibly be expected to know what my client was thinking."

"Overruled," replied, the judge. "Please answer the question, Miss Christopher."

"Oh, yes, sir. We'd talked about that before and she knew."

The attorney paced back and forth across the front of the room, stopping in front of the witness.

"Miss Christopher," he asked, "is it possible that your husband would still be alive if his hand hadn't been untied that night?"

"Yes, sir, it's possible. The doctor said he could live a long time on that ventilator, but..."

"Just answer the question, please," he interrupted. "Do you believe she knowingly untied his hand?"

Alex clinched her fists and stared down at her lap as she waited for Miss Christopher to answer.

"Mister," Miss Christopher replied, "don't nobody but Miss Alex know the answer to that question. But what if she did? Is that so wrong? My Prince was a suffering and if he hadn't died that night, he'd still be a suffering. Whether she accidentally untied his hand or whether she rightfully untied it ain't nobody's business. Prince pulled his tube out himself. He made the decision to die. She didn't have nothing to do with it, so why don't you leave that poor girl alone?"

The lawyer pinched his top and bottom lips together and pulled them out. In a quite voice he mumbled, "No further questions, your honor."

Alex took a deep breath and raised her head slowly until she made eye contact with Miss Christopher. The old woman's eyes twinkled.

"Thank you," Alex mouthed silently.

Eloise Christopher nodded ever so slightly as she curled the corners of her lips up in a smile.

- 38 -

The third day of the trial brought Alex to the witness stand. She tried to appear poised and confident as she took her place, hoping to conceal from the jury her fear and anxiety. Her heart pounded rapidly as she looked around the courtroom searching for a friendly face. Her father smiled, nodded, and winked his encouragement when her eyes met his. She felt the moisture in her palms as she rubbed her hands together. Elizabeth had convinced her to wear her navy blue dress with the white sailor's collar, telling her it made her look wholesome. She hoped she was right.

"Raise you right hand. Do you solemnly swear to tell the truth, the whole truth and nothing but the truth, so help you God?"

"I do," Alex said softly.

"You may be seated."

Alex watched as her lawyer took a stack of papers from his briefcase. He slid his glasses down to the tip of his nose and peered over them as he walked closer to her.

"Alex, is your family present in this courtroom?" he asked.

"Yes, sir," she replied.

"Could you point them out for us and tell us their names?"

"That's my father, Philip Lowe, on the third row in the navy suit," she said, pointing to the right side of the courtroom, "and my sister, Elizabeth, sitting beside him."

"And is your mother with them?" her lawyer asked.

"No, sir."

"Where is your mother?"

"My mother is dead," Alex replied.

"I'm sorry to hear that. When did she die?"

"Mom died when I was a junior in high school," she replied.

"And that would've been about six or seven years ago, would it not?" he asked.

"Yes, sir," Alex replied.

"Your mother must have died at an early age. What did she die from?"

"From colon cancer," she answered softly.

"Cancer," he repeated, nodding his head. "I don't proclaim to be a medical expert, but I've had friends who've died from cancer. It can be a rather long and drawn out process filled with pain and suffering, both emotional and physical. Did your mother suffer?"

"Objection, your honor," yelled Jason Corley, the prosecuting attorney. "Whether the defendant's mother is alive or dead has no relevance to this case. If counsel has a point, he needs to make it clear to this court."

"Mr. Hutchinson, is there some reason for this line of questioning?" asked the judge.

John Hutchinson gave a nod of his head.

"Your honor," he said, "if the court will bear with me for a short time longer, I will show how the death of the defendant's mother is quite relevant to this case."

"Mr. Corley, your objection is overruled, for now," the judge replied. "Mr. Hutchinson, please get to your point quickly."

"Yes, your honor," he said, smiling triumphantly at his opponent. "Alex, if it isn't too painful, could you tell the court about your mother's death?"

Alex closed her eyes and nodded.

"When Mom was first diagnosed with colon cancer, we all thought there had to be a mistake. She was so vibrant and healthy. She felt fine and looked good. But things changed quickly. By the time she was admitted to the hospital, she was losing weight and having severe pain."

"I'm sure it was difficult seeing your mother in so much pain," he said.

"Yes, sir, extremely difficult."

"Did she suffer very much?"

"Yes, sir. She suffered more than most of the people in this courtroom can even imagine. She had tubes everywhere. Her body swelled to the point that we were afraid her skin would burst. I guess one of the hardest things for us was when she began coughing up blood and gasping for air."

The lawyer shook his head slowly.

"It sounds like she suffered a great deal before she died," he said. "Were you relieved when she finally died?"

"Yes, sir, I was relieved but saddened. When you see a loved one suffer, like Mom did, it changes the way you look at things."

"It changes the way you look at things," he repeated. He paused, rubbing his chin with his left hand. "How so?" he asked.

"Up until the time mom became sick," Alex replied, "I was afraid of death. It was the worst thing I could imagine ever happening to anyone. But after watching her suffer so much, I found myself wishing she could die. On the one hand, I didn't want to give her up, but on the other hand, if death meant the end of her pain and suffering, then I hoped she could die. For the first time in my life, I realized there are things in life worse than death."

"Did you grieve when she died?"

"We all grieved, but I think I took her death harder than Dad and Elizabeth. I took it personally. Here was this person who'd taken care of me all of my life and now she was gone. I found myself disillusioned with life and withdrawing from those around me. I had a lot of unanswered questions."

"What kind of unanswered questions?" he asked.

"Questions about God and how He could allow my mother to be taken from me. And if He knew she was going to die, then why'd He make her suffer so long? It all seemed so unfair. And I guess, truthfully, I had feelings of guilt. After all, I'd prayed that if death was the only way for her to stop hurting, then let her die. As a seventeen year old who'd prayed for her suffering to end, I believed I was partly responsible for her death."

"How well did you cope with her death?"

"Not well at all," she replied. "For months, I had nightmares, nightmares where I'd see Mom struggling and crying out for help, but I couldn't do anything. At times, I thought I was going crazy."

"Alex, have you seen or spoken with your mother since her death?"

"Objection," yelled Mr. Corley, rising to his feet. "Counsel has established that Miss Lowe's mother died many years ago."

"I agree," replied the judge. "Mr. Hutchinson, can you explain your line of questioning?"

"Your honor, if you will allow my client to answer the question, I believe it will become very clear."

"Overruled," replied the judge. "Miss Lowe, please answer the question."

"I've seen my mother on several occasions," Alex answered.

"Seen as in dreams?" her lawyer asked.

"No, sir," Alex replied, shaking her head. "I've seen her just like I see you and everyone else in this courtroom."

"Now, Alex, we've already established that your mother died many years ago so can you please explain to us how you've seen her."

"I know it's difficult for you to understand, Mr. Hutchinson," Alex said, "but my mother has visited me on several occasions."

"Does she appear at your request?" he asked.

"No, sir. I wish she did, but I never know when she'll appear. The first time I saw her, I was terrified. I mean, who wouldn't be? I was afraid to tell anyone about it."

"Afraid of what?" he asked.

"Afraid they'd think I was crazy. Let's face it. If I told you I'd talked to someone who'd been dead for several years, wouldn't you think I was crazy? I questioned my own sanity."

"So, you've not only been visited by your mother, you've spoken with her?"

"Yes, sir. She always speaks to me when she appears."

"Are you telling me you actually hear her talking?"

"Oh, yes, sir," Alex replied. "We've had some long conversations."

"Let me get this straight. You and your deceased mother have conversations on a regular basis."

"I wouldn't say on a regular basis," she replied, "but we've had several conversations."

"When was the last time she appeared to you?" he asked.

"She came to visit me in jail before the trial began," Alex replied.

"Did anyone else see her or talk to her?"

"No, sir. As far as I know, I'm the only one she's ever contacted."

"When was your first encounter with your mother's ghost?"

"Not long after I started working at Richland Memorial, I was taking care of a young man named David Watson. It was a tragic situation, one in which he had a great deal of pain and suffering. I'd gone for months without the nightmares, but I started having them again, only this time they were worse. I had dreams where I'd see Mom and David crying out in pain, asking me to help them. Shortly after that, I had my first encounter with her. It was late one night in the ICU. Everything was quiet, or at least it seemed to be. I noticed an unusual light coming from David's room. When I went into the room, I saw Mom sitting in a chair beside his bed. I was scared to death."

"What'd she say?"

"She told me not to be afraid, that she'd come to comfort me. She looked so peaceful and healthy. I felt uneasy, but I also felt a sense of relief. At least I knew she wasn't suffering any more."

"Was that all she said?"

"No, sir," Alex replied, shaking her head. "She told me that David and his family were suffering, suffering needlessly. She told me he was going to die, but unless someone intervened, it would be after several more years of suffering and with financial ruin for his family."

"Did she ask you to take his life?"

"No, sir," Alex replied. "But she said some unusual things that night."

"What sort of unusual things?"

"She said they were allowed to work with troubled souls on earth to tempt fate and alter destiny."

"They were allowed to work with troubled souls?" he asked, sounding puzzled. "Who was she talking about?"

"At that time, I wasn't certain," Alex replied. "The only thing she said was that a group of people who had experienced undue suffering before they died were allowed to exert their influence on earth to try and prevent others who were destined to die to keep from having to suffer unnecessarily. When I told her I didn't understand what she was talking about, she told me not to worry that one day I would."

"Did she say anything else?"

"No, sir. Someone outside of the room called my name. I looked out for just a minute and when I turned back around, she was gone."

"Alex, could you tell the court what happened then?"

"Yes, sir. I was terribly shaken and in my confusion, I made a horrible mistake."

"What was your mistake?" he asked.

"I accidentally injected a syringe of potassium into the patient's I.V. tubing."

"Excuse my ignorance, but I thought everyone had potassium in their body."

"We do, but when a large amount of potassium is given too quickly in the vein, it can cause heart arrhythmias."

"Again, I must plead ignorance," he replied, "but what is a heart arrhythmia?"

"It's a generalized term for an abnormal heart beat. In the case of intravenous potassium, the arrhythmia is ventricular fibrillation."

"Alex, can you tell the court what happens when one's heart goes into ventricular fibrillation?"

"Ultimately, if untreated, that person dies."

"I see," he said, nodding his understanding. "Did David Watson develop ventricular fibrillation and die?"

"Yes, sir. He did."

"So, you killed David Watson?"

"No, sir, not on purpose. I made a terrible mistake that cost him his life, but I didn't intentionally kill him."

"Did you have any remorse about what had happened?"

"Yes, sir. I was deeply troubled, at first."

"At first?" he asked, surprised.

"Yes, sir. Right after it happened, I was quite upset. But then I learned that what had happened had happened for a reason. David's parents had been struggling emotionally and financially. When he died, they were able to pull their lives back together and start over. And David was certainly better off. At least through death, he no longer had to endure all of the pain and daily suffering."

"Did David's parents tell you this?"

"No, sir."

"Then how do you know? How do you know that his parents, even today, aren't emotionally devastated by the loss of their son?"

"David told me," Alex replied, shrugging her shoulders.

The judge pounded his gavel to quiet the buzzing courtroom.

"Order in the court," he yelled. "Another outbreak like that and I'll clear this courtroom. Counsel, continue your line of questioning."

"Before he died?" the lawyer asked.

"No, sir. It was after he died," Alex replied.

"I'm afraid I don't understand. How could a dead man talk to you?"

"Not long after he died, I was taking care of an old man on a ventilator. His lungs were in such bad shape that he couldn't survive without the ventilator. He'd suffered a stroke in the hospital and could only move one side of his body. We had to keep his arm tied down so he wouldn't pull out his breathing tube. I felt so sorry for him. I thought about Mom and how frightened and uncomfortable she had been on a ventilator. I knew that regardless of what the doctors did, this old man was going to die. I asked him if he understood that if his tube were pulled out he could die. He just nodded his head and smiled. I remember thinking that if he got his hand untied, he might very well extubate himself, and since there was an order that he wasn't to be reintubated, he'd probably die. I untied his hand and left his room. Sure enough, he pulled out the tube and just like I expected, it was only a matter of hours before he died. But I didn't kill him. I may have given him the choice, but he took his own life. Can you blame him? He had no future and no hope for improvement. He only needed a little help in taking his life. If what I did was wrong, then I know some doctors who break the law every day of the week."

"When did you talk to David Watson?"

"After Mr. Christopher died, I saw the same strange blue light I'd seen before, this time coming from Mr. Christopher's room. When I went in the room, my mother was there and so was David. I was terrified. It frightened me seeing mom again but seeing someone who'd died because of my mistake was even more frightening. Mom tried to reassure me and told me not to be afraid. And while her voice was calming, the fact that she and David appeared so healthy and happy was even more reassuring."

"Was that the extent of your conversation?" the lawyer asked.

"No, sir. David told me that everything was okay. My mistake had turned out to be a blessing for him and his family. After he died, he learned he was supposed to live another year or two in a coma in a nursing home if I hadn't intervened and his parents were to suffer through financial ruin with the stress in their lives ultimately leading to their divorce. When David died, he got a new body and was freed from his pain. He told me his parents grieved over his death, but they were able to rebuild their lives. He and Mom told me they knew how much I had struggled with his death. That's why they came back, so they could assure me that David's death was for the best."

Her lawyer folded his arms across his chest, looking first at the jury and then at Alex.

"Alex," he said, "those of us who've never seen a ghost, if that's the correct term for what you say you've seen, have a difficult time believing or understanding what you say has happened to you."

"I can understand that," Alex replied, bobbing her head up and down. "At first, I thought I was going crazy, you know, having conversations with dead people. But then Mom explained how I'd been chosen by the council and that's why she and David had been allowed to contact me."

"I'm sorry," he replied, shaking his head, "but I'm not sure I understand. You were chosen by whom and for what?"

"Mr. Hutchinson, people in our society believe events happen randomly, and most of the time that's true," Alex explained. "But some things happen because chosen people are placed in positions where the decisions they make will drastically alter another person's life. Mom explained that I was chosen by a higher authority to be placed in situations where I'd have the opportunity to influence destiny, primarily situations dealing with pain and suffering. David was a test for me. I found out later that I was allowed to make the mistake of wrongly administering the I.V. potassium. Someone could have walked in on me or asked me if I'd hung the potassium drip on my other patient and prevented my mistake, but they wouldn't allow it."

"Who wouldn't allow it?" he asked.

"The council, the group who selected me," she replied.

"Your honor, this is absolutely ridiculous," interrupted Mr. Corley. "This witness is on trial for murder. I fail to see the relevance of this testimony in which she's giving us the details of a very vivid imagination."

"Sir, it's not my imagination," Alex replied, rising to her feet and leaning toward the prosecuting attorney. "I've had these conversations and whether or not you choose to believe me is entirely up to you."

The judge pounded his gavel loudly.

"Mr. Corley, you're entitled to your opinion but I strongly advise you to keep it to yourself. I find Miss Lowe's testimony quite interesting and relevant. If you doubt her story, you'll be given ample opportunity to cross-examine her. Now, if you will please take a seat and allow her to continue."

The prosecuting attorney shook his head and sat down. If she truly believed she'd been visited by dead people, then she was crazy.

"Alex," her lawyer continued, "do you believe that a council of higher authority in the afterlife has singled you out to alleviate pain and suffering?"

"I know they have," she replied. "I've been told so. But it's not just any pain and suffering. I've only been placed in situations where the individual has a poor quality of life and is suffering unnecessarily, like in the case of Prince Christopher. Mr. Hutchinson, our society works too hard and spends too much money trying to keep people with terminal conditions alive. We prolong their misery and put unbelievable financial and emotional burdens on their families, not to mention the financial drain on our health care system. As a society in a country where we can no longer afford the rising costs of health care, we need to re-evaluate our views of death and the terminal stages of life."

"Your honor, this is all an opinion and is not relevant to this case," the prosecuting attorney yelled.

"Sit down, Mr. Corley," the judge ordered, "or I'll find you in contempt. Please continue, Miss Lowe."

"Alex," Mr. Hutchinson continued, "you've told us about your experiences with David Watson as well as Prince Christopher, and I think we all understand that you feel you've been chosen to manipulate destiny in the lives of certain people, but two isolated events doesn't necessarily set you apart from anyone else in this room. Do you have other examples in which you feel you were given the opportunity to alter fate?"

"Yes, sir. Several months after the incident with Prince Christopher, I had the opportunity to take care of a young man named Billy Jackson who'd been diagnosed with AIDS. His health was failing him but the worst thing was that his family had disowned him. It destroyed him. He knew that with no cure available for AIDS, he was dying. And he could accept death, but he couldn't accept the fact that his own parents had rejected him. Every day, he asked me to help him die. And finally, one day, he got through to me. I injected a syringe of morphine into his vein, knowing that the large dose would make him stop breathing. He died the following morning. When the doctor called his parents to tell them he'd died, they seemed more aggravated by the inconvenience than concerned that he'd died. They wouldn't even come to the hospital."

"Do you realize what you're telling us?" he asked. "You're admitting under oath, in a court of law, that you administered a medication with the sole intent of taking someone's life."

"He asked me to help him end his life," she replied, raising her voice. "What was I supposed to do? Ignore him and allow his suffering to continue? I've been appointed to help those who are suffering when the opportunity arises. I can't refuse to help, especially when someone willingly asks for my assistance."

"Do you believe what you did was wrong?"

Alex nodded her head.

"By the man made laws governing our society, yes, sir, it was wrong. Do I personally think it was wrong? No, sir," she said, shaking her head. "I acted out of love and compassion. If the opportunity arose, I'd do it again."

"Did anyone know about your conversations with your mother?"

"I told my sister, Elizabeth, about them," Alex replied.

"What'd she think?"

"She's here. Why don't you ask her?" she quipped.

"She may end up on the witness stand before this trial is over," he replied, "but for now, I'd like to hear your opinions. What did Elizabeth think when you told her about your conversations with your mother?"

"She thought I was crazy," Alex said, smiling.

"And are you?" he asked.

I don't think so," she replied, "but that's not for me to decide."

"Have you been involved in any other deaths?" he asked.

"Yes, sir."

"More patients in which you believe you were selected by higher powers to alleviate pain and suffering?"

"No, sir," she replied, staring blankly ahead.

"Did your mother return and ask you to take the lives of these patients?"

"No, sir."

"What about David Watson? Did he instruct you to take the lives of other patients?"

"No, sir."

"Alex, did anyone instruct you to take the lives of other patients?"

"Yes, sir."

"And who would that have been?"

"Mr. Warren," she replied, searching the courtroom for his face.

"Do you mean Gerald Warren, the administrator of Richland Memorial Hospital?"

"Yes, sir," she replied, staring at him in the back of the courtroom.

"Do you realize the serious nature of those allegations?"

"Yes, sir, I do. But it's true. He forced me to take the lives of several patients at the hospital."

"He forced you to take their lives?" he asked. "How'd he do that?"

"He found out about the deaths of David and the others and told me if I didn't go along with their plans, he'd go to the authorities and destroy me and my family."

"Let me back up. You said Mr. Warren found out about the deaths of the patients under your care. How'd he find out?"

"I didn't realize it, and I'm sure most people aren't aware of it, but Mr. Warren has surveillance cameras placed throughout the entire hospital."

"Why would he place cameras in the hospital?"

"The hospital was losing money, so Mr. Warren and his associates came up with a plan to cut the hospital's losses. They decided they could save the hospital money by taking the lives of patients who were costing the hospital more money than they were generating. Their only problem was that they needed someone with patient contact to carry out their plan."

The prosecuting attorney stood up and shook his head.

"Your honor," he said, "I object to this line of questioning. Counsel has already established that Miss Lowe has a vivid imagination. Now she's being allowed to use that imagination to implicate one of our city's leaders as being involved in her string of murders."

"Overruled," replied the judge. "Mr. Corley, whether this testimony is real or imagined remains to be seen. Miss Lowe has been sworn to tell the truth. Now, if you're privy to information showing that what she says is not the truth, you'll have the opportunity to cross- examine the witness and refute her testimony. Until that time, I expect you to sit there without interrupting and listen to what she has to say. Do I make myself clear?"

"Yes, your honor," he replied as he sat down.

"You may continue your questioning, Mr. Hutchinson," the judge said.

"What was the purpose of the cameras?" the lawyer asked.

"To spy on the employees. Everyone was being observed. If anyone made a mistake, Mr. Warren and his group knew about it. They knew that at least three patients had died under my care and they showed me the video to prove it. I didn't think I'd done anything wrong but I couldn't be sure that other people would see it that way. Mr. Warren explained his plan to me and threatened to ruin my life if I didn't cooperate."

"Exactly what was his plan and what was to be your role?"

"Mr. Warren and his group would select patients who were costing the hospital money rather than generating money. I'd be assigned to take care of these patients with the sole purpose of terminating their lives."

"Who else was involved with Mr. Warren?"

"Bob Carlson, Tim Alford and before she died, Lib Dillard."

"So, this group of four instructed you to kill certain patients because those patients were losing money for the hospital?"

"Yes, sir. Only, they never used the words kill or murder. It was called limiting resources or terminating resource utilization."

"How many people did you kill for them?"

"Four total. Two for them, one by accident, one out of love and compassion to end her suffering."

"Are you admitting to involvement in four deaths in addition to those which you've already described?"

Alex looked him squarely in the eyes.

"Yes, sir, I am," she said.

"How did you kill them?"

"With injections of lethal doses of medications."

"What types of medications?"

"Morphine or potassium initially, but later on we used a

poison mixture that Mr. Alford ordered from Mexico."

"Do you remember your first victim?"

"Yes, sir. She was an elderly lady named Maggie Cooper."

"How did you kill Miss Cooper?"

"I gave her some sort of medicine in her vein."

"What type of medicine?"

"I'm not really sure, but I think it was morphine. When I got to work that night, there was a syringe filled with medicine and a note in my locker telling me who I was to terminate. I didn't ask any questions. She was old, had no family, and a do not resuscitate order. When I looked at her, I had no doubt in my mind that she'd be better off dead than alive."

"Did you have any remorse about taking her life?"

"Not really," she replied, grimacing. "I don't mean to sound cold, but why should I have remorse? She had a miserable existence. I did her a favor that night by allowing her to die. She's at peace now. But it did bother me that I was being forced to take someone's life and had no choice in the matter."

"Who was next?"

"I don't remember his name," she replied. "He was a young man in the ICU. It was my first night to take care of him but I could tell by reading his chart that he was experiencing pain and suffering. His situation was hopeless. I remember thinking how he could very easily have been someone whose path crossed mine because of fate and not just because of Mr. Warren's plan. I took his life because I feared what Mr. Warren would do to me and my family if I refused. But in my heart, I knew I had done him a favor. I didn't have any remorse about his death either, at least not until Mr. Warren paid me the following morning."

"He paid you?" he asked, surprised.

"Yes, sir. The five of us met in his office early the next morning and everyone was given an envelope of money. He said it was a reward for a job well done. Apparently Mr. Carlson had determined how much money the hospital would save because of each patient's death. I guess part of the savings were passed on to each of us. I think Mr. Warren believed he could strengthen the team loyalty by paying everyone, but personally, getting paid made me uncomfortable, like I was a paid killer."

"Correct me if I'm wrong," Mr. Hutchinson said, "but I thought the purpose of taking lives was to save the hospital money. It seems odd that Mr. Warren would turn around and divide the money the five of you."

"That's what I thought," Alex replied, "but apparently what we received represented only a small part of what was saved. According to Mr. Warren, Richland Memorial has been running in a deficit for several years and the hole is just getting deeper. The problem wasn't strictly that the hospital didn't have its share of paying patients, but rather that it had an unusually high percentage of nonpaying patients. If they could manage to prevent the losses from those patients, the hospital could generate large profits from the paying customers."

"Tell me about your third patient," he said.

"It was the very next night. I was assigned to take care of an elderly lady who looked so old and decrepit. I knew she'd be better off dead. When I called her name, the lady in the bed next to her answered. It startled me. I began talking with the patient in the second bed and found out that she was actually the patient I was to terminate. I went back to the nurse's station and reviewed the records on each patient. I thought there had to be some sort of mistake. Miss Davis, the lady in the first bed, needed to die." Alex looked down at the floor and slowly shook her head. "She was in such bad shape. I felt sorry for her. I knew she had to be hurting. But the other lady, Miss Hibbetts, she was old, but she was spry for her age and she certainly didn't appear to be suffering. She would've already been discharged except there wasn't a nursing home bed available and she had no family to take her home."

"Did you take Miss Hibbetts' life?"

"No, sir. Like I said, I thought there had to be a mistake. There was no reason for them to want Miss Hibbetts dead."

"Did you kill Miss Davis?"

Alex nervously rubbed her palms together and glanced about the courtroom.

"That sounds so harsh," she replied. "I gave her the poison and she did die, but I don't feel like I killed her. Mr. Hutchinson, she was pitiful. Death was the most humane thing I had to offer her."

"Was the group upset when they found out you hadn't terminated Miss Hibbetts.

"Oh, yes, sir. Miss Dillard was the first to find out and she was madder than a wet hen."

"How'd she find out?"

"She was the night nursing supervisor and I believe it was her responsibility to see that I received my instructions as well as the syringes of medication. Because of that, she knew I was supposed to terminate Miss Hibbetts that night. It was strange. The intern on call had just pronounced Miss Davis dead when Miss Dillard appeared at the nursing station wanting to know who'd died. I could tell by the surprised look on her face that she was expecting me to tell her it was Miss Hibbetts, not Miss Davis."

"What'd she do when she found out it was Miss Davis and not Miss Hibbetts who'd been injected?" he asked.

"She was furious. I tried to explain that I felt there'd been a mistake in my instructions, that Miss Hibbetts didn't deserve to die. She told me in no uncertain terms that the only mistake was the one I'd made."

"What'd she mean by that?" he asked.

"She meant the poison was intended for Miss Hibbetts."

"But you said Miss Hibbetts didn't appear to be suffering."

"She wasn't, and I guess that's when I finally realized how ruthless Mr. Warren was."

"Why do you say that?" he asked, shaking his head.

"Pain and suffering was never a consideration in selecting Miss Hibbetts," Alex explained. "It was strictly a financial decision. Miss Davis was a paying customer who was generating money for the hospital. It didn't matter to them whether she was suffering or not. No, sir. They wanted to keep her alive because she was making money for the hospital. But Miss Hibbetts was costing the hospital money. That was her only fault. It didn't matter that she wasn't suffering. She was costing the hospital money so they wanted her dead."

"What happened next?" he asked.

"Miss Dillard told me to meet her in Miss Hibbetts' room," Alex replied.

"And did you?"

"Yes, sir."

"What happened then?"

"Miss Dillard pulled a syringe from her pocket and told me to inject it into Miss Hibbetts' I.V. tubing."

"Did you?"

"No, sir. I knew it was filled with poison and I refused. She told me I didn't have a choice, but I knew differently. Mom had told me I always had a choice, that I never had to take anyone's life if I didn't believe it was for their benefit. Then Miss Dillard said if I wouldn't give the medicine, she would, but she'd tell Mr. Warren and he wouldn't be happy with me."

"Did she give it?"

"She tried, but I wouldn't let her. I couldn't let her. There was no reason to take Miss Hibbetts' life."

"How'd you stop her?"

"When she put the needle into the I.V., I grabbed her wrist. We struggled and the needle came out."

"And?"

"And it stuck in her thigh."

"And the syringe was full of poison?"

"Yes, sir. We both knew she was in trouble. Mr. Alford had warned us that the poison was extremely lethal. A few drops could kill you. She had a look of sheer terror on her face as she ran from the room. I followed after her, but by the time I reached the nursing station, she'd already collapsed across a chair. We tried to resuscitate her but it was no use."

"She died?"

"Yes, sir," Alex answered softly, "unfortunately, she did."

"How'd you feel about that?"

"I felt sorry for her. She didn't deserve to die any more than Miss Hibbetts did. I don't think she wanted to participate in Mr. Warren's project anymore than I did."

"Then why'd she go along with his plan?"

"I don't know, but I figure he must've known something about her which she didn't want known. I think she went along to protect her job."

"Did you intentionally kill her?"

"No, sir!" Alex replied loudly. "I've never taken anyone's life unless I honestly believed they'd be better off dead than alive. Mr. Hutchinson, I've taken the lives of some people, but I'm not a ruthless killer. I believe in right and wrong. I went to the authorities after Miss Dillard's death because I finally realized how wrong it was for me to do what Mr. Warren was making me do."

"Did Mr. Warren know of Miss Dillard's death?" he asked.

"Yes, sir. In retrospect, he probably knew within a few hours after it happened."

"How'd he react?"

"He called me to his office early that morning and asked me if I knew anything about it. I didn't realize that he already knew what had happened so I told him she'd probably died from a heart attack."

"You lied to him?"

"Yes, sir. But I was afraid to tell him what had really happened."

"What happened then?"

"Mr. Carlson was with him and became very upset. He slammed his fist on the desk and said I was lying. That's when Mr. Warren showed me the videotape of what had happened that night. He had everything on tape."

"Everything?" he asked, dropping his chin to his chest and looking upward at Alex.

"Yes, sir," Alex replied, "everything."

"What happened when you realized they knew about Miss Davis and Miss Dillard?" he asked.

"I got scared. Mr. Warren wanted to know if I'd gotten my assignment and if so, why hadn't I followed my instructions. He blamed me for Miss Dillard's death. He said if I'd done what I was instructed to do, she wouldn't have died."

"How'd you feel about that?"

"It's like I told him. I didn't stick the needle in her thigh. She did. Any way you look at it, an innocent, undeserving person was going to die that night because of Mr. Warren's desire for power and self preservation."

"Was that the end of your meeting with Mr. Warren?" he asked.

"No, sir," Alex answered. "Mr. Warren told me that Miss Dillard's death had been officially listed as a myocardial infarction. He'd gone to great lengths to assure that an autopsy wouldn't be performed. He said if anyone discovered that she'd died from poisoning, it would draw too much attention to us and force him to stop his operation. I couldn't believe he planned to continue taking the lives of innocent people simply because they were costing the hospital money, not after what happened to Miss Dillard."

"Did you tell him that?"

"Yes, sir, I did. He told me everyone was sorry Miss Dillard had died, and how she'd been such a vital part of our team, but that her death was no reason for him to hold off on his plans."

"So, did he ask you to kill again?" he asked.

"Yes, sir," Alex said, nodding her head. "He told me he expected me to terminate Miss Hibbetts that night. He never said kill. It was always terminate. I couldn't believe what I was hearing. I thought I'd made it clear to him that I wanted out."

"You wanted out?" he asked.

"Yes, sir. I wanted out."

"Out of what?"

"Out of my association with the three of them, out of their lives. I didn't want to be involved with their plan any more."

"Was Mr. Warren surprised when you refused to take the lives of any other patients?"

"No, sir. I think he expected it."

"Why do you say that?"

"After I refused to kill Miss Hibbetts, he told me he had enough evidence against me to send me to prison, and possibly to the electric chair. That's when I told him that I wasn't afraid of prison or death. You see, Mr. Hutchinson, he hasn't seen the other side. He doesn't know what I know. He hasn't had conversations with someone who's passed beyond. He doesn't understand death the way I do. Death doesn't scare me. The only reason I took those people's lives was because I knew death offered them a new beginning with freedom from pain and suffering."

"How'd he react to your reaction?"

"That's when he told me that my boyfriend, Ben Folmar, was involved in his operation."

"What was his involvement?"

"He wasn't involved. They only wanted me to believe he was involved so I'd cooperate. They told me he was a drug addict who was hooked on morphine. They showed me order forms with his signature authorizing the shipment of the poison to the hospital pharmacy and told me they had syringes filled with the poison with his fingerprints on them."

"Did you believe their story?"

"No, sir. At least, I didn't want to believe them. I knew Ben was too good to be involved with such a ruthless group of people. But as I thought about it, I considered myself too good to be involved, and yet I was."

"Was that the end of the conversation?"

"Almost. When I told them I didn't believe what they were telling me about Ben they showed me a drug screen with his name on it where he'd tested positive for morphine. They even told me to confront him, but for me to expect him to deny it. They said if he denied it, I should look at his arms."

"And why was that?" he asked.

"Mr. Warren told me if I looked closely, I could see the needle marks from the morphine injections in Ben's antecubital fossa."

"I'm sorry," he said. "You'd see the needle marks where?"

"In his antecubital fossa," Alex replied, "in the crook of the elbow, the place where most junkies shoot up."

"Did that make you believe their story?"

"It made it hard for me not to believe it. They were very confident and cocky. Before I left, Mr. Warren told me to confront Ben and to look for the needle sticks. If they weren't there, then everything I'd been told was a lie and I should go to the police. But if they were there, then he was telling the truth and I'd ruin both of our lives and our family's name if I went to the authorities."

"Did you confront him?"

"Yes, sir," Alex replied, "and he denied everything."

"What about the needle sticks?" he asked. "Were they present?"

"Oh, yes, sir. Both arms. It made it hard for his to convince me that they were the ones who were lying rather than his."

"How'd he convince you?" he asked.

"I'm not sure," Alex said, slowly shaking her head. "He told me that everything they'd told me was a lie and that he wasn't involved. I guess when he finally swore on his mother's grave, I knew he was telling me the truth. Ben never swears on his mother's grave."

"But what about the needle sticks on his arms?"

"It was all part of their elaborate plan to frame me and Ben if anything ever went wrong. For weeks, Mr. Alford had been drawing blood from my Ben's veins. He told him he was doing a study on electrolyte levels in acutely ill patients and wanted to use him as a control subject. The repeated venipuncture gave the appearance of intravenous drug abuse. They were scared that sooner or later I'd refuse to cooperate with their plans, so they went out of their way to fabricate evidence and lies about Ben to ensure my long term participation."

"But you turned yourself and them in to the police. Evidently, their plan wasn't quite elaborate enough."

"No, sir. When Ben convinced me that he wasn't involved, I broke down in his arms and cried. I knew I was in trouble, but I was afraid to go to the police. I was afraid that if Mr. Warren found out he'd have me killed. But he made me realize that each time I took a life, it was captured on videotape, videotape which they'd use against me if the need ever arose."

"So, you and Ben went to the police station and told them just what you've told us today?"

"Yes, sir, except I didn't tell them anything about my visits with Mother."

"Why not?"

"I didn't think it was necessary," she replied. "I mean, I didn't want them to think I was crazy and just blow me off. If they didn't take me seriously, then they might not believe what I was telling them about Mr. Warren. And if they didn't go after Mr. Warren, then I'd turned myself in for nothing."

John Hutchinson nodded his head as he walked back and forth in front of the jury.

"When you told the police your story, what was their response?" he asked.

"Disbelief at first," Alex replied, "but then intrigue. It's not often that someone walks into the Richland police department and confesses to a series of murders, and then implicates some of the town's leaders as being involved."

"Have you been in jail since then?"

"No, sir. I wasn't locked up until after they arrested Mr. Warren and the others the following morning."

"So, you turned yourself in, admitting to them that you'd committed several murders, and they let you walk out of the police station? Why?"

"Mr. Warren had given me instructions to terminate Miss Hibbetts that night. I was afraid if I didn't show up for work, they'd know I'd talked to the police and if they thought I'd gone to the police, I was afraid they'd kill Miss Hibbetts. I felt they were afraid of her and what she might've known about Miss Davis' death. When I told the detective my concerns he felt they'd need more evidence to convict someone of Mr. Warren's social status and asked if I'd help them get it."

"And did you?"

"Yes, sir. I carried out my instructions that night and went by Mr. Warren's office the next morning. He had taped everything and seemed very pleased. We talked about what had happened that night and what the plans for the future were. I was wearing a wire so the police could hear our conversation, including when he admitted to paying me for terminating patients. Before I left his office I placed a microphone on the leg of his desk. After I left his office, the police recorded a conversation in which Mr. Warren, Mr. Alford and Mr. Carlson talked about getting paid when the patients were terminated."

"Did the three of them actually admit to killing patients?" he asked.

"No, sir," Alex said, shaking her head, "because the three of them never actually killed anyone. But they admitted to paying me to kill patients. Doesn't that make them accomplices?"

The lawyer ignored Alex's question.

"No further questions, your honor," he said.

- 39 -

Alex shifted nervously in her chair as Jason Corley walked slowly toward the witness stand. The golden frame of his glasses reflected the sun's rays coming through the window. He removed his glasses and dabbed his forehead with a red, silk handkerchief. John Hutchinson had tried to prepare Alex for this moment but no amount of coaching could calm her fears. "Stay calm and keep your poise," she said to herself, remembering his advice. "There's nothing Mr. Corley would like better than to see you get upset and lose your temper in front of the jury."

"That's quite a story you've told everyone today, Miss Lowe. Quite a story. I only wish I believed it," he began.

"Objection. Mr. Corley is accusing my client of perjury," Mr. Hutchinson interrupted.

"Sustained," replied the judge. "Counsel will keep his opinions to himself."

Mr. Corley nodded his agreement.

"Miss Lowe," he said, "you've admitted your involvement, either directly or indirectly, in the deaths of at least seven people. Is that correct?" he asked, pacing back and forth.

"Yes, sir. But..."

"But, were it not for your actions," he said, cutting her off in mid-sentence, "how many of those people do you feel would still be alive today?"

"Objection," yelled her lawyer. "There's no way for the witness to know what the future held for any of those people."

"Overruled, Mr. Hutchinson. The witness will please answer the question."

"I don't know," Alex answered. "They could all still be alive or they could've all died because of other reasons."

"They could all still be alive," he echoed slowly. "Did I hear you correctly, Miss Lowe?"

"Yes, sir," she replied, "but they could also all be dead."

"I don't deny that, seeing that everyone will die some day. But the fact remains that had you not intervened, each of those individuals could still be alive. Correct?"

"Yes, sir," Alex replied softly.

"You don't know for a fact that any of your victims would have died were it not for your actions, do you?"

"No, sir."

"Miss Lowe, do you believe in miracles?" he asked.

"I don't know," she said, shaking her head. "I've never witnessed a miracle."

"Have you ever seen the wind?" he asked.

"No, sir."

"Do you believe there is such a thing as the wind?"

"Yes, sir," Alex replied, nodding her head and wrinkling her brow.

"Even though you've never seen it?"

"Yes, sir."

"Let me ask you again," he said. "Do you believe in miracles?"

"I don't know. I prayed for a miracle when my mother was dying, but nothing happened. She only got worse and had to endure more pain and suffering than you can imagine. If miracles exist, then why didn't my mother receive one?"

"Miss Lowe, I will ask you again. Do you believe in miracles?"

"Yes, sir," she replied reluctantly. "I guess I do, it's just that I've never seen one."

He smiled and nodded having coaxed the answer he wanted from her.

"Isn't it possible, Miss Lowe," he asked, "that one or perhaps all of those patients could have received a miracle and been restored to good health?"

"Well, yeah, it's possible," she replied, "but..."

"Earlier today, you told us you were not a ruthless killer and that you believed in right and wrong. Is that correct?"

"Yes, sir."

"Miss Lowe, do you believe it's wrong to kill someone?"

Alex paused, staring off into space.

"Mr. Corley, I believe it's wrong for someone to have to suffer needlessly when there's no hope for their future."

The lawyer smiled and nodded.

"I agree," he said, "that it's unfortunate that some individuals have to endure severe pain and suffering during their lives. But we established earlier that we don't really know what the future holds, not if we believe in miracles. Now, do you believe it's wrong for one person to take another person's life?"

"According to the laws set down by our society," Alex replied, "it's wrong to take another person's life. What you've got to try and understand is that even though I'm obligated by man to abide by the laws imposed upon society, I've been chosen by a higher authority to do whatever I can to alleviate pain and suffering."

The prosecuting attorney walked back to where he had been sitting and opened his briefcase. He held a black book high in the air as he turned to face Alex.

"Do you recognize this book?" he asked as he walked to the witness stand and handed Alex the book.

"Yes, sir," she replied.

"And could you tell the court what book you're holding?"

"The Holy Bible," she answered softly.

"Are you familiar with the teachings in the Bible?" he asked.

"Yes, sir," she replied, "I was raised on its teachings."

"Could you turn to page eighty-nine, please?"

Alex leafed through the thin paper pages of the Bible until she found page eighty-nine. She stopped and looked up at him.

"Have you found it?" he asked.

She nodded.

"If memory serves me correctly, you are in the book of Exodus, specifically, chapter twenty. Could you read verse thirteen aloud to the court?"

Alex cleared her throat and swallowed hard.

"Thou shalt not kill," she read in a low voice.

"Could you read it again, only this time, a bit louder?" he asked.

"Thou shalt not kill," she said, raising her voice.

"Miss Lowe, do you know whose words those are?"

"Yes, sir."

"Whose words are those?" he asked.

"They're the words of God as recorded by Moses," Alex replied.

"In fact, Miss Lowe, isn't that one of God's ten commandments, one of His laws?"

"Yes, sir," Alex said, staring at the floor.

"Was it God who authorized you to take the lives of those people?"

"No, sir."

"Miss Lowe, do you know of any power or authority in heaven or on earth who you would say is higher than God?" he asked.

"No, sir."

"But yet, you say you were chosen by a higher authority to alleviate pain and suffering, even if it meant taking someone's life to achieve that objective. Miss Lowe, there is no authority higher than God, is there?"

"No, sir," Alex replied.

"In fact, you've not been authorized by any so-called higher authority to alleviate pain and suffering, have you? In your mind you've created encounters with your mother and others who have died to try and rationalize actions that you know are wrong. Thou shalt not kill. You're correct in saying it's a law of our society. But you were raised to know that it's a law of our society only because it was first a law of God. Miss Lowe, you've never spoken to your deceased mother or to David Watson, have you?"

"Yes, sir, I have," Alex argued earnestly.

The judge pounded his gavel, quieting the courtroom audience.

"Miss Lowe, perjury is a crime," the attorney said. "I will ask you again. Do you truly believe you've had conversations with your deceased mother?"

Alex's lawyer jumped to his feet.

"Your Honor, Mr. Corley is badgering the witness," he yelled. "She has already answered his question."

"Sustained," replied the judge. "Prosecution will not repeat questions which have already been answered by the witness."

Mr. Corley nodded his acknowledgment.

"Miss Lowe," he said, "do you know if anyone else has ever had contact with your deceased mother?"

"No, sir, not that I'm aware," she replied.

"Don't you find it a bit unusual that your mother would choose to appear only to you, and not to your father or sister also?"

"No, sir."

"And why not?"

"Because they weren't chosen to alter destiny," she replied.

The lawyer lowered his head and paced back and forth in front of the juror's box before coming to a stop directly in front of Alex.

"Do you think you're mentally unbalanced?" he asked. "After all, in our society, people who hear voices and claim to speak with dead people are considered mentally ill."

“If you’re asking me if I’m insane, the answer is no,” Alex replied defiantly. “Mr. Corley, I understand how hard it is for you to believe my story. I doubted what I was seeing and hearing in the beginning. I thought I was losing my mind, but then I realized I wasn’t crazy. I was having contact with someone who had passed beyond this life as we know it. I’m sure you won’t believe me when I tell you this, but my mother appeared to me the night before the trial began and told me that my only hope for not going to prison was to pursue insanity as my defense.”

“Did you ever stop to think that she may be right?” he asked.

“Oh, yes, sir,” she replied. “Mr. Hutchinson and I discussed it, and I realize that since I’ve openly admitted my involvement in these cases that insanity may be not only my best defense, but in many people’s eyes, my only defense. But, you see, sir, I’m not insane and I’m not a murderer. I’ve done nothing more than some of our physicians have been doing for years. Our courts don’t convict them when they assist terminally ill patients with suicide. There comes a time in life, when the joy of living is completely overshadowed by the pain and suffering of survival. A time when, without a miracle, death is the ultimate, humane pain killer. I can’t count the number of times during my mother’s illness when I found myself thinking that she would be better off dead, that we would all be better off if she was dead. I hope and pray that if my health ever deteriorates to the point that I’m unable to enjoy life because of physical pain or the lack of intellectual capacity that there will be someone who has enough compassion and courage in their heart to hasten my exit from this world.”

The prosecutor found himself at a loss for words and stared blankly at Alex. She freely admitted her involvement in the deaths of which she was accused, and now she adamantly denied that she was insane. In fact, her reasoning would lead one to believe that she was quite rational. His goals had been to establish her guilt and to prove that she was competent to stand trial. He had met his goals but as he looked into the eyes of the jurors, he feared that he had taken his line of questioning too far. He knew that her final statement had completed the picture that he had tried so hard to distort. She wasn't a ruthless killer. She was a caring and compassionate individual who had acted out of love. If the truth were told, she was the kind of person he would like to have take care of him if he were to ever find himself in such a hopeless situation.

"I have no further questions, your Honor."

"The witness may be excused," replied the judge.

John Hutchinson hugged her as she sat down beside him.

"You did great, Alex," he said. "You really did!"

"This court is adjourned and will reconvene tomorrow morning at nine o'clock," the judge said, pounding his gavel on his desk.

The officer placed the handcuffs on Alex's wrists and led her out of the courtroom. Her father kissed her on the cheek as they made their way down the courthouse steps.

"I'm proud of you," he said. "You handled yourself well today. Your mother would've been proud if she could've seen you."

Alex smiled and leaned her head against his shoulder.

"She knows, Dad," Alex replied. "She was there today."

"You saw her?" her father asked.

"No, sir. I didn't see her, but I know she was there. She wouldn't have it any other way."

"Get some rest, honey," he said. "We'll see you first thing in the morning."

- 40 -

The courtroom was packed when Alex arrived the following morning. Her palms were sweaty as she took her seat near the front of the room. She scanned the face of the jurors, hoping to find a glimmer of hope in their eyes.

John Hutchinson paced back and forth in front of the juror's box delivering his closing argument.

"...and what she did is not unprecedented in our society," he said. "This young lady, my client, acted out of love for her fellow man. Her only desire was to put an end to the needless pain and suffering which these people were being forced to endure. If she were a prominent physician, her actions would be looked upon as assisted suicide and she would be appearing on television talk shows telling our nation why she did what she did. But she wouldn't be facing the possibility of life in prison. Our courts have already ruled in cases like this and have found those physicians innocent of any wrongdoings. The issue you must decide today is not whether Alex Lowe took anyone's life or whether her actions allowed others to take their own lives. She has admitted to that from the very beginning. The issue you must rule upon today is whether or not she is guilty of wrongdoing because she is a nurse rather than a doctor. Do we have a double standard in our society? That is what you must decide."

"A double standard? That's not what this trial is about." Jason Corley stopped near the corner of the juror's box and wiped the sweat from his brow. "I don't think anyone here doubts the fact that Alex Lowe is a caring and compassionate individual. After all, she is a nurse. Her chosen profession has compassion as its very cornerstone. Miss Lowe has openly admitted that she's taken the lives of no less than seven people. Whether or not these people were suffering is not the issue. In fact, how can she know that someone who can't communicate, someone like David Watson or Minnie Davis, is suffering. The question we must decide today is whether or not it is wrong to take another human being's life, regardless of the circumstances. The prior court rulings in which physicians have assisted patients in committing suicide have no bearing on this case. The circumstances are completely different and should not influence your decision today. If you find the defendant not guilty, you'll be sending a message to nurses everywhere that it is okay to indiscriminately kill patients who they feel are experiencing unnecessary suffering. I don't know about you, but I find that scenario frightening. We cannot give our nurses licenses to kill. Alex Lowe knows that what she did was wrong. She has admitted that it is against the law to take someone's life. She told you that there is no higher authority than God and read to you from the Bible that 'thou shalt not kill'. A double standard? The only double standard is for her to say that killing is not wrong when it's carried out under the pretense of compassion. You can't allow her to walk out of this courtroom as a free woman, free to take the life of anyone she perceives as suffering unduly."

He walked across the courtroom and closed his briefcase. Her future was out of his hands.

"Ladies and gentlemen of the jury, you've heard the testimonies of these witnesses," the judge said. "It's your job to determine whether Alex Lowe is guilty of the charges brought against her."

Mr. Hutchinson took her by the hand and, after the courtroom cleared, led her to a small room adjacent to the courtroom. Alex sat down backwards in a wooden chair, her chest pressed tightly against the back of the chair, her chin resting on the top rung of the chair as she stared out the window.

"Is it hot in here, or is it me?" she asked.

"I think it's you, Alex," he replied. "I'm comfortable and I've got my coat on."

Alex bounced her feet rhythmically up and down on the wooden floor and nervously tapped her fingers on the rungs of the chair.

"How do you think it went in there?" she asked.

"As good as we could hope," he replied. "I'm proud of the way you handled yourself. You could've done yourself a lot of damage if you'd allowed Jason to upset you. He would have loved for the jury to see some anger in you."

"It was hard not to get mad, but I remembered what you told me," she replied.

The soft knock on the door startled Alex. Her heart jumped into her throat.

John Hutchinson opened the door and smiled at Alex. "Relax," he said. "It's just your father, sister and boyfriend."

Alex breathed a sigh of relief.

"I thought they were coming to tell us the jury had reached a verdict," she said. "I was afraid they'd found me guilty if they had reached a decision that quickly."

"They probably haven't even selected a foreman, yet," her father said, placing his arms around her. "I bet it'll be a while before we hear anything."

"I tend to agree," John echoed. "There's a lot of evidence for them to consider."

"Regardless of the outcome, John, I want you to know we think you've represented Alex well," Philip said. "I believe everyone in that courtroom, other than the prosecuting attorney, knows that Alex did what she did because of her love for those people."

"Thank you, Philip, that means a lot to me," he replied. "But don't be upset with Jason. He's a good lawyer who plays by the rules. He's only doing his job."

"Well, I think he needs a new rule book," Ben said.

"I understand how you feel, but he didn't do anything I wouldn't have done if the shoe was on the other foot," the lawyer replied.

Philip walked across the room and pressed his nose against the window. He sighed deeply as he turned back around.

"I hesitate to bring this up," he said, "but if the jury does return a guilty verdict, what happens then?"

"You must think they're going to find me guilty," Alex said, bursting into tears.

"No," her father replied, "I don't necessarily believe they'll find you guilty, but we should be prepared. They've only got two choices, guilty and not guilty. If they find you not guilty, and I pray they do, then we all smile and go home. But if they find you guilty, then we need to know what to expect."

John nodded his head.

"If the jury returns a guilty verdict, Alex will be taken back to jail until she's sentenced. Sentencing usually shouldn't take too long. And then we begin the appeals process. I won't rest until we get a not guilty decision."

The next five hours passed slowly as the four of them sat in the cramped room making small talk to pass the time. With each knock on the door, Alex's heart raced. Late that afternoon, with the sun slipping behind the trees, the word came that the jury had reached their verdict.

"Say a prayer for me," Alex said, kissing Ben on the cheek and squeezing her father's hand.

"I've been praying for you since this ordeal began," Philip replied as he embraced her tightly.

A hush fell over the crowd as the jury made their way back into the courtroom. Alex rocked slowly back and forth as the jurors took their seats. Her father placed his arm around her sister and lowered his head anticipating the verdict.

"Have you reached a verdict?" the judge asked.

"Yes, your Honor."

"Would the defendant rise?"

Alex squeezed her lawyer's hand as she stood.

"Would the foreman please read your verdict for the court?"

"We, the members of this jury, find Alex Ellen Lowe not guilty of the charges brought against her. We would like to make it clear to this court that we do not condone her actions but we do understand her actions and believe her actions emanated from a strong love and compassion for her fellow man. With your honor's approval, we would like to recommend that she receive psychiatric evaluation and counseling, and in addition, that she perform a minimum of two hundred hours of community service."

Alex put her hands over her face and lowered her head, trying to hide the tears streaming down her cheeks. The judge pounded his gavel to quiet the noisy courtroom.

"Miss Lowe," he said, "the jury has found you not guilty of murder. Why? I'm not sure. I don't know that I agree with their decision, but it is a court of law and I'm obligated to abide by that decision. I hope and pray that you'll recognize the error of your ways and quit living in your make believe world of apparitions and councils of supreme beings who've chosen you to alleviate pain and suffering. Don't misunderstand me. As humans, we're obligated to help our fellow man, but we're not given the right to take another's life under any circumstance. I'll take the recommendations of the jury under advisement and within the next seventy-two hours will notify you of my decision regarding psychiatric evaluation and community service. I see a lot of wasted potential in you. You've taken a noble profession and disgraced it. I hope, for your sake, I never see you in my courtroom again. This court is dismissed."

- 41 -

Marcus Steele was well known in Richland as much for his good looks as for his abilities. With his slicked back, black hair, chestnut eyes, and muscular build, he presented an imposing figure in the courtroom. Since he hadn't lost a case in over five years, it came as no surprise when Gerald selected him for his defense. The two of them looked as if they'd stepped off the cover of GQ magazine when they entered the courtroom wearing expensive suits and wing tip shoes. They appeared confident to the point of arrogance as they made their way to the front of the room. The brash lawyer liked nothing more than being center stage with all eyes focused upon him.

Alex sat with her father, Elizabeth and Ben in the rear of the warm, crowded courtroom listening to the opening statements from the two opposing lawyers. The strands of hair around her face curled into tight ringlets as she perspired as much from the heat as from her anxiety. She fanned her face rhythmically with a cardboard fan stapled to a tongue depressor handle. Her stomach churned as she watched Marcus Steele strut in front of the jurors.

"I think I'm more nervous today than I was before my trial started," she whispered to Ben.

"It's okay," he answered softly, "they can't hurt you now."

"Ladies and gentlemen," Mr. Steele said, "I stand before

you this morning representing Gerald Warren, a man known to many of you as one of the leaders of our community. As the administrator of Richland Memorial Hospital it's been his job to ensure the financial soundness of our hospital. And that has not been an easy task. But while hospitals of comparable size in cities similar to our own have been shutting their doors, he's had the vision to move Richland into the twenty-first century. Through innovative, cost saving initiatives he has insured the survival of our town's hospital. Unfortunately, he is also responsible for many of the cutbacks and lay-offs which have occurred at Richland over the past twenty-four months. Hard feelings often arise when employees are terminated and it's human nature to wish harm on the one who has harmed you. My client has been accused of masterminding a plan in which patients at his hospital were murdered under the guise of saving the hospital money. Those of you who know Mr. Warren understand how inconceivable these charges are. His accuser has recently been tried for murder, but was found not guilty. We're not here to question that verdict or to try and have that verdict reversed. But what I will do in the coming days is show you beyond a reasonable doubt that the accusations against my client are entirely false, and in fact, were made by an individual whose sanity we must question. His accuser has admitted, under oath, that she took part in the events that culminated in the deaths of these patients. When she learned that my client had gathered evidence against her and was preparing to go to the police, she turned herself in to the authorities and fabricated an elaborate story in which she accused him of having patients killed in an attempt to save the hospital money. His accuser has a very vivid imagination, even to the point of believing she's had conversations with dead people. My client is not the evil man she has portrayed him to be. He is the true gentleman whom the people of this community have known for years and when the evidence is presented, it will show that he is an innocent man."

"They can't send me to prison," Alex whispered tearfully, "but they can hurt me."

Mr. Steele surprised everyone by calling his client as his first witness. There was an air of confidence about the hospital administrator as he made his way to the witness stand. As he sat down, he faced the jurors and methodically looked each of them in the eye showing that he had nothing to hide.

"Mr. Warren, could you tell this court what you do for a living?" his lawyer asked.

"I'm the administrator at Richland Memorial Hospital."

"How long have you served in that capacity?"

"Twelve years," he replied.

"Twelve years," the lawyer mused. "That's a long time. You must be a very capable administrator for the hospital to retain your services for that many years."

"I like to think so," he replied.

"During those twelve years, has Richland Memorial experienced any financial difficulty?"

"No more so than any other hospital of comparable size."

"So there have been some financial problems?" his lawyer asked.

"Yes, sir," he replied. "I'd dare say that any hospital with less than three hundred beds has had some financial difficulties in today's environment of medical change with lower reimbursements, DRG's, and increasing percentages of Medicare and Medicaid patients."

"Have you taken any actions to try and strengthen the economic position of the hospital?"

"Yes, sir. Last year we were forced to lay off about twenty percent of our nursing staff. We've also implemented programs designed to lower the costs of the care rendered for certain medical conditions. From a personal standpoint, I haven't accepted a raise for the past five years. I realize it's not much, but I can't justify taking a raise when my institution is trying to cut costs to survive."

"By laying off nurses, you undoubtedly saved the hospital money, but if you have fewer nurses taking care of the same number of patients, haven't you compromised patient care?"

"Unfortunately, yes. Our nurses are overworked and can't possibly provide the same level of care they provided before the cutback. Now, that's not to say we don't provide excellent care at Richland, because we do. But if you look at the trend nation wide, the level of care provided in most hospitals today is inferior to the care given just five years ago. I don't mean to say that today's nurses are less competent. They aren't. They're just overworked, and under-paid. I put the blame on the government and third party payers. As reimbursements continue to decline, quality of care will mirror that decline."

"We're definitely overworked and underpaid," Alex mumbled.

"Mr. Warren, you mentioned the implementation of programs to help save money. What types of programs?"

Gerald sat up straight in his seat and adjusted his coat.

"Well, for example," he said, "if you're admitted to our institution with pneumonia, your physician may order an antibiotic which is very expensive. We now have protocols in place that allow us to substitute a less expensive antibiotic without that physician's approval. We have similar protocols for treating most common infections as well as protocols to follow for heart failure, chest pain, and back pain. I'm not convinced that protocols, or cook book medicine, as the physicians so fondly refer to it, provide the best care for the patient, but there's no doubt it saves the hospital money. In today's market, if you don't reduce costs and conserve money, you don't survive. None of us enjoy the changes we're being forced to make, but we really don't have a choice."

"Mr. Warren, are you familiar with the charges brought against you?" the lawyer asked.

"Yes, sir, I am," he replied, smoothly.

"You've been accused of orchestrating a rather elaborate

plan in which you've had people, patients at your hospital, killed in order to save your hospital money. Is that true?"

"That's the accusation, but it's a lie," he answered, shaking his head. "I've never been involved in any such situation."

"He's lying," Alex whispered to Ben, squeezing his thigh.

Ben placed a finger against his lips. "Shhh," he said. "Let's hear what he has to say."

"Does your hospital have cameras in the hallways and in patient's rooms?" asked the lawyer.

"Yes, sir, it does."

"Are cameras commonly found throughout most hospitals?"

"No, sir."

"Could you explain, then, why your hospital is equipped with so many cameras?"

"We began installing cameras about two years ago for two reasons. The primary goal was to enhance our security efforts. There are very few places in our hospital that are not under surveillance. It gives our staff an added sense of security knowing that not only the hospital, but also the grounds and the parking deck are being monitored. We live in a world of violence where there is no respect for human life. The monitoring system gives our employees a sense of security. The second reason was to improve patient care. We selectively monitor our employees and the job they do. We've already discussed the fact that because of the financial climate we're short-staffed. The video cameras allow us to monitor the interactions between our employees and our patients. If we see employees not working or not providing quality care, we terminate them. There's too much competition in the market place for us to provide inferior care. The nearest hospital is over an hour away, but if we don't provide excellent care for our local people, they'll go elsewhere."

"Was Alex Lowe one of your employees?"

"Yes, sir. Miss Lowe was a registered nurse at our hospital."

"Was she a good employee?"

"Yes, sir, one of our best, at least at first."

"At first?" the lawyer asked, cocking his head. "What do you mean?"

"She'd worked at our facility for about a year. If memory serves me, she came to us straight out of nursing school. She was always pleasant and worked hard. Patients and coworkers had nothing but praise for her. On the surface, she appeared to be the ideal employee. But I guess it's like the old saying, you can't judge a book by it's cover."

"How so?" his lawyer asked.

"The cameras had been installed for only a few months when we began to take notice of Miss Lowe's actions. When it was first brought to my attention, I was horrified. Here was one of our most respected employees committing the unthinkable."

"And what was that?"

"We had taped footage of Miss Lowe injecting a medication into a patient's I.V."

"But she's a nurse. Isn't that what nurses do?"

"Yes, but this time it was different. After she injected the medication, she had a terrified look on her face, as if she'd done something terribly wrong. The tape showed her leaving the room only to have the patient experience a cardiac arrest. The medical staff responded to a code blue, everyone but Miss Lowe, that is. They worked frantically, but the patient died. It seemed odd that Miss Lowe wasn't involved in the code seeing that it was her patient."

Alex sat quietly in the back of the courtroom and shook her head. How could he sit there and lie? David Watson was a 'No Code'. There hadn't been any frantic attempts to resuscitate him.

"Do you know where she was?" the lawyer asked.

"I learned later that she was in the snack bar," he replied. "One of the employees on the night shift working the snack bar had seen Miss Lowe that night. The employee thought she appeared distraught, almost dazed I believe was her exact description. When Miss Lowe left the snack bar, she pulled something from her pocket and discarded it in a paper cup. The employee's curiosity got the best of her and she pulled the cup from the trash can. When she unfolded the cup, she found an empty syringe. She gave the syringe to Lib Dillard, the night supervisor. When Miss Dillard confronted Miss Lowe about the syringe, she denied that she had been the one who'd thrown it away."

"Was your employee able to identify her as being the one who'd discarded the syringe?"

"Yes, sir, she did. But Miss Lowe denied that she'd even been in the snack bar. When Miss Dillard told me about the incident, we reviewed the tapes from that night. That's when we saw Miss Lowe inject something in the patient's I.V. just before he died. It seemed too coincidental. We had the lab analyze the few drops of liquid remaining in the syringe, and that's when we became suspicious."

"What was in the syringe?"

"Potassium chloride."

"Mr. Warren, what's the significance of finding potassium chloride in the syringe?"

"Potassium chloride, if given too quickly or in too large of an amount intravenously, can kill a person. When we reviewed the records of the patient who died that night, the same patient who Alex Lowe had been caring for, we found that his blood contained toxic levels of potassium. He'd died because of an injection of potassium chloride. Alex Lowe had killed him."

"If you felt certain she'd killed him, then why didn't you go to the authorities?"

"We had no doubt that she'd administered the potassium, but we didn't know if it was intentional or accidental. Miss Lowe had always been a model employee, so we wanted to give her the benefit of a doubt. Murder is a serious charge to bring against someone."

"Was she disciplined in some way?"

"No, but we began monitoring her every move. We knew to which patients she was assigned and what types of care those patients would require. If she made a move, we captured it on tape."

"Were your suspicions confirmed?" he asked.

"Unfortunately, yes," he replied, nodding. "Shortly after the potassium incident, another patient met an untimely death under Miss Lowe's care."

"What happened this time?"

"She was taking care of an elderly gentleman with end-stage emphysema who had suffered a rather debilitating stroke. It was an unfortunate and sad situation. He was on a ventilator and was having difficulty weaning from the machine."

"In laymen's terms, Mr. Warren, what do you mean when you say he was having difficulty weaning from the machine?"

"His lungs were in terrible condition, so much so that whenever his doctors tried to take him off the ventilator, he was unable to breathe on his own. If he came off the ventilator, he would die."

"And what happened to him?"

"As I said, he'd experienced a devastating stroke which left him paralyzed on one side of his body. His good hand had to be restrained to prevent him from pulling out his I.V. line and his endotracheal tube. That night, Miss Lowe untied his good hand and left him unattended. As soon as she left the room, the old fellow pulled out his endotracheal tube. Since his family had made him a 'No Code' he couldn't be re-intubated. He died within hours."

"Is it possible that Miss Lowe just made a mistake?" the attorney asked.

"Anything's possible, and that's why we still didn't go to the authorities. We didn't feel comfortable accusing her of murder without having more concrete evidence. Two patients had died under her care, but both deaths could have been accidental."

"Did you acquire more evidence?"

"Yes, sir, and, unfortunately, it didn't take long. A few nights later, we taped her as she injected a medication into the I.V. of another patient, another patient who died, that is. But again, we didn't have absolute proof that whatever she'd given him had caused his death. Unlike her first victim, this patient didn't die for almost two hours, so it couldn't have been potassium that she gave him. When we looked closely at the videotape, we noticed that his breathing slowed considerably just before he died. It raised our suspicions that she'd given him a narcotic or a sedative. His autopsy confirmed high levels of morphine, but when we reviewed his chart, he wasn't on morphine."

"Let me get this straight. You've now witnessed three deaths which you think were engineered by Miss Lowe, but still you elect not to go to the authorities. That seems a little strange, doesn't it?" Mr. Steele asked.

"Not really," Gerald replied, shaking his head. "We still didn't believe that the evidence was strong enough to convict Miss Lowe. After all, we had tapes showing her untying one patient's hand and giving I.V. medications to two other patients, things which nurses normally do."

"We? Who else knew about the video tapes?"

"I suspected we had a problem when Lib Dillard first brought me the potassium syringe, so I asked her to help me monitor Miss Lowe's actions. I knew if my suspicions were accurate, I'd need other witnesses. Because of that, I showed the tapes to our chief financial officer, Bob Carlson, and to the head of our pharmacy, Tim Alford. I probably would've come forward sooner had it not been for them. They were the ones who urged me to proceed slowly and cautiously. 'Don't turn her in until you are certain of what she is doing.' That's what they told me."

As if involved in a carefully scripted play, Bob Carlson and Tim Alford nodded their heads in unison.

"Did she kill again?" the lawyer asked.

"Yes, sir. Not long after that, she was videotaped injecting a medicine into the I.V. of an elderly patient. Maggie Cooper, I believe, was her name."

"Did Miss Cooper die?"

"Yes, sir, and quickly. It wasn't more than five minutes after she injected the medication into her I.V. that the old lady began jerking like she was having a seizure. When the seizure stopped, she was dead."

"Was that her last victim?"

"No, sir. She killed three more times. Her next victim was an elderly lady named Minnie Davis. We captured everything on tape. This time we felt certain that she'd committed murder. The tape clearly showed her injecting a medicine into the patient's I.V. line. In only a matter of minutes, Miss Davis' body began jerking violently, like Miss Cooper had done. Then, she went limp. Whatever Miss Lowe had given her had obviously taken her life."

"Did you go to the authorities at that time?"

"No, sir. We didn't learn of Miss Davis' death until the following morning when we reviewed the tape. It was then that we learned that Miss Lowe had also taken the life of Lib Dillard. It was horrible sitting there watching the tape."

Mr. Steele paused and rubbed his chin as if in deep thought.

"Up to this point," he said, "Miss Lowe had only taken the lives of patients. Why do you suppose she elected to kill a fellow employee?"

"I can't be sure," the administrator replied. "The three of us watched the tape several times, but without having the audio available, we could only speculate as to what transpired between the two of them that night. We assume that Miss Lowe was attempting to take the life of another patient when she was confronted by Miss Dillard. When Miss Dillard tried to stop her, a struggle ensued. During the struggle, the needle stuck in Miss Dillard's leg. Whatever was in the syringe must have been potent. Miss Dillard was dead within minutes."

"That's a lie and you know it!" Alex screamed as she jumped to her feet.

Ben quickly grabbed her arm and pulled her down to the seat.

"Order," the judge yelled, pounding his gavel. "Order in the courtroom." He shook his finger at Alex. "Young lady," he said, "one more outburst from you and I'll be forced to remove you from this room. Do you understand?"

"Yes, your honor," Alex answered softly, collecting herself and slumping down in her seat. "It's all lies," she said, grinding her teeth. "All lies and he knows it."

"I know, honey, but you can't yell out like that, not if you want to stay in the courtroom. You'll get your turn to speak," Ben whispered as he wiped the tears from her eyes.

"So, now you feel confident," Mr. Steele continued, "that Miss Lowe is indeed murdering patients, and not only patients, but one of your own employees who was aware of her activities. But yet, you still didn't go to the authorities. Why?"

Gerald Warren shifted his weight and sat up straight in his chair.

"Bob, Tim and I discussed it at length," he said. "We needed more than just the tapes and our suspicions. If we could determine what she'd injected into Miss Davis and Miss Dillard, then we could go to the police. Tim recommended we search the pharmacy and reminded us that Miss Lowe's boyfriend, Ben Folmar, was one of his pharmacists. He'd been concerned about him for some time, but had never imagined that he could be involved with Miss Lowe's activities. When Tim went through the pharmacy's purchase orders, he found something quite disturbing. On two occasions, Ben Folmar had ordered crotalotoxin."

"Son of a," Ben whispered, biting his lip. "Now he's lying about me. I'd never heard of crotalotoxin until your trial and

I'd certainly never ordered it."

"Mr. Warren, what is crotalotoxin?" Mr. Steele asked.

"We were uncertain ourselves," he replied. "Tim phoned the company from which Mr. Folmar had ordered it. You can imagine our shock when we learned that it was a mixture of poisons so deadly that when only a few drops were injected, death ensued within minutes. From there, it wasn't hard to put two and two together. Mr. Folmar and Miss Lowe were conspiring together to take patient's lives. Mr. Folmar was ordering the medicine and preparing the syringes. Miss Lowe was using the poison to take the lives of innocent people."

Mr. Steele opened his briefcase and withdrew a pink sheet of paper and a plastic bag containing a syringe that he handed to his client.

"Mr. Warren, do you recognize these items?" he asked.

Yes, sir. The paper is the order form containing the authorization to ship the crotalotoxin to our pharmacy. It's signed by Ben Folmar. The plastic bag contains a syringe."

"Do you know anything about this syringe?"

"Yes, sir," he replied, nodding. "That's the syringe Alex Lowe used to kill Lib Dillard. One of the nurses on the night shift saw it fall from Miss Dillard's hand just before she died. When the contents were analyzed, it confirmed our suspicions. The liquid in the syringe was the crotalotoxin."

Mr. Steele took a sheet of paper from his pocket and handed it to the judge.

"Your honor," he said, "you have before you the results of forensic testing on the syringe and its contents. You will note that the syringe was found to have the fingerprints of only three people, Alex Lowe, Lib Dillard, and Michelle Banke, the nurse who turned it in to my client. As Mr. Warren stated, the analysis of its contents revealed a mixture of various toxins and poisons, any one of which when injected is potentially lethal."

Alex slid down in her seat and closed her eyes. She'd fully intended to return to the nurse's station and retrieve the syringe but had forgotten to do so. At least it hadn't been introduced as evidence against her in her murder trial. Obviously, Gerald Warren had felt the syringe would be more beneficial in proving his innocence than in proving her guilt.

"Have you had a chance to review this report?" the judge asked, turning toward the prosecuting attorney.

"Yes, your honor," Stacey Pitts replied.

"You may resume your line of questioning, Mr. Steele."

"Did you go to the authorities after you received this toxicology report, Mr. Warren?"

"I received the report on the morning of my arrest. Unfortunately, by then Miss Lowe had killed again."

"When did she strike again?"

"On the night before my arrest, the night after she killed Lib Dillard and Minnie Davis. We knew then that she had to be stopped."

"Who did she kill?"

"Ella Hibbetts," he replied, shaking his head, "one of the sweetest ladies I've ever known. Miss Hibbetts and her sister lived next door to me when I was a child. She practically raised me."

"So, you knew this victim?"

"Yes, sir. She was like family to me. I would have given anything in the world if I could've prevented her death."

"How was she killed?" he asked.

"I reviewed the tape just before I was arrested. Miss Hibbetts convulsed after Miss Lowe injected something into her vein. She died within minutes. It had to be the poison."

Alex smiled and clinched her fist.

"Were you surprised when you were arrested?" the lawyer asked.

"In a way, yes, but in a way, no," he replied. "We'd asked Miss Lowe questions about some of the patients who had died. She was always very defensive. When I questioned her about Lib Dillard's death, she became indignant with me. The very idea that I would think she was involved in Miss Dillard's death astounded her. I even showed her the videotape and told her I knew she'd wrestled with Miss Dillard before she died. She told me she'd stumbled upon Miss Dillard trying to inject something into Miss Hibbetts' I.V. When she confronted her, they began fighting. The needle plunged into Miss Dillard's leg. The court knows what happened after that. I told Miss Lowe we'd be keeping a close eye on her. When she left my office that morning, I had a very uneasy feeling about her. I didn't trust her but I never imagined she'd concoct such an incredible story and try to shift the blame to me."

"Mr. Warren, are you aware that Miss Lowe was found innocent in her recent trial?"

"Yes, sir. And it's certainly not my job to question our judicial system, but frankly, I was quite surprised by the verdict. I mean, with the evidence presented against her and the fact that she confessed to the murders, it's difficult for the average citizen to understand how she could be found innocent. Now, to top it off, I'm being forced to stand trial because of her accusations."

Mr. Steele nodded his agreement.

"I have no further questions, your honor," he said.

Wiping the sweat from his forehead, he returned to his seat, never taking his eyes off the jurors.

"Your witness, Mr. Pitts," said the judge.

Stacey Pitts walked slowly to the front of the courtroom, the metal taps on the heels of his shoes clicking as he walked.

"I would like to remind the jury," he began, "that we're not here to retry Alex Lowe. She has been tried in a court of law and found to be not guilty. I believe we all understand that she has openly admitted that some actions on her part did indeed result in the deaths of several patients. That's not the issue today. The question we're faced with is whether or not Gerald Warren, after learning of Miss Lowe's actions, coerced her into taking the lives of other patients for the sole purpose of saving money for Richland Memorial Hospital."

He stopped pacing and looked at the accused.

"Mr. Warren," he said, "you stated earlier that Richland Memorial has been experiencing some financial difficulties. Is that correct?"

"Yes, sir."

"Is it unusual for a hospital like Richland to lose money?"

"No, sir. Not at all."

"For how many years has Richland been losing money?"

"We've lost money for the last three years."

"For the last three years," the prosecutor echoed, nodding his head. "How far in the red is your hospital, Mr. Warren?"

"By making cutbacks in our staff," the administrator replied, "we significantly decreased our losses last year, and at the current rate, we'll break even this fiscal year."

"Mr. Warren, how much money has the hospital lost over the last three years?" he asked.

"We've lost four and a half million dollars," Gerald replied.

"That's a lot of money, Mr. Warren. A whole lot of money," Mr. Pitts replied. "I understand that by laying off almost a fifth of your nursing staff last year, you were able to save the hospital a tidy sum of money. Is that correct?"

"Yes, sir. We reduced our operating costs by almost six hundred thousand dollars."

"That's very impressive," he replied, "very impressive. Six hundred thousand dollars is quite a savings. But how much money did your hospital lose last year?"

The witness' voice was low, almost muffled. "Half a million," he replied.

"Could you speak up, Mr. Warren?" the prosecutor asked. "I'm not sure everyone was able to hear your answer."

"Half a million dollars," he said, raising his voice. "We still lost half a million dollars."

"Mr. Warren, you stated earlier that the hospital had implemented programs to save money. Were those programs in place last year?"

"Yes, sir."

"So, with all the layoffs and money-saving programs which had been instituted, your hospital still lost five hundred thousand dollars. Is that correct?"

"Yes, sir."

"Mr. Warren, when does the fiscal year begin for Richland Memorial?"

"We run from October through September."

"If my math skills serve me, with this being March twenty-third, you're about six months into this fiscal year. Did I understand you to say that so far this year your hospital is almost breaking even?"

"That's correct," Gerald replied, holding his head high in the air.

"That's quite a turn around, Mr. Warren. Did you make further cuts this year in your staffing?"

"No," he replied. "There haven't been any more layoffs, if that's what you're asking."

"What about new programs?" he asked. "Do you have any new money-saving programs in place this year which weren't operative last year?"

"As a matter of fact, yes. We've added a new protocol which has reduced our operating costs."

"What type of protocol?"

"It's a cardiovascular protocol," the witness replied. "Our cardiologists have been using Isodye, a new, cheaper contrast agent to perform arteriograms, and by doing so are saving us about eight hundred dollars per catheterization."

"And does that account for the roughly two hundred and fifty thousand dollars which you have miraculously saved over the first six months?"

"No, but I'd estimate that it's saved us at least seventy-five thousand dollars."

"That leaves approximately one hundred seventy-five

thousand dollars in unaccounted savings. How did you save that much money, Mr. Warren?"

"We've cut deals with several pharmaceutical companies. Those deals are saving us about fifteen thousand dollars each month."

"Six months at fifteen thousand dollars per month," Stacey Pitts replied, pulling a calculator from his coat pocket. "Ninety thousand dollars. That still leaves roughly eighty-five thousand in unaccounted savings. What have you done to save Richland Memorial that much money?"

Gerald fidgeted nervously in his chair. "I don't know exactly," he replied, clearly irritated by the line of questioning. "There are a lot of small things. A thousand dollars here, five thousand dollars there, another ten thousand dollars somewhere else. I can't keep track of everything."

"But isn't that your job?" asked Mr. Pitts. "Aren't you the hospital administrator?"

"Yeah, I'm the administrator," Gerald replied through clinched teeth, "but it's not my job to know how much money is saved by each little change we make. It's my job to look at the bottom line, and the bottom line is that we've taken the necessary steps to ensure the survival of Richland Memorial Hospital."

The defense attorney stared at his client until they made eye contact with one another. He wrinkled his forehead and motioned with his hands for his client to calm down. Gerald took an extra breath, momentarily closed his eyes, and nodded his acknowledgment.

"And I would admire your efforts, Mr. Warren," the prosecuting attorney continued, "were it not for one thing. The additional savings which you can't explain were generated by taking the lives of nonpaying patients." He rested his hands on the wood railing of the witness stand and leaned forward. "Isn't that true, Mr. Warren?" he asked.

"I don't know what you're talking about," Gerald replied,

shaking his head.

"Mr. Warren, do you know the approximate cost for a day of treatment in your intensive care unit at Richland?"

"No, sir. There are so many variables that it would be almost impossible to determine a day's cost without knowing the specifics about the patient's condition."

"True, Mr. Warren, very true," he replied. "The exact cost of care definitely depends upon the patient's condition. But for simplicity's sake, let's assume a patient who requires the very minimum level of care. How much would that cost per day?"

"I can't say for certain, but we've done studies which suggest a minimum cost of one thousand dollars per day in ICU."

Mr. Pitts looked at the calculator in his hand.

"So, even with a conservative estimate, it costs your institution roughly seven thousand dollars per week to care for a stable ICU patient?" he asked, showing the defendant the total on his calculator.

"Yes, sir," the administrator replied.

"How much does it cost each day to care for the typical patient not in an intensive care unit?"

"Again, I'm guessing," Gerald said, shaking his head, "but probably between three and five hundred dollars per day."

"Roughly, two thousand to thirty-five hundred dollars per week," the prosecutor replied, again looking at his calculator. "Is that correct?"

"You're the one with the calculator," Gerald snapped.

Marcus Steele raised his eyebrows and glared at his client who shrugged his shoulders.

"Please answer the question, Mr. Warren," the judge said disdainfully.

"Yes, sir," Gerald replied. "That sounds about right."

"Do you have any patients at your facility who are unable to pay their hospital bills?" the lawyer asked.

"That's a ridiculous question. Of course we do. All hospitals do."

"Are some of those patients cared for in the ICU?"

"I'm sure some of them are."

"And are any of them cared for outside of the ICU?"

The witness sighed and stared in disgust at the prosecuting attorney. "Yes, they are," he said.

Mr. Pitts folded his arms across his chest and raised his chin. "When an uninsured patient without private funding is admitted to your hospital, who pays their bill?" he asked.

"Usually no one," Gerald replied, stiffly.

"And what happens to that bill?"

"We try to collect as much as we can, but usually write off the majority of it."

"You write it off? Do you mean your hospital assumes a loss on the care of that patient?"

"Yes. We assume a loss on the care of that patient," he replied, sounding quite aggravated.

"You told us earlier that your hospital lost approximately five hundred thousand dollars last year. Isn't it true, Mr. Warren, that most of those losses can be directly attributed to the relatively large volume of indigent patients who receive their care at your institution?"

Marcus Steele jumped to his feet, his face beet red.

"Objection!" he shouted. "The number of indigent patients in our community has absolutely nothing to do with the charges brought against my client."

"Overruled," replied the judge. "Please answer the question, Mr. Warren."

"Because of our demographics, we do have a large number of indigent patients who receive medical care at our hospital. And since we're a federally-funded hospital we have no choice but to provide medical care for them."

"I will ask you again," Mr. Pitts continued. "Isn't it true that your hospital has been losing money because you have so many nonpaying patients?"

Gerald rubbed his eyes and ran his fingers through his hair. The entire courtroom waited in complete silence.

"Yes," he stated, "we lose money each year because we take care of so many patients without funding."

The prosecutor smiled ever so slightly and nodded his head.

"Mr. Warren, let's suppose you have a chronically ill patient on a ventilator occupying one of your ICU beds. And let's suppose that this patient is uninsured and his family is unable to pay his bills. Now, I assume that the longer this patient stays in your hospital, the more money your institution loses. Is that a fair assumption?"

Gerald looked at his attorney who shrugged his shoulders and nodded his head.

"Yes, I suppose that's a fair assumption."

"The only way for you to cut those losses is to get that patient well so they can be discharged or else for that patient to die. Do you agree?"

Gerald paused and glanced uneasily around the courtroom. "Yes, sir. I suppose you could look at it that way."

"Mr. Warren, do you ever have patients who teeter on that fine line between life and death, patients who are too sick to ever leave the hospital but too strong to die?"

Gerald folded his arms across his chest, clearly disgusted by the line of questioning.

"I imagine that sort of situation occasionally arises," he spat.

Mr. Pitts smiled and nodded his head ever so slightly.

"Do the names Ella Hibbetts, Jason Bradley, and Maggie Cooper mean anything to you?" he asked.

"I'm familiar with them," he replied. "If memory serves me, they're three of the patients that Alex Lowe admitted to killing."

Alex closed her eyes and lowered her head. It hurt hearing someone say that she had killed the three of them.

"Your memory serves you well," Mr. Pitts replied, "for indeed they are. Are you also aware that the three of them were costing your hospital a significant amount of money each day they were kept alive?"

"No, I wasn't aware of that."

Alex shook her head from side to side. "How can he sit there and blatantly lie under oath?" she whispered where her father and Ben could hear. Ben put his arm around her shoulder and pulled her close. Her father patted her lightly on the thigh.

The attorney walked to the table, his shoes clicking as he walked. He took a piece of paper from his briefcase and handed it to the defendant.

"Mr. Warren, do you recognize this document?" he asked.

"No, I can't say that I do," he replied.

"Can you tell the members of this court exactly what you see on this document?"

"There appears to be a list of names."

"Just names?" he asked.

"And some numbers, too," he replied.

"What's the first name on the list?"

"Maggie Cooper."

"And the second name?"

"Jason Bradley."

"And the third name?" Mr. Pitts asked.

"Ella Hibbetts," he replied, the tone of his voice never changing.

"How many names are on the list?"

"Ten," he answered.

"And I believe you said there are numbers beside each name. Is there a heading above the column containing the numbers?" Mr. Pitts asked.

"Yes, sir."

"Could you please read that heading for us?"

"Loss to date," he answered softly.

"Is there anything different about the first two names?"

"No, sir," Gerald replied, shaking his head.

"Is there a line drawn through each of the first two names?" the lawyer asked.

"Yes," he replied flatly.

"Mr. Warren, would it surprise you to learn that out of the other eight names on that list, five are in your hospital, too sick to go home, but too strong to die? And the other three names are the names of former patients, two of whom went home several weeks ago, and one who died last month?"

Gerald stared blankly at the back of the courtroom.

"Please answer the question, Mr. Warren," the judge instructed.

"I wasn't aware of that. But no, it doesn't surprise me."

"Is this your handwriting, Mr. Warren?" the lawyer asked.

"No, it doesn't appear to be," Gerald replied.

"Do you recognize this handwriting?" the lawyer asked.

"No. Can't say that I do."

"Is this Bob Carlson's hand writing?"

"How should I know?"

"He's the hospital's accountant. I thought you might recognize his writing. For the record, a handwriting expert has confirmed that this is indeed Mr. Carlson's handwriting. Mr. Warren, have you ever seen this piece of paper?"

Gerald shook his head.

"No, I can't say that I have," he replied.

"Are you certain?" Mr. Pitts pressed.

"Absodamnlutely!" Gerald replied angrily in a loud voice.

"A simple yes or no will suffice, Mr. Warren," cautioned the judge.

"Mr. Warren, isn't it true that the names on this list are the names of patients who were selected to be terminated because they were costing your hospital money, and in fact, the first two names have a line drawn through them because they've already been killed?"

"That's absurd, Mr. Pitts! If what you're suggesting is correct, then Ella Hibbetts would have a line drawn through her name."

"Mr. Warren, I believe the only reason Ella Hibbetts

doesn't have a line drawn through her name is because you were arrested before you had time to cross her off the list. No further questions, your honor."

"The witness may be excused," the judge said.

Gerald Warren walked slowly from the witness stand, never making eye contact with the jurors, the cocky swagger now absent from his walk. He sat down by his lawyer and stared blankly off into space. Marcus leaned over and whispered in his ear.

"You did fine," he said. "It was my mistake to put you on the stand first. I'll call Tim next. He'll shift the focus back to the Lowe girl and her boyfriend."

- 42 -

Tim Alford appeared nervous and uncomfortable as he took the witness stand. His forehead glistened with sweat. His starched white shirt appeared tight around his neck. He tapped his fingers nervously as Mr. Steele approached.

"Mr. Alford, what is your responsibility at Richland Memorial?" asked Mr. Steele.

"I'm a pharmacist," he replied.

"Are you in charge of the hospital's pharmacy?"

"Yes, sir, I am."

"Would you be considered the senior pharmacist?"

"Yes, sir, I guess I would be."

"Do you order the medications for the hospital?"

"Yes, sir, I do."

"Is anyone else allowed to order medications?"

"Yes, sir. All of our pharmacists can place orders."

"Mr. Alford, are you familiar with a product called crotalotoxin?"

"I am now," he replied. "I'd never heard of it until we learned of Miss Lowe's and Mr. Folmar's activities."

Alex and Ben looked at one another.

"It's not enough to drag me through the mud," Alex remarked. "They've got to drag you into this, too."

Mr. Steele unlocked his briefcase, the latches making a

loud noise as they popped open. He unfolded a sheet of pink paper and handed it to his witness.

"Can you identify this paper?" he asked.

"Yes, sir," Tim replied nodding his head. "It's a purchase order from our pharmacy."

"Mr. Alford, is crotalotoxin one of the products being ordered on this form?"

"Yes, sir," he replied.

"Could you please tell us who authorized the purchase of these products?" he asked.

"Ben Folmar."

"That's horse shit," Ben mumbled to Alex.

"And how do you know that Mr. Folmar is the one who ordered the crotalotoxin?" Mr. Steele asked.

"He signed the request," he replied.

"Mr. Alford, have you ever ordered crotalotoxin?"

"No, sir."

"You're a lying sack of sh...," Ben began, catching himself before catching Alex's cold stare.

"Do you know of any medicinal uses for crotalotoxin?" Mr. Steele asked.

"No, sir," Tim replied. "Like I said, I'd never heard of the product until we became suspicious about Mr. Folmar and I stumbled across a purchase order for it hidden in a drawer in the pharmacy."

"Can you explain to the court what crotalotoxin is?" the lawyer asked.

"What little knowledge I have strictly comes from the package insert which accompanies the product. But from what I could tell, it's an extremely potent mixture of several poisons, any one of which in sufficient amounts can be lethal. When combined, the ingredients are extremely deadly, with just a few drops of the material capable of causing death instantaneously."

"How is it administered?"

"Any way you choose," the pharmacist replied. "It can be given orally, subcutaneously, intramuscularly or intravenously. Death occurs the quickest if it's administered intravenously."

"What actually causes the person to die?" Mr. Steele asked.

"It could be any one of the ingredients, but more than likely, it's the neurotoxin which ultimately causes respiratory paralysis and death."

Mr. Steele rested his hands on the wooden railing of the witness stand and leaned toward Tim.

"Have you ever administered crotalotoxin?" he asked.

"No, sir," Tim replied, shaking his head quickly from side to side.

"Mr. Alford, were you ever instructed by Gerald Warren to order or administer crotalotoxin?"

"No, sir."

"To your knowledge, did Gerald Warren ever administer or order any one else to administer crotalotoxin for the purpose of taking a life to prevent hospital losses?"

"No, sir, not to my knowledge."

"Thank you, Mr. Alford. No further questions, your honor."

Stacey Pitts, eager to begin his cross-examination, was standing beside the witness box before the defense attorney had reached his seat.

"Mr. Alford, could you look at these signatures for me?" he said, handing the witness a piece of paper. Tim wrinkled his forehead as he stared at the signatures.

"Do you recognize the name, Mr. Alford?"

"Sure," he replied, "it's Ben Folmar."

"Now, compare these signatures to the one on the purchase order which you reviewed moments ago. Do any of these signatures match the one on the purchase slip?"

"They all look very similar," he replied.

"You're right," Mr. Pitts replied. "They all appear similar, but interestingly, Mr. Alford, each one is a forgery, written by me."

"Objection, your honor," shouted Mr. Steele. "Mr. Alford has never claimed to be a hand-writing expert."

"Sustained," replied the judge. "Mr. Pitts, if you have a point to make, please do so."

"I'm sorry, you honor. My point is that when Ben Folmar's deposition was taken under oath, he knew nothing of crotalotoxin and denied having ever ordered crotalotoxin. Mr. Alford, you testified moments ago that you had never ordered crotalotoxin. Is that correct?"

"Yes, sir."

"Are you aware that perjury is a crime, punishable by imprisonment?"

The defense attorney jumped quickly to his feet and pounded his fist on the table in front of him.

"Your honor, I must object," he shouted. "Mr. Pitts is badgering the witness."

"Sustained," replied the judge. "Make your point, Mr. Pitts."

Mr. Pitts handed the witness a pink piece of paper, much like the one introduced previously by Marcus Steele.

"Mr. Alford, you have in your hand a purchase order from the pharmacy at Richland Memorial Hospital," he said. "Do you agree?"

Tim Alford stared at the sheet of paper.

"That's what it appears to be," he replied, cautiously.

"Is crotalotoxin among the items being ordered?"

"Yes, sir, it's on the list."

"Mr. Alford, could you tell the jury the name of the person authorizing the purchase of the crotalotoxin?"

The witness scrolled down the list until he reached the bottom of the page. The color rushed from his face.

"Tim Alford," he said in a shaky voice, "but there has to be a mistake! I've never ordered anything like this. It must be a forgery!"

"Mr. Alford, what would you say if I told you that a handwriting expert has conclusively identified that signature as being of your handwriting?"

"Well, I've never ordered any crotalotoxin," he replied, his voice higher pitched than before. "If that's my signature, then Ben Folmar must've altered the form after I signed it."

"Mr. Alford, isn't it true that you were ordering the poison at the request of Mr. Warren to be used for the sole purpose of killing patients who were costing his institution money?"

"No, sir. I never ordered it!"

Mr. Pitts shook his head.

"Please, Mr. Alford," he said, "for your own sake, remember that you're under oath. If you didn't order it, then why is your name on the order slip?"

"I've already told you," he replied. "Ben Folmar must have altered the request form."

"And why would he do that?" Mr. Pitts asked. "You've already testified that he had signed a request form in which crotalotoxin was ordered, though I must admit I doubt the authenticity of that signature."

"I don't know why. Why don't you ask him?"

"I'll tell you why," Mr. Pitts said, raising his voice. "Because you forged his signature on one order form so that you and Gerald Warren could implement him in case your scheme was ever uncovered. The reason your name is on this order form is because you were the one that Gerald Warren had persuaded to order the poison so his plan could be carried out. You're as guilty as he is, and trust me, Mr. Alford, you'll have your day in court. No further questions, your honor."

Tim Alford sat on the witness stand, not moving, the starched white shirt appearing even tighter around his neck. He looked as though he wanted to speak, but said nothing.

"Mr. Alford, you're excused," the judge said. "Please return to your seat."

Tim shook his head and made his way slowly to the back of the courtroom. He hadn't realized that a purchase order with his name on it had been discovered.

- 43 -

There was electricity in the air when Alex arrived at the courthouse the next morning. Some people were shouting, others whispering quietly in hushed voices. She and Ben were trying to push their way through the crowded lobby to the courtroom when they were stopped by Stacey Pitts.

"Are you ready to take the stand today, Alex?" he asked.

"As ready as I'll ever be," she replied.

"Try to keep your cool," he said. "I can assure you that Marc Steele will do his best to get under your skin."

"I don't doubt that," she said, "but I'll be fine. I've been through this before."

"What's all the commotion this morning," Ben asked. "Did Warren plead guilty before we arrived?"

Mr. Pitts laughed softly. "No, I'm afraid not. The commotion's about Tim Alford. You haven't heard?" he asked.

Ben shook his head. "Apparently not," he replied. "What's going on with Tim?"

"He wrecked his car last night, almost died from what I heard."

"Really?" Ben asked, raising his eyebrows. "What happened?"

"He was driving out on Belmont Lane and lost control of his car. The car apparently went into a spin and flipped end over end down the hill. Sounds like he was lucky to survive it."

"Was he hurt?" Alex asked.

"Yeah," the lawyer replied, nodding his head. "He suffered a severe concussion, but he's conscious and communicating this morning. He broke both legs and several ribs. And he ruptured his spleen. Dr. Haskins did emergency surgery on the spleen last night."

"Belmont Lane's out near your neighborhood isn't it?" Ben asked.

"Yeah, it is," Mr. Pitts replied. "In fact, he wrecked on the section of road that leads up to my house. I was sitting on the screen porch when it happened. I heard his brakes squealing and then I heard the awful sound of metal scraping and glass breaking, but I couldn't see anything, at least not until the car exploded."

"The car exploded?" Ben asked.

"Yeah, it burst into flames when it reached the bottom of the hill. When I saw the flames, I immediately got in my car and drove down there. I found Tim wrapped around a tree about halfway down the hill."

"Did he say what happened?" Alex asked. "Was he driving too fast?"

Mr. Pitts shook his head.

"Not really," he replied. "He said a car came flying up behind him, within a foot or two of his bumper. The driver kept his lights on bright and seemed anxious to pass, but Belmont's so curvy that he couldn't get around him. Tim said when he reached a straight stretch of road, he slowed down and motioned for the car to pass. When the driver pulled out to pass, his front bumper caught Tim's left rear bumper and spun him out. Once the front wheels left the pavement, the soft shoulder gave way and he began flipping down the hill. He was fortunate to have been thrown from the car. There's no way he could have survived the fire."

"Did the other driver stop to help?" Ben asked. "He had to know what happened."

"No, the police are treating it as a hit and run."

"What was Mr. Alford doing out on Belmont Lane?" Alex asked. "He lives on the other side of town."

Mr. Pitts shrugged his shoulder and shook his head.

"I don't know and he didn't say. But I do know one thing. He's lucky to be alive. Looks like we're going to have a packed house again today," he said looking around the lobby. "You two may want to go on in and find a seat. I saw your dad earlier. Where's your sister? Is she coming?"

"No," Alex replied, "she had to work last night, so she's sleeping in this morning. She wants to see Mr. Warren brought down, but she likes her sleep." Alex elbowed Ben and motioned with her head as the defendant and his attorney walked by. "Speak of the devil," she said. "Looks like they're ready for their GQ photo shoot."

"Image is everything," Mr. Pitts replied with a smile. "I'll see you inside."

Ben and Alex pushed through the crowded lobby and made their way to the courtroom where they took a seat beside Philip. The prosecutor was right. The courtroom was filling up quickly.

"Look at the three of them," she said, pointing toward the front of the room.

Philip stretched his neck as he sat up straight in his seat. "Planning strategy, no doubt," he remarked.

"I don't know," Alex replied. "Mr. Carlson seems pretty upset. Looks like they may be arguing."

Philip nodded as Bob Carlson shook his finger at his former boss.

"You may be right," he replied. "Look how red his face is."

Alex smiled. "Mr. Warren can do that to you," she said.

A hush fell over the courtroom as the judge entered. The crowd of people stood in unison as they waited for him to be seated. He pounded his gavel to call the court into session. When he instructed the audience to be seated, Marcus Steele remained standing and strolled to the front of the room. Alex's heart pounded when her name was called as the day's first witness. She tried to appear calm as she walked to the witness stand. She hoped her blue dress was good to her again.

"Miss Lowe, are you a registered nurse?" he asked after she was sworn in.

"Yes, sir," Alex replied.

"From where did you receive your degree?"

"Felton State Community College."

"When you graduated from nursing school, did you immediately seek employment?"

"Yes, sir."

"Where was your first job?" he asked.

"Richland Memorial," she replied.

"Are you still working there?"

"No, sir."

"Did you quit?" he asked.

"No, sir," Alex replied.

"Did you resign?"

"No, sir," Alex responded, shifting her weight uncomfortably in her chair.

"Then why are you no longer working there?"

"I was given a leave of absence," Alex replied.

"And why was that?"

"You know why."

"Yes, ma'am I do," he replied, "but this court would prefer to hear it from you."

"I was accused of taking the lives of several patients," Alex replied, "and because of that I was given a leave of absence until my trial concluded."

"And what was the outcome of that trial?"

"I was completely exonerated."

"You were found innocent?" he asked.

"Yes, sir. I was."

"Am I mistaken, Miss Lowe, or did you not confess that you played an active role in the deaths of several patients?"

“Objection, you honor,” shouted Mr. Pitts. “We’re not here to retry the case of Miss Lowe.”

“Sustained,” replied the judge. “Mr. Steele, do you have any questions which directly relate to this trial?”

“Yes, your honor. Miss Lowe, did my client ever directly instruct you to take a patient’s life?”

“No, but...”

“Thank you,” he said. “A simple yes or no is sufficient. Are you aware of any instance in which my client actively participated in the death of a patient?”

“Mr. Warren forced me to administer medications to several patients which resulted in their deaths.”

“He forced you to administer medications? How’d he do that? Did he hold a gun to your head?” Mr. Steele asked, folding his arms across his chest.

“No, sir, but he told me that if I didn’t cooperate with his plans, he’d go to the authorities and accuse me of killing patients.”

“Why would that bother you, Miss Lowe, unless of course you were guilty?”

Alex sat stunned, staring blankly ahead. The attorney unfolded his arms and walked to where she was sitting. He placed his hands on the wooden railing and leaned toward her.

“Miss Lowe, you didn’t answer my question. Were you killing patients?” he asked in a loud, threatening voice.

Alex lightly bit her bottom. “I did some things which led to the deaths of several of my patients,” she replied carefully.

“Isn’t it true, Miss Lowe, that my client had evidence in the form of videotapes showing you committing random acts of murder, and because of your fear that he would go to the authorities, you fabricated an elaborate story in which you accused him of arranging the deaths of patients who were costing the hospital money?”

“I didn’t fabricate anything,” Alex said. “What I’ve told is the truth.”

"Miss Lowe, is your mother living?" Mr. Steele asked.

"Objection, your honor," shouted Mr. Pitts. "Whether the witness' mother is alive or dead is totally irrelevant."

"Overruled, Mr. Pitts," replied the judge. "Please answer the question, Miss Lowe."

"No, sir," Alex said. "She's dead."

"She's dead?" Mr. Steele asked. "When did she die?"

"When I was in high school."

"Have you seen or spoken to your mother since her death?" he asked.

"Yes, sir. I've seen her and spoken to her."

"Even though she's dead?" he asked, raising his voice.

"Yes, sir," Alex replied softly.

The judge pounded his gavel to quiet the buzzing whispers of the audience.

"Have any other family members or acquaintances had contact with your mother?"

"No, sir, not that I'm aware of," Alex replied.

"Do you personally know of anyone, other than yourself, who has had conversations with a deceased person, whether it be your mother or someone else?"

"No, sir."

Mr. Steele tilted his head and frowned.

"Don't you find that just a bit unusual?" he asked. "I mean, why would your mother appear to you and have conversations with you, but not with anyone else? Do you think she loved you more than she loved your sister or your father?"

"No, sir," Alex replied.

"Then why you?"

"She came to me because I was chosen by a higher authority to alleviate unnecessary pain and suffering. She let me know that what I was doing was okay, that the people who were hurting and suffering, those whom I had helped to die, were better off dead than they would've been if they were still alive."

"So, you were doing a good deed by taking lives. Is that

what you're trying to tell me?"

"Yes, sir. I know it's hard for you to understand," Alex admitted, folding her hands in the praying position and moving them up and down as she spoke, "but some of us are put on earth to alter the course of others' lives. I don't know why I was chosen, but I was."

"Miss Lowe, isn't it true that your attorney believed your best defense against your murder charges would be a plea of insanity?"

"I'm not crazy," Alex said.

"Then why would he suggest that you plead insanity as your defense?" the lawyer asked.

"I don't know why," she replied, shaking her head. "He's sitting in the back of the room, why don't you ask him?"

The courtroom audience broke into laughter causing the judge to pound his gavel.

"You're quite amusing, Miss Lowe," Mr. Steele said, smiling, "but you didn't answer my question. Perhaps, as a lawyer, and having defended murderers before, I can answer for you. He suggested that you plead insanity because you're mentally unstable." The lawyer stretched the open palm of his right hand toward the jurors. "I ask the jury to listen to what you're telling us. You killed patients because you were told by your dead mother that you've been chosen by a higher authority to alleviate unnecessary pain and suffering. How can we possibly be expected to believe your accusations regarding my client when you're so delusional that you believe you can talk to the dead? Your honor, I have no further questions for this witness, but with the court's permission, I would like to show the ladies and gentlemen of the jury videotapes which captured the cold-blooded, ruthless nature of this seemingly kind and gentle lady."

The judge nodded his approval, his wavy, white hair bouncing as his head moved.

"Permission granted," he said.

Alex sat with her hand partially covering her face as the tape rolled while Gerald Warren looked on as if he were watching an award-winning movie. The tape concluded with the image of Ella Hibbetts jerking in her bed minutes before she presumably died. An eerie stillness filled the room.

Mr. Pitts walked quickly to the witness stand, reaching Alex before the defense attorney had settled in his seat.

"Miss Lowe, do you remember the first patient who died under your care?" he asked.

"Yes, sir," Alex replied calmly.

"Could you describe that incident for us?" he asked.

"Yes, sir. I was working the night shift, taking care of a young man named David Watson. He'd been hospitalized for weeks following a car wreck. He was unconscious and was given no hope for recovery by his doctors. The only time he responded in any way was when something painful happened to him. And even then, his only response was a grimace. It was emotionally draining for his family as well as for me. Each day that he lived, his parents died a little bit. And each night after I took care of him, I had nightmares about him and his suffering."

"What about the night he died? Can you tell us what happened that night?"

Alex nodded and cleared her throat before giving a detailed accountant of the events that occurred on the night of David Watson's death.

"So David's death was accidental?" Stacey Pitts asked when she concluded.

"Yes, sir," Alex replied.

"The second patient, as I recall from previous testimony, Miss Lowe, was an elderly man with end-stage emphysema whose hand you untied allowing him to extubate himself. Is that correct?"

"Yes, sir. He had suffered a stroke and had been placed on a ventilator. I had taken care of him previously and knew that he didn't want to live that way so I untied his hand and gave him the option of life or death. He chose to die."

"So, again, you did not actively and purposefully take his life, did you?"

"No, sir."

"Did Gerald Warren know about the deaths of David Watson and Prince Christopher?"

"Yes, sir, apparently so."

"Miss Lowe, who was Billy Jackson?"

"Billy was a young man who was dying with AIDS. He asked me to help him die and I did."

"What did you do?"

"He asked me to give him an overdose of morphine."

"And did you?"

"Yes, sir."

"And it was after his death that Mr. Warren confronted you?" he asked.

"Actually, it was Lib Dillard who first contacted me," Alex replied. "One night, several hours before my shift ended, I injected a large bolus of morphine into Billy's I.V. He died the next morning after my shift ended. It was the next night at work when Miss Dillard contacted me."

"You're referring to Lib Dillard, the night nursing supervisor, correct?"

"Yes, sir."

"What did she say to you?"

"At first, it was just casual chit chat. How'd I like working nights? Was I adjusting to sleeping during the day? Those sort of things. But then she asked me to join her in her office and I knew something was wrong. The only reason a nurse was invited to Miss Dillard's office was to be reprimanded."

"So, you went to her office expecting a reprimand," he said. "Did you have any idea why she might be reprimanding you?"

"Not really," Alex replied, "at least not at first. But as we walked to her office she said there were some concerns about a couple of patients who had been under my care. I wondered what I'd done wrong. Which family or which doctor had I offended?"

"When you got to Miss Dillard's office, was she alone?"

"No, sir. Mr. Carlson, Mr. Alford, and Mr. Warren were there, too."

"Didn't you find that a little bit unusual?"

"Oh, yes, sir, quite unusual. It was two o'clock in the morning. I wondered why they weren't home in bed."

"What happened at that meeting?"

"Mr. Warren asked me about the deaths of David and Mr. Christopher and then he showed a video of me injecting the morphine into Billy's I.V. After the tape ended, he told me his plan."

Mr. Pitts stared at the defendant. Gerald avoided eye contact and shifted nervously in his seat.

"What was his plan, Miss Lowe?" Mr. Pitts asked.

Alex sat up straight in her seat with her eyes focused on the defendant.

"He planned to kill patients who were costing Richland Memorial money," she said.

"Did he say why?" Mr. Pitts asked.

"Not specifically," Alex replied. "The best I could tell, he was going to eliminate patients who were losing money for the hospital. He called the five of us a resource utilization team."

"How'd you feel about that?"

"I didn't like it."

"But you agreed to go along with it?"

"No, sir. Not at first. But when he threatened to turn me in to the authorities, it scared me. I didn't believe I'd done anything wrong, but when I saw myself on the tape and heard his threat, I didn't feel that I had any other choice."

"Gerald Warren threatened to turn you in to the authorities?" he asked.

"Yes, sir," Alex answered, nodding with her entire upper body.

"And he had enough evidence against you to make you doubt your own innocence?"

"I never doubted my innocence, but I doubted our legal system. I doubted that a jury would understand that I was acting out of love when I helped Billy end his life. But I guess I was wrong."

"Miss Lowe, did you take the lives of patients at Richland Memorial hospital because you were ordered to do so by Gerald Warren?"

"Yes, sir," Alex replied.

"How many patients did he direct you to kill?" he asked.

"Three."

"And did you take the lives of all three?"

"No, sir, only the first two. The first two patients he selected fit my idea of people who would be better off dead, people who were suffering needlessly. The third patient was a lady named Ella Hibbetts. When I went to her room that night to take her life it was obvious that she wasn't suffering or experiencing pain. There was no reason for me to take her life. She didn't need to die."

"But Mr. Warren wanted her dead?" the attorney asked.

Gerald shook his head from side to side as the lawyer spoke.

"Yes, sir," Alex replied. "I felt certain they'd made a mistake. I thought it had to be Miss Davis, her roommate, whom he wanted killed. She was the one who was suffering and would benefit from death. I thought maybe my instructions were wrong. Maybe they had the right room but the wrong bed. I went back to the nurse's station and pulled both charts."

"And was there a mistake?"

"No, sir. He wanted Miss Hibbetts killed."

"But you didn't kill her?" he asked.

"No, sir," Alex replied. "I gave the poison to Miss Davis. I couldn't stand to see her suffer and I saw no reason to take Miss Hibbetts' life. That's when I realized that what he was making me do was wrong. Until then, I'd rationalized that the patients they'd asked me to kill were patients who would've been better off dead anyway. But when I looked into Miss Hibbetts' eyes, I finally understood that they didn't care about alleviating pain and suffering. They were only concerned about saving the hospital money."

"What happened when they found out you'd taken the life of Miss Davis and not Ella Hibbetts?"

"Miss Dillard found out first. She appeared on the floor shortly after Miss Davis was pronounced dead. She walked up behind me at the nursing station and asked me who died. I could tell by the look on her face that she was expecting me to say Ella Hibbetts. When I told her it was Miss Davis, she asked me how Miss Hibbetts was doing. She seemed surprised when I told her Miss Hibbetts was fine and asked me why Miss Hibbetts was still alive."

"And what did you tell her?"

"I told her I felt there had been a mistake and that I'd given the medication to Miss Davis."

"You'd given the medication to Miss Davis? By medication do you mean poison?" he asked.

"Yes, sir, the poison," Alex replied.

"How did Miss Dillard react to that?"

"She was furious and told me that the only mistake was my own, that the medicine was intended for Miss Hibbetts, just like my instructions had said."

"What happened then?"

Alex sat up straight in her seat and folded her hands in her lap as she retold the story of her argument with Lib Dillard. A light perspiration popped out on her brow when she recalled how their ensuing struggle ended with the nursing supervisor plunging the needle of the poison filled syringe into her thigh.

"Did the poison get injected into her leg?"

"Yes, sir, it did. Not much, but unfortunately, enough to kill her."

"Lib Dillard died?" he asked.

"Yes, sir," she replied. "We both knew she was in trouble as soon as the needle stuck in her leg. She ran from Miss Hibbetts' room to the nurse's station where she collapsed. We worked on her for about forty-five minutes, but we couldn't save her."

"Miss Lowe, did you intentionally kill Lib Dillard?" he asked.

"No, sir," Alex stated. "She didn't deserve to die any more so than Miss Hibbetts."

"Would Miss Dillard still be alive if Mr. Warren hadn't ordered you to kill Ella Hibbetts?"

"Yes, sir, I think she would," Alex replied.

"Did Mr. Warren order you a second time to kill Ella Hibbetts?"

"Yes, sir."

"Did you?"

"No, sir. I couldn't. There was no reason for her to die."

"But the videotape we saw showed Miss Hibbetts dying."

"It only looked that way," Alex explained. "When I left his office I went to my boyfriend's apartment and confronted him about his involvement with their plan and about his drug addiction. It was hard for him to do, but he finally convinced me that Mr. Warren was lying and that I had to go to the authorities to stop him."

"So, you went to the police, told them your story and were put in jail until your trial?"

"I went to the police and told them my story, but I wasn't put in jail until the following day."

"Isn't that rather strange, Miss Lowe," he asked. "Why would the police allow you to walk free after you confessed your involvement in several deaths?"

"I was afraid that if I didn't report for work, Mr. Warren and the others would know something was wrong. And if they suspected anything, they'd kill Miss Hibbetts. When I told Mr. Horton, the homicide detective, he agreed that I should report for work. With his help, we made it appear that I had terminated Miss Hibbetts that night."

"You made it appear that you had terminated Miss Hibbetts?" he asked.

"Yes, sir. We knew Mr. Warren would be taping the events in Miss Hibbetts' room. That night a female police officer dressed as a nursing student worked with me. We went to Miss Hibbetts' room and explained our plan to her, about how we wanted to make it look as if she'd been killed. About an hour into the shift I went to her room and injected a syringe of water into her I.V. She thrashed about in the bed for a few minutes after the injection and then lay perfectly still as if she'd died. Detective Horton had arranged everything. A police officer posing as a doctor pronounced her dead and two other officers dressed like workers from the transportation department put Miss Hibbetts on a stretcher and carried her to the morgue, only they didn't take her to the morgue. There was an unmarked police car waiting outside the morgue to take Miss Hibbetts to a nursing home. When I went by Mr. Warren's office the next morning, he seemed pleased that I'd killed her."

"But you didn't kill her."

"No, sir, but he thought I did."

"So, the last patient on the video which the defense showed us is still alive?"

"Yes, sir, she is," Alex replied. "She's sitting in the back of the courtroom."

Mr. Pitts turned, facing the rear of the courtroom and stretched his neck looking for Ella Hibbetts.

"Miss Hibbetts, if you're present," he said, "could you please stand up?"

The old lady, smiling from ear to ear, stood up and waved at Alex. Gerald slowly turned his head until he saw her. When he realized she was alive, he lowered his head until his chin rested on his chest. He tightly closed his eyes and slowly shook his head.

"No further questions, your honor."

Marc leaned over and whispered in his client's ear.

"Did you not have a clue that she was still alive?" he asked.

"How was I supposed to know?" Gerald whispered. "We told the girl to kill her and it looked like she did."

Marc inhaled deeply, his chest stretching the fabric of his navy blazer. He puffed out his cheeks as he slowly exhaled.

"Then the old lady knows everything as well," he said. "This is not looking good, Gerald, not looking good at all."

Gerald's face flushed with anger.

"For the money I'm paying you," he whispered angrily, "you better make it look good. You promised me you could do the job. Now, damn it, do it!"

- 44 -

Marcus Steele buttoned his navy blue blazer and rose to his feet. Particles of dust floated on the beams of sunlight above his head.

"Your honor, the defense calls Bob Carlson to the stand," he said.

Bob walked quickly to the witness stand, his eyes darting around the courtroom, making contact with friends and family, but never meeting the eyes of Gerald Warren. He rubbed his hands together nervously as he sat down.

"Mr. Carlson what is your job at Richland Memorial Hospital?" Mr. Steele asked.

"I'm the chief financial officer," he replied.

"Is it your job then to know the financial soundness of the hospital?"

"Yes, sir, it is."

"Is Richland financially sound?"

"No, sir, it's not," he said, shaking his head.

Mr. Steele nodded.

"Mr. Carlson," he said, "Gerald Warren told this court yesterday of changes which have been made at the hospital to allow it to become more financially sound. Are you aware of those changes?"

"Yes, sir."

"And have they helped?"

"Yes, sir. We're close to running in the black this year."

"As you're aware, Mr. Carlson, my client has been accused of cutting losses further by eliminating nonpaying, revenue consuming patients. To your knowledge, did Mr. Warren kill any patients at your institution?"

"No, sir."

"Before this morning, have you ever had the opportunity to view the tape which was shown to this audience?"

"Yes, sir," he replied.

"When would that have been?"

"I've seen it on several occasions. Gerald and I have known each other since childhood and have developed a mutual trust and friendship through the years. Because of that, he tended to confide in me. Whenever something happened at the hospital that bothered him, he discussed it with me."

"Did Mr. Warren appear overly concerned that one of his employees was apparently taking the lives of patients?"

"It definitely concerned him."

"Did it concern him enough to have meetings with her and discuss her behavior?" Mr. Steele asked.

"Yes, sir."

"Who was present at those meetings?"

"The Lowe girl, me, Gerald, Tim Alford and Lib Dillard."

"Was Miss Lowe made aware that the four of you suspected her of killing patients?" he asked.

"No doubt about it," he replied. "Gerald was open and candid with her from the very start."

The lawyer paused momentarily, looked down at the floor, and then looked at his client. As if reading his mind, Gerald nodded his approval.

"Mr. Carlson, did Mr. Warren ever ask Alex Lowe to take a patient's life for the sole purpose of saving his hospital money?"

Gerald's heart pounded. His throat tightened as he waited for the answer. Bob licked his lips and swallowed hard. He glanced quickly at Gerald.

"Yes, sir, he did," he said, nodding his head. "And he told her if she didn't cooperate with him, he'd turn her in to the authorities and use the tapes to prove his case against her."

In the back of the silent courtroom, Alex squeezed her father's hand and fought hard to suppress the smile stretching across her face. Bob fidgeted uncomfortably on the witness stand as Gerald glared at him, slowly shaking his head from side to side.

"Mr. Steele, do you have further questions for your witness?" the judge asked.

The defense attorney stuttered and stammered, searching for the right words.

"No, your honor, sir, not at this time," he replied.

He looked at his client with hollow, defeated eyes and walked slowly back to his seat. It was too late to withdraw his question. His strategy had failed. His witness had refused to lie under oath.

Stacey Pitts' shoes clicked happily on the wooden floor as he approached the witness stand. He found himself unprepared to question a non-hostile witness.

"Mr. Carlson, I introduced as evidence yesterday, a pink sheet of paper containing a list of names in your handwriting. Do you recall that piece of paper?" he asked.

"Yes, sir," he replied.

"Is this your handwriting?" he asked as he handed him the sheet of paper.

"Yes, sir, it is," Bob admitted, rocking nervously back and forth in his seat.

"Do you recognize these names?"

"Yes, sir, I do," he replied.

"Can you tell this court what this list and the numbers beside each name represent?"

Bob sighed and took a deep breath. He stared at Gerald as he spoke.

"Those are the names of the ten patients who at the time this list was constructed were losing the most money for the hospital each day. The numbers out to the side represent our estimate of how much money the hospital was losing on each patient each day."

"The first two names have a line drawn through them," Mr. Pitts said. "Why is that?"

"When a patient was terminated, we scratched their name off the list," he replied, lowering his head.

"Mr. Carlson, who developed this list?"

"It was a team effort," he said. "Since I was involved in the financial operation of the hospital, I had ready access to each patient's account and insurance status. Lib Dillard turned in names of patients whom she felt were going to be difficult to get out of the hospital from a nursing standpoint. The ultimate decision of who was placed on the list, however, was up to Gerald."

"How were the patients killed?"

"The first couple were killed with potassium or morphine, I think, but I'm not really sure. It was my job to determine who was costing the hospital the most money, not how to kill them. I do remember that after the first two deaths, Tim suggested that we switch to some type of poison."

"Why the change?" Mr. Pitts asked.

"There was always the possibility with potassium or morphine that the patient might not die, especially if a code was called. And morphine was too closely regulated and too easy to trace. With the poison, people died, and they died quickly."

"Who ordered the poison?"

"Tim did. He ordered it and filled the syringes."

Mr. Pitts paced back and forth across the front of the room as he questioned the witness.

"Mr. Carlson why would you or anyone else go along with Mr. Warren's plan?" he asked. "Did you approve of what he was doing?"

"That's a hard question," he replied. "I think we all understood why he was doing what he was doing. If Richland continued to lose money, there'd be no option but to close the doors. Our city couldn't afford that. But from an ethics standpoint, I don't think any of us agreed with what we were being told to do."

"Then why'd you go along with him?"

"Truthfully?" he asked. "We didn't have a choice. Gerald had information about things in our pasts, things which could destroy our lives, which he threatened to disclose if we didn't cooperate with him."

Mr. Pitts stopped pacing and stared at Gerald as he spoke.

"Mr. Carlson," he asked, "did Gerald Warren order the deaths of Maggie Cooper and Jason Bradley for the single purpose of saving money at Richland Memorial Hospital?"

The witness closed his eyes and nodded.

"Yes, sir, he did," he replied softly.

Ben draped his arm around Alex's shoulder and pulled her close. Tears trickled down her face and landed silently in her lap. The prosecuting attorney paused and took a deep breath.

"Your honor, with the court's permission," he continued, "I'd like to play a conversation recorded in the defendant's office on the morning of his arrest, a conversation between the defendant, this witness and Tim Alford."

The judge nodded his head.

"Permission granted," he said.

The district attorney placed the cassette player on the railing in front of the jury box and turned it on.

"Gentlemen, come in. I think you'll be pleased with what you're about to see."

For several minutes there was complete silence on the tape.

"I don't know about the two of you, but I'll certainly rest easier tonight knowing she's a team player. I must admit, I had my doubts about her when she left my office yesterday."

"I think we all did. Did she talk to her boyfriend?"

"Yeah, she did. He denied everything, just like we said he would. I think the needle punctures in his arms were what really convinced her that her boyfriend was lying. We're fortunate. If this situation had arisen a few days earlier, we'd have had a difficult time convincing her that her boyfriend was hooked on morphine."

"What about tonight? Is she going to terminate another revenue loser?"

"She's agreed to carry out one more termination and then take a few nights off. I think the stress is getting to her. I thought we would terminate the young man in bed four of the ICU, the fellow who was in the car wreck and has no insurance, but she's still hung up on her belief that it's wrong to kill these patients if they're not suffering. With that in mind, I think our next best option is to terminate a lady up on four west who's been here for three weeks with no insurance. She's costing us about seven hundred dollars a day and since she's a stroke victim, our little angel of mercy shouldn't object too strongly. Is that agreeable with the two of you?"

"I've got no problem with it."

"Nor do I."

"You know, I almost feel guilty making money by killing these poor people. But hell, I'm doing it for the good of the hospital. And what's good for the hospital is good for our community. In fact, we should get recognized at the Kiwanis Club for our community service."

Mr. Pitts turned off the cassette player. The silence in the room was deafening.

"Mr. Carlson, is your voice one of the three voices on this tape?" he asked, holding the tape high in the air for everyone to see.

"Yes, sir," he replied.

"Do the other voices belong to Tim Alford and Gerald Warren?"

"Yes, sir, they do."

"In fact, Mr. Carlson, is it not Gerald Warren who says, and I quote, 'You know, I almost feel guilty making money by killing these poor people. But hell, I'm doing it for the good of the hospital'?"

"Yes, sir. It is."

Mr. Pitts wiped the sweat from his brow with the back of his hand.

"No further questions, your honor," he said.

"The witness is excused," the judge replied. "This court stands in recess until one o'clock."

Gerald glared at his friend as he made his way from the witness stand to the back of the courtroom. Though unable to hear his words, Bob could read his lips.

"I thought you were my friend," Gerald said.

"I was," he mouthed silently, "until last night."

Marc Steele looked at his client.

"What'd he mean by that?" he asked.

"I don't know," Gerald replied, shaking his head. "I just don't know. We've been friends since childhood."

The lawyer shook his head.

"That's what I thought," he replied. "I never had any indication he'd turn against you. If I had, I would have never asked him what I did. I'm sorry, Gerald."

"You're sorry?" he asked, raising his voice. "What's that supposed to mean? You're sorry?"

"It means I'm sorry. I never thought Bob would turn against you. Now I'm afraid there's no way we can hope for a favorable verdict. I think it's time we come clean and ask for leniency from the jury."

"Do you think I'm going to prison?" Gerald asked, his voice filled with fear.

"At this point, I'd have to say that your chances don't look good," he replied. "If you're asking my opinion, I think we should plea bargain for a light sentence."

"What if you put me back on the stand and let me tell my side of the story, no holds barred, only the truth?"

"I don't know, Gerald," he replied. "If that's what you want to do, I can't stop you. It's hard to imagine that you could do any more harm than has already been done."

- 45 -

Gerald appeared nervous as he walked to the front of the room when the court reconvened. His heart raced as he took his place on the witness stand. He wiped his sweaty palms on his trousers and tried to swallow the cotton ball growing in his throat.

"Mr. Warren," the judge said, "this is a most unusual request, but the prosecution has agreed to let you speak to this court without interrupting you to ask questions. Mr. Pitts does, however, reserve the right to question you after you complete your remarks. Is that agreeable to you?"

"Yes, sir," he replied without making eye contact. His voice was low and soft.

"Ladies and gentlemen of the jury and members of the court audience," the judge said, "at the close of the last session, the defendant, Gerald Warren, asked for, and was granted, permission to address this court on his behalf." The judge nodded to the defendant. "The floor is yours, Mr. Warren."

"I wonder what kind of lies he's going to tell now," Alex whispered in her father's ear. Philip didn't answer, but silently shook his head.

Gerald looked worried. He cleared his throat and tugged on the collar of his shirt. His voice quivered as he spoke.

"I asked that I be allowed to speak directly to you, the

members of the jury, so that I could present my side of this story, the true side," he said. "Some of the things I told you yesterday when I was on this witness stand are not true. Rather than recounting those things, I'd like to take this opportunity to explain how all of this has come about. As you're well aware, the health care field has experienced enormous changes over the past decade. These changes, unfortunately, have led to the closure of many small hospitals across the country. Richland Memorial has not been isolated from those changes and as such has been operating in the red for a number of years. The reimbursements to our institution have fallen drastically as the percentage of HMO patients has risen. The money that was once paid to hospitals and physicians who provided the care is instead now paid to corporate America. Ten years ago, we could afford to take care of the indigent population because we made money off of our insured patients. Before Medicare and private insurance companies began cutting reimbursements, our hospital benefited by keeping patients alive. Since I wasn't able to prolong lives, I had to find another way to scam the system. Bob Carlson, our chief accountant, and I had been friends since we were kids. There were things we knew about one another's past that no one else knew, and I used some of that privileged information against Bob to convince him to assist me with my plan. At first, I forced Bob to falsify the books by billing Medicare and private insurance companies for procedures that weren't actually performed, generally to patients who had died, patients who couldn't dispute the insurance claims. Since neither of us had the medical expertise to know which procedures could be billed with a particular diagnosis without raising red flags in an audit, we sought the help of someone with medical training. Bob had attended college with Lib Dillard and knew that she had, well, suffice it to say he knew something about her that she didn't want known. Lib helped us link the tests and procedures with the proper diagnoses to lower our risk of an audit while improving our profits. We were just beginning to see the fruits of our efforts when Lib had a wonderful idea. Jim Curry, one of our more talented physicians, had a reputation for prolonging the lives of terminally ill patients, and in her words, 'ordering every test under the sun.' If we could ensure that Dr. Curry took care of our insured, critically ill patients, we could increase our profits without committing insurance fraud. Strings were pulled so that Dr. Curry was appointed Chief of Staff and given the authority to oversee the care of all patients admitted to the intensive care units. He was delighted with his title and we were delighted with the increased revenues.

Unfortunately, times changed. Medicare and insurance companies cut their reimbursements, and today we barely break even on our insured patients. And we can no longer afford the expense of caring for our uninsured patients. Several years ago it became painfully clear that if we didn't make some radical changes, we'd be forced to close Richland's doors. We began by laying off staff and instituting protocols to cut costs. The changes we made helped, but we still lost money. During a brainstorming session, someone jokingly said that if we could close our doors to the indigents of our area, we could save a lot of money. But if we closed our emergency room, then we would be defeating our reason for existence. We're here to serve the health needs of our county. It was then that I began investigating how much money we were losing by providing care for nonpaying patients. The figures were astounding. It didn't take a Harvard graduate to realize that if we could eliminate the terminally ill who were consuming resources rather than generating revenues, we could keep Richland Memorial afloat. With the dirt I had on Bob and Lib, I felt certain they would cooperate with my new plan but I worried about Jim Curry. He thrived on saving lives and was unconcerned about the costs. I hate to admit it, but I was relieved when he died in a car wreck. His death made it much simpler to carry out my plan.

With Bob and Lib's help, I uncovered some dirt on Tim Alford, the head pharmacist at the hospital. After securing

Tim's cooperation, the only thing that stood in my way was finding a nurse or a physician to carry out my plan. I authorized the installation of cameras throughout our hospital for the sole purpose of monitoring the activity of our staff, hoping to catch someone making a mistake, a mistake so bad that I could make them go along with our plans. Lib worked as our night supervisor and knew whenever anyone died on her shift. After two patients died under Miss Lowe's care, we began investigating her activities. The tapes clearly showed her doing things that led to patient's deaths. I honestly believe that she felt she was acting in the best interest of those patients when she took their lives, but her motives didn't matter. We knew we had found our nurse. From the manner in which we presented it to her, I'm not sure she had any choice but to go along with us. Her biggest concern was whether or not the patients who were being terminated were experiencing pain and suffering. You've heard her testimony and even today she persists in the belief that she's been chosen to direct destiny by intervening in the lives of people who she feels are suffering needlessly. It was that belief which ultimately led to our downfall. If I hadn't gotten greedy, and had continued to have her terminate only those patients who fit her ideal picture of undue pain and suffering without regard to consumption of resources, none of this would've ever erupted, and Richland Memorial would be in the black. My mistake was in asking her to terminate Ella Hibbetts. When she saw and spoke with Miss Hibbetts, she saw that even though Miss Hibbetts was elderly, she was not in pain, nor was she suffering. The only reason I selected Miss Hibbetts was because she was consuming resources in excess of the revenue she was generating. Miss Lowe balked, and that's when our operation began to fall apart. You've heard her testimony and how the events of that night resulted in the deaths of Maggie Cooper and Lib Dillard. When we learned of Lib's death we got scared, scared that Miss Lowe would go to the authorities. I called her into my office the next morning and confronted her. The three of us, Bob Carlson, Tim Alford, and I, fabricated an elaborate story of how her boyfriend was a drug addict and was as involved in all of this as she was. We tried to convince her that her boyfriend was ordering the crotalotoxin and was aware that patients were being killed with it. We thought we had convinced her, but obviously, we hadn't. I had no idea, until today, that Miss Hibbetts had not been terminated. And whether you choose to believe it or not, I'm thankful that she's still alive."

He paused, closed his eyes tightly, and took several slow, deep breaths. Looking around the crowded courtroom, he found Miss Hibbetts and briefly made eye contact. "I know that what I've done was wrong, but you've got to try and understand my reasoning. I'm not a heartless, cold-blooded killer. I'm a hospital administrator who was trying to save a dying hospital and ensure that our town would have medical care available for its citizens. I'm a visionary who's seen the future of health care and elected to move forward. What I've done seems wrong by today's standards, but this is the future of health care. Our country has reached the point where we can no longer pour out billions of dollars on our terminally ill. We spend far too much money providing care to those who have no hope for meaningful survival outside of the hospital. We've become too concerned with prolonging life while ignoring the quality of the life we're prolonging. We put feeding tubes down our elderly to keep them alive after their brains stop telling their bodies that they need to eat. We take our smokers whose chronic tobacco abuse has destroyed their lungs and put them on ventilators when they can no longer breathe on their own. We take our young people with irreversible brain damage from car wrecks who have no hope of meaningful survival and spend millions of dollars to keep them alive. When are we going to wake up and realize that we can't keep going like this? We don't have the financial resources available in this country to do everything medically possible for everyone in every situation. We have wonderful health care available to us in our country, but we can't afford to continue spending billions of dollars in situations where, no matter what we do, the end result, whether it be one day, one week, one month, or even one year, is ultimately death.

What I've done is wrong if you judge me according to the laws that govern our society, but what I've done is no different than what is already being done in many foreign countries where they understand the financial ramifications of prolonging life unnecessarily. We don't prosecute our physicians when they decide that someone has a terminal illness and elect to withhold treatment. And in a way, what I've done is no different than what they do every day. But I'm not a physician, so I'm viewed differently. I ask you to weigh the consequences of my actions. If you believe I've done wrong by trying to reign in the run away costs of health care and preserve our hospital, then you have no choice but to find me guilty of these charges. But, if you are open minded enough to see the future, to understand that this is the future of medicine, and realize that my actions have been beneficial to all involved parties, then I ask that in your infinite wisdom, you find me not guilty."

He tugged at his collar and nodded to the judge.

"Mr. Pitts, do you have any questions for Mr. Warren?" the judge asked.

"No, your honor. No questions," he replied shaking his head.

Gerald sighed deeply. He pulled a handkerchief from his pocket and wiped the perspiration from his face. Marc Steele shook his hand firmly when he returned to his seat.

"You were great, Gerald, just great," he said. "The only thing we can do now is wait on the jury and pray. And if you're a praying man, you need to be praying hard."

"Do you think I convinced them?" Gerald asked.

"I don't know," he replied, "but if you didn't, then nobody could."

- 46 -

Gerald Warren searched each expressionless face as the jury made its way back into the courtroom. As each juror walked through the door, his anxiety rose, giving him the sensation that his heart would explode within his chest. He squeezed his lawyer's hand when the judge told him to stand for the reading of the verdict.

"Has the jury reached a verdict?" the judge asked.

"Yes, your honor," replied the foreman.

"Would the foreman of the jury please read your verdict?"

Alex squeezed Ben's hand and closed her eyes. Her dad patted her lightly on the thigh.

"We, the members of the jury, find the defendant, Gerald Xavier Warren, guilty as charged in each of the three counts of conspiracy to commit murder."

Alex loosened her grip on Ben's hand and buried her face against his shoulder, unable to stop the stream of tears pouring from her eyes. Ben draped his arm around her shoulder and pulled her close.

Gerald loosened his grip on Marc's hand and sat down. Tears filled his eyes. "I never meant to hurt anyone," he said. "I only wanted to save the hospital for the sake of our town."

"I know, Gerald, I know," Marc replied. "This thing isn't over. We'll appeal all the way to the supreme court if needed."

"I won't go to prison," Gerald replied. "I can't."

"You won't," his lawyer assured him. "We'll win this thing on appeal."

"I need to speak to the jury one more time."

"Gerald, it's too late. They've already made their decision. The only thing we can do is appeal to a higher court."

"I've got to say one more thing. Please ask the judge if I can speak before they clear the courtroom."

Marc moved hurriedly to the front of the courtroom. The judge nodded his approval and pounded his gavel to restore order in the courtroom.

"Mr. Warren," the judge said, "this is a most unusual request, but this has been an unusual trial from the very beginning. I'll give you five minutes to address this court."

Gerald's legs wobbled as he walked the short distance to the front of the courtroom to face the jury.

"I want each of you to know that while I don't agree with your decision, I do respect your decision and can only wonder how I would've voted had I been in your shoes. Sometime in the future, Bob and Tim will have their days in court. I could not live with myself if I didn't defend them and their actions. They did what they did only because I forced them to do so. They had no other choice. As many of you know, Tim Alford was critically injured in a car wreck last night by a hit and run driver. I was that driver. When court adjourned yesterday, Bob and I followed Tim because I was afraid he was going to tell the prosecuting attorney the truth about the activities at our hospital. When Bob realized that I intended to run Tim off the road to prevent him from talking, he made me stop the car so he could get out. He refused to be a part of what he was afraid was going to happen. After he got out, I caught up to Tim and rammed his car from behind. When he lost control of his car, it flipped end over end down the hill. When it exploded, I assumed he was dead. I didn't realize until this morning that he'd survived the crash. Five years ago, I did the same thing to Jim Curry, but he wasn't as fortunate as Tim. My determination to save this hospital has driven me to desperation, even to murder."

Marc looked around the courtroom until he found Bob. "You knew didn't you?" he mouthed silently.

Bob's lips were pressed together tightly. He nodded his head slowly up and down.

"Yeah," he replied.

"When Bob got out of my car last night," a broken Gerald Warren continued, "he told me I was a sick man. While I was sitting here waiting for you to return with your verdict, I realized that he was right. I have become a very sick man. Sick men are either kept alive in our hospitals or in our prisons, and as I've tried to explain, our country cannot afford to keep every sick person alive. I will not be accused of being a financial drain on our system. I apologize to Tim and his family for my actions last night. I'm truly sorry. If what I did at Richland Memorial caused harm to anyone, again, I apologize. But from my perspective, I had no choice. I couldn't bear the thought of Richland closing and our community being left without hospital services." He paused as his eyes searched the crowd. "Bob, I'm sorry for dragging you into this. I never intended for it to end this way."

Bob swallowed hard against the lump growing in his throat and nodded his head to his friend.

"Miss Lowe," he said, locating Alex, Ben and her father in the back of the room, "I'm sorry for the pain I caused you and your family. Miss Hibbetts, I hope you can find it in your heart to forgive me."

Alex forced a weak smile and closed her eyes. Her father put his arm around her waist.

"There won't be any appeals, Marc," Gerald said as he pulled a syringe from his pocket. "It's over."

In one smooth motion, he pulled the cap from the needle and thrust the needle into his thigh. The crotalotoxin burned as it infiltrated the tissues of his leg. He smiled knowingly as

Marc rushed to his side and pulled the needle from his leg. It was over. Death would come quickly.

Printed in the United States
132798LV00001B/1/P

9 781934 937495